KT-512-457

Cancelled

4721800039276 4

Family
Business

Muriel Bolger is a well-known Irish journalist and award-winning travel writer. In addition to her works of fiction, she has also written four books on her native city, including *Dublin – City of Literature* (O'Brien Press), which won the Travel Extra Travel Guide Book of the Year 2012.

@MurielBolger

Also by Muriel Bolger

Consequences
Intentions
The Captain's Table
The Pink Pepper Tree
Out of Focus

Family Business

MURIEL
BOLGER

HACHETTE
BOOKS
IRELAND

Copyright © 2017 Muriel Bolger

The right of Muriel Bolger to be identified as the Author of
the Work has been asserted by her in accordance with the
Copyright, Designs and Patents Act 1988.

First published in Ireland in 2017 by
HACHETTE BOOKS IRELAND

First published in paperback in 2017

1

All rights reserved. No part of this publication may be reproduced, stored in
a retrieval system, or transmitted, in any form or by any means without the
prior written permission of the publisher, nor be otherwise circulated in any
form of binding or cover other than that in which it is published and without
a similar condition being imposed on the subsequent purchaser.

All characters in this publication are fictitious and any resemblance
to real persons, living or dead, is purely coincidental.

Cataloguing in Publication Data is available from the British Library

ISBN 9781473606678

Typeset in Caslon by redrattledesign.com

Printed and bound in Great Britain by Clays Ltd, St Ives plc

Hachette Books Ireland policy is to use papers that are natural, renewable and
recyclable products and made from wood grown in sustainable forests. The logging
and manufacturing processes are expected to conform to the environmental
regulations of the country of origin.

Hachette Books Ireland
8 Castlecourt Centre
Castleknock
Dublin 15, Ireland

A division of Hachette UK Ltd
Carmelite House, 50 Victoria Embankment, EC4Y 0DZ

www.hachettebooksireland.ie

*To my wonderful friends, with whom I've shared and built such
a huge pile of happy memories to keep in my mental filing cabinet.
They pop into my mind when I least expect them
and make me smile.*

Chapter One

Inside the offices of Cullen–Ffinch, solicitors and barristers-at-law, Anne Cullen gathered up the stacks of files she had been scrutinising.

'Whoever predicted that computers would herald the end of paper was so wrong. If anything they've created an even bigger mountain than before.'

'Charlie Lahiffe won't be worrying about things like that,' Anne's assistant, Paula, said, 'whether he wins his case or not. He could well afford to plant a whole rainforest with the money he's paying his senior counsel to screw that poor wife of his. Though maybe poor is the wrong word to use. Wasn't it her family's money that made him what he is today? In hindsight that's probably why he married her. Rich lists, a helicopter that survived the Celtic tiger nosedive and a few homes close to his tax-dodge investments. He'd have none of those without her.'

'Absolutely,' Anne replied, 'but it makes me sad to see what's happened to them. They were such a golden couple when I was growing up. They were always part of our lives, at dinner parties and bashes and skiing holidays. I always liked him, and Dee and Mum have been friends forever.'

'It kinda shatters your faith in marriage, doesn't it?' Paula said. 'The alarm bells should have started ringing when he got that meno-Porsche.' They laughed. 'His *red* meno-Porsche.'

'He's such a stereotype, isn't he?'

'Meno-Porsche?' Maurice Cullen asked from the doorway. 'What's a meno-Porsche?'

Paula laughed. 'It's an integral part of the male menopause for some who can afford it; others settle for anything low, sleek and noisy!'

'Where have I been hiding? All that seems to have passed me by, but I have to agree with you, Anne, as a couple they were well suited.' Maurice said, 'Your mum and I had some great times with them through the years, before this business. In fact we always felt they looked on you as the daughter they never had.'

'He let money and his ego go to his head,' Paula said, gathering up the files. 'It does that to some people. They have to show it off and that's when they begin believing they can buy anyone and anything they want.'

Maurice nodded. 'Sadly he won't be able to buy his way out of this mess. Bigamy is not looked on favourably in this jurisdiction. I really wish we weren't involved, but we are, so you get down there to the courts and show them. You can easily win this one for Dee.'

'I'm still not happy to be handling this, Dad, and you know it.' Anne said.

'Let's not go over old ground again. We had no choice. Dee needs our support and our professionalism at a time like this. How do you think I feel acting against my friend? It's a lose–lose quandary. If I'd said no to her I'd have had your mother's anger to contend with on top of everything else. And I know Charlie feels I've just abandoned him to his fate when he really needs a friend.'

'He brought it on himself,' Maurice said to Anne.

'He'll have plenty of time to reflect on his actions after today,' Paula said.

'I'd like to be there for you, and wish I could go too,' he said.

'I know that, Dad, and I do understand why you feel you can't. I hope I don't disappoint either of you. Dee deserves to win.'

'She will,' he replied.

'Of course she will, although it won't be easy,' Paula said. 'She's been handling it all with such control and graciousness so far, but whatever the outcome she'll be hounded by the media after this.'

'Tell her to keep doing whatever she is doing,' Maurice said, looking at his watch. 'You'd better get off – you don't want to be late. I know it's a big case at this stage in your career; just have faith in yourself.'

'I will, Dad, but you never know what way Downey will go. He's not known as "the Inscrutable" for nothing.'

'That's an act. Just remember that. He may not show his thoughts, but he is fair. Your case is very strong, and no matter what happens, it's Charlie who is guilty, one hundred per cent, not Dee. She's done nothing wrong.'

She nodded. 'I know that. I also know he has Daniel Hassett as his senior counsel and truthfully that man still terrifies me!'

'Why?' Paula asked, looking from one to the other.

'I don't honestly know; I felt like that since the first time I saw him as a law student. He strutted around the place with the confidence of someone who is totally comfortable in his own world. He has this sense of entitlement which both intrigued and petrified us all, male and female.'

'He's very easy on the eye.'

'I have to agree he is,' Anne said, 'but we were all in awe of him since first seeing him in action. Back when we'd amble in to the courts to get a feel for how everything worked, watching how the different barristers and judges conducted the proceedings, Daniel Hassett would arrive on a Harley, clad from head to toe in black leathers only to appear transformed into a terrifying adversary once he'd changed into court dress. He, his successes and his lifestyle were the ones we all wanted to emulate.'

'I can't wait to see him in action,' said Paula, 'and to see you take him down off his perch!'

This was to be the first time Anne faced him in head-on battle, and although her father wouldn't physically be there she knew she had his full support. This was without doubt her highest-profile case to date and she was nervous. By comparison she was a relatively inexperienced junior, a lightweight pitted against a heavyweight. She tried to steer her thoughts away from such anxieties. It was a watertight case and she had to remain positive and confident.

As they waited for Dee to arrive, Paula said, 'I wonder if the other wife will be there. If it were me I'm sure I'd be curious to see what my predecessor looked like in the flesh.'

'I believe she will be, although I don't know if I would do that. I think it would be much harder on Dee, thinking of him with her, courting her, buying her presents, taking her out to dine, proposing, while she waited at home for him, unsuspecting.'

'I think I'd want to castrate him,' Paula declared.

'It's just as well that's not on the statute books. Remember he's made a fool of her too. I'm sure she wants her revenge. Otherwise why would she fly halfway across the world when she isn't entitled to a penny from him legally?' Anne argued.

'To make sure he gets his comeuppance; to see him squirm when he's faced with his two wives in the one place and to be there when he's sentenced.'

'Oh, you are evil, Paula! Remind me to keep on your good side.'

Dee arrived just then and together they made their way downstairs to the taxi.

'Nervous?' Anne asked.

'Yes and angry, disappointed and hurt,' Dee replied. 'A total mess, if I'm honest.'

Anne hugged the older woman. 'Leave it to us.' She held Dee's hand on the short drive to the courthouse, squeezing it as she noticed the waiting mob jostling for the best vantage point.

'Right, here we go,' said Paula. 'Heads up – time to show the opposition and the paparazzi that we're ready for battle.'

I just hope that'll be enough, Anne thought to herself, wondering how long a road they had ahead. It might be a protracted trial; no one could predict. It had been postponed twice already as new evidence and clarifications were deemed to be necessary before it could proceed. She'd have to make sure to get the point across that this had caused further anguish and upset to her client. While the accused was seen around town projecting an image of a carefree and untroubled man, Dee had become a virtual prisoner in her home.

'Don't make eye contact with any of them,' Anne told Dee, 'and say nothing, no matter how they provoke you.' Someone opened the car door from the outside, and cameras clicked and flashed as they made their way though the frenzy to the relative quiet inside the building.

Chapter Two

Anne had read law reluctantly at first. All through school she had found study easy, and, although a straight 'A' student, all she had wanted was to become was an artist, a career choice that had brought on her mother's conniptions any time she'd mentioned it; Sheila Cullen had bigger plans for her two girls. From a very early age if Anne had argued a point with her parents or her younger sister Gabby, her mother used to tell her she had a big future ahead of her. 'That one will be a wig when she grows up, the way she has with words,' she'd say to her husband.

For a long time Anne hadn't understood what she'd meant. 'But I don't want to be a wig. I like my plaits and I want them to grow so long that I can sit on them.'

'You can keep your plaits, no one will touch those,' her mother had told her, 'although I doubt you'll still have those by then.'

Her father had explained the etiquette of courtroom hierarchy and its attire. She'd listened and argued. 'I won't need a wig. I'm going to be an artist, a painter!'

'You can do that in your spare time, not as a career,' her mother had dictated. 'You'll never make a living drawing little pictures for people.' Such remarks had confused Anne because she'd often seen her mother proudly showing the same 'little pictures' to anyone who'd cared to look.

Her father had often stepped in. 'There's plenty of time to make your mind up,' he'd told her, 'so let's postpone the arguments until then. I've no intentions of going anywhere and the firm will still be there if you want to join us. I'd love if you did, but it's your life and if the thoughts of working alongside your old man freak you out that'll be fine too. It'll be your decision when you're old enough to make it.'

They had a bond, her and her dad, from the time she could toddle and he'd sit her on his knee and draw animals for her. Together, like conspirators, they knew how to handle her mother.

'The first thing you must do is to let her think she has won. The second is to let her win, occasionally,' he'd told her once, grinning. 'That's the secret. Choose your battles and be prepared to lose some for the sake of all of us! But hold on to your dreams and go for them. We only have one life here so make the most of it.'

'Did you, Dad? Did you follow your dreams?'

'Yes, every one of them and I enjoy my life. Of course there will be challenges – there's no opt-out clause for those in anyone's journey here – but if the rest is in place you'll get through them too.'

She had taken his advice back then and as she grew she saw herself working in a studio in Provence, or the Algarve, becoming recognised for her art. But when the time came to make decisions to bring her there, against her instincts she opted for law because she knew it was what her parents really wanted. Her painting was relegated to spare-time relaxation, and then her spare time seemed to shrink as study and a very enjoyable social life got in the way.

It made sense, reading law as her father had done. It had been his whole life. He had joined the old and eminently respected firm of Ffinch and Ffinch when he qualified. A father and son enterprise, when Ffinch senior died Maurice was given the opportunity of becoming Peadar Junior's partner. Despite being quite senior in years that moniker stuck and Peadar continued to be referred to as Junior.

'I don't want to spend my life handling traffic offences and house sales,' she'd argued after several work experience stints. 'I'd die of boredom. I'd like to do something more rewarding, more fulfilling even.'

'Then look at family law,' her father advised. 'That'll never be dull. It will always be fulfilling and often frustrating, but it'll certainly never be boring.'

The idea of that interested her.

'You only have to look at the complications that arose when Darcy's parents died.'

Her best friend Darcy's parents had never married and died in a road accident when she was in her teens. Neither had made wills and it took several years for their affairs to be sorted in favour of their only child, and that had only happened after relatives she had never known existed had made claims and counterclaims on her parents' estates. Anne had often heard her father say, 'Where there's a will there are relatives and where there's no will there are always more!'

When Maurice had suggested she should handle Dee's case she had protested.

'I'm not sure if I'm qualified enough to take it on. She needs a senior counsel.'

'You are, and having you on her side will give Dee some much-needed support. Besides –' he had grinned at her '– from an ethical stance you can't say no to me. The Bar's code of conduct requires that a barrister must accept a brief from a solicitor to appear before a court in a field in which the barrister practises or professes to practise. You've specialised in family law …'

She laughed. 'So no pressure then, Dad?'

'Absolutely none! I would never suggest you take it on if I thought this brief was outside your skill or capacity. I'll work with you preparing the arguments and opinions. We can't let her down on this.'

'I'd hate to do that.'

'You won't. You've been trained to be independent and objective.' He smiled at her. 'I have every faith in you.'

Anne was upset that Dee was in this position at all: Dee needing this representation because she'd discovered her husband had another wife – one he had married in America – one he had neglected to tell anyone about. No one had ever suspected that anything had changed. When the news about Melody Maddock had broken they had all been shocked.

'Having an affair would have been despicable enough, but getting married to the woman and keeping the duplicity up is incredible. How come none of us never noticed anything?' Maurice had asked his wife on several occasions since the disclosure.

'How Charlie thought he'd never be found out is beyond me. He's not a stupid man. Did he never wonder what he'd do when it came out, as it was bound to, or wonder what it would do to Dee?' Sheila had asked.

'I don't think he was thinking at all.'

'If he was it wasn't with his brain. He's destroyed Dee. She's in bits.'

'I know,' he'd agreed.

The gossip columnists were having a great time rehashing the few facts that were in the public domain and rarely a weekend passed without a photo of Charlie and Melody appearing alongside another speculative storyline.

'She's exactly as I would have expected him to pick,' Anne had said when the photos had begun featuring under headings like, 'Decorator to the Stars Duped' and 'Melody's Mistake Bagging a Bigamist'.

During the time they were preparing the case, several other revelations hit the papers about Charlie Lahiffe regarding alleged irregular business dealings. These purported that he had bribed a number of council officials to get approval for some regeneration projects in the inner city. Files pertaining to these accusations were being compiled for the Department of Public Prosecutions, but Maurice had refused to get embroiled in discussions about these.

'You've already pushed the bonds of friendship too far, Charlie. You're on your own on this one. Make sure you have plenty of funds available, legal ones. With your lifestyle you'll not be getting any free legal aid and these cases, as you know too well, can drag on for years and time is money.'

'I'll probably lose everything in the bigamy case.'

'I won't discuss it, Charlie. You're not a child. You knew your actions had consequences. Now they have to be faced.'

Chapter Three

Anne escorted Dee in to court through the mob of cameramen and the assault of multicoloured microphones that were shoved in their faces.

Anne's good friend, Alan Seavers from the *Chronicle*, stood a little apart from the mob. He caught her eye and gave her a wink. She didn't acknowledge him. She couldn't. They were on opposite sides of the fence now – he a court reporter, she the sometimes target of these reports. Professionally they behaved as decorum dictated. Personally he had always had a thing for her, a fact he never tried to hide, although he no longer actively pursued her, yet seeing him there warmed her and made her feel she had an ally in this hostile arena.

The jostling began again and someone shouted, 'The other one is here.'

The cameras turned and reporters scattered to surround the car that had just pulled up at the kerb. Anne had to resist looking back to catch a glimpse of this woman. Instead she ushered Dee inside to get seated.

A few minutes later Melody Maddock arrived, not togged out in the flamboyant colours Anne had expected from those she had seen her wear in the photos, but dressed demurely in black. Her skirt stopped just above her knees. A narrow orange scarf that matched an oversized handbag with an unmissable logo and chunky chain shoulder strap broke the severity of her appearance. She took the seat indicated by her counsel, nodding in acknowledgment.

'So that's what I was up against,' Dee whispered. 'She's so thin.'

'No, she's not,' Paula answered, 'she's like a knitting needle with ginormous breasts. I'm surprised she doesn't topple over. She didn't get those from Mother Nature, or from eating maple-syrup pancakes.'

'Paula, you're a tonic,' said Dee.

'Well, it's true, isn't it? Enhanced and enlarged.' She laughed. 'Makes my thirty-four Cs look stunted.'

Before Dee could reply a murmur went around the courtroom as Charlie Lahiffe made his entrance, arms swinging, walking briskly in, smiling at everyone, two solicitors flanking him. Daniel Hassett, who was a good head above this trio, followed a few seconds later, his gown billowing behind him as he walked up to the front of the courtroom, bowing in recognition, almost imperceptibly, towards Anne. Anne smiled back. She was nervous, extremely nervous, but she knew from her training and experience that she couldn't show it, to either her client or to their opposition. She took a deep breath before the door opened at one side and the judge entered. She had to keep her head, be ready to counter all his arguments with facts and clarity.

'I have to admire her composure,' Dee said, after that first morning session. 'Melody never let her gaze wander in our direction, even for a split second. It took me all my willpower to stop watching her. I feel a bit sorry for her. There she is – sitting on her own – I don't think she's ever been in Ireland before. At least I have my friends here to support me.'

'Maybe she doesn't have many, or maybe she wanted to be on her own to avoid further ridicule. Can you imagine how foolish and gullible he's made her feel,' said Anne.

She watched Dee cringe as the court reporters made notes on what they perceived to be the juicy bits of the trial. She was disgusted with Charlie's attitude. Anyone looking at him could be forgiven for thinking he was playing a role on stage instead of being tried for making suckers of two women who had been unfortunate enough to fall in love with him. Charlie, or CP, as it transpired he was known to his other wife, sat brazenly there, immaculately turned out in his perfectly tailored suit and silk tie, avoiding eye contact throughout with both Mrs Lahiffes. They all knew that later on these details and facts would be given their own spin to suit the publications present, and they were all there, the nationals, the provincials and the broadcast media.

'Your friend from the *Chronicle* never stops scribbling,' Paula remarked as they gathered their papers at the end of the first day's proceedings. 'I think he must be writing a thriller. Any time I look in his direction he's scribbling away.'

'Alan's not writing. He's drawing. He does those artist's impressions you see sometimes on the news during trials.'

'I never knew that.'

'He doesn't advertise the fact – they're never signed anyway. He writes poetry too.'

'A man of many parts. How did you find that out?'

'We go back a bit. He dated one of my friends through college.

He was the darling of the debating society. Even then he used to draw the speakers as they argued. He's very talented.'

The verdict was delivered just in time to make the main evening-news bulletins.

'You strike me as being an intelligent man, Mr Lahiffe,' the judge announced in a voice full of authority. 'If you had put your cunning to better use you could have walked away from this courtroom with a tidy divorce settlement, which the law in its infinite wisdom would have forced me to make to you, although it would have been against my better judgment. Instead you have duped these women, playing on and with their emotions, marrying two at the same time. Greed is never a nice trait, be it in a child or a grown-up. Neither is deceit. Together they are despicable. Bigamy, however, is a criminal offence and as such demands punishment by law. Legal precedent in this country permits me to give a custodial sentence for this offence of up to seven years.'

Charlie's mask slipped and he looked over at Dee. Anne could see the panic in his eyes, his knuckles white as he grasped the wooden barrier between him and the court. She heard Dee gasp.

'However, I'm recommending that this will be reviewed at a later stage, as I am reliably informed that there are further proceedings in train against you for charges of embezzlement and corruption. You may not leave this jurisdiction in the interim and will surrender your passport. You will also relinquish any hold on the title of the family homes, cars and possessions. You may visit the Dublin home, with Mrs Dee Lahiffe's solicitor present, to collect your personal belongings, and after that you are barred from visiting or making personal contact with her. I am also granting her a legal separation from you to facilitate divorce proceedings when the correct amount of time has elapsed. Any other joint possessions shall be disposed of as she so wishes.'

The reporters were scribbling furiously.

'Miss Maddock,' he continued, looking at Melody, 'I know you did not choose to take proceedings in this country, but I wish you well in your endeavours when you do. I do hope this experience does not colour your opinion of the Irish male. There are decent ones among us. Unfortunately you didn't meet one.'

Someone in the gallery applauded. The judge looked up as though to admonish them and seemed to decide against it. Instead he stood up and left the bench. They could hear the noise outside escalate when the doors opened and the reporters had their story. As Charlie was being ushered out he mouthed at Dee and Anne, 'I'm sorry, really I am.'

'The car won't be outside for a few minutes,' Paula told them. 'Wait a bit and then we'll make a run for it.'

As the seats emptied Daniel Hassett came over then and extended his hand to Anne. 'Well done, that's a big one to put on the portfolio.' Surprised, she muttered her thanks and he went to walk away. He turned back and said, 'It's a bit of a scramble out there, ladies, stick together and follow me.'

He divided the reporters and camera people like Moses separating the sea. Together the women pushed through the collection of microphones that were thrust in their faces, refusing to say anything. Anne saw Alan and he gave her the thumbs up and a wink. She smiled back and realised how tense she had been. She could feel her face relax as cameras flashed. Melody Maddock was enjoying her moment in the limelight and took the media focus away from them temporarily as she answered their questions. They took the opportunity and made their getaway.

As they sat in the evening traffic on the quays Anne asked Dee how she was feeling about the judge's decision.

'I don't know how I feel – parts of me are elated, sad, mad, and all at the same time. I can't believe it's ended like this. It's so final and yet it's not. I don't know what to think, what to do next. And I'm starving. Let's go somewhere quiet where we can talk.'

'I'm glad to hear that. You've eaten like a bird all week.' Anne took her phone out to ring a restaurant and book a table. There was a message from her mother: 'Come back here for dinner – I won't take no for an answer.'

She showed it to Dee who laughed. 'Good old Sheila.'

'Let me out and I'll head home,' Paula said.

'You'll do no such thing – you're practically one of the family and I know they'd never forgive me if I let you off like that.'

'Of course you have mixed feelings about the outcome,' Maurice Cullen told Dee as he poured drinks for them. 'It's a pyrrhic victory. Your life has just changed forever; that'll take some adjustment.'

'I know he hasn't been around for the past while but now that it's official I feel alone, really alone, for the first time. The house seems far too big. Maybe I should sell it.'

'You'll do no such thing, Dee. I won't let you rush into anything like that,' her friend said, putting the last-minute touches to the meal.

'Sheila's right – no hasty decisions,' Maurice said, 'and you know we are always here for you.'

'I'd never have got through all this without you all, but you know that.' She raised her glass to toast them. 'And I want to see all those cuttings you have.'

'There's nothing to be achieved by that,' Sheila told her.

'Maybe there is and maybe there isn't, but I want to know what Miss Maddock knew about his – our – life, and what he told her to win her over.'

'There's no need. She's telling it on the evening news,' Anne said coming in from the kitchen, then turning on the television in the corner.

'Of course I'll pursue him in the American courts. No one makes a fool of Melody Maddock, and I'll make sure Charlie Lahiffe will pay for trying to. I was oblivious of his deception. Imagine how I felt when I came across a photo of him with his wife that someone had posted on Facebook. And the wife wasn't me! He couldn't deny it. It was taken at an Irish racetrack, and the date was on a poster behind them.' She paused to listen to the next question. 'Yes, he did buy me these diamonds.' She waved her manicured fingers in front of the camera. 'And he's not getting them back either.'

Another reporter jumped in.

'No. Of course I don't want him back,' she answered. 'I wouldn't take him even if he came crawling. He's humiliated me both personally and professionally.'

Dee sighed. 'I know he's a bastard for doing what he did, but he was my bastard and I loved him. It's not easy to turn my emotions off to order. I actually felt sorry for him when he said he was sorry. He looked so lost and vulnerable. Yet sorry is such a little word for such a big hurt, isn't it?'

They all agreed.

Chapter Four

The next morning the papers were full of the judgment. The tabloid journalists were enjoying their moment. They had been gagged for months, ever since the story broke, restricted by snippets already in the public domain, afraid to say anything fresh, or to report all they already knew, for fear of prejudicing the case. Photos of the two wives were splashed across the front pages.

The headlines shouted:

'Victory for wife number one and two.'

'One man one wife'

'When one just isn't enough.'

'Two into one won't go.'

Paula read the beginning of Alan Seavers' piece to herself: 'The Battle of the Spouses – property developer and speculator Charlie Lahiffe charged with bigamy.' She continued to read. 'At the end of a spectacular trial the swingeing judgment given in court yesterday will ensure Charlie Lahiffe will be absent from the social columns in the foreseeable future. In a ground-breaking case the judge came down heavily on Dee Lahiffe's side, handing over their suburban mansion, with all its contents, to her, after the court heard it had been bought originally with her money. It also agreed on a substantial settlement to the wronged wife, a settlement that will not be affected by any future financial orders. A further trial is pending regarding allegations of corruption in Mr Lahiffe's business involvements. The fate of his other properties, here and abroad, will be decided then. These are all currently held in the sole-trading name of Charlie Lahiffe.'

After reading a bit further, Paula put the papers down on Anne's desk. 'Did you see what Alan wrote in the *Chronicle*? What he said about Daniel Hassett and you?'

'Don't mind him. He's always at that – hinting we're an item. He loves trying to get back at me in the nicest possible way because I won't go out with him.'

'You never told me that before,' her assistant said eyeing her intently. 'I'll read him with new interest now that I know that.'

'Let me see what he's saying this time.'

Paula handed the paper over.

After a minute Anne laughed out loud. 'Oh, Daniel will love this. "Sparks flew and ignited across the courtroom this week as Dublin's most attractive legal adversaries battled it out over the Lahiffe fortunes and misfortunes. Junior counsel Anne Cullen took on the prince of Dublin's legal hierarchy. Looking like stars from central casting for some courtroom drama rather than actual working wigs, they may have been sundering one couple's union, but my money is on them creating a different one of their own in the near future, perhaps even more than just a personal arrangement too. There's still a vacancy at Cullen–Ffinch since Peadar Ffinch retired. Hassett shepherded Cullen and party as they left the courts, after chatting very amicably too. He didn't seem too upset by having just lost one of the most significant family law cases of the decade. Miss Cullen looked triumphant."'

'Well, you can't argue with that. It's a lovely picture, wigs atilt, hair and gowns flying.'

'That was taken during the week.'

'Whenever … you still make a dashing couple,' Paula teased.

'Don't you start. They've Photoshopped those. We never left together like that suggests,' she said, scanning the photo and folding the page. She smiled. They did look good in it.

'He's not the only one speculating.'

'You make us sound like something from Jane Austen,' Anne said. Her phone buzzed. It was her sister Gabby.

'I see you made headlines again,' Gabby said, as soon as Anne answered.

No 'well done', or 'congratulations', just a blunt and almost accusatory statement. Anne knew she should be used to this by now but she wasn't. She'd never understand her only sister's resentment at everything she did. Why could she never be happy for her?

'He's very attractive. Are you interested in him?'

Anne laughed the photo off. 'Gabby, there's no truth in any of this. It's just tabloid sensationalism. They have to fill their pages with something. Did you read on and see what one of them said about the two wives looking as though they wanted to stab one another? Nothing could be further from the truth.'

'Did Dee did talk to her afterwards?'

'Of course she did. Dee's a lady. She shook hands with her and said she was sorry.'

'What had she to be sorry about? She did nothing wrong.'

Anne sighed. Her sister never made conversation easy.

'Sorry that her slime-bag husband had tricked and deceived her as well. Melody was an innocent in this too, you know?'

'I suppose,' Gabby replied.

Anne was about to ask her to meet up that evening to celebrate but thought better of it. Gabby would read that the wrong way too, celebrating when, according to her, life never went her way. Instead she heard herself saying, 'I'm popping over to the folks on Saturday. Will you be there? I haven't seen you for a few weeks.'

'No can do. I'm playing golf.'

'What about Sunday?'

'No. There's a banker's outing to Wooden Bridge – I'll be gone all day.'

'Well, I'm sure we'll catch up soon.' Sometimes she didn't know why she bothered.

No sooner had that call finished than an email from her friend Darcy arrived in her inbox. 'Looking good, missus,' it read. 'You're all over the papers, and wow, that's a fabulous photograph in the *Chronicle*, and yer man's not bad either. Congrats by the way, well done. A great victory. Tell me *everything*. I want all the details.'

Anne sat looking at the screen deciding on her reply. Why couldn't her sister be more like that – happy for her, even a little pleased? Before she had too much time to dwell on those dark thoughts, Paula buzzed. 'Daniel Hassett's on the line, do you want to take it?'

Puzzled, she said, 'Yes, put him through.' What could he want? Surely he wasn't going to ask her to work for him, or with him even. Was he? She found herself smiling as she heard his voice.

'Good morning, Anne.'

'Good morning, Daniel. No matter who you're representing, you can't afford me. I'm not for hire.'

'That's just as well because I'm not hiring. This is a social call. I've just been leafing through the redtops and it seems we are today's hot gossip –' he laughed '– so I got to thinking that as speculation is rife perhaps we should give the hacks something to talk about. Would you have dinner with me?'

'I'm not sure that's the most romantic reason anyone has ever given me for asking me out …'

'Sorry, I realised as I was saying it how clumsy it sounded. It was just an excuse anyway. I'd love to take you out –' he hesitated '– if you'd like, that is.'

His reply amused her. 'Is the eloquent Mr Hassett having a hard time finding the right words?' she asked, smiling.

'Shush, don't let anyone hear you, or my reputation could be frayed.'

'And I can't certainly be responsible for that, so I suppose I'd better say yes, and thank you.'

'Good. What about this Friday?'

'Sounds good to me.'

'That's settled then. Do you have any favourites? Italian, French?'

'Surprise me.' She laughed.

'I'll do my best. Until then,' he said as he rang off.

Her dad popped his head around the door.

'You look happy. I've just had Peadar on the blower – he sends his congratulations. He's probably calculating what this victory means to the value of the partnership.'

'If he ever decides to let it go. That was nice of him though, considering how much he resisted you taking me on here in the first place.'

'You did help to drag him into the real world. When he started working with his father women didn't deal with business matters. They couldn't even have bank accounts in their own name or buy property of their own without a male guarantor to vouch for them. Peadar's still a bit of a misogynist, but he has come a long way.'

'They really were the dark ages.'

'They seem like that now. We didn't think so then, but I'm holding you up. I'll let you get on with your day. Well done again.' He went back to his office, whistling.

Anne sat there for a few moments wondering whether she had really just had that conversation with Daniel Hassett. Had she actually agreed to have dinner with him? As students, half the women fantasised about catching his attention and she had been numbered amongst them. She picked the paper up again and looked at the photo – yes, he certainly was easy on the eye. She looked back at her screen and tapped a reply to Darcy: 'Have I got news for you?! You won't believe what just happened – drinks tonight – on me – usual place!!' Still grinning, she pressed send.

'Mystery and intrigue – can't wait. Can I have a clue?' The instant reply pinged back.

'Definitely not!' was shot back, just as quickly.

That evening she told Darcy about the unexpected turn of events.

'I bet you never thought you'd be thanking a journo for getting you a date.'

'Have you any idea how pathetic that makes me sound, as though I was incapable of getting one myself? And I might not have anything to thank him for yet – it might turn out to be a complete disaster.'

'Or a huge success. Maybe Alan's finally given up on you.'

'You know I've never looked at him in that light. He was just part of the college gang, and he had that long-term girlfriend then – the artist with the dull, straggly hair. She was always stoned and took things from pubs and restaurants. Every mug, plate and glass in her bedsit was filched from somewhere, the cutlery too. I wouldn't be at all surprised if her clothes had been lifted as well.'

'Maybe that's why he went in for court reporting!' Darcy said. 'But seriously, he's a genuine guy – and you get on well – were you never interested in him?'

'Maybe, fleetingly, a long time ago. What an impossible combination that would be now, the junior counsel and the legal hack! It would compromise both our careers and integrity, and no one would trust either of us.'

'I noticed that he was in court all through the trial.'

'He's very good at what he does.'

'It's funny, I never saw him becoming a journalist. He was much more interested in the theatre, head of Dram Soc and all that.'

'Life is funny. I never saw you as a teacher either.'

'Neither did I. Did you hear from Gabby today – did she see the papers?'

'Yes, and yes. She did.' Anne sighed.

'I take it she wasn't over the moon for you.'

'You know her as well as I do, Darcy.'

'It's about time she got over herself. She's spent her life resenting you. We're not back in school now, and I'm sure she did have to put up with the teachers telling her "you'll never be half as good as that sister of yours," but that's standard treatment for younger brothers and sisters, isn't it?'

'I don't know, but she has turned life into a competition between us. I hate the way she does that and I hate the way it makes me feel towards her. She resents me working with Dad. You'd think we had a conspiracy between us to exclude her. I don't resent the time she spends with Mum, or their shopping trips abroad.'

'Admit it. You were a hard act to follow, being her big sis.'

'That's nonsense, Darcy, and I was never aware of any of that.'

'Look at it from her perspective. You were elected games

captain every year and led the school to victory in several of the inter-schools finals.'

'But I enjoyed sport, and the fun and companionship that went with it. Anyway, we're grown women now, not school kids. Doesn't she realise life is not about being the first at everything?'

'That's easy for you to say. She doesn't see it like that, obviously; I reckon that's why she took up golf,' Darcy said.

'Hitting a ball with Dad on a Sunday evening hardly qualifies.'

'I always remember the evening the pro told you that you'd need to practise as you weren't a natural. Her eyes lit up and I could see the determination on her face. She'd found something she could do better than you and, boy, did that motivate her.'

'I never thought of it that way.'

'You wouldn't,' Darcy replied. 'You're too nice to think like that.'

One never knew how long trials would go on. Both her father's and her own experience had taught her that it was better to err on the longer side than find yourself torn in half, trying to satisfy two clients at once. In this case, Lahiffe versus Lahiffe finished earlier than the three weeks they had allocated so Anne had some unscheduled, but very welcome, free time. She decided to take the Friday afternoon off and prepare for her dinner date at leisure. She chose a sleek, emerald-green dress, which made her tawny eyes look more green than amber, and wore her hair back behind one ear. The only adornment she wore was a gold belcher chain necklace and bracelet that her father had given her when she qualified.

Daniel arrived, looking every bit a casually elegant version of the man he portrayed in chambers. Everything about him advertised breeding, money and the self-confidence that comes naturally to those who never had any reason to doubt themselves. He glanced approvingly at her and said, 'You look very good, Anne.'

'Why, thank you, kind sir. You've scrubbed up well too.' She leaned forward to give him a kiss on the cheek, as she normally did when greeting friends, then she felt uncomfortable and pulled back. She was actually blushing. He laughed.

'It's a bit awkward, isn't it? Let's pretend we don't know anything about each other and start as strangers – no work talk at all.'

'That's a great idea.' She smiled at him and held out her hand. 'My name's Anne Cullen and I just beat this ace barrister in court this week. Tell me about yourself.'

'I'm Daniel Hassett and I was beaten by a rookie in court this week. I don't like losing.' They laughed and he led the way into the bar.

I know very little about you, she thought, as they waited for their drinks to arrive, but when he smiled at her she found herself responding easily. He was even more attractive close up. She noticed his hands, perfectly manicured and expressive, his eyes intense and interested.

'Hello,' he said breaking her reverie.

She blushed. 'Sorry, I was daydreaming.'

'Am I that boring? This could be a long evening if I've lost your attention already.'

'You haven't. I was just thinking how funny life is. I'd never have predicted that I'd end up sitting here drinking with you. I thought minions like me were virtually invisible to you.'

He grinned and looked at her intently, saying, 'Not all of them.'

After drinks they walked to a French bistro she had been in a few times before. The meal didn't disappoint, and even though Daniel appeared to be knowledgeable about the wines, he consulted her before ordering. They chatted easily.

'Why law?' he asked.

'If I'm totally honest it was my second choice, probably because of a mother whose ambitions for her daughters pushed me in that direction, and a father who felt the same but who kept those thoughts to himself.'

'I know Maurice, and old Peadar too. Is your sister in law too?'

'No – she's in banking.'

'And your dad, is he still into his bikes?'

'How did you know he liked them?'

'We bikers are a strange breed. I like tinkering with them too and he procured an old manual for me once, one that I'd been looking for for ages.'

'Did you always see yourself wearing horsehair and a jabot?'

'I think I probably did. It's in the blood. My grandfather was a judge. He used to let me play with his wig and gown and I'd go around his house banging an old gavel on any surface that made a noise. With an uncle who's a high-court judge and two who are senior counsels I suppose there was an inevitability about my career path, even though it skipped a generation in my father's case; he became an investment banker and my mother is a consultant in a clinic just outside Dublin.'

They chatted easily for the rest of the evening, and Anne couldn't believe how late it was when he dropped her off at her apartment block.

'I had a really lovely time,' she told him, and she meant it.

'So had I. I'll take that as an indication that we might repeat the exercise again sometime soon.' He took her hand and kissed it.

Afterwards she could hardly remember what she had eaten. Instead she kept smiling as fragments of the conversations they had had kept floating into her consciousness and she found it difficult to go to sleep.

'I was impressed by the fact that he didn't seem to be well known in the restaurant,' she told Darcy the next day. 'At least it didn't appear to be a place he'd brought successive girlfriends, like some of the guys I've dated.'

'You really weren't going to let him away with anything, were you?'

'I hadn't realised that, but you're right, as usual.' She smiled. 'Then I haven't been as lucky with men as you though, have I?'

'Maybe that's about to change.'

'I've only had one date! I really expected him to be conceited and full of himself, but he wasn't arrogant at all. He was really nice and interesting as well as being interested in what I was saying.'

'Nice? Is that the best you can do?'

'Will charming do? He was very complimentary about the way I handled Dee's case.'

'I thought you'd agreed not to discuss business.'

'We had, but it was inevitable that it would pop up every now and then, with knowing so many of the same people and moving in the same professional circles.'

'You're putting up a good argument for him, but are you going to see him again?'

'Probably.' She found herself grinning as she answered. 'Yes, probably.'

And they did, as often as possible over the following months, dining around town, meeting each other's friends and heading off into the country at weekends.

'I'm delighted to see you so happy,' her mother told her.

Anne laughed. 'I know that look but I wouldn't go buying a new hat just yet.'

'No, but—'

'No buts of any kind. I hardly know him a wet weekend and you have us walking up the aisle!'

Chapter Five

It was Saturday morning and Maurice Cullen was in his man cave, fiddling with one of his old motorbikes. It was a matter of pride for him and his two equally enthusiastic friends Eoin and Paddy to keep them all in factory condition and to give them an airing on an occasional run out to Wicklow or over the Sally Gap. It also gave him an excuse to escape the girly talk in the kitchen where his younger daughter and wife were catching up.

'So how is the big romance?' Gabby asked Sheila, standing beside her at the kitchen counter. 'Has my sister met her match?'

'Who knows?' Sheila replied. 'She doesn't wear her heart on her sleeve. What about you? How is Paul? Is his new job going well?'

'It's pressured, as sales always is, but he likes the challenges and it means he's not stuck in an office all day. But it's all about meeting targets, targets, targets. I'd hate it myself.'

'I don't think I'd like it either. What about the bank?'

'Same old, same old, but I'll be moving up a grade in two months and I've applied for flexi-time. That'll give more time for golf when the evenings get longer. I'm hoping to cut a stroke off my handicap shortly.'

'Good for you. You really enjoy golf, don't you?' Sheila said, putting some pastries on a plate. 'I could never get that enthusiastic about it. Take that mug and those pastries, will you? I'll bring the rest out after you.'

As they walked across the side passage to the garage, Sheila added, 'Those men think they're still in their teens. I know Paddy is a lot younger than the other two, but look at your dad there – since he got his new knee he can hardly get his leg over the saddle.'

'It's not a horse, Mum,' Gabby said, entering the hallowed sanctuary.

'It might as well be,' said Eoin, wiping grease off his hands on a piece of old mutton cloth.

Sheila laughed. 'When Maurice gets up on one of his machines he thinks he can conquer the world.'

'Words spoken with the resignation of someone who doesn't appreciate the beauty of this old girl,' Maurice told Gabby, stroking the shiny chrome of the Ducati he and Eoin were restoring.

'I don't know how you two ever got together,' his daughter said. 'You're so different.'

'It's called love,' Paddy chipped in. 'It makes fools of us all.'

'It's called compromise,' Eoin said.

'Or a bit of both. Remember that, Gabby,' Paddy said, wagging a finger at her. 'So think hard before you make the leap.'

'But it's true,' said Maurice. 'It's a funny old business, isn't it, love?' he said making a lunge towards his wife.

Laughing, she jumped out of his way. 'Don't come near me with those grubby paws.'

Gabby turned her eyes up to heaven and muttered, 'Oh, please!'

At her reaction, cynical as always, Maurice Cullen couldn't

help thinking about his second daughter; he loved her but their relationship was very different from the one that he enjoyed with Anne.

Gabby was the polar opposite of her older sister. As a baby she had cried, and cried a lot; she had hardly slept for the first year and a half, demanding and getting attention. As she grew he often remarked to his wife, 'You'd never think they were from the same gene pool. Gabby's glass is never half full, never mind overflowing. It's barely damp!'

'Give her time,' Sheila would tell him. 'She'll grow out of it.'

'I hope for her sake she does. If she doesn't she's going to make life very difficult for herself,' he used to say.

From a very early age he could see how she'd resented her older sister. Instead of being happy for her, she'd begrudged her everything that came her way and Anne was completely unaware of Gabby's insecurities.

Suddenly Maurice was snapped back into the present when Eoin spoke.

'Life … it's such a lottery,' Eoin was saying. 'I'd have put money on Charlie and Dee staying together.'

'So would we all. I never thought all those years ago when I was at the match in Parc des Princes that I'd meet Sheila on the flight home. And the rest, as they say, is history.'

He had found himself seated beside her on the way back.

'A birthday treat,' she'd explained, as he offered t o p ut h er expensive-looking shopping bags in the overhead bin. 'A shopping trip to Paris.'

'Lucky you,' he'd said, smiling at her. He had been aware that he was being scrutinised by the older woman with her – her mother, obviously, and probably the bestower of the gift. He had also been aware of the faint smell of expensive scent.

'Were you over for the rugby?' she'd asked.

'I was – but it was a match I think we'd prefer to forget,' he'd said. 'Twenty-two to nine.'

'Maybe our expectations were too high after doing so well last year.'

He hadn't expected that reply. 'You obviously follow it.'

'In a houseful of men it's impossible to avoid,' the older woman had said, then introducing herself and her daughter, Sheila. 'I'm not sure if the boys or their father are the worst. That's why we decided we deserved a treat – to get away from all the talk and debate about who did what wrong and who should have tackled whom.' She had smiled and in that moment he could see a strong family resemblance between the two of them.

'And you end up beside me.' He'd laughed as he'd buckled up. 'Let's move on – have you been to Paris before?'

'No,' Sheila had replied. 'This was my first time and I loved it. It's vast and there's so much I didn't get a chance to see. I'll definitely come back.'

'So will I.'

And they did – three years later – as husband and wife, and the following year again, for his fortieth birthday.

He often teased her about her expensive tastes.

'I should have seen the signs when you pranced on to the plane, weighed down with those designer bags, before designer bags became commonplace. Yes, I should have read the signs then and I'd have saved myself a fortune.'

She'd just laugh at him. 'I didn't prance.'

'Yes, you did.'

She was an awful snob, as was her mother, and this was something he found mildly amusing, as he didn't notice what anyone wore, or if their suits were bespoke or off the peg. He never remembered the juicy bits of gossip either. She always talked about 'My husband, Maurice ... he's a solicitor,' and later, 'My husband Maurice, he's a partner in Cullen–Ffinch, the law firm.'

'Honestly I don't care a whit about position and who earns what,' he would tell her. He'd never had to worry about things like that. Whenever they discussed such matters she'd tell him, 'That's because you mix in the right circles. As do my both my brothers and their wives. We need to make sure our girls stick within those and meet the right sort. That's why their schooling is so important.'

'And so expensive. We could afford a villa in the south of France for what that's going to cost over the years.'

'You can't put a price on class and connections.'

Oh, yes, you can, he had wanted to tell her, but he didn't. There was no point. She had their girls' futures mapped out in her mind. She knew well that his friend Eoin Maleady had come from a decidedly working-class clan, with far too many children, not enough money and an address that was definitely not within her desirable post-code range. Eoin had won a scholarship to the private school, which is where Maurice first met him; they became friends on their first day of secondary school. He also got through medical school without having to find funds to do so, thanks to his academic prowess and scholarship grants. His mother and, later on, two of his sisters worked in the supermarket close to the inner-city council flat where he had gown-up. Sheila chose to put these facts aside because Eoin was now a renowned cardiologist, and addressed by his patients as Mister.

Sheila had vetted their girls' friends from an early age, encouraging friendships with those she thought 'suitable' companions and discouraging those she didn't. Despite Anne's obvious artistic ability Sheila had never countenanced any notion that she should make a career out of it.

Maurice had tried to get around her. 'Are you sure it's not because you don't want the prospects of her hanging around with long-haired scruffy arty types, with no hopes of an ology of any sort after her name?'

'Don't be ridiculous. That has nothing to do with it.'

'Are you sure?' he'd urged.

'Maurice, she could be anything she wants, with those grades.'

'And what if being an artist is that?'

'Of course it's not. It's only a fad.'

There was no point in arguing with Sheila when she was in such a frame of mind, but he'd encouraged Anne to work towards having a portfolio ready just in case.

'If you don't you might regret it later on.'

She'd taken his advice and he'd admired the tenacity and endless hours she'd dedicated to it and had been thrilled for her when she'd been offered a place in the National College of Art and Design. Maurice spent a lot more time in his man cave that winter as Sheila had vented her disappointment when Anne had started her course.

Even Dee and Charlie Lahiffe had agreed with Anne's choice.

'If I'd been fortunate enough to have a daughter,' Dee had commented, 'I'd be more than happy to let her follow her dreams. Her watercolours and portraits are amazing.'

'No one is asking her to stop doing them, just not as a profession.'

'Well, I think you're wrong,' Dee had replied, never afraid to take her friend on in an argument.

The only one who had seemed happy was Gabby – happy that Anne was out of favour with their mother for a change.

Immediately after that Christmas, the family had gone skiing to Bad Gastein. New Year's Eve had seen them heading for the spa and the radon caves in Radhausberg mountain. Dee had been there twice and raved about them.

It had started off as a bit of an adventure but then Sheila began to panic – they had been a mile inside the mountain and had the rickety little train journey to endure before reaching daylight. Maurice had seen her have a panic attack once before, in the National Concert Hall in the middle of a packed row, and the middle of Beethoven's *Sonata Pathétique*. He'd managed to get her out before the third movement, and it hadn't happened since. Eoin had assured them it happened to lots of women at menopause and the pre-menopausal stage and was nothing to be overly concerned about, unless it became a frequent occurrence. It hadn't and, apart from making sure they always booked tickets at the end of a row, they'd practically forgotten all about it.

The radon caves wouldn't have been top of his to-do list but his women had been excited at the prospect and he'd gone along with it. Sceptical about the benefits that were attributed to this excursion, he had changed into togs and a robe along with everyone else, but had found the whole experience a bit weird. They had seemed to be travelling deeper and deeper inside the mountain and instead of feeling colder it was actually getting warmer. The train had stopped, and they'd disembarked, and dispersed to find a wooden bed on which to relax. They'd spent the next half an hour lying on these in their swimsuits, in silence, using their robes as pillows, in the hot innards of the hewn-out passageways. He'd listened to the sounds of humanity around him, a cough, a sneeze, a tummy rumbling, a deep sigh; further along someone began to snore, loudly. He'd resisted the urge to laugh and realised how tense he was. He hadn't liked it in there. He had had to try very hard not to think of trapped miners and cave collapses, or of the poor devils who had quarried out the labyrinth of tunnels in the first place, mining for the gold that had funded most of the large estates around. The miners may not have been well paid, but they had enjoyed other unexplained benefits. Their ailments had just vanished while they'd worked in the radon-rich environment.

He had been relieved when their time was up and he'd walked back to meet the women. One look at Sheila and he'd known that she was not happy. As they'd waited to board the little train she'd grabbed him with a vice-like grip, her eyes desperate, her face white, despite the heat, and he'd known she was in trouble. He'd seen Anne looking at her, her concern clearly visible too. There was no quick escape route.

'Just take slow, deep breaths, we'll be outside in no time at all. We can go straight back to the hotel and have a rest before dinner,' he'd said as they climbed into the little train. He'd put his arm protectively around her back and pulled her close.

Anne had sat across from her, their knees almost touching. Gabby had squeezed in opposite Maurice. She'd prattled on about feeling great, how soft her skin felt, oblivious to her mum's anxiety. Sheila had been finding it hard to breathe. Maurice had held her, willing her to stay calm. 'Close your eyes,' he'd told her, 'and pretend you're on a beach somewhere warm and sunny, or think of whatever New Year's resolutions you're going to make tonight.'

'I can't.'

Anne had leaned over and taken her free hand; the other one was still clutching Maurice's. 'Yes, you can, Mum, we'll only be a few more minutes, nearly everyone is on now. Just breathe slowly. Slowly, Mum.' She'd raised her voice above the clackety-clack racket of the wheels. 'Look, we're moving off already.'

'You're doing great,' Maurice had said.

'I can't stay here, I can't,' Sheila had said irrationally, looking wildly around her.

'Breathe slowly, try not to pant like that,' he'd advised, as they'd wended their way along the two kilometres of dark, rock tunnel.

'Mum, you're doing great. We're all here and we're on our way back out. And I wanted to tell you something – something important – something that I know will make you very happy for the New Year. I was going to wait until midnight.'

Maurice had felt the pressure on his arm slacken somewhat. He'd looked at his daughter, succeeding to take his wife's mind off the situation when he hadn't managed to, but he hadn't been prepared for her announcement either.

'I've decided to apply for law. If I get it I'll finish out this year at NCAD and then switch. What do you think of that? Mum, did you hear me? Aren't you pleased?'

'What, yes, I did. I heard you. Of course you'll get it,' she'd said, opening her eyes and then closing them again immediately, before tightening her grip once more.

'That's terrific news, isn't it, Sheila? She can join me in the company. We can start a dynasty.'

'I hope you're not including me in that,' Gabby had said. 'I want more excitement in my life.' Even in the gloom Maurice's look had stopped her from continuing.

'I think I see the terminus lights up ahead, Sheila. Are you OK? We'll be there in a few seconds, love.'

She had just nodded. The train had slowed to a halt at Spa Robe Station and Maurice had felt himself relax.

Once back upstairs, they'd found loungers and rehydrated with sparkling water.

'Don't hang around for us if you want to go back to the hotel,' Anne had said, as she and Gabby had headed to try the hydrotherapy pools. 'We'll see you there for dinner.'

'Don't ever let me do anything like that again, Maurice,' Sheila had said when the girls had gone. 'I really thought I was going to suffocate in there.'

'I'm sure a lot of people feel like that.'

'I suppose that's why they have doctors on duty, although when I saw them doing their walkabout wearing nothing but swimming trunks and a stethoscope I thought I'd laugh out loud.'

He'd laughed, relieved her anxiety had passed.

'Are you up to trying out these pools?' He'd stood up and given her his hand.

'I am.' Together they had jumped in at the deep end and had swum a few lengths, forgetting the earlier drama.

The hotel had looked splendid that night. They had gone all out with preparations and the tables had been moved together to make longer ones so that no one felt excluded. The Cullens found themselves seated with the friends they had met at the après-ski fun during the week. A Danish couple had told them they were celebrating a wedding anniversary and had ordered champagne for them all. Maurice had protested and offered to contribute but the man had confided, 'This time last year Margareta was wired up in hospital fighting for her life after an aneurism. We never thought she'd see the first of January. And she did, and now here is another one coming up. What's not to celebrate? Such occurrences make you realise how important every minute is. Now we intend to celebrate each one, so let's raise our glasses before we go out to ring in the New Year.'

Snow was falling outside in large, fluffy flakes as strains of Austria's equivalent of 'Auld Lang Syne', 'The Blue Danube Waltz', spilled out of restaurants and homes and people danced in the streets. The church bells rang out from all the little churches around the valley and fireworks had tinted the scene in rainbow colours as they'd exploded from various points in the surrounding mountains.

'I can't believe we're really here again,' Sheila had told Maurice as they'd all crowded outside on the verandas to welcome in the first of January.

'And if all goes well, we'll be here again next year too. And the year after that. I think we should make it an annual event, without the caves!'

They lit the sky lanterns that they had been given as they'd left the dining room. They released them and watched them soar up and out of sight, little halos of light disappearing amid the snowflakes, taking their wishes and resolutions out into the magical night. The fireworks stopped and stillness descended for a few seconds as though everyone had been holding their breath in anticipation of new beginnings. Then the revelling had revved up again. Before they'd gone back inside Sheila had told them, 'I'm sorry for spoiling the cave experience for you all today.'

'There's no need to, Mum; you didn't spoil it,' Anne reassured her.

'We've had a great year, all of us, so let's be thankful for that,' Maurice said. 'Now we've got a new one ahead of us so let's drink a toast to us and to those who are important in our lives: each other.'

It had been only at the airport the next day that Maurice had finally gotten the chance to talk to Anne alone.

'Was that declaration yesterday about doing law a spontaneous one to distract your mum, or did you mean it? If it was, it worked, and if it wasn't, I want you to know I won't mind.'

'It wasn't. I promise. It makes sense. Art College is fun and I still want to paint, but not doing the sort of projects we are doing on the course. I enjoyed being in the office last summer, but I knew I had to explore other avenues, like you told me,' she said, grinning at him. 'Besides how many of my peers have a ready-made job opportunity just sitting waiting there for them? I'll work hard and you'll be proud to have me.'

'I've no doubt about that. I just want you to be happy.'

'I will be, Dad, I know it.'

Gabby's reaction to her news had surprised even Anne. They were back home when Gabby asked her, 'Did you get tired of dyeing pieces of cloth with tea and making collages?'

'Gabby, grow up! You're doing your Leaving Cert next year and you can make your own choices then. I assure you I won't be sneering at whatever you decide to do.'

'Of course you won't. You'll be too busy trying to worm your way into the family business. The golden girl strikes again. You'll probably be a partner before you're thirty.'

'There's nothing stopping you following the same path, or being a partner either, if that's what you want to do.'

'And follow you around in your shadow forever more? No, thank you.'

'That's nonsense and you know it.'

'Not from where I'm standing, it's not. I'm sick doing that. Saint Anne the Infallible.' Gabby had slammed the door on the way out, leaving Anne standing there wondering what her problem was.

When Darcy had rung Anne to see how the holiday had been and if she had told her folks about college, Anne filled her in and then told her about Gabby's reaction.

'Pay no heed to her – she was born angry.'

Anne had had to laugh at that.

'Maybe she was – that would explain a lot.'

Chapter Six

Daniel and Anne had been dating for a few months. The more she got to know him outside his professional sphere the more she realised they had in common and the more she liked him. She looked forward to his phone calls, and to his texts, which popped up when she least expected them. They socialised together as often as their work schedules would allow. Their romance had not gone unnoticed by the gossip columnists and social diarists who kept an eye on such trivia.

'Let's go away from prying eyes for a weekend. We could hop over to London.'

'I'd love that. You know, I've never spent any time there.'

'You've never been to London? I can't believe that.'

'No, never. I suppose it's Ryanair's fault – it always seemed more romantic to head off to Budapest, Vienna or some such place rather than London.'

'Then may I offer my service as your tour guide? We'll do it together. Isn't your birthday on the horizon?'

'Yep, in early October.'

'That's when we'll do it. Leave it to me.'

And she did. Daniel Hassett proved he knew how to treat a lady. He had thought of everything, including a deluxe suite at Brown's Hotel in Mayfair. He knew the city well and had managed to get bookings in a few of the top restaurants.

'I thought you'd like the Courtauld Gallery, they have fantastic impressionist and post-impressionist collections, and we'll take in the Turner collection at the Tate Britain if you'd like too.'

'You're quite the aficionado, aren't you?' she remarked when he showed her some of his favourites.

'My grandfather on my mother's side lived in London for several years; he was the only artist in our family. He was in the RHA when he went back to Dublin. I used to spend holidays with him here when I was growing up and he used take me and my uncle Clive, who is only five years older than me, to these places and he'd take us for high tea afterwards. You must know Clive, he's a Senior Counsel now.'

'Clive Kilucan? I didn't know you were related.'

'One and the same. Grandpop treated us both the same, despite the generation gap.'

'So he's responsible for both your knowledge and your expensive tastes.'

He grinned. 'I suppose you could say that. He would have loved you,' he said, pulling her closer to him. She had a feeling she would have loved him too.

She thoroughly enjoyed being escorted around and took an extra day away from the office to recover before facing back in to the workload that she knew was waiting on her desk.

Darcy dropped in on her way home from school and teased Anne when she told her all they had done on their few days away.

'Hold on a minute, run that past me again, the bit about the navy Rolls Royce that conveyed you to afternoon tea at Quaglino's ... from Brown's Hotel? If I remember rightly they're hardly miles apart, now are they?'

'No, they're not, but the Prohibition Afternoon Tea was all part of Daniel's plans for the birthday and our driver gave us a little tour en route. I felt like something out of *The Great Gatsby*. All razzle-dazzle, art deco and decadent cocktails. I was floating by the time we got to the theatre.'

'He certainly knows how to treat a lady. Our two trips to London saw us eating in the Aberdeen steak houses and buying matinee tickets from the ticket booth in Leicester Square. And we thought we were being posh!'

'It was lovely being totally spoiled; I'll not deny that. I enjoyed every minute of it, even the window-shopping ... and as for Harrods' food hall – that reminds me I brought you back some of their truffles.'

'Calorie free?'

'Are there any other kind?'

'It sounds as though you got on famously. And you look happy. Will we be hearing wedding bells anytime soon?'

'Wedding bells? Darcy, I hardly know the man and he does make me happy, but just because you've tied the knot doesn't mean you have to marry us all off.'

'"Hardly know the man". Well, I'd never have got that impression,' her friend said. 'You have to admit though, don't you, that this relationship has room to bloom?'

Anne laughed. 'It has, and he has hinted about moving in together, but I don't want to do that yet.'

'What's there to wait for? Daniel's a dish – charismatic and attentive and your mother likes him!'

'I know she does, but even if she didn't, if I loved him that wouldn't stop me,' she said.

'Then what *is* stopping you?'

'Nothing really. I'm enjoying life as it is – there's no need to rush into anything more permanent, not yet. Besides Gabby and—'

'I knew it,' Darcy interrupted. 'You're holding back because of Gabby, aren't you? You're waiting for her to make the first move so she doesn't feel you're upstaging her again. Isn't that it?'

'Yeah, maybe you're right. She'll never forgive me if I do and she does seem to be serious about Paul. I think they'll be taking that step soon.'

'You can't put your life on hold because of her, that's not how it works. And he's as dull as they come.'

'I'm not doing that, I promise.' Her friend gave her one of those 'who do you think you're kidding' looks and she replied, 'Maybe a bit of me is, but I just want to be sure. And I have to agree with you about Paul, he'd never suit me, but he's her choice.'

'I don't know what she sees in him. He's a weedy little fellow, certainly no Bradley Cooper, and he's seriously challenged in the conversation stakes. I've never heard him talking about anything only his golf swing and trying to get his handicap into single figures.'

'That'd do it for her – they met at the club and she talks about little else herself these days. Her sole ambition in life seems to be to become lady captain one day,' Anne said.

'How pathetic. I bet she only wants to do that because she knows you never will. What does dear Mama think of him?'

'That he's not perfect …'

'How tactful. Does that mean he's not as perfect as Daniel?'

'Well, that has been mentioned. She feels Gabby could do better.'

'Oh God, don't tell me she told her that.'

'Of course she did. You know subtlety is not one of Mum's virtues, but Gabby is her little girl and she's prepared to compromise for her happiness. Paul didn't go to college and she's the first to admit that she had higher hopes for her younger daughter than a stationery and print sales rep. That didn't feature on the list of suitable son-in-law material.'

'That almost makes me feel sorry for Gabby, and I never thought I'd hear myself say that!'

'Neither did I!' exclaimed Anne. 'But if they love each other isn't that all that matters.'

'And do they?' asked Darcy.

'I would assume they do. Even Gabby is not foolish enough to commit herself for life to anyone just to get back at me for whatever it is I am supposed to have done to ruin everything for her.'

'I wouldn't give her that much credit, but then I'm not as nice as you. On the other hand if I had the chance of moving in with Mr Eligibility, I wouldn't be holding back. I'd be there in penthouse paradise in a flash.'

'You better not let Richard hear you saying that. Married less than a year and already lusting after someone else and you pregnant too ...'

'No, Richard's safe – he's a keeper. So is Daniel.'

'We'll see,' said Anne.

'Well, you have nearly three months to decide, because we'd like you both to be the baby's godparents.' She rubbed her bump protectively.

'I'd be honoured, but don't mention the godfather bit to Daniel just yet.'

'Afraid it might scare him off?' she asked.

'No, just because …'

'OK, I promise. Now I'm whacked and need to go home and get my beauty sleep.'

'And I need to get my head back into work mode for the morning.'

She waved her friend off. She'd love kids of her own, but not yet. They didn't feature in her immediate plans; advancement in her career did. In a way she envied how certain Darcy was about everything, despite having her life shattered when her parents died in a car crash. She knew what she wanted to do with her life and had just got on with it. She had no doubts once she had met him that she and Richard would marry. They were both secondary school teachers and graduated and got their master's together. And now they were starting the family they knew they would have.

She looked through her diary for the coming week, but her mind kept wandering. Darcy's news had unsettled her. If anyone had asked her where she saw herself in five or ten years' time she couldn't have answered them. She couldn't visualise what lay ahead.

She definitely loved Daniel, but she wasn't sure if she was in love or if she was using this as an excuse to hold back. There was a tiny niggle of doubt. It had been injected in her subconscious after she won the Lahiffe case and had started being seen about town with him. She hadn't paid any attention to it then, but when her journalist friend, Alan Seavers, mentioned it, it registered on some level. The original piece he wrote had hinted that the rumour machine was speculating on whether Daniel's love interest had been sparked by a desire to get his hands on Peadar Ffinch's share of Cullen–Ffinch when he finally let it go. It had been written in a light-hearted way and she dismissed it, but when Alan referred to it again when they bumped into each other in the courts one day it had struck a chord – a dissonant one.

From time to time it popped into her mind and she had to ask herself if there could be anything in it, but Daniel never mentioned anything to give rise to any sort of suspicion. Such introspection then prompted the other niggle: if she really loved him would she even be giving doubts like these any headspace at all? Whatever, she needed more time and she knew she couldn't discuss these thoughts with anyone.

Chapter Seven

It was a sub-zero morning and Maurice was foostering about with his project in the garage. He looked up to greet his daughter. He'd heard her car drive up and her footsteps on the gravel. The girls always came in by the side door.

'All on your own this morning, Dad?'

'Yep, the boys both have family commitments.'

'It's freezing and you'll get pneumonia if you stay out here. Leave what you're doing for a bit. I've brought some warm croissants – come on in and join us. I see Gabby is here already.'

'Why do you think I'm hiding out here?' he said. 'She's just told your mother that she and Paul are announcing their engagement – tonight.'

'Tonight? Where?'

'Where do you think?' he said, raising his eyes to the sky. They both said, 'The golf club!' and laughed.

'How do you feel about the news, Dad?'

'Between you and me, I have mixed feelings about him. He's

no Daniel and frankly he wouldn't be my first choice for her,' he replied. 'He's very cocky. I think he tries too hard to make an impression, and in my book that's always a sign of insecurity. Mind you, the prospects of being Sheila's son-in-law would probably make any suitor feel a bit apprehensive, so I suppose I should allow for that.' He straightened up and grinned.

'She could have given us more notice. We have a dinner party tonight and I don't think Daniel would be too pleased if I reneged on that – he's been trying to introduce me to these friends of his for ages.'

'And I know your mother told me we have plans but I can't for the life of me remember what. Don't let her know I said that, but you know her and her social calendar. She tells me and I pretend to be all excited! OK, let's go in together – a united front!' He winked.

Anne opened the kitchen door to the smell of something delicious bubbling away on the cooker. She walked over and embraced her sister.

'Dad tells me you've great news. I'm delighted for you.' She automatically glanced at her sister's left hand.

Gabby noticed and said, 'No, I've no ring yet. Paul is giving me his grandmother's one but it needed to be resized. It was too big.' Gabby had never had the growth spurt she had hoped for in her teens and disappointedly remained at least five inches shorter than her sister. She had tiny hands and feet, as befitting her five-foot-two stature. It gave her something else to be resentful about.

'We're going to tell people about it tonight at dinner in the golf club.'

'Gabby, I'm afraid we already have a commitment. Could you not have given us a little more notice?' Anne said.

'I didn't think you'd be bothered. Besides this is my night, not yours.'

Maurice glanced at his wife. Had she mentioned their plans?

'Paul's parents have a table booked,' Gabby told her mother. 'They go there every week. I'm sure they won't mind if you join them.'

Sheila hesitated. 'Shouldn't we wait to hear from them? I wouldn't like to just show up.'

'Please yourselves,' Gabby said. 'It's obvious that you have other things to do.'

'Darling, it's not like that,' her mother said, looking at Maurice for help, 'but don't you think if his parents wanted us to join them they'd have contacted us?'

'Perhaps we could drop by for a toast?' Maurice suggested.

'I wouldn't dream of asking you to put yourselves out. Why can't you ever be happy for me?'

'Of course we're happy for you, Gabby,' said Anne. 'It's really exciting news. A wedding to plan – it'll be such fun.'

Maurice could see his wife was trying hard not to say the wrong thing and he interjected. 'I suppose it's too early to think about dates.'

'Paul wants us to have the reception in the golf club and he got a few options. Places get booked up very quickly, and they don't like closing the dining room to members on Saturdays. Because Paul's dad is vice captain, he'll be captain by next summer. He's using his influence to get the first available date, one of the Saturdays in June. He's already offered to pay for any losses they'll incur in the bar because of it. I don't want to have to wait too long and there's so much to do.'

Maurice noticed a look pass between Sheila and Anne. That venue was obviously not what either would have chosen, but Anne prevented Sheila voicing her displeasure. 'You can count on me to help in any way I can. This is really exciting, planning my little sister's wedding. It's been a week of good news.'

'Don't tell me you and Daniel – in London,' Gabby exploded. 'That would be just typical of you.'

'Me and Daniel nothing. I was going to tell you all that Darcy and Richard want me to be their baby's godmother.'

'Oh,' was all Gabby could manage, before Sheila said, 'We're so happy for her. She always said she wanted loads of kids. I suppose being an only child must be lonely sometimes.'

'What are you talking about, lonely? She practically lived with us,' Gabby said. 'She was always here.'

'As were your friends,' Maurice reminded her. 'And she was always a delight to have around the place.'

'She still is,' Sheila agreed. 'She's due sometime in March – a spring baby will be lovely.'

'She thinks the world of the pair of you. She was saying yesterday how she'd probably never have finished s chool, n ever mind college, if it hadn't been for you,' Anne said.

'Her parents would have done the same for you if the situations had been reversed, which thankfully they weren't,' Sheila said. 'It's sad that they won't be around to see their first grandchild.'

'Do you hear that, you two?' their father said. 'I'm not getting any younger. I'd like to think I'd still be around to see some of our next generation, so don't wait too long, will you?'

'You're such a softie, Dad,' Anne said.

'No, I just want to be able to upstage Eoin and Paddy when they go on about their little marvels, carrying photos of them around on their phones. It's something I never envisaged – grandchildren envy!' He laughed. 'And theirs are both budding geniuses, if you believe them.'

'Well, I'll be sure to tell Paul that,' Gabby said before adding, 'Doesn't anyone want to hear about my plans and not about fantasy embryos?'

'Of course we do,' Sheila said and Gabby launched forth. It was obvious to them all that her thoughts had been occupied by nothing else for quite a while.

Later, once they had left, Maurice turned to Sheila and asked, 'What do you think of the golf club as a venue?'

'Need you ask? That child does my head in. How many times did she mention the bloody golf club? You'd think it was the be-all and end-all of everything! I think it's totally unsuitable and *nouveau* – it's the O'Reilly's obsession with telling the world they think they've made it. For god's sake, just because they play golf there. He was a brewery rep when he became a member, and that was only because that publican cousin of his proposed him. He's an insufferable little man now,' she said pausing for breath. 'I can't imagine what he will be like next year, when he's captain … and Paul is a carbon copy of him.'

'Closing the bar and restaurant to members on a Saturday – if they permit that it'll set him back a fair few grand in penalties,' Maurice said.

'I don't think that will bother him - he enjoys flashing his cards around.'

'I know I may be old-fashioned, Sheila, but I always saw myself paying for the girls' weddings. I've no intention of going head to head with him, but I can just imagine the spin he'll put on this in the club – he'll give the impression he's taking the tab for everything.'

'Oh, he'd enjoy that.' She busied herself putting cups in the dishwasher then said, 'It's as though our daughter has been brainwashed. It's all been hijacked already. I always thought that their engagements would be something we'd celebrate together. I don't feel like gate-crashing their table with a sideways invitation like that.'

'Nor do I. We can always take them out to dinner next week and do it our way then.'

'That's a good idea. I always imagined that their wedding receptions would be somewhere nice and intimate, with lovely gardens, not somewhere as impersonal as the clubhouse.'

'It's not that bad, Sheila, when it's all decked out.'

'Don't get me wrong, Maurice. It's functional and pleasant, but there's nothing special or even cosy about it. No amount of prettifying will disguise that it's still just a draughty clubhouse, like every other draughty clubhouse around the country too. And,' she added, 'its locker room smells.'

Maurice threw his head back and laughed. He got up from the table to put his arm around her. 'I get the point, although I'm not sure if I agree about the smell. It won't be until next year anyway and we might get around her to choose somewhere else in the meantime.'

'I wouldn't count on that. This is Gabby we're talking about, not Anne,' Sheila said. 'She seems to have it all worked out. Or rather she and her new family seem to have.'

'She is a big girl now and we have to accept that these are her decisions, even if we don't agree with her. Maybe when it's Anne's turn she'll give you the day you visualised.'

'Do you think that's likely to happen?'

'I do, but on her terms. I don't think she'll rush in to anything and I admire her for that,' he replied. 'And I like Daniel, if he's to be the one.'

'Do you think he might not be?' she asked

'Let's not meddle. That's up to her, not us. Isn't it?'

'You're such a guy, aren't you?' his wife said. 'You see everything in black and white. You'd think I'd be used to you by now. I'm going to ring Dee and tell her about Gabby's engagement and plans.'

He laughed. 'That's my cue to go back to my man cave! And I'm sure it won't be my ears that will be burning.'

She laughed and threw the tea towel at him. It missed.

He picked it up, grinned and put it back on the counter top.

The following week Sheila and Maurice hosted their daughters, their future son-in-law, Paul, the O'Reillys and their daughters, Darcy, Richard and Daniel to a celebratory dinner to mark the engagement.

Once seated they all admired the ring, which Paul and Gabby had collected that morning from the jeweller's, his mother telling them twice how it had belonged to her mother, who always wanted her first-born grandson to keep it in the family. When conversation flagged, the topic of golf plugged the holes, until Daniel spun it around.

'Isn't it strange how you never hear anyone talk about their prowess at water polo or snooker the way they do about golf?'

'Well, they're hardly the same thing, are they? I mean, do you play either of them?' one of Paul's sisters asked.

'I played on the Legal Eagles water-polo team at one stage, and I do confess I could give my peers a decent challenge at the snooker table.'

'I didn't know that,' Anne said.

'Exactly. That just goes to prove my point.'

Paul's father laughed at that, and his wife interrupted. 'Don't they say being good at snooker is the sign of a misspent youth?' she asked.

'They do,' Paul's father said, 'but our Danny here hasn't done too badly for himself, has he, so it's clearly not true.'

Maurice saw Daniel sit up straighter and knew he was bristling at being called 'our Danny'. He recognised the signs that this evening could all go downhill very easily and he didn't want Gabby's engagement to be remembered for the wrong reasons.

'Don't tell me those are empty glasses I see. Let's have some more champagne.'

Maurice, Sheila and Dee went to Bad Gastein for Christmas. The first snowfalls had already happened and had been welcomed with glee, as there had been unseasonably high temperatures the previous year and no skiing at all. It hadn't prevented them enjoying themselves and they had taken the opportunity to tour around places they had never seen because they were usually too busy on the slopes.

Anne spent the holidays with Daniel, meeting more of his friends, going for long walks along the beach and enjoying each other, both in and out of their bedrooms. Gabby and Paul's social time was spent with their club friends and in making and re-making schedules and plans, while Darcy and Richard shopped in the sales for all their nursery requirements.

On the Saturday after Christmas Anne woke to that particular stillness that accompanies snow. It had started during the night and would continue all day. It was still early and dark and she left Daniel in bed and went into the kitchen to make coffee. Pulling her dressing gown around her, she opened the doors to the balcony and stood staring down at a world of humpbacked shapes, the snow swirling in a choreographed ballet around the streetlamps. She was happy. Daniel's mother had asked them to a party that evening, her usual Saturday-after-Christmas bash. It was the first time Anne had been invited to their home, and the first time she would meet his parents, and she was looking forward to it.

'What are you doing out there?' she heard a sleepy voice coming from behind her. 'Come in or you'll get your death of cold.'

She laughed. 'I'm a real kid when it comes to snow – I just want to run outside and play!'

'You're full of surprises and there's so much I still have to learn about you. But as regards playing, I have something else in mind. Come back to bed and I'll warm you up.'

She didn't argue.

Darcy and Richard dropped by later and they had gone outside like children and built a snowman. When the guys began pelting each other with snowballs Anne said, 'That's our cue to go inside. I don't want to be responsible for you slipping. And I don't want to turn up at the Hassetts with my arm in a sling.'

'Are you nervous about meeting them?'

'No, not really, but I'd like them to like me.'

'Of course they will,' her friend assured her.

Daniel's parents couldn't have been nicer. She could see where he got his looks from. His mother was long-limbed and elegantly dressed in a rust-coloured outfit that brought out the amber in her eyes. His father was an older version of Daniel, his dark hair silver at the temples. The phrase ' distinguished-looking' sprang to her mind as he welcomed her, saying, 'It's been a while since Daniel has introduced us to a lady friend.' She wasn't sure about the significance of that. She met some people she had met before and lots of new ones as they moved from room to room in the tastefully decorated home.

'You were a big hit with the folks,' Daniel told her as they made their way home in the wee small hours.

'I'm glad they approved,' she said, tucking her arm through his.

'So am I. Maybe now you'll think about moving in.'

'Maybe I will,' she said and knew she meant it.

Chapter Eight

In the first few months of the year Anne and Daniel did spend more and more time together and no one was surprised when she finally decided to make the move. They had been photographed together at the races, a fundraising ball and a gallery opening and featured several times in the gossip columns over that period.

'I don't know what I used to do with my free time before I met him,' she told Darcy when she came to see where she would be living. 'It'll be strange getting used to being together all the time.'

'But you spend lots of nights together now anyway.'

'I know we do, but he's such a social animal, he'd go out every night if he didn't have to appear in court the next day. Sometimes I can hardly keep up with him. Then when he's immersed in a case he hardly comes up for air.'

Darcy was overwhelmed by her friend's new home and punctuated her tour of inspection by wow-ing and aah-ing at every gadget and piece of modern furniture.

'If I had bought this penthouse,' Darcy said, 'I'd never want to go out at all. This must have cost a fortune to furnish, never mind to buy.'

'According to Daniel, he got it for a fraction of what it would have cost when it was built during the boom. It had been empty for three years when he bought it. The vendor was so thrilled to find a cash buyer that apparently he accepted a vastly reduced price to the one advertised. He showed me the write-up it got when it was launched back then and it was described in the property pages as "a swanky architectural space, suitable for an urbanite or couple with good taste and an appreciation of refined design", whatever that meant. He put in an offer after the first viewing.'

'Lucky him. We'll never aspire to anything like that on our teachers' salaries, although I do love our little pad in Ringsend.'

'So do I. Between us, I find the architectural space a bit cold and depersonalised, but those views back towards the Pigeon House and across Dublin Bay to Howth make up for the other shortcomings.'

'I can see why. They're stunning,' Darcy said, 'and you can add your own touches now. Loads of your own art work and squidgy cushions and—'

Anne laughed. 'I think I'd better wait a while before I start doing that.'

Gabby tagged along with their parents when they came on their first visit and Anne could see she was impressed. However, instead of being generous about its good points, Gabby remarked, 'Some people prefer to live in a house, with their own garden.'

'I know,' Anne said, deciding not to mention the roof garden to her. 'Darcy was just saying that when she came over – they love that about their place, although their garden is really tiny: she refers to it as her outside box room.'

'We were hoping to get something with one a bit bigger than that,' her sister said and before Anne could reply she heard Daniel telling her father, 'I was badly stung when I bought my first place, out Blanchardstown way – the builders were pretentiously describing it as West Dublin's D4.'

Anne knew Gabby and Paul had been looking at places in Blanchardstown, and so did their father.

'It might have become that if the collapse hadn't happened,' Maurice said.

'I doubt it. I think they were taking a bit of creative licence there. The property journos were probably on fat backhanders to write such drivel, maybe even getting a share from the sales. The upshot is they built too many estates out there and forgot about the landscaping and trees – consequently there are acres of soulless little grey boxes everywhere.'

Anne and their mother tried to distract Gabby, but when Daniel had the floor he made full use of it and he was in full flow here. 'Anyway, my builder went bust and that left us early buyers living in one half-filled block of what should have been, and I quote, "a three-block enclave amid an idyllic sylvan setting with parkland and amenities". They never materialised either. The undeveloped lands turned into the meeting point for cider parties and for dumping.'

'I'm sure there are some very nice parts.' Sheila said.

Gabby remained silent.

'Not where I bought, there aren't. It went further downhill when someone decided it would be a good idea to fence it off from our blocks and fill the empty units with people on social lists. I think they had to have at least ten kids each to qualify.'

'You do exaggerate.' Anne laughed, trying to lighten the mood. 'No one has ten kids these days.'

'Believe me, that's what it sounded like – babies screaming and kids shouting. I couldn't wait to get out of the place.'

'I'm not surprised,' her mother said. 'It sounds awful and you'd have to feel sorry for the young people they put in them.'

'And for those who are now stuck in negative equity. You must have taken a hit when you sold it,' Maurice said.

'I did, but it was worth it to get out – it'll never come back up in value.'

'Well, you hit the jackpot here, didn't you?' Gabby said, opening the French doors and going out on to the veranda. 'From this height you can look down your nose at the minions below.'

Daniel looked puzzled and Anne whispered, 'I'll tell you later.'

'Did you do the décor?' Sheila asked, trying to change the subject.

'No, I hired an interior designer to remove the chintzes, the flounces, and the fancy standard lamps. It was very girly before and not really to my liking at all. We had a few fights before I won her around. She'd swapped the busyness for a more "pared-down ambience", I believe she called it, a sophisticated look of leather, suede and chrome instead. And – *voilà* – that's what I now have.'

She'd left the large picture windows free from drapes so that the views were unrivalled.

'It's the ultimate bachelor pad,' Anne had exclaimed the first time she'd seen it.

'All it's missing is the bachelorette,' he'd replied. 'And I'm interviewing, if you're interested.'

'I wonder how many women you've said that to.'

'Honestly? Not many, until now.' And she'd believed him. He hadn't pushed her on the subject then, and she had been happy to let things progress at their own speed.

He loved music and had had a techie friend work with him to ensure the whole place was programmed for any device he would ever need. Before such gadgetry had become mainstream, he could turn his heating and lighting on and close the blinds on his big windows remotely if he wished. His surround-sound could play different t racks i n d ifferent ro oms. The apa rtment eve n had a mezzanine, with floor-to-ceiling windows, a space that he seldom used. He enjoyed entertaining and the wrap-around verandas were a great hit with his friends who loved sitting out there, enjoying a drink and the views.

'Don't sell your own place, Anne,' her father had advised when she'd told him she was going to move in. 'Life doesn't always go as planned and it's good to have something of your own to fall back on if you should ever need it.'

'That's not exactly a vote of confidence.'

'I didn't mean it like that, and you know it,' he'd said. 'I'd be giving you that advice no matter who you were planning on sharing with. Ask your mother. She'll tell you the same.'

Anne's place was in Blackrock and also enjoyed sea views of Dublin Bay, a vista that changed totally when the lights went on across the city, redefining the landscape. After her father's advice she had found tenants, a couple who were coming to Ireland on a fifteen-month secondment from Silicon Valley. She gave them a lease for the period of their contract. They weren't due to arrive for a month and that had given her time to get everything freshened up and to do her move in easy stages. She and Daniel had been back and forward between their places numerous times already.

'Yes, Gabby and Paul offered to help one day, but they had to get away early – something to do with their wedding plans,' she'd told Darcy, who wanted to muck in. 'There's no way you're going to help, lifting boxes in your condition.'

'I'm pregnant – not feeble,' Darcy told her.

'In fairness, they are house hunting too, so they haven't got much time.'

'What did they say when they saw this place?'

'Verbally not a lot – facially volumes!'

'That doesn't surprise me, but there must be something I can do.'

'There is – you can help me cull my collection of shoes and handbags and go through things I haven't worn for ages.'

'Can I take things you don't want? For when they'll fit me after the bump is gone?'

'You look radiant and you know it. Feel free to help yourself.'

'It's great having rich friends; ones with good taste, too.'

'I'm not rich,' Anne had protested.

'You are, you know. Mum used to tell me there are more ways to be rich than having money, and when I think of that I can still hear her voice. Yet I can't remember anymore how it sounded when she said my name.' She had begun to cry.

Anne hugged her friend who, when she finally released her, had said, 'Pay no attention to me – it's the baby hormones. I cry when I'm happy and when I'm sad. As for when I'm watching soppy television, I'm a blubbering wreck.'

The process of bringing her possessions to Daniel's had taken a few weekends. She had tried to find new homes for everything as she had gone along and had finally whittled it down to the last two cars full of stuff.

He laughed as he held the door open for her with his foot.

'Can I put my painting things up in the mezzanine?' she asked as she carried her easel out of the lift.

'Of course, there's no need to ask. *Mi casa es su casa* etc., but

I didn't think you still did any art,' Daniel said, nodding in the direction of her easel as he led the way. She deposited it on the floor with the boxes they'd brought in earlier.

'I don't, I mean I haven't done anything since I met you. I haven't exactly had much free time, have I?' She grinned.

'And what makes you think that you'll have any more, now that I have you here in my nest?' he asked, pulling her to him. They kissed and responded hungrily to each other. She yielded and they made love on the couch in the mezzanine, as though sealing a bond, the promise of a future shared. Afterwards she'd said, 'If I'd known it would be like this I'd have moved in months ago.'

'I did try to tell you!'

'OK, you were right.'

'Don't look at me like that or we'll never get this stuff sorted and there's still more in your car.'

'Let's go down and get that and then you can show me what a good chef you are.'

'That won't take long – I have a folder full of the nearest takeaway menus.'

She laughed. 'You neglected to put that in your list of enticements.'

'How could I have forgotten?'

'Easily and intentionally, I should imagine,' she'd said, pushing him gently out the door in front of her.

'I'm a good cook, but like your excuse, I haven't exactly had much time to buy provisions this weekend.'

When she was next at her mother's Anne told her, 'Getting used to living with someone is a lot easier than I thought it would be, once we'd established a few basic house rules, like the lid on the toothpaste, keeping the toilet seat down and the like.'

'I'm delighted to hear that. You know, often it's silly little things like that which actually start friction between a couple.'

'Did you and Dad always get on so well?'

'Don't be fooled by that – I had to house train him in the beginning too. But I'm very happy for you. I like Daniel.'

'So do I, Mum.'

'I should hope so!'

The noise of the rain driving against the picture window woke Anne. She looked at the clock and couldn't believe it was time to get up. She stretched and reached for Daniel, but he was already showered and had the kettle boiling and bread in the toaster.

'I was going to sneak out without disturbing you,' she said.

'I had the same idea, great minds and all that.' He came around from behind the counter and wrapped his arms around her.

'I'm so glad you moved in.'

She smiled and kissed him. 'So am I, but despite my heart telling me one thing, my head is telling me another and I have to listen to it.' She pushed him gently away. 'I'll make it up to you tonight.'

It was one of those dark mornings when Howth had vanished in the mists and the rain visibly slanted down in great swathes across the sea. The traffic was horrendous. It snaked its way into town as she half-listened to the same bad news stories that had been on the radio for months now. Dire warnings from economists of a fluctuating world economy: yet more fiscal instability ahead. Dah-dah dah-dah – she'd heard it all before. The windows kept steaming up. She switched to lyric fm and listened to Marty Whelan, who never seemed to allow the predictions of the imminent collapse of the world impinge on his good humour. She arrived almost half an hour later than she had planned.

'Maurice would like to see you in his office,' was Paula's greeting as Anne shook the rain from her hair. Anne was working on a really tricky case and didn't want to be disturbed; however, a meeting in her father's office was a command that could not be ignored. She had seen him the previous Saturday at home, but he made it a rule to keep business in the office. He never brought office talk home with him, unless it was of vital importance. This was something that she and Daniel were trying to develop. They found it hard to keep to, though, and invariably ended up talking about cases they were working on or consulting with each other on points of law or precedence. In such matters Maurice was more disciplined than she. For him weekends were for his family, the occasional golf game, his bikes, and that usually included his biker buddies too.

She was surprised to see Peader Junior sitting in her father's office. He made to stand up and greet her as she entered, but she told him not to. He had grown frail in the few years since he had been actively involved in the firm. He was a lot thinner too, she noticed, his shirt collar too large around his neck, his linen jacket no longer hugging his bony shoulders, blue veins showing through the paper-thin age-speckled skin on the backs of his hands. When had that all happened?

'I know I've said it before but you really brought the old firm up in the world with the move.' Peadar nodded his approval. He had just returned from his farm in France, where he'd been since Christmas. The business had relocated the previous year, a move necessitated by the ending of the lease in Pembroke Place, their address since the 1930s.

'As a traditionalist I love those old buildings, they have character and a solidity about them that these turn-key places lack, but there's a lot to be said for this – it's so bright and airy,' he said as he crossed the room to look down on the tree-lined canal below.

'Yes, the overall reaction has been very positive,' Maurice said, 'and from a personal perspective it's such a bonus being able to park and to have enough room for several of us to meet clients without having to book the space and know someone else is waiting outside the door to take over the room when we leave.'

'And there's a proper kitchen and modern cloakrooms too,' said Anne, who was always getting complaints that the water in the ladies' room in the old place was either too cold or scalding.

'We tried to replicate your old den as best we could. The panelling is new but the desk, chairs and bookcases, with their tomes, your tomes, are all the originals. There's just a bit more space in here for them.'

'Yes, that gets my approval too,' he said. Before he sat down he half stood and seemed to be examining the desktop. Then he reached out and ran his finger across a discoloured mark.

'I did that with a cigar that fell off the ashtray.'

'I never knew you smoked,' Maurice said.

'I didn't. I was trying to be one of the big boys and was determined to learn how to inhale like a pro. I nearly choked and went off to get water. I forgot all about the bloody cigar and when I came back to the office it had burned down and fell on the wood. My father wasn't happy at all – that desk was an antique even then!' He laughed. 'Don't things like that seem so trivial when you look back at them? At the time it seemed monumental.'

'There are lots more antiquities in here. Some of those statute books go way back in British Rule.'

'Aye, and so do a lot of our rules,' Peadar said. 'Those books belonged to my father.'

'If you ever want any of them back—' Maurice began.

'Good god, no – when I die it's going to take a bin lorry to clear my possessions. I've always been a dreadful hoarder and—'

Paula's knock and enquiry – 'Coffee for everyone? Do you still take it black with two sugars?' – interrupted his reminiscing.

'Well remembered, it's just like old times being back in here,' Peadar said again and smiled at her. When she left he continued. 'You're probably wondering why I asked for this meeting. It's because I've been made an offer for my side of the business. It's a generous offer but I wouldn't feel happy taking it without telling you first.' He turned to Maurice. 'I always told you I'd give you first refusal if and when I decided to sell.'

'I appreciate that, Peadar. Does this mean you have finally decided to call it a day?'

'Yes, I think it's time I put my affairs in order and to admit that I'm old!'

'You know, when I was younger I always saw us buying you out someday.'

'You didn't think I'd last this long did you?' He chuckled.

'Probably not, but when you're young you think fifty is old,' said Maurice. 'Now that I'm past retirement age myself, I can appreciate where you're coming from. And I'm not ready to give up yet either.'

'Poor Sheila, that may be a bit unfair on her – being a younger wife. I bet she's not ready to have you under her feet all day just yet.'

'Probably not. I can't believe I'll be seventy next birthday. It's flown by.'

'Good god, if you're going to reach seventy that makes her sixty. Where has it all gone?'

'It just creeps up, doesn't it? I'd like to keep going as long as you,' he said to his partner, 'so I'm sure you understand that I'm not quite ready to dry my quills off just yet.'

'I never think of you being old, Dad,' Anne said.

'Young lady, that makes me feel less ancient.' Peadar laughed. 'How do you both feel about the future of the company?'

'Anne and I have never had a formal discussion about whether in time she wants or would be willing to take on the responsibility for all this, or whether she'd be happy with my share and a new partnership. Owning only forty-nine per cent hasn't been an issue while you're still involved, but with a new partner we'd always have a lesser say. We'll have to talk it over properly.'

'Young lady, what's your opinion?' Peadar Ffinch asked her directly.

'It's a lot to think about and it would depend very much on who made the offer and whether they'd have the same business ethics and ideals as we have.'

'Now that's an interesting thing – and I can't give you any help there. The approach was made by a third party, and he was instructed that the bidder's identity be kept out of any negotiations.'

'It's all come a bit out of the blue. We'll need time to think and talk about it,' Maurice said.

'Of course, take as much time as you like. I'm off to France for a few weeks. And remember, I'm not holding a gun to your heads, although I never thought I'd see the day when a woman would be in control of my late father's family business. See, I may be a fossil, Anne, but I have moved with the times. I'm no longer a prejudiced one. I just wanted to inform you both of the offer.'

'We appreciate it,' she replied. 'Thank you, Peadar, and I should never have called you that.'

'You were right to. I was prejudiced and if you hadn't called me on it you wouldn't be sitting there. I have to say you dragged me out of my comfort zone and I know I didn't appreciate it at the time, but I'm glad you did.'

She laughed. 'That wasn't an impression I ever got.'

'I know, and you were probably right, but you wore me down.' He smiled at her and then at her father. 'This young lady made me realise just how misogynistic I was being.'

'Now the fairer sex is taking us over, in this practise anyway. We now have nineteen solicitors on the payroll. More than half of them are women. It's hard to believe nowadays, isn't it?' Maurice said. 'How things have changed in such a short space.'

'Before you two start recollecting, can I ask a question? How much time do we have before making a decision?'

'They've made no stipulation about that, so we'll talk about it whenever you're ready. You can call it.'

Paula came back in with the refreshments and Anne stood up. 'That's great, now can I be excused and take my coffee in my office? I've a case that requires some urgent work.' They nodded and she said, 'It's always great to see you, Peadar, and when I'm boss you'll always be welcome to stop in for a cuppa and a chat.' She put her hand on his frail shoulder and he smiled up at her.

'You might even ask my advice sometime,' he said.

'That's a very distinct possibility. Now I really have to go.' She went into her office, and glanced at her watch. So much for an uninterrupted morning, she thought, as she settled back to study her notes.

After a while she heard Paula call a taxi for Peadar. Maurice walked him to lift and escorted him down and out to the car. That done, he came to Anne's door.

'That was a bit of a bolt out of the blue, wasn't it? I'd love to know who put that offer in.'

'Maybe he's bluffing to get you to make a better one and buy him out.'

'I doubt it. He's a sharp old boy, but that's not his style. Peadar always called the shots as they were, and I've no reason to suspect he'd do anything different at this stage, but let's keep our eyes and ears open and see if we get any hints as to whom the bidders might be. And let's keep this between ourselves until we decide what to do?'

'Does "between ourselves" exclude Daniel?'

'For the moment I think it should, if you've no objections. That way if anyone talks to him he won't find himself in an awkward situation.'

'OK, but Dad, I have this domestic abuse case on this week – I can't give the offer any consideration until that's over.'

'That's no problem. It'll give me chance to go over some of the figures and the paperwork. Even if we're not going to sell, or merge, a good audit of best practise is well overdue. We really need to consider a dedicated e-commerce and data-protection division.' He nodded in the direction of one of the glass-partitioned rooms. 'It's got too big for just two to handle.'

'You don't want to do a Peadar Junior on it and hang on while everyone else passes us out.'

'You're right. I can see it's the way forward, Anne. We're getting more and more enquiries about piracy, brand protection and cyber crime – they seem to be the zeitgeist nowadays and we have to stay abreast of developments in these sectors.'

'I agree. It's too easy to fall behind with the speed things are moving.'

'And I'm no techie whiz kid …'

'Right, Dad,' she said, moving to push him gently out of her room. 'That's it for me. My head's spinning already. Techie whiz kid or not, go back to your own office. There's a big Do Not Disturb sign going up on my door for the rest of the day.'

He looked at her, then at Paula and said, 'She'll make a good MD!'

'Out! Now!'

Chapter Nine

Anne reheated some soup, and put some meatloaf that was left over from the previous night on a plate. Not for the first time was she grateful that Daniel was a good cook. He enjoyed experimenting and always made enough of everything to last two days, to cut down on preparation. She added some salads and ate at the breakfast bar, her favourite place in the gleaming high-spec kitchen. She hadn't turned on the main light. She enjoyed sitting here like this. The counter spots dropped little pools of light on the black marble surfaces. Polished steel glowed and beyond the picture window the lights of Howth reflected in the waters of Dublin Bay.

She always felt this sleek kitchen was the sort of state-of-the-art space you saw people having parties in the movies. She realised that, although they often had a few guests around, they hadn't had a proper party since she'd moved in. She'd have to rectify that, but she'd wait until she knew his friends a little better, and until the wedding was over. To have it before would probably antagonise her sister, who would be sure to let her know she thought it was an effort at upstaging her again.

She sighed. Gabby could be so petty, and she certainly had no reason to be. They had had a charmed life, when she thought of the one her client, Perdita, was enduring. Despite being less than a mile away from each other geographically, their worlds were light years away from each other. She wondered did anyone ever call on Perdita with flowers or show her any kindness? In her experience the friends of people in her situation often disappeared, not wanting to get involved. What happened that some lives could go so horribly wrong? All most people want is love and a bit of security and she and Gabby had had both, excesses of both, and enough to embrace Darcy too.

Daniel was talking on the phone when she'd finished eating. She would love to have snuggled up beside him on the sofa but knew he wouldn't welcome such distraction. She took herself up to the mezzanine, which they now referred to as the studio, and began sketching some ideas. It was after eleven when she looked at the time. She realised how engrossed she'd been. She had switched off completely and hadn't thought about the complexities of the pending case or her sister's wedding for hours. She was more relaxed than she had been for a long time. Daniel had dropped off on the couch downstairs, his papers scattered on the floor where they had fallen. She gathered them up and put them beside him. He woke, and put them in their proper order.

'You look tired,' he said.

'So do you, I just want my bed,' she said. 'I'm whacked.'

A few minutes later as he put his arm around her and she snuggled up to him he said, 'What are we like? Too tired to make love. We need a break.'

'There's not much chance of that at the moment. I'm snowed under and we've asked Paul and Gabby over on Saturday.'

'To listen to them going on about the wedding.' He laughed. 'I'm sure the last royal one didn't take as much organisation as theirs.'

'Don't get me started. Paul's as bad as Gabby,' she muttered. 'Honestly, I know she's my sister and I am pleased for her, although it may not seem like it, but I'm finding all the wedding business a little overwhelming, not to mention very time-consuming. She keeps ringing me and asking my opinion and no matter what suggestions I make she dismisses them. I'll ask Darcy and Richard along too,' she said but Daniel's breathing told her he was already asleep.

She turned over and eventually slept too.

Chapter Ten

Darcy's baby arrived in early February. She had no time to tell anyone labour had started. Three weeks early, this tiny, cherub-like little girl with dark curls had decided she couldn't wait to meet the world. Richard made the phone calls at six thirty in the morning – he couldn't wait to tell everyone the news. They hadn't wanted to know the sex in advance and were thrilled they had delayed finding out. She was immediately loved by everyone who saw her. Her besotted parents had to wait a few anxious days before they could cuddle her for long or take her home.

'Just precautionary,' the medics had assured them. 'It's pretty normal with premature babies – it just gives their lungs a few more days to develop and expand. Have you got a name for her?'

'We have,' Darcy had said, smiling with pride. 'We're calling her Samantha Anne. Samantha after the grandmother she'll never know, and Anne because she's going to be the auntie we hope will be very much part of her life.'

Anne was thrilled for her friends. Once she was allowed she

held the baby and marvelled at how petite she was and how alive. In the strict sense, Anne was no blood relation but she was perfectly happy to assume the role of auntie. Darcy had been Anne's friend since they had sat beside each other on their first day at secondary school. A few years later the road accident that claimed her parents' lives left her orphaned and it was the Cullen family who took her into their care. The two had been inseparable ever since.

Their bond was stronger than the one between Gabby and herself. She'd confessed this to Maurice one time, and he'd told her, 'You may be the same bloodline, and family should always stick up for each other, but it doesn't always mean they like each other. Although, in my humble experience, when sisters grow older they often grow closer to each other, especially when they marry and have families of their own.' Anne couldn't see that happening in the foreseeable future. Maybe Samantha would be the catalyst.

Darcy had become a member of their family after the accident, although they all knew that they could never replace what she had lost, someone of her own flesh and blood to love and cherish. That had all changed, and Anne was delighted that they now had a little one to indulge too. She didn't know how she'd feel about being a mother; she wasn't anywhere near that stage yet.

She and Daniel hadn't discussed kids. Was it too soon to discuss them? Would he run scared if she did? Maybe she'd bring up the topic soon. Maybe not. She smiled to herself when she had these thoughts. Her future mightn't be with Daniel anyway, although as they'd settled into co-habiting she was finding i t h arder a nd harder to visualise a future without him being part of it.

She shook herself. Since Samantha was born she'd been pensive and couldn't wait to see her again. Stop the daydreaming and focus, she told herself. You have a case to fight and a way to go to advance in your profession. She turned her attention back to the notes on her desk.

She decided to detour and pay her little niece a visit on her way back from the courts. She brought some flowers and a cake. She also wanted to ask Darcy what she should buy Samantha as her welcome-to-the-world present. They gazed into the baby's crib, fascinated by her perfect little ears, eyelashes, fingers and fingernails and the way she opened her tiny fist and closed it as though dreaming.

'Do you know what I would absolutely love? One of your watercolours, painted specially for her.'

'I haven't done anything for ages.'

'I know, and you should, but I could honestly set up a shop with all the baby presents she got. Your mum and dad have been really generous too. They opened a bank account in her name.'

'They look on you as their third daughter, which makes this little one theirs too.'

'They have always been there for me. Your mum knows I want them to be Samantha's honorary grandparents.'

'She told me, and they're delighted too.'

'If you can tear yourself away from her for a few minutes, come see what she got. We won't have to buy the child anything to wear until she's at least two, and look,' she said, picking up a pink and black zebra, 'we could open a stuffed animal zoo with all the toys she's been given. I'd like her to have something special from you that she can have forever; something that's not pink, preferably.'

'OK, let me have a little think about it.' Anne drank a hurried coffee and said, 'Now, much as I hate to leave you both I really have to go. I have to pop back to the office for a bit.' She kissed her fingertips, then touched them to the baby's downy forehead. She hugged her friend and left.

Anne was engrossed in the preparation for her client Perdita's acrimonious marriage break-up case and she needed to keep a clear head. Family law was complicated and always challenging, reasons she had chosen it as her speciality. No two cases were ever the same. It was difficult not to be judgmental and to stop becoming too involved. It could be draining too.

She worked late that night. When she got home Daniel asked, 'Did you get it all wrapped up?'

'I hope so, although that won't stop me going over and over it again in my mind all night.'

'Poor you, I know that feeling, worrying in case you've missed anything. I'm afraid I'm caught up in something myself here. Do you mind if I keep going at it? I've already eaten.'

'Of course I don't,' she said giving him a peck on the cheek. 'I'll get myself something. You carry on.'

The case Anne was working on was settled out of court, and she wasn't a bit happy about that. She was defending her client against a man she had disliked the moment she had met him. Without being told anything about him she would have put him in the category of a bully who was capable of violence. His body language spoke volumes: the way he looked at women and his whole attitude to why he was on trial at all gave him away. It was too easy to be judgmental and she had had to work on that as a student. Never make snap decisions and concentrate on the facts – the facts were where the truth lay, not in someone's tattoos, piercings, accent or haircut. This wasn't a snap decision. She had developed the ability to be much more clinical, even though her instincts mostly proved to be right. And they turned out to be right on all fronts in this case.

Perdita was looking for a barring order. He had admitted to Anne that he had 'slapped her around a bit' occasionally, but that he hadn't ever meant to hurt her. The wife was claiming that after several documented injuries, some that had required medical attention, she now felt that their son were in danger too. Recently he had lashed out at Johnny, an eleven-year-old, when he tried to step in front of his mother to protect her.

'I'll never understand why women keep doing this – taking men like that back?' Daniel said when they were relaxing and discussing their day that evening after dinner.

'I don't know either. I would have spotted her as a victim a mile away, a thin little woman, dressed in dark clothes with a haunted look. She looks at least fifty and she's younger than me. She'd be a hundred times better off without him. So would the boy. Can you imagine what it must feel like to be in a home like that, seeing your father beat your mother?' Anne said. 'Waiting for the next punch to land, or hearing a bone snap?'

'It's just too awful to imagine. Did you see that report in the papers about the archbishop who sparked outrage in Spain by saying that domestic violence occurs because "women do not obey men"?'

'I don't believe it.'

'Yep,' he said. 'Some enlightened chap in Toledo, Braulio Rodriguez, I think he's the Primate of Spain, told his congregation that wives could avoid being hit by doing what they are told and not asking for a separation.'

'What sort of message does that send out in this day and age? It's the twenty-first century.'

'Not a very encouraging one,' he agreed

'Doesn't that let men like Perdita's husband off the hook, giving them a reason to be physical? It's too easy to promise to try mediation and anger-management therapy, but it means nothing for the victim or victims.'

'No, but it gets the perpetrator off a custodial sentence.'
'That's why I have a problem with his ilk. He just keeps reverting to type, especially when he has drink taken. I'd say half the time there isn't enough food in the house either. Then he stops for a few weeks, begs to come back, swears undying love for her and the children, falls off the wagon and it all begins again. I really wanted her to walk away with a sense off freedom and security, knowing there was an end to the torture. Instead I just felt sick today when they told me they were going to give it another shot. I'd love to think that it will work out for them, but I have my doubts.'

'Women will always be an enigma to me. They can be so strong and cope with enormous challenges, yet some always pin their hopes on such losers and bullies.'

'They stay with them because they love them and because they're optimists. They always think they'll be able to change them.'

'I'll never understand that. You can't change anyone,' he said.

'It's also because they feel trapped and conflicted. It can't be an easy decision to make when there are kids involved – deciding to leave or to have a partner barred.'

'It's a big thing to keep them from their father, but it's a fact, some fathers aren't fit for that role.'

'Don't you ever think it's wrong for us to defend people we know are guilty?' she asked.

'Everyone deserves a fair trial.'

'But it's not fair, is it?' she argued. 'Perdita and wives like that don't deserve to be beaten, no matter what goes on in that home.

Kids don't deserve to see such violence, Daniel, yet because he has money he can pay someone like us to get him away with it. That's not justice and it bothers me.'

'So you think we should only represent the innocent parties.'

'In an ideal world, yes.'

'So what happened to innocent until proven guilty?' he asked.

'That's just semantics in a case like this – that guy was guilty before being proven anything and we all know it.'

'God, Anne, I love you,' he said, pulling her close to him and kissing her on her cheek. 'You're good. I hate to think what you'll be like when you're a senior counsel. Please don't come up against me too often, or you'll have me doubting every argument I've learned to make.'

She laughed and stepped back.

'That's exactly what I will do. Be warned, my learned friend, I'll show you and those old fuddy-duddies on the bench – and that archbishop fellow too, if I get the chance – what strong women are really like! Now I'm going up to the studio. I want to work on little Samantha's pressie or I'll never have it finished in time for the naming ceremony. When I finish this case let's go away somewhere close. Somewhere we can drive to – with no airports involved?'

He nodded. 'Right, somewhere romantic and remote where we don't have to think about reality.'

'That sounds wonderful. Surprise me.'

'I will,' he promised.

She left him downstairs and went up to the studio. She stood looking out to the city lights, feeling happy, and trying to imagine what others were up to behind their curtains, where life in all its guises was being played out on mini stages everywhere and where the abnormal and unconventional were the normal and the conventional to those involved.

She sat at her desk and toyed with several glimmers of ideas. Perhaps she'd use the letters in Samantha's name. She looked up its meaning, which according to some sources meant 'listener' or 'listener of God', while one gave 'sexy booty' as its explanation. Nothing to go on there. She found flowers – a rose, campanula and a verbena all called Samantha, but they didn't inspire her either. She began to think of toys and flowers, characters from fairy tales. Darcy had said she wanted something her little girl could keep forever. She hit upon the idea of a collage of things that were significant in her childhood – and probably would be in Samantha's. Could she create something that could be a permanent link between their lives?

She rang her mum and told her she'd pop in after work the next day to go through the photo albums for inspiration.

There were several of these on a bookshelf in her home. Her mother had loads of photographs dotted around. The ones that captured occasions that required hats, caps and gowns and the like were strategically placed. These had silver frames. They couldn't be missed by anyone calling.

'I'd love to see you, Anne, and bring Daniel along. You know your dad always enjoys a good chat with him. Despite everything, I know he misses having Charlie around, although he met up with him last week.'

'He never mentioned anything to me about that.' But then, she thought, no one said much about Charlie any more. They were all still smarting from his behaviour and how he had deceived them.

'Maybe I shouldn't have either, so don't bring it up unless he does.'

At dinner next evening her father did bring it up.

'He's lost a fair bit of weight, but apart from that he actually seems to be coping with life much better than I thought he would. I suppose he's trying to keep focused for the next trial.'

'Does Dee know you saw him?' Anne asked.

'Yes, I've seen him a few times but I didn't feel happy about not telling her, so I gave her a ring. She understood. He was my friend for years. I don't approve of how he conducted himself, and she knows that, but it just didn't feel right abandoning him to his fate. He needs his friends more now than ever.'

Sheila smiled at her husband. 'You're a good man, Maurice Cullen. I bet many of his so-called friends haven't been near him.'

'You're right there,' he said, 'it's amazing how they all have suddenly become so engrossed in their lives that they can't fit him in.'

'Why didn't you say anything before, Dad?'

'I didn't tell you, Anne, because I had just found out that he had asked Daniel to act as counsel for him again. I wasn't sure if you knew that and I didn't want to make things awkward.'

Anne looked at Daniel. He hadn't told her that either.

'Actually, that came as a bit of a surprise to me too, after the outcome of his bigamy case,' Daniel said. 'I never expected to hear from him again.'

'He hadn't a hope of winning that.'

'Thanks, Dad,' Anne said, 'for a great vote of confidence.'

'I didn't mean that, and you know it. I meant he needs the best he can afford and, without doubt, that's Daniel,' Maurice said. 'He's living a pretty solitary life these days. He's even given up on his golf and you know what that means to him.'

'In the light of everything you can hardly expect him to be welcome in the club with open arms, can you?' Sheila said. 'A lot of those people are Dee's friends too, and—' but Maurice stemmed this line of conversation.

'That's enough shop talk.'

'I agree,' Daniel said. 'That spiced salmon was delicious, Sheila. I can see where Anne gets her culinary skills from.'

'I don't get to use them that much, except at weekends. I never feel much like cooking when I come in after work, whereas Daniel finds it relaxing to potter around the kitchen.'

'Pottering – that's the best you can do to describe my delicious dishes? You sure know how to hit right at my heart.' They laughed at his melodramatic gestures. 'Don't look so worried,' he said to Sheila. 'We make a good team, but my efforts wouldn't match this. I suppose I'll have to add your homemade brown-bread ice-cream and raspberry coulis to my menu if I'm to keep her from running home for a feed.'

'That sounds like a sensible plan! Why do you think I stuck around for so long?' Maurice said.

The men cleared away and the women put the photo albums out on the table in the sitting room. It was Anne's favourite place in the house, overlooking the back garden. It got the evening sun and even on gloomy days the purple settee and lime-green cushions made it feel warm and welcoming. It led to the conservatory that spread all across part of the back of the house. At the other side sliding doors opened into the room they called the study. Nowadays this doubled as the place where the computer lived, along with shelves of legal reference books and opinions, and a selection of the latest novels. Both her parents were avid readers. The dividing doors were usually kept closed, but when the Cullens had their friends over for a bridge night, every other month or so, they put the card tables up in the two rooms.

There were three of Anne's watercolours hanging here, detailed botanical studies. The first was of the passionflower creeper that covered the side of the garage with its rampant growth and spectacular delicate green and purple flowers. Th e mi ddle on e was of her mother's favourite clematis, 'Apple Blossom'. Even looking at it now she could imagine the masses of vanilla-scented flowers that opened from rosy-pink buds to full blooms, contrasting beautifully against the bronze-tinted foliage. The third was her favourite, naked ladies or Bowden lilies, which flowered s pectacularly a gainst t he e vergreen h edges y ear a fter year, their Barbie-pink flowers looking feminine and dainty. She remembered doing the sketches for those and how she nervously presented them as part of her portfolio when she was interviewed for a place at the National College of Art and Design. Would she ever have met Daniel had she continued on that path?

'Do you remember that hat?' her mother's question broke her reverie.

'God, yes. It had peacock feathers on it and Granny wouldn't let you wear it in the house.'

'She always believed they brought bad luck.'

'She was a great one for her superstitions,' Anne said, turning the pages of an early album. 'I haven't looked at any of these for ages. I've forgotten half of them.'

'I often take them out and sit here going through them. They bring back so many memories of good days and of special ones too. They also remind me how quickly time flies and of how lucky I am. Come to think of it, no one ever seems to take photos on the bad days, do they?'

'Maybe that's why everyone thinks everyone was happier back when,' said Anne.

'Possibly. But we *were* happy and all these photographs remind me of things I'd forgotten. You and Gabby on the swing at your gran's.' She turned the page over. 'That lime tree in their garden that you used to call the singing tree.'

'I'd forgotten it. Why did I call it that?'

'Because you said it was always buzzing with insects on sunny days. You always said they were singing and it sounded as though they were. You could hear it as you approached.'

'Remember those matching party dresses Gabby and I had? We wore them at some party or picnic and they itched like mad and gave us both rashes on our legs.'

'I was never sure if it was the raspberries we picked or the material that caused that.'

'Ah, there's Patches. I loved Patches,' Anne said, as she saw her six-year-old self, gazing adoringly at the little three-coloured cat. 'Gabby used to tease her unmercifully and pull her tail when she thought no one was looking.'

There were others of Anne and Gabby at various stages and ages: there were a few of Anne and her stuffed pink bunny, a constant companion until her younger sister decided to cut its ears off, telling them all it was an accident; in the garden with her grandfather, holding his hand on the patio as they watered the flowers with a toy watering can; baking with her mini rolling pin; playing doctors and nurses with a motley collection of creatures with handkerchiefs bandaging wounded limbs; another showed her holding an empty ice-cream cone, crying.

'Now there's one taken after a catastrophe,' Anne said. 'I remember that day in Dun Laoghaire. We were going to walk the pier. The ice-cream toppled out before I had even had one lick and the raspberry juice spilled over my new T-shirt and shorts. Look at me there, Mum. That's delightful.' She laughed. 'I look distraught – it's no wonder the woman gave me another one.'

'She didn't have much choice with you wailing like a banshee, scaring her customers away.'

They moved on. There were several of their birthdays over the years, with cakes, cousins, wrapping paper and candle blowing.

'You and Dad have your big birthdays coming up in a few months. Have you plans to celebrate? We could have a party for you.'

'I think Dad may be planning to take me to Paris. I walked in on the end of a phone conversation. He hasn't said anything, but I have an inkling, so check it out with him first.'

'Even if you are going away we have to do something together, all of us, to mark the occasions.'

'I know but let's get the wedding out of the way first, then we'll settle on something.'

'Ah yes, the wedding. Don't get me wrong, Mum, but honestly, does it really have to take so much preparation?'

'No!' she said rolling her eyes heavenwards. 'It doesn't, but it is her special day and I'll agree to anything if it makes her happy. And she's marrying into the O'Reilly family who seem to think they will impress their circle by inviting the whole golf club to the bash. Anyone would think he'd been knighted the way he's going on since he became captain. He'll probably have his handicap engraved on his headstone when he dies.' She lowered her voice, nodding in the direction of the conservatory where the men were deep in conversation. 'Why couldn't she have met a professional like Daniel? He has breeding.'

'I'm not marrying him,' she hissed back.

'Maybe you will,' Sheila said, turning back to the album.

'And maybe I won't.'

'We'll see.'

Anne laughed. 'You never give up, do you?'

'No, but I just want to see my girls settled and happy.'

'Mum, it's the twenty-first century. Women don't need to be "settled" to be happy.'

'Well, I'll settle for happy for you then.'

'But I am, very. And looking at this lot has certainly jogged my memory, Mum, and made me realise what an easy life we've had.'

'I agree and I've really enjoyed the evening.'

'So have I. We must do it again, with Gabby,' and together they finished her sentence, 'when the wedding is over!' and they laughed like a pair of conspirators. Forever after things were categorised into two in Anne's mind: things that happened before or things that happened after the wedding.

On the way back home she asked Daniel why he hadn't told her he was representing Charlie Lahiffe.

'It must have slipped my mind. I don't tell you everything, you know. Do I have to?'

'Of course not. I just thought as their bigamy case brought us together it might have seemed important enough to share.'

'It's not important enough to have a row over, is it?' he said, turning his car in to the slip road to the underground car park of their building. He punched the code in and the barrier lifted.

'Of course not,' she replied, somewhat perplexed. 'What were you and Dad chatting about?'

'About his bikes. He was also telling me how he came to join the firm and become a partner with Peadar Ffinch. He's an interesting guy, your old man. I have a lot of respect for him.'

'He has for you too.'

Over the next few free nights she painted small and detailed individual paintings of a pink bunny, a playhouse, a calico cat, a decorated watering can, an artist's palette, a stack of picture books, a pair of party shoes, hockey sticks and tennis racquets. On a larger piece of heavy watercolour paper, which she washed in pastel colours first, she painted a swing in the centre. Around this she randomly arranged the smaller pieces of art, and stuck them down. She selected a mount and along the bottom margin in pastel colours, a different one for each letter, she wrote Samantha Anne.

She heard Daniel coming up the stairs to the studio.

'It's late, love,' he said. 'Are you ever coming to bed?'

'I've just finished. What do you think?' She held the large collage up for inspection.

'It's really beautiful, Anne. Well done. That's so much detail. You're amazing. I hadn't realised how talented you are.'

'It's a pity she won't be able to understand it until she's older.'

'Her parents will, though. And she will one day. That's the first piece you've finished since I met you. You must do something for here.'

'I will. I can't tell you how much I enjoyed it. It was a complete switch-off. I'll leave this to dry overnight and drop it in to be framed tomorrow.' She turned around and he came up behind her.

'Great, now come to bed,' he said, kissing her on the neck. He put his hands on her shoulders and began massaging her. She moaned softly, relaxed, and leaned in to his pressure. He continued up on to her neck and into her hair. She felt herself responding with a wave of desire as he kissed her ear and ran his hands around to cover her breasts, moving slowly in circles until he found her nipples beneath her flimsy blouse. He let one hand slip to her waistband and slid it inside over her flat stomach and beneath her panties. She went to turn and he said, 'No, stay like this. You're delicious. I just want to feel you and satisfy you.' She groaned as his fingers stroked and probed, slowly at first, the momentum gathering until she could hold back no more. She cried out with pleasure and satisfaction. He held her like that for a while then he scooped her up and carried her downstairs and laid her on the bed.

'Are you happy?' he asked.

'Blissfully,' she sighed and smiled up at him. 'And you?'

'What do you think?' he said lying back down beside her.

Chapter Eleven

Despite discreet enquiries and being extra vigilant, neither Maurice nor Anne could find out the source of the offer made to Peadar Ffinch. He hadn't furthered the trail either. They had a meeting with their financial people, who discussed the various options and advised them not to take it, saying it was undervalued by a long way. If they were happy with a new partnership they should ask for considerably more. If, however, they wanted to acquire it and become Cullen and Cullen instead, they needed to keep the price down. Alternatively they could buy one per cent from Peadar and no matter who came on board they'd be equal partners. If he'd agree to allowing them have two then they'd be the majority shareholders.

Maurice hadn't seen Anne at the weekend to discuss these options. She and Daniel had gone away somewhere, and he knew she'd want to ask Daniel what his thoughts on it were. He also knew once she gave her word not to talk about it that she wouldn't. Perhaps he'd been unfair asking her not to tell him – he always shared everything with Sheila – but he preferred to keep it that way for the moment. Now if it were Gabby, she'd have blurted it out within hours. Anne was also immersed in an upcoming custody case that was keeping her focus elsewhere these days and he didn't want to interfere with that.

A week later Maurice and Peadar met for lunch.

'You've still no idea who the bidder is?

'Not a dickey bird, although, if I was asked to put money on it, I wouldn't be surprised if it were the Benton brothers. I seem to recall the twins did a lot of quizzing about my future plans the last time we met, and that was just after Anne won the Lahiffe case.'

'We could do a lot worse than go into business with them. They're a highly reputable and respected company,' said Maurice.

'Or it could be Corr and Feeney. But what I don't understand is why they'd want us, apart from knocking the competition off their pedestal.'

'Like us they may be looking at increasing their corporate-litigation profile.'

'It's possible, I suppose, and we already have the structures in place. Have you talked to Anne? How does she feel about the situation? After all it'll affect her more in the long run?'

'Honestly, I know she'd be more than capable of running the whole show when I retire …'

'I sense a "but" coming after that.'

'Not really,' Maurice replied. 'We've not yet had the chance to sit down and have a serious talk about it. I know having a good career is important to her, but there should be more to life than work and its worries. I'm just a humble solicitor and I wish I had spent more time with my family, especially when they were younger. She'll be a senior counsel soon and that's responsibility enough for anyone, without all the other trappings of life. I often think that women's lib didn't solve everything for the fairer sex, especially from what

I see of those working here who have kiddies at home. Their lives are hardly stress-free.'

'Well, you know my views on those matters. I never doubted that women were every bit as good as men at their jobs, but in my antediluvian ways, I just think that there should have been another layer of society to take over the role they played before they had to work. It was fine when they had the choice, but that's no longer an option; most have to do it for financial pressures.'

'And Peadar, no amount of discussion is going to change that. It's the status quo now, however we feel about it. Anne has to make her own choices; at least she can do that, but I won't put pressure on her.'

'You always had a clear head and I respect you for that,' the old man said with a twinkle, 'but I have every confidence in her – she's a chip off the old block! I'll say no more.'

When Maurice did get a chance to talk things over with her a few days later he asked, 'If you could wave a magic wand would heading this place be your dream?'

'Put that way, no, of course it wouldn't. It would be to run an art school or an artist's retreat somewhere sunny and warm and host people from all over the world. That would be my pipe dream. What about you?' she asked, and waved her arms about. 'Is this what you wanted to do with your life? Control your own little empire?'

'Realistically, no. I always saw myself heading along Route 66 on a Harley or bombing around Australia, the Great Ocean Road and all that, and just going wherever the wheels took me. Practically, though, I saw myself here. I had responsibilities, a family to look after and a career I was committed to. They've been a good and rewarding life in so many ways, and I'm not giving up just yet. It could be your future too, if you so choose.'

'I don't really want to have to think about that yet, Dad. You still have years here ahead of you.'

'I hope I have too, but I am nipping closer at a new decade and whilst I feel great I don't necessarily feel like starting over again with a new partnership and new people. Maybe it is time I stepped aside.'

'But Dad –'

Maurice put his hand up to stop her from continuing. 'If we sell out we may be faced with letting staff go, and ultimately that would have unpleasant repercussions. We've always been one big family and the ones who have been here the longest will probably have to take redundancy or gardening leave or whatever.'

'Surely we'd have some bargaining power.'

'Of course we would, but we'd have to make room for the bidder's key players too, and if changes like those have to be made it would be easier all around if I made them and then left, or moved over. That way you'd be starting off without recriminations and no old grudges to fend off.'

'You have thought this through, Dad, and I can see the logic to what you're saying but you'd hate being idle. You know you would. You'd miss all this,' she said, 'and do you really want to take on the financial burden of buying Peadar out?'

'I'd never be idle. Your mother and I could do that trip to Australia to visit her brothers – she's been promising to do that for the last twenty years – and there's the Camino, on both our bucket lists, for the scenery, and the challenge.'

'But financially?'

'Despite all the advice and sure-fire tips that I got when things were good, many from Charlie, I never bought in to the property frenzy, so I never lost heavily like some of my advisors did, and because of that I could do it. Money is cheap right now and it would be a good investment for the future – probably the surest return we'd ever get. If you're happy with the options then so am I.'

'And if you're happy to throw our hats in the ring then you can count me in too, Dad.'

'I thought you might say that,' he said, grinning. 'I'll ring Peadar and let him know.'

'Maurice, old friend,' Peadar said, when he heard the news. 'One should never say I told you so, but you can draw your own conclusions!' He chuckled. Maurice knew how he loved being right and getting his own way. He was even more delighted when both happened together. It was a long time since he had heard him as energised as he now sounded.

'I won't screw you on price. If you want to buy me out then you can have my fifty-one per cent for the price of the bidder's original offer. Most of it will go on taxes when I die anyway.'

'That's very decent of you. Much appreciated.'

'Nonsense. I'd be happy to see you at the helm. If you don't want the pressure, I'll sell you the necessary two per cent, then we'll up the ante and we'll enjoy watching the sport.'

'Wicked as ever. I'll get back to you on this. I just need to run over the figures. And I'd still love to find out who wanted in?'

'Then let's not let anyone know we've come to this arrangement and we'll feign interest to smoke them out.' He chuckled again. He was enjoying himself.

That weekend Maurice told his girls he had something he needed to discuss with them. He asked Peadar along too. He'd practically had to send an official invitation to his younger daughter to ensure she'd be there. Gabby was always busy these days. She arrived late, as though to prove how much she had been inconvenienced by this summons. She came in to the conservatory where the others were already sitting. She had Paul in tow.

'I didn't think anyone would mind me bringing my fiancé along,' she said, looking pointedly at Anne and introducing him to Peadar. 'Unlike Daniel, Paul is practically family now.'

'That's why he's not here,' Anne replied.

'But his car is outside,' Gabby said, clearly embarrassed at her faux pas.

'I'm driving it,' Anne replied.

It was obvious to Maurice that Sheila was making an effort to be as warm and courteous to her future son-in-law as she always was to Daniel, and he could see she was struggling with it. For his part he found his soon-to-be son-in-law a 'pleasant enough, if somewhat limited young man', while he knew his wife couldn't get past his awful 'nouveau riche' parents.

'I'm making plans for the future of the firm, changes that will affect you both down the line; that's why I asked Peadar to join us.'

'Don't look so worried, Gabrielle,' Peadar said. 'He assures me he's not sick. He's still *compos mentis* and, he's not giving everything to a donkey sanctuary, whilst I on the other hand might just do that – save handing my hard-earned shillings to the revenue.' They laughed and he continued. 'I'll be brief.'

Maurice caught Sheila's eye and they exchanged a look. Both knew that when Peadar prefixed a sentence with that that it would be anything but brief, and it wasn't.

'I have decided to pass on the business to your father, my long-term and trusted partner. Your mother has been apprised of this, but allow me to explain the vicissitudes of a buy-out by Cullen of Cullen–Ffinch …'

Gabby looked at Paul in exasperation and Maurice could see her impatience. Even to his trained ear Peadar did seem to be going around and around. After a bit he was suddenly aware that Peadar was winding up when he heard him say, 'I just want you to be clear of your options.'

'That doesn't seem fair to me,' Gabby said, when he paused for breath. 'I mean, when Mum and Dad are gone will the firm simply be signed over to Anne? Just like that, she'll get everything.'

'Of course she won't,' Maurice interrupted. 'You'll both get your entitlement, but without having to close the company or sell it off, unless that is what you'll both want to do. We'll draw up proper agreements if we go ahead and make sure everything is watertight. As Peadar said, nothing will happen overnight.'

Anne was furious at her sister's reaction. 'Actually, Gabby, we don't have any right to tell Mum and Dad what to do with their estate. If they want to give everything away while they are still alive that's their decision. Likewise if they decide to leave everything to that donkey sanctuary, Brother Kevin's soup kitchen or to little Samantha, that's their decision to make too. They don't have to consult us.'

'I was thinking of our future,' she said looking at Paul, who had hardly uttered a word since he'd shook hands with the old man. 'We might have children who do law, and they might want to go into the business in the future.'

'You might, Gabby, and so might Anne,' their father said, 'and I'd love to think all my efforts would go on long after me and benefit them all, but I'll probably not live to see that and I don't have a crystal ball.'

'I think your father is being very fair,' Sheila said. 'A lot of my friends never discuss anything like this with their children.'

'And that brings its own problems with it. I saw it all too often in the office,' said Peadar.

'I agree,' said Maurice, 'and I have no intention of trying to be a clairvoyant, or of trying to predict how big or small your families will be. I'll make sure you are both treated equally and you, Gabby, can decide whether you'd like your share in equity in the company or in bonds. But whatever happens that's all hypothetical at this stage as my estate will become your mother's property if and when – and that's not so big an if, as men tend to die first, and I am that much older – but if I do predecease her she will have the power to change things as she wishes.'

Gabby was about to object to that bombshell when Anne said, 'I hope that won't be for a very long time.'

'So do I,' said Maurice, 'but I just wanted to say these things to you both personally, so that there will be no cause for disputes or questions. Your mother and I have discussed these matters in depth and I trust her completely to make the right decisions if she wishes to change anything when I'm gone. These are my wishes. Hers are her own.' He smiled at his wife and took her hand. 'I don't want these matters discussed again. When the sale goes through, and that will probably take some months, I'll have the necessary paperwork drawn up and go through the fine print with you both then. Oh, and by the way, what Sheila does with her own money is up to her too.'

'That's enough of all this, and those morbid thoughts,' Sheila said. 'I've made some lemon drizzle cake, your favourite, Peadar. So who's for tea or coffee?'

He smiled at her. 'You always spoil me when I come over here. My one regret is that I never had a daughter, or daughter-in-law.'

Anne went in to the kitchen to make the tea and when she came back in she heard Gabby make her excuses.

'Not for us. We have to go,' Gabby said, looking at her fiancé, who was already standing up. 'We're having dinner in the golf club tonight with Paul's parents.' Anne could have sworn she heard her mother mutter, 'Of course you are'. They said their goodbyes and left. Maurice knew his younger daughter wasn't happy, but then she never was. He didn't hear her say to Anne as she waved them off, 'It seems like you've fallen on your feet again – a ready-made company for you to take over.'

Anne didn't reply, but went back inside. She stayed a while longer before getting ready to go back home to Daniel, armed with a cake her mother had made for him.

'Anne's the one who is supposed to be wooing him, not you, Sheila,' Peader teased. He had stayed on to enjoy the company, and he knew there'd be another one already wrapped in tin foil for him to take with him. There always was.

'I'm not wooing anyone!' Anne said.

Sheila laughed. 'I don't think anyone woos anyone any more.'

'Well, that's a pity. It worked for me. Be sure to give my regards to your young man,' he said to Anne. 'He always impressed me.'

'I will.' She kissed them all and left, wondering how all the changes would affect them.

Daniel and she were going to a house-warming dinner party that night. He had been playing golf that afternoon and hadn't left much time to get ready. When they were dressing she flicked along the rail and chose a patterned silky dress in red and black.

'I always considered having a walk-in wardrobe would be the ultimate in luxury and decadence, and now that I have one I know it is!'

'You're easily pleased.'

'I know – didn't I end up with you?' She laughed. He slapped her playfully on her bottom as she reached for some black stilettoes on one of the shelves filled with her shoes. She completed her outfit with a red clutch bag with a bow-shaped diamanté clasp.

'What was the family council about or is that too personal a question?'

'Dad is putting his affairs in order, and he wanted to keep us in the loop.'

'Sensible fellow. He's not ill, is he?'

'No, nothing like that. And Peadar Ffinch asked to be fondly remembered to you. He said you were an impressive young chap or some such.'

'He's a formidable old fellow, always knew his stuff, but why was he there?'

'He's finally decided to opt out of the business.'

'That's all very sudden, isn't it?'

'Not really. I've known for a little while.'

'You never said anything before. How long is a little while?'

'Just a little over a month. Dad asked me not to mention it to anyone – someone made an offer to buy Peadar out. Dad's been trying to find out who and he didn't want to put you in an awkward position. Did you hear any rumours?'

'Why would I?'

'Well, you know how people talk?'

'I must say I'm amazed you never mentioned a word about this. And it shows how much your father really thinks of me,' he retorted. 'I thought the fact that I'm sleeping with his daughter might have elevated me above the "anyone" status.'

'Is that how you see our relationship, Daniel? Am I just the woman you're sleeping with?'

'Don't try to be clever, twisting my words. Did he know about this the night we were talking at your house?'

'He did, but he had told Ffinch Junior that he'd keep schtum too.'

'So it's a done deal?'

'There's nothing on paper yet.'

Daniel said nothing.

'Do you mind?' she asked, surprised by his reaction. 'You do understand, don't you?'

'No, I'm just a bit surprised that you all felt I was not to be trusted.'

'That's not true. And that certainly wasn't our intention.'

'It looks like that to me. Now are you ready yet?'

'I just have to pop up to the studio and get the painting I did for tonight.' She had already covered it in bubble wrap and gift paper.

'You look lovely,' he said when she came back down the stairs, but she felt it was almost as an afterthought. She was bothered by his reaction. Initially she had wanted to tell him but surely he understood the sensitivities involved. The legal circles were very small and very tightly woven. If it got out that Peadar was finally letting go of the reins more offers would certainly follow and the price could rocket. It simply made good business sense to keep those who knew to a minimum.

On the way to the party she said, 'I'd rather not mention anything about Cullen–Ffinch to anyone tonight.'

'Well, I won't bring it up – I'm not well enough versed to be able to answer any questions on the matter,' he said, as the taxi pulled up outside the cottage.

Once inside introductions were made.

'And this is Frank and his much better half, Alzbeta Kocheryozhkin-Murphy.'

Anne laughed. 'I'll never remember that!'

'It's quite a mouthful. Just call me Alphabet – everyone does.'

'Alphabet?'

'Really – they do,' said Frank. 'Apart from sounding like it, her name has the same amount of letters!'

The people at the party were mostly Daniel's friends, and consequently mainly in legal circles too. He had grown up surrounded by uncles and cousins who had all chosen the law as their profession. He has shared a student house with the male of the couple, Greg, whose father was an eminent high court judge. The female half of this partnership, Carole, had dated Daniel for over a year some time beforehand and Anne felt herself being scrutinised from head to toe as though she were a rival. Carole accepted the gift, hardly giving it a second glance, although everyone else loved it.

'It's fabulous,' Greg said, studying the pen and wash representation Anne had made of their pink cottage. 'How on earth did you manage to get inside the gates to do that?'

'I didn't. I looked up the property page archives, found it and rang the estate agent's to see if they still had a brochure on file. They were highly suspicions of me. I think they thought I was trying to case the place for a robbery.' They laughed at that. 'He grudgingly let me borrow it, but only after I had proven I was reputable.'

'You could have been up to anything,' Carole said.

'I could,' Anne agreed, and smiled at Greg. 'I'm glad you like it.'

'I do, we both do, don't we? Where will we hang it?'

'Don't waste time on that now, dinner will be spoiled.' She took it from him and put it against the wall behind an armchair.

He looked embarrassed. 'It'll be safe there for tonight.'

When they were seated, one their friends called Clive asked, 'Do you do a lot of painting?'

'I haven't for a while but funnily enough this is my second one in a few weeks. The other is for a naming ceremony tomorrow – I'm to be the little one's fairy godmother.'

'Fairy godmother?' asked Alphabet.

'Yes, cute, isn't it? The parents are not religious, but they want me to be part of her life, so they've created this honorary role for me.' As she was answering she realised this Clive was Clive Kilucan, the uncle with whom Daniel had spent his school holidays at his grandfather's in London. She hadn't recognised him without his wig and gown.

Alphabet's husband, Frank, had been listening to their conversation. 'Do you take commissions, Anne?' he asked.

Before she could say anything, Daniel answered for her. 'No, she just does it as a hobby.'

'That's a shame. I'd love one of our house,' he said.

Alphabet agreed. 'I was thinking the same thing but didn't like to ask.'

'I'd be delighted to do one for you if you were interested,' Anne heard herself saying.

'Really. That's fantastic. Thank you.'

She smiled. She could see Daniel was annoyed and, if his face was like a darkening rain cloud, then Carole's was like a thundery one, but she was still shocked when she heard her say, 'If you've finished drumming up business, Anne, perhaps we can serve dinner.' She felt her cheeks redden and looked towards Daniel to offer some support but he turned to the woman next to him and began talking to her.

The other four couples all seemed to know each other very well, and it was obvious their hostess hadn't done herself any favours in their eyes. There was an instant's silence after her barbed comment before several started talking at once. They chatted to Anne and asked her about her life and interests.

'Daniel, you've been depriving us of this woman's company for too long. You have to come and see us next,' Alphabet said. He just nodded and she felt she had to rescue the situation.

'That would be lovely, thank you,' she said.

'Have you seen anything of Melissa lately, Daniel?' Carole asked him.

'No, she's in the West End at the moment, coming to the end of some run or other. She's just landed the lead in a new BBC costume drama.'

'Oh, how exciting. Do you know her, Anne - Melissa Coddle?'

'I don't recognise the name, but may recognise—'

'Of course,' Carole said, cutting across her. 'I suppose Daniel doesn't talk too much about her, what with their history. We all thought they were a perfect match, then out of the blue you turn up.'

Her husband tried to stop her. 'Your glasses are empty. Anne, Alphabet, let me top them up.' There was a moment's awkward pause then they all began talking at once.

When the evening came to an end they had two further invitations to dinners. Her nasty hostess hadn't thawed towards her. Anne could feel her hostility and she knew she wasn't imagining it. She watched Carole hug and kiss Daniel with exaggerated gaiety before offering her a limp hand. No matter how unbothered she tried to be the slight was obvious. Greg, on the other hand, was genuinely warm and thanked her again for her painting. As they left the porch, Carole called, 'Be sure and give Melissa my love when you're talking next.' Daniel smiled and waved back at them.

She was still thrown by his reaction earlier and his indifference to her throughout the evening. Trying to break the tension as the taxi drew up, she asked, 'Did Carole have a problem with all your girlfriends, or was it just with me?'

'What do you mean?' He opened the door for her. 'I've no idea what you're talking about.'

'Well, she certainly didn't seem to enjoy having me there.'

'Perhaps if you hadn't monopolised her friends so much …'

'Monopolised? Oh, please, Daniel, grow up.' she whispered, aware the taxi driver was tuned in to the goings on in the back of his cab. He didn't reply and they didn't speak another word on the short ride home. They undressed in silence and when they got into bed he didn't reach for her as he normally would. All this as a reaction to her not telling him about her father's plans? Two can play at that game, she thought and moved further away in the super-king bed.

The sun streaming in through the windows woke her. Her first thoughts were that it was Sunday, lie-in day, and they had Samantha's naming ceremony at lunchtime. Then she remembered the previous night. She turned to find Daniel was already up. She hoped he'd have got over his moodiness by now. This was a side of him she hadn't seen before and as she lay there trying to decide if she'd get up just yet or not she remembered her mother saying how important it was to really know someone before you committed to them. She hadn't committed herself to anything, she argued with herself. Had she? Was moving in considered a commitment? If so, what sort of commitment was it? One aimed at getting to know each other better, surely? One that prepared them for a life of sharing everything and that meant the good, and the unexpected? Forever.

She had no answers and was just deciding whether to get up when Daniel came in.

'You looked so peaceful I had to leave you there.' He placed a large tray down and she could smell the fresh coffee.

'I got the papers and some almond croissants while I was out.'

'What a decadent way to start a Sunday. I could get used to this.'

'You deserve some spoiling,' he said, kissing her on her forehead. 'You've been working very hard.'

'So have you.' Neither mentioned the tensions of the previous night.

Chapter Twelve

Later that morning they were all gathered at Darcy and Richard's house. The star of the day was sleeping, oblivious to the preparations her parents had made for her special day. Anne felt carefree again – these were her friends. People who genuinely meant something to her. Her parents were already there too. She handed over her present. Darcy tore open the paper and hugged her. 'You're brilliant. It's perfect. I love it – she'll love it. And I still think you're wasting your talents, girl.'

Richard agreed. 'I had no idea you were this good, although Darcy kept telling me you were. You ought to do a lot more of this. It's fabulous.'

'I have to say I did enjoy doing it. I hadn't realised how much I missed painting till I started doing it. It's a great way of switching off.' She was about to tell them about the commission but decided against it in case it annoyed Daniel or reminded him of the previous evening.

Her friends' firstborn was the centre of everyone's attention. Anne held her and marvelled yet again at how perfect she was.

Richard's brother was the fairy godfather and he stood beside Anne, who held the sleeping baby, while Richard and Darcy read a blessing they had written and they named their little girl.

Champagne corks popped and Sheila whispered to Anne, 'I may be an honorary grandmother, but I hope I don't have to wait too long before becoming a real one.'

'I'll let Gabby have that privilege. Where is she anyway? Weren't they supposed to be here?'

'They had to go to Paul's parents – they'll drop in later if they can. They had some chef coming to cook sample main courses for their reception – to see if they will be good enough! Did you ever hear the like? Rose O'Reilly's lost the run of herself this time.'

'The chef in the club must be delighted by that insult!' she said.

'When you and Daniel—'

'When you and Daniel what?' Darcy asked, coming to reclaim her daughter, who was beginning to remind everyone quite vociferously that it was her day and they were all only there because of her.

'When we nothing! Mum's fantasising. You know what she's like.' Anne laughed, handing the baby over.

'Look at your dad and Daniel over there, engrossed in conversation. They get on like a house on fire.'

Anne laughed. 'But that doesn't mean they are going to marry, does it, or that I have to?' She went over to join them.

'Your young man is trying to prise information out of me and I have to keep reminding him that I never mix business with pleasure.'

'My young man – you're beginning to sound like Peadar! And I've been trying to make him understand that since I moved in.' She smiled at him.

Daniel didn't return that intimacy. Instead he said, 'Obviously I'm proving to be a slow learner in that department. Now if you'll excuse me, I want to get a drink. Can I get either of you anything?'

They declined and he headed for the kitchen.

Chapter Thirteen

Paula put a call through from Alan at the *Chronicle* a week later.

'Hi Anne, no need to ask how you're doing ...'

'How are you, Alan? And why am I suspicious when I get a call from you?' She laughed.

'I haven't an idea, but I'd like to talk to you about something. Can we meet for a coffee?'

'Come on over – I'm here all morning.'

'I'd prefer not to come there. Let's make it somewhere else, somewhere neutral.'

Neutral – that was a strange word to use.

'Why the intrigue?' she asked when they were sitting down an hour later.

'I overheard a conversation ...'

'I hope you're not going to tell me something about anyone in any of my cases, because if you are I have to stop you there. I won't discuss them with you and you know that.'

'I'm not, Anne, but I think what I heard might be of interest to you. You've had an offer for Ffinch's share of Cullen–Ffinch.'

How did he know that? She said nothing, but let him continue.

'Your father is thinking of bypassing it and buying old Ffinch out. Am I right?'

'Is that a statement or a question?'

'Anne, this is me you're talking to. Alan, your friend, not an opportunist hack. I'm telling you what I know, as that. I don't have an agenda and this conversation is strictly between us.'

'What if what you've said is fact, how does it concern you?'

'It doesn't, but it does concern you. Trust me on this, Anne, we've known each other a long time and I'm on your side. Someone rang the paper to leak the story to us. I happened to take the call and passed it on to the commercial desk. I hovered around to hear what I could and whoever it was wanted it to make the business pages tomorrow. From what I could gather there's a much bigger offer in the pipeline, one that Peadar Ffinch won't be able to refuse. Someone is keen to take you over and from the tone of the conversation it seemed that they don't care what it takes to do it.'

'But Alan,' she said, 'and this is strictly between us: Peadar and Dad have an agreement, a gentleman's agreement about the firm's future.'

'I've learned that there are few agreements that can't be altered by money.'

'I'm not sure I feel reassured by that.'

'I wasn't sure if I should tell you, but my journalistic curiosity reacted and that aroused my suspicions. There was something about the way my colleague answered – it was almost as though he was in on something – I just can't put my finger on it, but something makes me feel it could be an offer from someone on the inside track. I just thought I should tell you.'

'I am intrigued, Alan. Only a few people know that there have been any discussions about this, and they certainly were not for public consumption.'

'Obviously someone has blabbed and it'll be public knowledge when tomorrow's paper comes out.'

'Well, I appreciate the head's up, Alan. I'll let Dad know what to expect.'

'And I'll let you know if I hear anything else.'

As Alan had predicted, news of a prospective merger made the business pages. There was little more in the paragraph other than what he had told her. Although he was expecting it after Anne's meeting, her father was furious. So was Peadar, who had appeared unannounced at nine fifteen.

'Only a fistful of people knew about this, so it had to have been leaked from someone we thought we could trust,' he told Maurice.

'I know and we'll get to the bottom of it. Meanwhile we talk to no one in the media and we'll put our plans on hold for a month or two.'

They w ent t hrough t hose w ho k new a nd e liminated t heir financial a dvisors, w ho h ad w orked w ith t hem f or d ecades. A s they skimmed the shortlist both Maurice and Anne came to the conclusion that the most probable suspect was Paul. It seemed to register with Peadar at the same moment.

'What about Gabrielle's young fellow? Could he have talked?'

The more they thought about it the more convinced they were that he had obviously told his parents everything that had been discussed at their house. Anne thought Gabby was probably equally to blame; she was probably delighted to have some news that would keep her in favour with the O'Reillys, and they would have touted it about in the club. Anne kept that suspicion to herself though.

The partners were even more annoyed now and Anne was afraid Peader would have a heart attack right there in the office. She'd rarely seen him so angry. She got Paula to make tea and bring some scones up from the canteen to try to defuse the tension.

'Actually, Dad, maybe we are to blame. We didn't make it clear that we didn't want it to get out until the deal was done.'

'Has that dullard no sense at all?' Peadar asked, keeping on the trail like a beagle on the scent of a fox. 'He must have blabbed royally to divulge the fifty-one/forty-nine share split. Until now no one only Maurice and I ever knew about that.'

Eventually Peadar left. Anne was relieved to see she had back-to-back appointments until the afternoon and when she was finally free Maurice popped his head in.

'I can't concentrate. I'm going to call it a day. I'm going home to do my crossword and have a G & T with your mother, before I tell her about this fiasco.'

'Maybe you should have a word with Paul,' Anne suggested.

'Maybe I should, but it's all very awkward. I don't want to cause bad blood before he's even officially in the family. I'll have to think about the best way to handle it!'

'Good luck with that.'

She left shortly afterwards and was surprised to find Daniel back at the apartment before her. He was sitting on the sofa reading the papers.

'Both slumming it at the same time, now that's an unexpected treat,' he said when she'd put her laptop and bag down. He got up and kissed her. 'Let's go out and have a nice meal somewhere, just the two of us.'

'That sounds lovely, but do you know what I'd really prefer – to stay in. Let's cook something simple and have a quiet night. We were out on Friday, Saturday and yesterday, the fridge is full and I'm social-ed out!'

'Anything the lady wants.'

'Anything?' she teased.

'Yes, anything.' He caught her in an embrace and over his shoulder she could see he had been reading the page with the piece about Cullen–Ffinch. Now was not the time to discuss this.

'Are you hungry?' she asked.

'Not for food.'

'Me neither,' she replied and she led him to their bedroom, where their passions were expressed and satisfied, feverishly at first, then more slowly, exorcising the bad feelings and resentments of the past few days. Sated they fell asleep still wrapped around each other and ended up ordering a takeaway just in time to catch the late-night news.

The next morning the world seemed to be a brighter place, but a day later terrorist attacks kept inconsequential matters such as a family-firm takeover out of the papers. The news bulletins and radio waves were filled with speculation, eyewitness reports and conjecture, making those watching and hearing realise how lucky they were.

Such world affairs did not impinge on Gabby's life at all. She was immersed totally in her plans and arrangements until Maurice broached the subject of the possibility of Paul's – and probably also her – indiscretion.

She was furious. She accused Anne 'of having a vendetta against the two do us'; of 'being jealous that we are getting married'. She threatened her parents that if they didn't apologise they could stay away from the wedding altogether. Maurice confided to Sheila that he was 'sorely tempted to, that way we could avoid the spectacle'. When this didn't quite have the reaction she was hoping it would she said, as she made to exit, 'And you needn't expect me to come visiting with him when he knows he's not welcome.'

But common sense prevailed eventually, thanks to Sheila's intervention, and Maurice had the chance to explain, as tactfully as he could, why discretion was needed and why Peadar and he felt that the leak to the papers had had to come from them or someone at the golf club.

'What about Saint Daniel? Couldn't he have talked to his high and mighty buddies?'

'He could have,' her sister explained, 'except that he didn't know anything about it.'

'And I'm supposed to swallow that?'

'That's up to you.'

'Girls, girls, please. Is it too much to ask for a little peace and harmony in my home?' their mother said. 'Can we declare a truce? Even a temporary one would be nice.'

Anne held her tongue. She was used to doing this in such circumstances. The hen party was scheduled in four weeks and she was dreading the thought of a whole weekend in a country-house hotel with Paul's sisters and some of their fair-weather friends. The only redeeming factor was that Darcy would be there too. Her mother, Dee, Paul's mother and his two aunts were going for spa treatments and for afternoon tea on the Saturday, for what Gabby called 'a little pre-wedding bonding'.

She hoped that once her sister was safely married that she might actually grow up and realise that life was not a golf match – one that she had to win.

Chapter Fourteen

The truce held, if somewhat tenuously, as the countdown began. There were twelve weeks to go before the big day. Sheila came home from shopping in town with the bride to be. She'd been out since early morning and was exhausted. Her daughter had wanted her along when she was having yet another fitting for her wedding dress. She hadn't been able to make up her mind about anything and now had two veils and a headdress put by – and three pairs of shoes – still awaiting the final selection. Gabby was hard going at her best and at her worst – well – today had been one of those. Sheila had felt sorry for the poor assistant who had been chosen to look after her and who'd tried as often as she could to tell her there was no point coming in again until two weeks before the big day, in case she had lost weight. But she might as well have been blowing bubbles against the wind.

The day had started with Gabby being annoyed that Anne wouldn't just drop everything and go along with them. Then she'd decided she'd like more sparkle on the bodice of the dress and had a tantrum when the dressmaker had said they might not be able to match the crystals already on it. The headdress she fancied hadn't been quite the same shade of ivory as her dress and she hadn't been sure it suited her either.

'I apologise for my daughter,' Sheila had told the seamstress when Gabby had gone back into the changing room, 'and if it's any consolation I can get nothing right either. No matter what I say she takes it up differently. When I say nothing I'm accused of not taking sufficient interest.'

'Don't worry. We've seen it all and she's not the worst by any means. We have some right divas in here from time to time. I blame it on those wedding-dress programmes. They seem to think they have oil baron daddies who can buy anyone and everything.' She'd smiled. 'And they can't, but weddings do that to some people. Generally they are nice, underneath!'

When Sheila finally got home she dropped her coat and bag on a chair in the hallway, went straight to the kitchen and made a cup of tea. She carried it through to the conservatory. It had started to rain and the drops pitter-pattered down on the glass roof. She loved that sound, and the feeling of being safe and dry inside. With a sigh she put her feet up on a stool and rang Dee. She'd missed her while she'd been away.

Dee was still trying to make a new life for herself since Charlie had been ordered to stay away. She had just returned from a month with some girlfriends in Santa Monica, where they'd shared a condo. She had asked Sheila to go with them, even for part of the time, but she had had to decline because of the timing. She couldn't abandon Gabby in the middle of all the preparations. In quiet moments Dee had admitted to Sheila that despite the way Charlie had deceived her, she was still lonely. She missed him and she missed the life they had enjoyed.

'Many of our so-called friends have just faded from sight since the court case. You've no idea how much I value your and Maurice's loyalty and friendship. Being included in your lives means more than you'll ever know.'

When she answered the phone Dee asked, 'Well, how did it go?'

'Let me just say I hope that when it's Anne's turn she elopes!' Sheila said, and the friends laughed. 'Consider yourself lucky that you don't have this to face. If I hear "Paul wants", "Paul's mum thinks" or "Paul's dad says" one more time I'll lose it altogether.'

'It can't be that bad.'

'It is! Paul's father has a new car ordered so it'll look good parked in the captain's reserved space on the day. A beamer, as he calls it, like a twenty-year-old wannabe boy racer. What a jumped-up Johnny he is.'

'Are you serious?'

'Never more so.'

'I thought his wife was nice.'

'She is, she's definitely much more genuine, but I think she's not yet grown used to the idea that just because you can afford something you don't have to have it, or tell everyone about it either. She just sits there basking in his captaincy. You'd think he'd won the Nobel Prize for physics or discovered a cure for dementia the way she talks, not that he's captain of a sports club for one year!'

'She's a bit obsessed with appearances all right.'

Sheila sipped her tea and went on. 'Wait until I tell you what happened when she saw Anne and Paul's two sisters, dressed in their bridesmaids rig-outs. They are short, like all of their family. She nearly had a fit because Anne is so much taller than them all. You'd think she was a giant the way she went on. They're the ones who are vertically challenged. She's asked Anne to wear flats and stand at the other end of the line when they're taking the photographs, so as not to dwarf her, *not to dwarf her*. And Gabby agreed with her. Anne's her only sister for god's sake, and she's supposed to be her chief bridesmaid. Dee, I know she's my daughter, but occasionally, just occasionally, I struggle to love her and right now she's really trying my patience.'

'Don't let her upset you. She won't be thinking about things like that on her big day.'

'Oh, I think she will. I think there she'll be inspecting everything to make sure it meets with her new in-laws' approval.'

'Isn't that the planner's job?'

'You'd think so, wouldn't you? I don't know how that poor woman hasn't resigned by now. I don't know why Gabby needs her either as she's doing everything herself anyway. I never realised how demanding she could be. Thank the stars we only have to go through this once more, if ever!'

'You'll need a holiday when this is all over.'

'You can sing that! Maurice and I are going to do something nice in September, but at this rate I'll never hold out for six months. I think we'll both need a rest after the first of June! Somewhere relaxing – anywhere relaxing – with sun.'

'How is Anne coping with all this?' Dee asked.

'With resignation. She's still not very pleased at Darcy not being included in the bridal party. She may not be a blood relative but she's lived with us since they were fifteen.'

'Gabby never really accepted her.'

Sheila paused to ponder this. 'No, she didn't, did she? She's probably afraid she won't have her figure back in time for the photographs.'

'Families are funny, aren't they?'

'Anyway, Anne's just happy that she's not expected to wear pink.

Oh, and that's another thing – Gabby doesn't want me to wear the turquoise ensemble I bought, because Paul's mother might be wearing red, *might be wearing red,* and they'd clash.'

'That's ridiculous.'

'I know. She's probably bought something to match the new car, sorry … to match the beamer!'

'Sheila, you're great!' They laughed like schoolgirls.

'I'm not. You're the only one I can say these things to. I feel like a prize bitch, but that family brings out the worst in me. They'll be telling the guests what to wear next. I'm surprised they didn't colour co-ordinate them too. You know I was delighted with myself having my rig-out all sorted. Now I have to go and look for something else.'

'Let's go out tomorrow and do that, then we'll have a nice lunch and a glass of wine somewhere and a proper catch-up.'

'That's a great idea, Dee, I'd love to. Sorry for bending your ear with my silly family stuff when you've been through much worse.'

'You're not. I've known your girls all their lives, Sheila, they're like the children I never had. Besides, look at what you've been through for me, all that sordid stuff with Charlie and his love nest, not to mention his so-called respectable business associates.'

'That's what friends are for.' It was true – they had always been there for each other. Dee understood her girls better than anyone else and she loved them too.

'Oh, Dee, I missed you and our chats when you were away. Emails are not the same. By the time I've tapped back a reply the spontaneity is lost.'

'I agree with you there and I hate Skype – it gives me chins I never had and I look like a woman possessed as I stare into the camera.'

'It does not. Now I'd better let you go. I look forward to tomorrow.'

'I'll see you at ten.'

She finished her tea and pushed the button on the recliner. She was glad Dee would be shopping with her – she had very good fashion sense. She looked at her watch. There was time for a quick power nap before Maurice was due home.

Chapter Fifteen

Maurice pulled into the leafy driveway of their Victorian house. Already the clusters of crocuses and snowdrops that had brought the first colour to the garden were vanishing. The car lights picked out the drifts of early daffodils that had pushed their way through the frosty soil over the past few weeks. The majority of them seemed to be waiting for some secret order telling them to open their heads and announce that, no matter what the calendar said, winter was gone, spring had come and it was their turn to emerge.

The house was in darkness. Sheila must still be out with Gabby. He remembered they were going in to town that morning to do wedding-y stuff. They never seemed to talk about anything else these days. He was glad he was a mere male and could stay clear of all that, although he reminded himself that he must give a bit of thought to his father-of-the-bride speech.

He let himself in to the garage. He wanted to check on something. He and Eoin had been working on his Ducati, but needed a replacement part before they could give it a test drive.

He'd got an email back from the supplier telling him there was a digit missing on the order he'd submitted. He was sure he'd verified it. He must have taken it down incorrectly. He reached for the manual, located the item and typed the revised reference into his phone. His girls would have laughed at him, he thought. They'd just photograph it and send that through. Maybe they had a point. He shivered.

The garage was cold and he hadn't bothered switching on the heater. The rain was pouring down, but he wouldn't be out there for long enough to get a chill. Sheila would see to that if she'd seen his car pull up. He finished his task, locked up and went back into the house.

He turned the lights on in the porch and the table lamp inside the door hall door. He noticed Sheila's bag and coat on a chair. She must have gone for a lie down after her day in town. He called her name, turned on more lights, pulled the blind in the kitchen and walked through to close the conservatory doors. Despite the double-glazing the heat bled in there on cold nights and the forecast was for a wild, windy and wet one.

He thought of the old adage, *March: in like a lion and out like a lamb*; it certainly hadn't applied this month. Quite the reverse in fact. Climate change seemed to have turned lots of things on their head. April was only a few weeks away and the clocks would be jumping ahead, but already the stretch in the evenings was evident and it had been mild for weeks. That was all about to change if the weather people were to be believed – they had just delivered a status yellow for later than night – and already the trees were rustling outside in anticipation.

It was then he saw her. Sitting there in the shadows in the reclining chair, leaning back, her hands on her lap. Sleeping. It must have been a marathon session with Gabby.

She was sleeping. Wasn't she?

He had an awful premonition She had to be only sleeping. Of course she was. What was he thinking of?

But he knew, with a sickening realisation, that she wasn't. She was too still.

Too dead.

He leaned over and shook her shoulder gently. There was no response. He felt her neck. There was no sign of a pulse or of her breathing. The awful stillness and silence seemed to be closing in around him and choking him. An emptiness he had never felt before was taking possession of his soul.

'Jesus Christ,' he muttered, grabbing her phone from the table beside her and frantically dialling. 'Ambulance. I need an ambulance. Now,' he screamed. He could hardly get the address out coherently. While waiting for help to arrive he fell down on his knees beside his wife and took her hands in his. They were still warm and he put his head on them.

'Sheila. Wake up, Sheila. Wake up. You can't leave me, my love. Sheila, please.' Nothing. Nothing at all. He cried like a wounded animal, his tears staining her skirt.

He straightened when the doorbell sounded, her scent, the one she loved best, still on his hands as he blew his nose. The paramedics from the rapid-response unit were professional and sympathetic, but there was nothing they could do to revive her. It was too late. Reassurances that she wouldn't have suffered or been distressed offered little comfort. One of them asked if she could call anyone for him.

'You shouldn't be on your own,' she said gently.

'My daughters. My daughters, but I have to do that myself. You can't do it.' He hesitated while he tried to compose himself.

He had to ring them. How could he tell them? He knew that the calls he was about to make would change their lives forever. He couldn't do that over the phone.

'Can you please leave her where she is until our girls get here – I don't want them to see her in the morgue. Can you do that for me? They aren't far away. Please.' They agreed.

He took a deep breath, exhaled slowly and used his phone to ring Daniel.

'Are you at home? Is Anne there? No, no – don't get her. Can you bring her over to the house straight away? It's her mum … she's—' His voice broke. He swallowed hard. 'She's had a turn. Yes. Now, Daniel. Right away.'

He tried Gabby – he didn't have Paul's number in his phone.

'If you've had more than one don't even think about driving – take a taxi … Well, cancel it, Gabby, you can finalise your hen party plans another time … I know it's important, sweetheart – so is this. Just get here as soon as you can.' Then he added 'please' and cut off before he vented. He hadn't called her sweetheart since she was a teenager, and she had berated him for calling her silly names in front of her friends.

The bloody wedding – what would happen about the bloody wedding? It was probably all the nonsense and fussing about that … that … he couldn't think about that now.

He needed Eoin. He'd know what to do next. He was still in his consulting rooms, but said he'd come over immediately. Then Maurice remembered Dee – he'd have to tell her. She and Sheila were like sisters. She should be here too.

Dee arrived before the girls did. The paramedics stood tactfully aside.

She was stunned. 'The ambulance … outside. What's happening? Where's Sheila, did she fall?'

He thought she might faint. He shook his head and took her by the hand and led her through. She stood staring at Sheila. 'I can't believe this. We had a great chat at about four o'clock and she was in terrific form … I can't believe this. It must have happened just after that. She brought me up to speed on all the wedding plans. We made arrangements to go shopping together tomorrow to get her wedding rig-out. I've booked a table in the Saddle Room. We were planning to have a long leisurely lunch to catch up.' She sobbed, clutching Maurice's arm. He couldn't speak. 'It's a month since we saw each other. I think that's the longest time we've ever gone without seeing each other. I just can't believe it, Maurice. What will we do without her?'

He just shook his head and tried to lead her to the sitting room, but she wanted to go to her friend.

Daniel arrived, his arm around Anne. She looked at Maurice and then at Dee, as though she sensed something awful. 'Dad, where's Mum? Why did you have to call an ambulance?' The emergency crew were keeping their distance at the entrance to the kitchen.

'There's no easy way to tell you – Mum is gone.'

'Gone? So why is the ambulance still outside?' Anne asked him. His look answered her fears. Daniel let his arm drop as reality struck. 'Oh, Maurice, Anne.'

'Noooo. No, Dad, she can't be. She can't be.' He put his arms around her and held her. Gabby came through the door at that minute. She looked around at their faces and her questions were full of fear.

'What's going on? What's happened? Where's Mum?' Anne went to hug her, Dee to take her hand, but she brushed them aside. 'Tell me!' she shouted.

'I don't know, love. I just came home and there she was.' His voice broke.

Eoin was next on the scene. He looked out of place to Maurice, appearing in his consultant's guise – an immaculately tailored suit, crisp shirt, colourful matching silk tie and handkerchief. Normally he was in casuals or his biking gear when he came to the house. He hugged them in turn and said, 'I loved her too, Maurice. We all did, but she's too young to go. What a tragedy for you all. Words are so inadequate.'

'The Gardaí want to ask a few questions,' one of the paramedics said quietly. 'It's normal procedure.'

He didn't know what to say. He hadn't even noticed them arrive. He nodded. He didn't know how long they were there or what he said. They were ushered out of the room while the paramedics sorted things out.

Darcy had Samantha in her car seat. 'I came as soon as I could when Dee phoned. Can I do anything? Is Sheila OK?' Before he could answer, the female paramedic called Maurice and said quietly to him, 'I'm afraid we'll have to take her now.'

He nodded and they followed him back to the conservatory where Sheila was now lying flat on the gurney, her face uncovered. He walked over and kissed her, a silent tear coursed down his cheek, wetting hers. He wiped this tenderly away with his thumb and moved aside to let the others say their goodbyes. They drew the sheet over her face and wheeled her out. He stood in the rain and watched them put the trolley into the ambulance. He watched them close the doors with a finality that was almost unbearable. He walked out behind it to the gates and stood looking after it as the lights faded in the distance.

Was this how it ended, their lifetime together, all their dreams and their plans vanishing with a trip to oblivion in a gaudy yellow vehicle?

'Your jacket's soaking. You better take it off,' someone said. He wanted to shout at them, what the bloody hell did that matter? What did anything matter? At that point his brain seemed to shut down. At some point later he overheard Anne and Daniel talking, huddled together on a sofa. They talked in hushed tones as though they might upset him. As if anything would ever matter again.

'She told me Dad was planning to take her to Paris for their birthdays in September,' he heard Anne say. 'Paris was their place.'

It *was* our place, he thought – the reason we met on the plane all those years ago, where we spent our honeymoon, and many romantic interludes since then. He felt himself well up again, his chest tightening, remembering the times they drank champagne and ate oysters in La Coupole in Montparnasse. Sheila loved the art deco décor and the ambience there, and it was where they always booked for their last evening. No, I definitely don't think I could ever go back there now, he thought. It has too many memories.

He felt his chest closing in and went out into the garden to get some air. The wind was picking up and whined through the trees. It all looked so normal. How could that be? There had just been a seismic and irreversible shift in their world, yet nothing seemed to have changed at all.

Dee came out and told him his other biking buddy Paddy had arrived and she persuaded him to come back inside. They talked about anything and everything, stunned, yet totally aware of the awfulness that had just visited each one of them in a different way. Later he had no recollection of who left, or when or with whom.

Paul appeared at some stage; Maurice did remember that and that he took care of Gabby. Neither mentioned the wedding.

Daniel and Anne stayed over. He hadn't needed to persuade them to do so. He couldn't have been there on his own.

He could still smell her fragrance on her pillow, her nightdress folded beneath it. She always slept on the left hand side and as he reached to her side the bed seemed much bigger than it ever had, and more empty.

He got through the night, the predicted angry storm adding to his feelings of helplessness. The old house creaked and groaned and the rain gusted against the windows. At some point he heard Anne going downstairs. It was still pitch dark outside and he was surprised to find it was already seven o'clock. For a moment he thought he'd imagined the events of the previous evening. If he kept his eyes closed maybe they would stay there and when he opened them everything would be back as it had been had. But he knew he couldn't fool himself.

He was amazed that he had actually slept at all. He had to get through the day somehow, despite the cold emptiness encasing in his soul. He kept asking himself why and what if? Would he have been in time if he hadn't gone into the garage when he came home? Eoin assured him it would have made no difference.

Afterwards the sequences of events and the time lines from those awful days blurred. He had either subconsciously decided to shut them out, or they were too painful to contemplate. He was never sure which.

Words, flashes, split-second images – the shock on the girls' faces. The ambulance doors closing, the morgue, questions by the Gardaí, form filling, more questions, the wait for the autopsy, the coroner's report, ruptured aneurism, instantaneous death, notices for the papers, choosing a casket as though he was buying shoes or a sweater, top-hatted car-park attendants in sombre long coats at the crematorium. Flowers, readings, phone calls. Peadar flying back from his home in Provence, seldom-seen relatives, one of Sheila's brothers flying in from Germany. He just happened to be in Europe on business; the other one still in Australia, unable to make it back because of a heart condition. He couldn't bring himself to tell him that they had been thinking of going out for a visit in the next year or so. Former colleagues. Eoin and Paddy watching him from a distance, making sure he wasn't alone. Half-hearing endless platitudes from sympathisers. And Dee, dear, kind broken-hearted Dee, a go-between putting on a brave face, welcoming everyone and making endless cups of tea and coffee for the endless stream of calls from their friends and neighbours. She fielded phone calls too.

When Charlie rang she answered. 'Of course you can come and see him. You're his friend. You were Sheila's too. Yes, I'll probably be here but that doesn't matter. Honestly. I doubt it will contravene your barring order. It's exceptional circumstances and you did ask my consent.'

Maurice couldn't bear the look of sadness on his daughters' faces. He wanted to protect them, comfort them, to tell them everything would be all right. He'd sort things out. Wasn't that what any father should be able to do? But he couldn't, because it wouldn't. It would never be the same again. It couldn't ever be. His sweet, snobby, sunny wife was gone and she had taken part of him with her, a huge part, wherever she was. He was bereft. His sadness was compounded by the fact that he hadn't had a chance to say goodbye.

The funeral was five days later. It was almost unbearable. Gabby suggested they invite people back to the golf club, but he knew Sheila would have deplored that. Dee took over and organised caterers. He asked their friends back to their house. Sheila loved to entertain and he knew she'd have approved.

Although he knew she was gone he kept looking around for her, hoping she'd come downstairs, or in from the kitchen, or usher someone in from the hall door. But she didn't: the realisation that she never would again began to sink in at some level.

Anne and Gabby were devastated and for the first time Maurice was glad that although they were independent woman they had men in their lives that they could depend and lean on while they needed to. He was more than willing to hand over the reins to them because he felt he had no solace to offer. Although Daniel hadn't been part of their family that long he was coming to look on him as a son. Despite his misgivings about him too, he could see that Paul was there for Gabby, and his mother had been very supportive of her. He felt rudderless and so alone.

Anne moved back home temporarily. She told Daniel, 'I'll stay just until Dad gets used to the house on his own.'

'Of course. Take as long as you need. It's been such a sudden shock – it'll be good for both of you to have each other,' he'd told her.

In the coming weeks if she had given any thought to the leak to the newspaper she never mentioned it to him or Maurice and he said nothing more about it to Paul.

Anne filled the rooms with daffodils, Sheila's beloved daffodils, the ones she'd planted the previous and preceding autumns, tall and short ones, cream, bright-yellow to dusky-orange ones. Even the sunshine of the petite and cute tête-à-tête ones failed to lift the pall of gloom that had seeped into every corner. It was quiet, far too quiet. She tried leaving the radio on so that they didn't have to come home to that awful silence. It didn't really help. Daniel stayed over some nights and Anne often left them alone to chat.

Maurice knew they were chaperoning him as he found his way in a re-ordered world, one that was so familiar, yet ominously strange and alien at the same time.

'Try to get back into a routine,' Eoin advised a few days after the funeral. 'Keeping busy is the best way to deal with grief. Nothing will fix it, Maurice; it's something you have to go through. Lean on your friends as much as you can and don't try to be too brave in front of the girls. They'll understand more than anyone and they need to be able to talk about her to you. You all need to be able to cry together.'

'Is that what you tell your patients?' Maurice asked.

'It is, and it's true. There are no quick fixes for grieving and loss, and I'd be lying if I told you it won't be painful, because it will be.'

Dee was the first one to ask. 'What's going to happen about the wedding, Maurice? Will they postpone it?'

'No one's mentioned it and I don't know how to handle it if they do. I can't even begin to contemplate it. All I know is that Sheila would never have done anything to upset their plans and although she hated all the awful flashiness they were planning, she was going along with it for their sakes.'

'Would you like me to have a word with Gabby?' she offered.

'Would you? I can't even think what it would be like without Sheila there. It's just too soon, and I'm sure she'll feel the same.'

'Leave it with me.'

The opportunity came up the following Sunday. Dee insisted that Maurice, Gabby, Paul, Anne, Daniel, Darcy and Richard come to her for lunch. It was nine days since the funeral and Maurice hadn't gone outside the house since. Collaring Gabby in the kitchen, Dee discovered she had no intentions of changing the date of the wedding. Her reaction when Dee approached her on the topic left little room for doubt or discussion.

'We can't do that, everything's arranged,' Gabby said. 'The invitations are printed. People have made plans around it and Paul's groomsmen are coming home from New Zealand specially. They haven't seen each other for three years and they booked their airline tickets months ago.'

'Oh, that is awkward,' she muttered.

'I know, but like I told Anne, Dad will be fine with it. Of course I wish Mum could be there, but it's almost three months away and I know she would have wanted us to go ahead.'

'Of course, you're right, she would,' Dee agreed, afraid she might say something she'd regret later. And Anne apparently had tried too. They needed to have this discussion, the three of them. There was nothing to be gained pussy-footing around it. It would be hell for Maurice, and he'd need as much time as possible to prepare himself for it.

She carried a gateau Diane in and put it on the table saying, 'Gabby was just telling me, Paul, that your best man is coming home specially for the wedding, all the way from South Island, New Zealand. That's some journey, isn't it? I can't imagine the jetlag.' She looked pointedly at Maurice and watched as the realisation of the message she was sending him filtered through.

'Anne, will you serve this up while I put the coffee on?' And she left them to it.

Anne had gone back to work in the middle of the previous week. She had had no choice. She had a case pending which had been postponed because of Sheila's death. She tried to persuade her father to come in with her, even for the morning, but he refused to budge. She rang Dee and asked if she'd check up on him and she went to two of her colleagues and asked if they could find some excuse, any excuse, to seek his advice or try to induce him back in again.

She put on a brave face knowing that she was the focus of her colleagues' attention and being reminded every time she spoke to someone else. Even knowing that her father was at home in the empty house seemed to add to the sense of loss she was feeling.

Paula plied her with tea and coffee, pastries and her favourite biscuits, but they had lost their taste and she had lost her appetite.

'It's not good for him to grieve on his own. At least if he's in here I can keep an eye on him and he'd have some distractions.'

'I agree,' Paula said, 'but it's early days still. He's bound to be in shock. Maybe he needs this time to come to terms with the suddenness of it all. How are you doing?'

'I don't honestly know. I'm in a kind of limbo, going through the motions. It's hard to believe I'll never see her again. I keep thinking of things I want to tell her. I even rang her phone the other day just to hear her voice on her message. Is that weird?'

'I don't think that's weird at all. I'd probably do the same. Why don't you go off early? You look as though you haven't slept and I've enough here to keep me going for the rest of the afternoon. We'll start again fresh in the morning.

She hadn't been sleeping. She missed having Daniel beside her as she tossed and turned. The solace she longed for at the end of each endless day didn't come and she was conscious of a palpable vacuum permeating the whole house. Perhaps sleep would come that night. If not she could try to focus on work matters to switch off her mind.

When she got back home Darcy's car was in the driveway, parked behind both her mother's and her dad's. Her mother's car. Another reminder. How could they contemplate disposing of anything belonging to her? It was too painful. For a second she was confused. Why was Darcy here? Then she remembered that her friend was still on maternity leave. She tried to sound more cheerful than she felt as she called out to them.

She found her father holding little Samantha while Darcy heated a bottle for her in the kitchen. He seemed perfectly at ease sitting there, rocking her gently. Dark, curly hair peeped out from under a lemon hat that matched her baby suit.

'I just popped in to let her have a cuddle from her honorary grandpa and to put a casserole in the oven.' The women hugged each other, communicating wordlessly. 'I thought she'd behave herself. But no, she's demanded attention since we arrived, hasn't she?' Darcy smiled at Maurice as she tested the bottle and told him, 'You're a dab hand at this. Be careful or you might find yourself on my babysitting roster.'

Maurice handed her over gently. 'If you're ever stuck, just shout. I always loved babies. Sheila told me –' his voice broke a little and he swallowed hard '– she used to tell me I was a natural. She felt it was something to do with having big hands – her theory was that they feel more secure in them.'

'And that worked?' Darcy laughed. 'I'll tell Richard that the next time this one decides it's morning at two or three-thirty!'

He smiled at that and Anne could have hugged her friend again for bringing a bit of normality back into their home, however briefly. When her dad left the room she thanked her.

'Don't be nuts. What else would I do? I figured the bit of distraction might do us both good and babies provide a way of talking around things. He tells me the wedding is going ahead as planned.'

'So I believe, although I think the balloons, the doves and the fireworks may get knocked on the head. Gabby said they'd scale things down a bit.'

'That's called scaling down?' Darcy said.

'At least she's making an effort. I can't help feeling sorry for her. It is her big day and God knows she's devoted the last year to making sure it would be perfect and suddenly it's in disarray,' Anne said.

'It's called life.' Darcy stopped. 'I'm sorry, that sounded cruel. I didn't really mean it to be. It's unfair and it's hard for you all, but if I'm really honest I'm a bit surprised that she wouldn't want to push things out a bit.'

'So am I, but apparently several of Paul's relatives have long-haul flights booked so I suppose it makes sense. Anyway that's her decision so we'll just have to make the most of it and make it a memorable day for them.'

'How long do you intend staying on here?'

'I'm not sure. Daniel asked me the same thing this morning. I'll probably go home for a few nights this week, and try to persuade Dad to go back to work, even just in the mornings. I don't want him moping about here on his own.'

'I'll drop a few hints.'

She did, but they had no effect. Nor had the calls from the office with pressing enquiries. Maurice wasn't interested in taking up his old life. He only went back to work when Peadar phoned him to tell him that there was another offer on the table for his side of the business.

'The timing is awful, and you know it wouldn't be my form to discuss such matters so soon after – well – after everything, but the bidder seems to be in hurry for an answer this time,' he explained.

Darcy was visiting him when he got that call. She'd been doing that every other day, arriving with homemade soup, some brown bread or cakes from the patisserie in the village. 'I never seem to have time for baking or anything more adventurous any more. I never realised how time-consuming a baby could be. I don't know how anyone manages work and kids,' she said, putting the baby seat on the sofa beside her.

'Let me make the tea and take her for a bit and you sit down there and rest.'

'You don't now how wonderful that sounds,' she said, kicking her shoes off. She was asleep when he came back in with the tray. He left her there and sat gazing at the little person cocooned in a warm, safe world. For a few minutes he wished he could swap places with her and begin again. What lay ahead of him or for him? He couldn't imagine. He was angry and filled with resentment and, as though she sensed this, the baby opened her big eyes and looked at him with an intensity that made him feel she was reading his mind and could see into his soul. No one but Sheila had ever had that effect on him before. He had a sense that she had moved over to make space for this vital little creature who had yet to discover the world and its sometimes unwelcome surprises. He could hear her saying, 'Never let the things you want make you forget the things you have.' She used to tell the girls that, Gabby particularly, when they were growing up.

He went over and took Samantha out of her seat and held her, remembering. He had had a good life and it wasn't over yet. This little girl needed a granddad to look up to and there was so much he could tell her, so much they could all have done together.

'Maybe someday I might even take you to Paris and show you the Eiffel Tower and the fountains at Versailles. I might sell out and just go, anywhere.'

'I'd like to come too,' Darcy said and he realised he'd been talking aloud to Samantha. He didn't know how much she heard and he didn't mind either.

'I'm going to make fresh tea,' he said, handing the baby over.

'Is that what you're going to do? Sell up?'

'I honestly don't know. Right now I'm not in the headspace to be making decisions, certainly not major ones. I'm thinking maybe I should just step aside and retire from it all.'

'Maurice Cullen, I don't believe what I'm hearing,' she said, cradling her daughter. 'You can't give up like that and walk away from your life's work because you can't be bothered. Have you considered that Anne may be feeling exactly the same? How would you react if she told you she was going to walk away because she wasn't in the right headspace, whatever that means?'

'I don't know what I'm thinking or doing right now,' he said wringing his hands. He was never indecisive like this before.

'It's called grieving and you can't hide from that unfortunately, but I'll tell you what to do while you work your way through that – go back to the office and take control again. Let whoever wants in to the company know who's the boss and who means business.'

He laughed and Samantha looked up at him, startled. She hadn't heard him do that before.

'You know, Darcy, you're absolutely right. I need to be doing something. I can't just let Anne carry the burden. I'll go back in for a while tomorrow.'

'It will get easier in time. I promise.'

'I know it will. I just wish I could hurry it along though.'

'You can't, unfortunately. None of us can.'

'Of course. You know.'

'The hurt doesn't go away – you just learn to live with it.'

'You're very kind to an old man.'

'You're not old and you, both of you, were very kind to me when I needed you and you still are. I miss Sheila too and I always will.'

'I know you do. Now let's have that tea I offered you an hour ago.'

'No, you stay there – I'll make it – this little lady wants another cuddle from her honorary granddad, then I'll feed her,' she said, handing her baby back over and giving him a kiss on the cheek.

Chapter Sixteen

Dee rallied around in the weeks before the wedding, doing all the little things she thought Sheila would have done. It was surreal, she felt, taking over in Sheila's kitchen, setting tables with her friend's best linen and becoming familiar with what lived in which cupboard. She felt she was walking in her shadow and it felt wrong, uncomfortable even. She felt she shouldn't be there, but there was really no other solution. She wanted to be there for Anne and Gabby. And for Maurice too.

She was surprised one day to get a call from Paul's mother.

'I've been thinking about the hen party. It's coming up very soon.'

'Yes, I was just thinking that – it's going to be difficult. It feels too soon to be celebrating, although I know having more time won't bring their mother back,' Dee replied, wondering what was coming next

'I agree and I feel there's enough stress on the girls without having to think about us older folk. Should we suggest they keep the hen to their generation and let them off to celebrate as they wish, without us being in the way?'

Dee was relieved. She was dreading the weekend away. She didn't feel like celebrating anything at the moment. She had lost her best friend, her confidante and the main support system she had had since Charlie had let her down.

'I think that's an excellent idea. Have you mentioned this to Gabby?'

'I thought you might prefer to do it?'

'No,' said Dee, 'I think it might be better coming from you – after all you're her new family, I'm on the periphery.'

'Hardly that,' she said. 'You seem to be an important part of all of their lives and I know you must be missing Sheila terribly. Just be sure to remember we are here if you need anything.' Dee thanked her. She hadn't thought that woman had that much compassion and was glad they had had this conversation, even though she would be the last person on earth she'd ever consider consulting. In such circumstances it would have been the most natural thing in the word for her to pick the phone up and tell Sheila, 'You'll never guess what?' But she couldn't and never would be able to again. She sat at her kitchen table and cried again. She never knew it was possible to cry as much as she had done in the last year, first for her marriage and now for Sheila.

Her whole world had turned upside down in that time. It was so true what people always said – no one knows what's ahead – and maybe that's the way it should be, she reasoned, although that didn't help even one little bit.

Then she thought about Maurice and how he must be feeling. He was beginning to rely on her quite a bit and that wasn't a good thing either. He had to learn to stand on his own feet and she was determined to step back after the big day had passed and to ease herself out of their daily lives. He was lonely and so was she. He had happy memories of his marriage. So had she of hers, until she started remembering what her husband did and how he had cheated on her. She shut her mind to his other deceptions and the reality of scamming their friends into investing in his quick-buck deals. These memories eclipsed the happier times. He was a bastard, but he had been her loveable bastard and they had had great times together – before Melody Maddock came on the scene and he couldn't decide between the two of them.

If he hadn't decided that he needed two different wives and two different lives at the same time he might have got away with the business stuff, like so many of their friends had. He could have relocated to England temporarily and declared himself bankrupt. Then after a certain period of time he'd have been free to come back and set up in business again, without implicating any of his erstwhile business associates. Instead he had authored his own fate, making his associates fearful that if he were to get a custodial sentence they'd lose their investments, and one by one his intricately woven network would implode on him.

Yes, he was a bastard for treating her the way he had and he'd escaped incarceration, for the time being anyway. Hurt and angry as she felt she didn't like to dwell on him spending time in a prison cell and that was what was facing him. He'd be back in the headlines when the next trial started and she knew she'd be plastered across the papers again as the hacks regurgitated his double life and compared his simultaneous wives. Sheila and she had discussed going off somewhere together while that was happening. She probably should go anyway. She hadn't been involved in his businesses so it was highly unlikely she'd be needed as a witness in the proceedings. She must ask Maurice about that sometime.

The girls kept telling her how invaluable her support was and how glad they were to have her in their lives, especially now. They meant it too. Even Darcy, who had taken a long time to let Dee into her life after she came to live with the Cullens, now seemed to trust and like her.

Dee went with them to the final fitting of their dresses, making Gabby's mind up on the shoes and which veil was best. She tried not to show how difficult she was finding all this. Sheila had seen the dresses. She had been here in the showrooms while her daughters had deliberated and no doubt, knowing Gabby, had argued over the options. She must have imagined how her younger child would look walking down the aisle on her father's arm, giving her away to start her new life as a wife. She could never have imagined that Sheila wouldn't be there, a few short weeks later, or that she would be standing in in loco parentis.

Anne was sitting on a gilded chair looking withdrawn. Dee imagined she was probably having similar thoughts and she put her hand over hers and smiled. It took some effort to keep the tears back.

'I hope you girls have no plans for the rest of the afternoon because I have,' Dee told them as they left the boutique. She led the way to the Merrion Hotel.

'Dee, this is very extravagant,' Anne said, when she realised that both the table and the chilled champagne had been pre-booked weeks before.

'It's important to do things like this and your mum and I had planned it … before. These are the things you'll remember when you're old and grey,' she told them, 'the things you can tell your girls if you're lucky enough to have some.' She perused the tea menu to distract herself from thinking like that. 'Assam Bari, Spring Darjeeling, Oolong, Earl Grey, Green China. Quite a change from a choice between Barry's or Lyons, isn't it? There's even an Irish Malt tea here. It says, "The extravagant flavour of Irish whiskey has a hint of cacao blended with a malty Assam". I wonder will I try that.'

They toasted the bride, and friendship, and Dee sat back and forced herself to make the most of the experience.

When the laden trolley arrived, Gabby said, 'If we eat all those sandwiches and cakes we'll be going back to have the dresses let out again.' They had both lost weight in the past two months.

'Nonsense, everyone needs cake now and again,' Dee insisted, 'and this is one of those occasions so let's enjoy it.'

The waitress overheard and said, 'Our Art Tea here is special. Someone had the bright idea of getting our pastry chefs to create miniature cakes inspired by some of our art collection, from the work of Jack B. Yeats, William Scott, Louis le Brocquy and other painters that are hanging here.'

'As they've gone to so much trouble we'll have to try them all,' said Dee.

'This is decadent,' Anne said. She laughed when yet another tiered arrangement arrived after they had made inroads on the savoury one. Despite their protestations they made good work of the fare. They laughed and reminisced and realised there hadn't been too much of that in any of their lives recently. A few hours later, as they stood up to leave, the waitress handed them a goody box. 'Take that home and make someone jealous at what they missed,' she said. And the girls both said, 'We'll give it to Dad.'

Admiring a painting in the hallway, Dee remarked, 'All this artistry might encourage your sister to go back to her painting again.' Gabby just shrugged her shoulders by way of reply.

Dee had always encouraged Anne. Her choice of career was the only time she and Sheila had actually fallen out, albeit very briefly, when Sheila had pooh-poohed the notion that Anne would take up her place in NCAD when she had also got more than the points requirement for law. Dee often took Anne to galleries and exhibitions when she was growing up and occasionally they'd go into this hotel or somewhere else afterwards for a treat.

On the way out that afternoon they bumped into Alan Seavers. Anne hadn't seen him since their meeting, although she saw his name in the book of condolences after the funeral. That was typical of Alan. He came along to pay his respects, and left without making a fuss. He knew Gabby and she introduced Dee, knowing he'd remember her from the court case. He shook her hand and made no reference to it.

'I'd love to chat, ladies, but I'm late for a meeting. We're launching my book of poetry here in two weeks and are doing a recce of the space. Maybe you'd like to come?'

'You finally finished it?'

'This one is more impersonal – no one wanted a collection of broken-hearted laments about my failure as a suitor – even if they were all inspired by your spurning of me.'

They laughed at him.

'You never give up, do you?' Anne asked, giving him a gentle push.

'No, I've just become resigned to growing old, alone and unloved.'

'Poor you.'

'Maybe you'll come to the launch, all three of you. I'll send you the invites. Now I have to go or they'll give up on me completely.' He smiled at them, kissed Anne on the cheek and ran up the steps.

Anne did go to the launch, but with Darcy, and she was delighted to meet up with some of their friends from student days. It was the first social event she had been to since the funeral. She was persuaded to join a group of them in the Cellar bar afterwards and Alan asked her quietly, 'Any more developments on that other matter?'

'There's another offer in from the same source, but Peadar turned it down. He felt the timing lacked respect and decency. I have to say I thought it was bit inappropriate too. Dad wasn't even back in the office when it came through. We still don't know who the bidder is, but they were pushing for a quick resolution, no doubt hoping to capitalise on the situation.'

'Yep. That does seem strange,' he agreed. 'No other offers since the article?'

'No, I think that may be out of respect rather than anything else. Or else Peader is shielding us.'

'That could explain it.'

'Well done on the collection,' Darcy said as she joined them. 'I'm looking forward to reading it, although I had you down as a bit of playwright rather than a poet. Remember that one you put on in college, with a cast of dozens?'

'No one wants a cast of more than a handful these days – too expensive to stage and fund. I'm flattered you remembered, although I was hoping no one would.' He laughed. 'But I'd like to think I've honed my skills a little since then.'

'So would I,' she joked, 'but seriously, well done on the collection. That's quite an achievement.'

'I agree,' said Anne. 'Well done. I enjoyed the ones you read very much and I look forward to reading the rest of them.'

'I'm glad they decided to scale down the rehearsal dinner,' Maurice told Dee in her garden. She had invited him to supper one evening a few weeks before the wedding.

'That's all so American, but I suppose if families don't know each other it's a way of meeting before the event. It probably does make things easier on the day when there are a few familiar faces rather than a load of total strangers.'

'Well, Sheila took care of that, unwittingly, didn't she?' he said. 'I had a surfeit of the O'Reillys and their friends around her funeral and after. I know things about them that I never needed to know!'

Dee smiled. She knew what he meant. He didn't often talk about Sheila to her although she did mention her more frequently to him. She couldn't let her become a taboo subject. She found comfort in talking about her, no matter how painful it was.

'They mean well and they probably didn't feel comfortable either. There's no blueprint for how to behave in such circumstances, and Gabby will be part of their family soon.'

'I didn't mean to sound like a curmudgeon, and Paul seems to be a decent enough sort. It's just this bloody wedding has turned into a full-time career for Gabby. I think if they'd had their way we'd even have black swans doing a synchronised swim-by on the Liffey.'

She laughed. 'It's certainly the centre of their universe at the moment.'

After a few minutes he said, 'Did you know Gabby wants to call at the cemetery en route to the reception, to put her bouquet on Sheila's grave? Thankfully Anne talked her out of that, suggesting that she should leave it until the following day. I don't think I could have coped with that on top of everything else. The day's going to be torture enough and I know I couldn't face the cemetery so soon again. I never want to go back there until it's my turn.'

'Don't talk like that, Maurice, and you will get through it. It's what Sheila would have wanted.'

'I still wish Gabby had postponed the whole thing. Is that an awful admission to make?'

'No. I thought she might too, but I honestly don't think it would be any easier even if she put it off for a couple of months.'

'We were a good team, Sheila and I.'

'You were,' Dee agreed.

Chapter Seventeen

Alan Seavers was standing in for his colleague Gerry, the *Chronicle*'s crime correspondent, who was on leave after being winged by a bullet that had been intended to do much more than shatter a shoulder and render its victim incapable of driving for a few months. He had simply been in the wrong place as a panicked thug in a getaway car aimed and missed his target, clipping him instead.

Alan hadn't been given much choice in replacing him, although he didn't relish the prospect. Crime correspondents were like gold nuggets in the newspaper pecking order and therefore virtually irreplaceable. Their contact books held the numbers of the mighty and the lowest of the low in the land and were something they shared with no one. By comparison, Alan's role as court reporter gave him a modicum of access to the underworld and he was happy with that distance. This unwelcome move would be a challenge. He was under no illusions about that and he knew he'd have to do his best to survive.

The wishes of the editor, or Corleone behind his back, were tantamount to high-court injunctions. You disregarded them at your peril. If he'd refused to stand in for his colleague he had no doubt but that he would have been put on the 'voluntary' redundancy offer list pretty quickly. He'd seen it happen to much more established journalists than he.

The paper, along with all the print media, was going through a rocky patch and penny-pinching had become the norm. There were fewer journalists than ever fulfilling a single dedicated role and the space they had once enjoyed in the newsroom was shrinking all the time. Now they were forced to hot desk with freelancers working on contract publishing supplements. They were expected to cover everything from weddings to garden festivals, events that had traditionally been given to the rookies and journalism students. Sometimes it felt the only thing keeping them all motivated in the *Chronicle* was a common hatred of Corleone and the whispered venting that went on after their mandatory daily editorial meetings and in the local pub.

Alan was at his desk, or rather the one he had managed to purloin that morning, finding there a place to put his laptop down and charge his phone. He'd been woken early with a call showing an unknown number. It was from one of Dublin's lesser-known criminals.

'I have a tip-off for yeh. Meet me in Newtownmountkennedy. At the entrance to the Coillte walk and don't tell anyone yer meetin' me. Do yeh know where it is?'

'I do. What's this about?'

'I'll tell yeh when yeh get there.'

Alan did some paperwork and made a few calls before leaving to head out along the motorway. He loved this stretch of road. Just a few miles from the city and he was out in the Garden of Ireland, its greenery a change from the busy, nosy, dirty city centre streets that normally contained him during the working week. As the Sugar Loaf's gravelly top caught the sun it gave the impression it had been dusted with snow. He drove, constantly checking his rear-view mirror to see if he were being followed. He never knew when he got a summons like that what he was being dragged into and gangland warfare had reached a new level of brutality in the past eighteen months. There had been several assassinations and the revenge attacks that followed were even more brutal and now almost commonplace. He didn't know for certain who his caller, Tommy, was working for, although it was most likely the Pierce brothers, better known as Guzzler and Diesel. In his experience these criminal acolytes tended to be loyal to each other in a most unlikely fraternity, living by the maxim keep your friends close and your enemies closer. Maybe they were right.

There were two cars parked at the entrance to the woodland walk, both empty. He pulled in and waited. A few minutes later an elderly man with two dogs appeared. He called them to heel, let them off their leashes and opened the boot of one of vehicles for them to climb in. As soon as he drove away Tommy emerged from the undergrowth down by the river. He sat into Alan's car. The information he gave him turned out to be a tip-off about the contents of a warehouse in an industrial estate in the west of the city. According to him, 'It's choc full of fuckin' counterfeit cigarettes that are about to flood the fuckin' market.'

'And you dragged me out here to tell me that? What are you playing at? You could have told me that on the phone.'

In itself there was nothing unusual about this information at all. After drugs, illegal cigarette smuggling was the next most lucrative black market enterprise and one that was not going to go away anytime soon. There was certainly no headline news here.

Alan's gut reaction was that this had been used as a decoy while something bigger was going on, something he should have had his eye on.

'Like I said, did you drag me out here to the back of nowhere to tell me that, Tommy? I could have told you that myself.'

'Ya' eejit yeh. That's not why ... them fuckin' cigarettes are poison – they have asbestos in them. I saw me father die from asbestos poisonin' from workin' in a factory where them fibres were floating around in the air, and it wasn't funny, so it wasn't. The pain was somethin' shockin' and he couldn't breathe for a long time. Me ma never got over it. She wouldn't let him go into a fuckin' hospital. He was jacked to a fuckin' oxygen tank with tubes up his nose. He couldn't smoke then. No one could light up near him in case they fuckin' well sent him to kingdom come with a fuckin' explosion.'

'That's awful, Tommy, but what makes you think this particular assignment has asbestos in it?'

'I've heard Guzzler braggin' about how he's struck gold with this new supplier. He's got another container arriving through Belfast any minute. The supplier was gettin' rid of them in the markets across the pond, but some fuckin' know-it-all squealed when he got caught, so they've been in storage for a few months till the heat died down. That's how he got them so fuckin' cheap.'

'Why don't you tell the Gardaí this yourself – use the confidential line?'

'I can't help the fuzz, besides I want this in the papers not on a bleedin' confidential report in a bleedin' cabinet somewhere, and Guzzler is watching me like a fuckin' hawk. I'm sure he has my phones bugged. He doesn't trust me since he saw me talkin' to a mate outside the courts one day, one of the Murphy runners, and I don't fuckin' well trust him either and he knows it.' He grinned. 'Call it fuckin' mutual suspicion.'

'If that's the case how did you contact me?'

'I went into the twenty-four-hour launderette with a load and I pretended my phone had died and the auld one who runs it – she knows me, she knows me ma too – let me use hers. Simple or fuckin' what?'

Not for the first time Alan thought if Tommy Boyle had had an education he'd be dangerous, or a politician, or both.

'Can you get me a sample of these allegedly contaminated goods?'

'I can do fuckin' better than that,' he said, pulling a yellow packet from his pocket with a large 'Smoking Kills' label stuck on it.

'Now that's fuckin' tellin' it as it is, isn't it?' He laughed. 'Can you do somethin' about it?'

'Probably, but I'm still not sure what's in it for you.'

'Listen, mate, I may be part of Guzzler's operation but I'm not a bleedin' murderer. I know what these can do if they are poisoned with asbestos and I owe it to the auld fella and me ma too. She nursed him and his fuckin' polluted lungs for years. That fuckin' asbestos ruined her life too. If I grass they'll only destroy these ones and there's millions more where they came from. If yeh do an exposure or whatever fancy name yeh have for it it'll alert others to the fuckin' dangers. Don't dump me in it.'

'OK, leave it with me, Tommy. I need to do a bit of digging first. Just don't expect to find it in the headlines tomorrow morning.'

'Don't hang around too long, though, will yeh?'

'I won't,' he said.

'Legend. I owe yeh one, mate.'

Alan didn't remind him he was no mate of his. He just lifted his hand in farewell as Tommy headed back to his car and towards the motorway.

Alan took the coast road. He stopped for coffee in Bray and rang a friend in forensics. 'I need some diagnostics done in a hurry.'

'What kind?'

'Contaminated cigarettes.'

'Jesus, not again. There's all sort of fillers in those cheap knock-offs. What makes you think they are any different?'

'What about asbestos?'

'That serious? OK, drop them off at the pizza place and I'll have them delivered here during the afternoon.'

'Have you seen this before or am I on a wild goose chase?'

'No, Alan, you're not. These can be seriously lethal, depending on their make-up. In the fifties using asbestos in cigarettes was nothing new. Some manufacturers in the States believed that asbestos dust stopped the cigarette from burning too quickly and the fibres in the filters stopped them from getting too hot and burning people's lips.'

'Are you serious?'

'Yeah, they got away with murder then. One manufacturer even took ads out in the medical journals, for god's sake, extolling the virtues of how their filters were the healthy option, trapping the nicotine and tars. It was all codswallop. They were the worst contaminant ever.'

'Christ. How long did that go on for?'

'Too long. There are many well-documented court cases if you want to do some research. They relate to something called mesothelioma, a type of rare and deadly lung disease directly related to exposure to asbestos. It didn't only affect smokers, but to those working with it or in environments where it was found.'

'So if these cigarettes do contain it they could be a serious health hazard?'

'There's no question about that. You've only to look at some of the claims and the millions in payments that the companies were liable for to understand how serious.'

'Great. I appreciate your help.'

'Any time. I'll get back to you as soon as we've had the analysis done.'

Alan went back to the office satisfied that he had a story, a real story, on which to work. He wasn't about to break it yet. He had some digging of his own to do first, but despite this there was an urgency about it, and he needed to be ready to run with it if the lab results revealed anything.

He unlocked the warped drawer he managed to hold on to as his own in the newsroom, gave it a tug to open and rifled though it to find some blank paper. He liked to sketch out his story, mind-map fashion, with facts and possibilities, improbabilities too, and work his way though the options. Technology had its place, but so did pen and paper and he had some missing pieces in another jigsaw of criminality that had fallen into his lap. The page he pulled out was a flyer for the Dublin Theatre Festival from the previous year. He had submitted something but heard nothing back. Ruefully he acknowledged that his ambition of having one of his plays staged some time was getting buried deeper and deeper beneath his job.

He loved the buzz and the adrenalin-rush that came from honing a real story. That was what attracted him to journalism in the first place. What he could never quite reconcile, though, was the other side of being a crime correspondent, of having to deal with the seedier side of life, the gangsters, the rapists, the murderers and drug dealers. Court reporting was one thing, this was quite another, and one he was sure would wear him down eventually if he had to do it all the time. He'd seen it happen to colleagues who had let it become their sole purpose in life, those who had become obsessional about a particular gang, a disappearance or an unsolved murder. Ultimately it took them over and he was determined that he'd never let personal crusades dictate to him like that.

With a sigh he turned the flyer over and began scribbling on the back of it.

Chapter Eighteen

There was a kind of unreality about the rehearsal dinner, which, albeit pared down, the O'Reillys had insisted on hosting at the golf club. The last time most of those involved had been together was after Sheila's funeral. Consequently conversations started and stalled and awkward silences punctuated the early part of the evening. Paul's college friends, the effervescent groomsmen who had arrived home from New Zealand, rescued it. They had worked at logging, on fruit farms, lambing and on cruise ships before getting immigration status and they regaled everyone with their adventures.

'Those guys had everyone eating out of their hands,' Daniel said as they made their way home.

'They certainly make a good case for emigration,' Anne said

'You know, it's the one thing I regret, not having travelled more when I finished studying, or even when I was a student,' Daniel said. 'Law doesn't really allow that indulgence; there's so much competition for places and advancement here that everyone is afraid they'll miss their slot.'

'That seems so important when you're starting out. But there's nothing to stop us now. We could always take some time off and go off to India, do one of those crazy train journeys, or a safari in Africa. Maybe we could head to Brazil and do the Amazon Trail or Iguazú Falls. They're all on my to-do list. What's on yours?'

He looked at her as though she had lost her mind.

'To head the supreme court, as chief justice,' he replied.

She was about to say, 'All work and no play ...' then realised that was really what made Daniel – he was driven by ambition and no one or nothing would stand in his way.

'I'd hate to grow old and have regrets for all the things I wanted to do and didn't. Mum and Dad never got to visit her brothers in Melbourne, although they always talked about going. Now it's too late.'

'That's life,' he replied. She knew he didn't dream her dreams. He operated on a single track and the stations on that track were called focus, ambition and achievement. Hers had many more junctions and sidings and if any one of them came to a halt or a dead end she'd have no problem backtracking and heading down another. Her stations included creativity, fulfilment and fun. Not for the first time did she think how different they were in so many ways. The bedroom was not one of these. In there their appetites were mutually matched and satisfied and when they lay entangled after a very passionate love-making session, such thoughts vanished and she was happy. Very happy.

Anne had made sure to keep her workload light and to take some time off to be around for Gabby before her big day. Although she didn't talk about it much, her sister knew it must be hard on her trying to pretend everything was normal, when the reality was that this new normality would never feel quite as comfortable as the old one.

Anne felt her mother's absence acutely each time she came though the hall door. She knew her father felt the same. Everything looked exactly the same, except nowadays there was no smell of home-baking to greet her. The stillness and lack of welcome was emphasised by the lack of flowers that Sheila had always kept in the hallway and on the mantelpieces. Without saying anything to him Anne started to go out and cut some from whatever was growing in the garden and fill the vases. That helped a little and slowly she noticed Maurice was doing the same. The garden had meant a lot to Sheila and Maurice told his daughter he felt sure she was watching him, willing him not to pluck her flowers, mistakenly thinking they were weeds. She even found him leafing through some of her mother's gardening books one evening and he admitted he was beginning to enjoy spending time out there.

'She was so good at it that I never got involved.'

She laughed. 'That's the best excuse I ever heard.'

Anne had got into the habit of spending one night a week with Maurice, but decided to move back in a few days before the wedding. She told Darcy, 'I keep telling myself it's to give him some moral support but, if I'm honest, it's as much for my own sake as his!'

Gabby arrived home the day before to spend her last night as a single woman with them. Dee insisted on cooking for them all that evening. They raised a glass to Sheila and they shed a few tears, their father insisting that they shouldn't be maudlin. 'This is a happy occasion and we all know now, more than we ever did, how important it is to appreciate these times when they happen.'

'Thanks, Dad,' Gabby said and gave him a hug.

'Enough of that, you girls better get your beauty sleep or you'll blame me tomorrow if you look tired,' he said as Anne started tidying up.

'Leave those, I'll do them,' said Dee. She didn't leave until everything was in its proper place, and returned at the crack of dawn the next day to oversee operations and to be there when the hairdresser and make-up artist arrived to work their magic on the bridal party. Paul's two sisters were dropped off soon afterwards and the excitement in the house was palpable.

The sun shone as though the whole world was carefree. The co-ordinator came directly from the golf club and assured them that everything was in place and perfectly so. She had their bouquets in her car and Maurice was despatched to bring these in: cream freesias and gerberas with dark-green contrasting foliage and trailing cream bows.

Dee watched him through the window as he opened the boot of the black and white Mini. He picked up a posy, held it to his nose and inhaled deeply. He stood there like that for a few moments before he took a handkerchief from his pocket, wiped his eyes and blew his nose. That was the only crack that he showed all day in his emotions, and even then he hadn't realised he was being watched.

He took the boxes from the boot and carried them inside announcing, 'Special delivery for the bride and her maids.'

'Is your buttonhole there too? It should be,' said Gabby.

He took her hands and said, 'Listen to me, Gabby, this is the last instruction I'm going to give you as my little girl. Stop stressing! The sun is shining, and even if the meat is tough or there are caterpillars in the salad we'll cope. So just switch off, have a glass of bubbly and enjoy yourself. Right?' They all laughed.

They had left things for Maurice to do so that he didn't feel excluded. Daniel arrived as planned and insisted on taking him off to the local coffee shop until it was time for them to get into their formal attire, and Maurice whispered to him, 'You're a life saver. I know I've been surrounded by women all my life and I should be used to it, but all this faffing and beautification is more than any mortal should have to endure!'

A few hours later, as he escorted his younger child in the wedding car, he told her, 'You look stunning, love, and very like your mum today. He's one lucky fellow, that groom of yours. I hope he appreciates you.'

'Thank you, Dad, for everything, but please don't make me cry and ruin all the effort I went to to look like this.

'Heavens forbid.' He laughed. He held her hand and they sat wordlessly like this for the rest of the short journey, both engrossed in their own private thoughts: hers of happy ever afterwards, or as near as it could be; his of memories and of dreams no longer possible to share. He helped her out of the car, and the bridesmaids made final adjustments before getting in line. Anne squeezed his arm as she passed him by and smiled at him. They took their places at the back of the procession.

At the porch door he hesitated, a rare moment of panic seizing him as he heard the murmuring of voices inside. The organist changed the tempo and began playing the 'Wedding March'. Come on, you can do this, he told himself. If you're out there somewhere, Sheila, looking at our little girl, help me hold it together.

He inhaled deeply and walked her proudly up the aisle, looking neither left nor right but focusing on getting her to the end. Symbolically he handed her over as Miss Gabby Cullen to her waiting spouse. She left the church as Mrs Paul O'Reilly. He smiled for the photos, welcomed everyone and made an effort at the table to keep conversation going with the other Mrs O'Reilly.

He remembered little about the ceremony afterwards, except

that he seemed to have been chaperoned all of the time by Darcy and Dee. He hadn't been back to the clubhouse on his own. There were lots of things he hadn't done on his own and as he pondered on this he supposed his life would forever more be filled with the challenges of going places and of doing things solo, things he had taken so much for granted when his wife was by his side.

'You're doing great, Dad,' Anne told him.

'I'm getting there. Once the speech is over I'll relax,' he told her.

'Don't worry about it – people will understand.'

At one point Anne said to Daniel, 'All the fuss and preparation seem to have been worth it. Everyone is talking about the food, the table arrangements, the dresses and all the add-ons that took so much planning.'

He agreed. 'I think I'd prefer to elope if I ever decided to take the leap.'

She laughed. She'd been thinking the same thing.

It was Maurice's turn to speak. He'd read his speech through to Anne the previous day and delivered it without notes, twice. He looked dapper and confident as he cleared his throat.

'I know how proud Gabby's mum was of her and how much she was looking forward to this day and to welcoming Paul and his extended family into ours. I don't know where she is now, but I know she'd want me to do that on her behalf.' He faltered slightly, looked as though he was going to continue, but didn't. He looked around and caught Anne's eye. She smiled encouragement at him. He could feel her willing him on. But he didn't continue for some reason. He seemed to have second thoughts and ended there with, 'So I ask you to raise your glasses to my new son-in-law, Paul, and his lovely bride, my little girl, Gabby.' There wasn't a dry eye in the room. Everyone clapped, probably for longer than necessary.

One of Paul's friends who had come back from New Zealand

for the occasion gave a brilliantly witty best man's speech, and had everyone laughing. Maurice was glad of that. It took the spotlight off him.

He danced with the bride, with her mother-in law and then with Anne and the other bridesmaids. Dee, Eoin, Peadar and their partners made sure he had no time to brood.

They left together and escorted him home, some following in taxis. They insisted o n going i n to the house for a nightcap. Eventually, when they were leaving, Peader asked, 'Are you OK being on your own tonight?'

'Perfectly. But thanks for asking and for being there today, all of you. Your support was invaluable, but now will you all go home? I'm exhausted!'

He ushered them out, locked the door and went back inside to gather up the glasses.

'God, Sheila, that was murder,' he said out loud. 'I don't know if you're anywhere any more, but I still feel your presence sometimes here in the house and I miss you so much.' His mind spun with snippets of the day, things they would undoubtedly have shared and discussed, and he was glad he had such good friends, friends who understood how difficult it had been. He was glad they had come back with him – he still hated coming in to the empty house and was particularly dreading it tonight of all nights. Instead they had tuned it into a private party where they all talked as only old friends could, without strangers who needed explanations of events and gatherings they had shared over the years.

He thought he heard a noise, a key in the lock, and for one fanciful split instant he thought it was Sheila coming back. Then the doorbell sounded. Who'd forgotten what? Anne was on the doorstep.

'What are you doing here?'

'You didn't think I'd leave you alone tonight.'

He looked at her for a moment and hugged her hard, overcome by all the emotions of the day. He cried, letting out his despair, loneliness and grief and Anne did the same.

'God, that was hell, wasn't it?' he said, when they could talk again.

'Every single minute of it,' she agreed, 'but you were wonderful, Dad. Mum would have been so proud of you. You gave Gabby her perfect day, despite everything.'

'I couldn't have done it without you. You've been marvellous these past few months. It can't be any easier for you. Where's Daniel? Is he coming over later?'

'No, he's leaving us to have some quiet time together. He said he needs his rest. That murder case he's working on starts on Monday and he said he'll do a bit more prep on it tomorrow.'

'He's a good one. He's been very understanding too.'

'He has. Do you want to go to the cemetery tomorrow? Gabby's bringing her flowers to put on Mum's grave.'

'No. Let her have her private moment. She doesn't need us there.'

'I agree. Now, it's been a long and very emotional day for all sorts of reasons, Dad, and I can't wait to get out of this dress. I'm going to bed and I think you should too.'

'When did this happen – you looking after me?' He laughed, turning off the lights and heading upstairs after her.

'I don't know, but enjoy it – it won't last,' she replied. 'Goodnight, Dad.'

'Sleep well.'

Chapter Nineteen

During the following weeks Daniel's tenseness and preoccupation with the murder trial were obvious and she tried to keep out of his way as much as possible. She was preoccupied too. There had been another offer for the fifty-one per cent share of Cullen–Ffinch, but again Peader called the shots.

'I'm having too much fun with this secret bidder,' he told them that morning when he dropped in to the office. 'I'm holding all the trump cards and I'm going to hold out until he ups the bid considerably – then I'll tell him you're buying me out, if you still want to.' He chuckled. Her dad hadn't answered. It was looking increasingly likely that her father would be happy to do that. In his new status of widower he was finding that he wasn't as committed to going on working for a long time yet, as he had always said he would. She was telling herself that she'd probably have to face a new partner and new practises at some point. Maybe it would be better to do it when her dad was no longer involved. Besides it mightn't be that bad.

She had tried to discuss the latest developments with Daniel, but he hadn't really engaged. She knew how it felt to be embroiled in a trial. He didn't want to discuss it, or anything. That was his way – she understood that.

She'd tried to show interest, more out of offering support to him than offering advice, but he had cut her off.

'You can't possibly know what you're talking about,' he'd told her. 'You weren't there. You haven't heard the facts or the other side and therefore your comments are not really pertinent at all. I don't need to hear them.'

Shocked by this outburst she'd replied, 'I wasn't trying to tell you what to do—'

'Well, don't. This isn't some cut-and-dried bigamy case like the Lahiffe one, where the outcome is clear before anyone turns up in court. It's much more complicated than that. I have to try and have that gobshite acquitted. And I'm still not sure if he's guilty or not.'

Was that what he really thought? That she was incapable of making representation in what he considered to be serious cases?

He turned to leave the kitchen.

Incensed she began following him.

'Daniel, I didn't—'

'Don't. This case is important to me; in fact, it's the most important one I've ever handled.'

'I do understand that.'

He swung around. 'You don't. You don't have an idea. If he gets off and there's an appeal it'll do no end of damage to my career and to my reputation, and if I get it wrong it'll scupper any ambitions of ever making it on to the bench. It's way out of your league. Just stick at what you do best.'

'Which is what exactly, in your considered opinion, Daniel?' she asked, following him into the lounge.

'Looking after Daddy's firm and settling piddly marriage disputes. Now would you please leave me alone? I have some serious work to do.'

'With pleasure,' she answered, and took her bag and jacket and said quietly, 'Heavens forbid that anything would tarnish Mr High and Mighty's image or, even worse, dint his fragile ego.'

She drove to Sandymount and parked her car. The tide was out and dog walkers were enjoying the sunny evening, watching their pets retrieve sticks and splash in the puddles the tide had left behind. Couples strolled along, sharing the familiar with each other. A dozen or so keep-fitters were being put through their paces at a boot camp session on the firm sand, the un-Lycra-ed parts of their bodies glistening with sweat, while joggers overtook the power walkers on the path and along the beach. Everyone seemed to be on a mission. They all seemed to know where they were going. She didn't. She felt lost and very much alone.

She was reeling from Daniel's attack. She was upset by what he'd said, but she was more confused by the unwarranted way he had turned on her and by the coldness, almost hatred, in his eyes. This was a side of him that she had never seen before. This trial might really be getting to him, but that didn't give him cause to take it out on her in such a hurtful way.

She sat for a long time, contemplating going in to her father's house that night. But she didn't want the situation to fester, and she didn't want to involve him either. You're a big girl now and you can't go running back to Daddy every time you have a disagreement with your partner, she told herself. They didn't often row. Overall they got on really well and the sex was more than she had ever hoped for with anyone. Was this really the man she wanted to go exploring the world with or spend her life with?

Was she over-reacting? She always thought of them as being

equal. In fact, she realised, as she sat there mulling over the conversation, she never thought about that at all. It was a given. She was brought up in a home where neither species was better than the other and, apart from old Peader Junior, who had had very definite ideas on the definition of women and their roles, she never felt or had been made to feel a lesser human being – until tonight. And she didn't like it one little bit.

Offshore a departing cruise liner dwarfed a ferry as they passed each other, headed in opposite directions. The ferry progressed towards Dublin port, the cruiser out into the open sea, taking its passengers to God knows where. She wished she were on it. She wished she were anywhere but in this unexpected situation. Gabby and Paul were in Venice on their honeymoon. They were probably being ferried along the canals in a gondola or dining in some romantic restaurant at this stage. What were they going to talk about now that the wedding had finally come and gone? Doing up the starter house they had bought? Starting a family? She had never got around to discussing such matters with Daniel. She hardly would now.

A couple stopped on the sand in front of her car. They cuddled, joked and kissed. She watched as he dropped one hand to her mini-skirted bottom and fondled a cheek. The woman laughed as she playfully pushed him away and then, with arms around each other, they continued on their way, safe in their own bubble of security and infatuation, completely unaware that hers had just been burst.

Anne blew her nose, reversed out of the parking space and headed back to the apartment. Daniel was nowhere to be seen, but she could hear water running in the shower. Realising she'd left her dinner untouched she went back to the kitchen to eat something. She heard him moving about. Surely he'd apologise.

She waited, but he didn't. The sound of the guest-room door closing told her was going to sleep in there that night. That was a first, and although she didn't want to go to bed with so much anger between them, she felt it wasn't her place to fix things. He had really hurt her and he ought to realise that. She needed to cool down too.

She slept fitfully and when she woke up she could hear him moving about. He was gone by the time she had showered and dressed. She was angrier now. How dare he treat her like this?

She was still furious by the time she got to her desk. She hardly heard Paula as she described in detail a documentary that Anne had intended watching the previous night.

She went for a walk at lunchtime to get away from everyone, but she couldn't get away from the voice in her head. When she got back to the office there was a vulgarly large bouquet of flowers sitting there, done up in layers of different coloured cellophane and tied with an enormous bow. Her immediate reaction was to throw it out the window, but she didn't. The card said 'Forgive me', not 'I'm sorry'. She tore it up and dropped the pieces in the bin. She took the bouquet and walked in to Paula's office. She had been aware of her watching her through the open door.

'They cost someone a pretty penny,' her PA remarked.

'Do you like them?' Anne asked.

'They're spectacular.'

'You can take them home with you.'

'I couldn't do that.'

'Then give them to someone in the office. I don't want them.'

'But why not?'

'Let's just say I don't accept bribes. I can't be bought with over-priced bunches of scentless flowers.' She pushed some papers aside, set the bouquet on the corner of Paula's desk and went back to her office.

She ate on her own that night. There was no message from Daniel about when he'd be home. It was after eleven when she went to bed and there was still no word from him.

The following morning the airwaves were buzzing with Alan Seavers' story. It had been kept under wraps until the drug squad gave him the thumbs up. Based on his tip-off and the forensic findings, they had plotted and executed a major raid on those they believed were involved. It had been called Operation Serpentine in official circles and during the previous twenty-four hours the ringleaders of the gang and those along the smuggling route for the asbestos-contaminated cigarettes had been arrested in Dublin, Dundalk and Belfast. Interpol were involved in continuing the highly lucrative trail and had been shadowing transactions for a while. The stash confiscated from four warehouses was worth a small fortune. As a pay-off for Alan's services, he had been given some privileged information from the authorities and his paper had the exclusive.

Anne caught the tail end of an interview with him from the criminal courts on national radio. In it he was explaining that, according to medical experts, the real benefit was not the huge haul they'd confiscated, but in the numbers who had been saved from exposure to these highly carcinogenic substances. He told the interviewer, 'Those buying them under the counter and in markets around the country may think they are getting a bargain, but the cost long-term could be incalculable.'

When she got in to her office she'd send him an email, she thought, congratulating him on his scoop.

In the end she didn't get around to it and as the morning wore on she forgot about it completely. Instead she became more and more upset at the way Daniel was treating her. He hadn't come home again the previous night. Paula had obviously read the signs and was giving her a wide berth. She was having a sandwich in the canteen when her father came in.

'I just heard Daniel's murder trial has collapsed.'

'Why? What happened?'

'Apparently one of the jury members had watched a video he'd recorded and it contained interviews with the accused and some of his mates about the life of crime he had lived before moving to one of the Costas. The juror proceeded to discuss it with the others, richly peppered with his personal views, and one of the lawyers for the victim's family overheard it and put in an objection. They're going to reschedule a retrial date. Daniel must be furious.'

'How can anyone be so stupid?' Anne asked. 'They know, and are reminded, not to watch sensitive subject matter, and not to discuss their opinions with the other jury members.'

'He was probably trying to impress them with his research.'

'I can't imagine anyone was impressed with his stupidity, least of all that poor family, having to go through all that again,' she said, thinking that Daniel now had no excuse for not contacting her.

'The judge was furious. Apparently he told them their duties as jurors were clearly spelt out and the man who had broken them was lucky he wasn't being sentenced to a custodial sentence for contempt of court, as well as for wasting the judiciary's time and money.'

'That should get the message across all right.'

The apartment was dark when she arrived home. She switched lights on, put on some music and did a bit of tidying around. She heard the lift doors closing and held her breath. She hadn't a clue how she was going to handle things. Daniel walked in and put his laptop down on the table. No greeting. Nothing.

'Did you get my flowers?' he asked, after a few awkward moments.

'I did.'

'And?'

'And I gave them away.'

He didn't respond.

'Did you honestly think that was all you needed to do? Lift a phone and give someone your credit card number and I'd forget the spiteful things you said?'

'Let me fix it, Anne. I was stressed with the case, which was aborted, by the way.'

'I heard, but Daniel, we work in a world of highly stressful situations. That's not going to change, but we're adults and adults should have respect for each other.'

'I apologised.'

'No, you didn't, and you stayed away for the past two nights without a word. What was I to think?'

'What did you think – that I was with someone else?' His eyes had turned flinty again, the way they had been on Sunday.

'Actually that didn't cross my mind.'

'A likely story,' he said, opening the fridge to see what was in there. 'I'm going out to get something to eat. Do you want to come?'

She realised she didn't – the thoughts of sitting across the table from him repulsed her.

'No,' she said quietly.

'Have it your way.' His phone rang and he answered it.

'Oh, hello,' he said. 'I can't talk now. I'll ring you in a few minutes.'

He put his phone back in his pocket, picked up his keys and when he reached the door he turned back.

'While I'm gone you might consider moving out. I think whatever we had has run its course.'

Had she heard him properly? *Whatever we had has run its course.* He couldn't have said that. It had never entered her head that Daniel could have been with another woman. Reflecting on that bothered her. Surely that said a lot about their relationship, either she didn't care enough or she cared too much and trusted him completely. Whichever way, she felt betrayed and deflated. Had he been with that girl Melissa, the actress, his on–off girlfriend they had talked about at that awful dinner party? Had she flown back into town for a few days or was she home to stay this time? With him?

She wondered had she been neglecting him? Putting work first? She didn't honestly think so, not in the headspace he was in during a trial, especially one as important as this. These times were the only ones that his sexual appetite decreased somewhat and that was normal, surely.

Now she had been dismissed like a call girl, her worth to him finished; she felt violated, worthless and used. She remembered the way he had referred to her as the woman he was sleeping with at one stage. Now she wondered was that all it was to him? What she couldn't understand was why he had wanted her to move in with him if that was all there was to it. Or how he could have kept this mean streak so well hidden. He was ambitious and self-confident but these were qualities she normally admired in people. She had happily crossed over from being in awe of him professionally to sharing his thoughts and being his companion and lover, to sharing everything. His behaviour the night of the dinner party should have rung louder bells, but she'd pushed them aside. Last night's cruelty was a new low and, this time, she wasn't prepared to compromise again. She felt she was suffocating in his palatial penthouse, the glass wall closing in on her. She had to get away.

Dee Lahiffe's car was in the driveway when she arrived at her dad's. They were still eating dinner in the kitchen. 'Sorry, but I only bought two steaks. I can rustle you up an omelette if you'd fancy one,' he offered.

'Don't worry about me, Dad. I'm not very hungry.'

'Now that the nuptials are out of the equation we decided to hold a post-mortem and celebrate,' he said with a mischievous grin at Dee. 'I'll get a glass for you if you're staying a while and you can join in.'

'Thanks, Dad.'

'I was trying to persuade Maurice to go off on his bike for a few days with those Hell's Angels friends of his.'

Anne laughed – that's what her mother used to call the three of them when they were out in the garage tinkering with their machines.

'I think that's a great idea – a bit of man time. You've had an overdose of women's chat in the past few months; a bit of male bonding is just what you need. I hope you'll think about it.'

'That's been the story of my life, a surfeit of women, but I will think about it, seriously. Eoin suggested it recently too. We haven't done a proper road trip for months.'

'I think it would do you good to get away for a bit,' said Dee. 'You too, Anne. Have you and Daniel got any plans?'

'No. Not at the moment.'

'I suppose Daniel is angry over the aborted trial. How did he take it?' Maurice asked.

'Not too well. It was the last thing he expected to happen and he'd put a lot of preparation into it.'

'It's a real anti-climax. It could take months to get a rehearing date,' Maurice replied, then, after studying her for a few seconds, asked, 'Are you alright, love? You look a bit off form.'

She felt herself stiffen. She didn't want to tell them, but they could see she was upset.

'It's nothing, just a silly argument, and I thought it better to give us both a bit of space. I hope you don't mind if I use my old room tonight.'

'Not at all, but you know what your mum used to say: never let the sun go down on your anger,' he reminded her.

She didn't tell them it had gone down several times already. When Maurice went to the bathroom Dee asked, 'Is it that bad?'

'Just about as bad as it can get. I don't want to worry Dad, but I think it may be the end of our relationship. I'm moving out. My place is rented and I don't want to come running back here. He needs to get used to living on his own, so I'm going to have to find somewhere short-term to rent, but honestly the timing is all wrong, I'm too busy at the moment to even think about it.'

'Don't be daft, Anne. I'm rattling around in the house on my own. You're welcome to come and stay with me for as long as you like. I'd love the company.'

'You've done more than enough already. You've been a great friend to us all through everything. I don't think Dad would have managed without you.'

'Darcy is the one who worked miracles with your dad, bringing little Samantha around and letting her worm her way into his heart. It was just what he needed. He adores her.'

Anne tidied away and Dee insisted again as she was leaving that her house was open to her if she decided she needed a bolthole.

Anne didn't tell her that there was no question of decision-making – she had been asked to go.

Getting ready for bed in her old room that night, she looked at the familiar: favourite books, early drawings and other mementos that had never been thrown away. The one-eyed teddy bear that her grandmother had given her when she was born. He had two eyes then, but after much loving and rough handling one had become detached. She had cried herself to sleep when they couldn't find it. Her mother tied a yellow silk handkerchief around his head and that's what he had looked like ever since. She sighed as she moved him to a wicker chair by the window. Life had been so uncomplicated back then.

So much had changed so quickly. Her mother was gone, her sister married, she was single again and her dad on his own, Charlie was facing prison and Dee was putting on a brave face as her husband's embezzlement and bribery and corruption trial loomed.

Alan's book of poetry was on the bedside table. She'd left it there after the launch. She picked it up, flicked through the pages and closed it again without reading anything. She needed to be in a certain frame of mind to appreciate that and, whatever that frame of mind was, she wasn't in it then. The book reminded her of how much time she had spent at her father's of late. Had Daniel resented that? If he did he never let it show. Was it unreasonable to expect him to make allowances for grief and for a family wedding? She needed someone made of sterner stuff, someone with a bit more compassion too.

She went over the whole disagreement with him again for the umpteenth time. It wasn't what had been said that upset her most, but the fact that she clearly didn't know the man she had been living with for half a year, and she didn't like what she was seeing now. Perhaps she had known deep down. She remembered Sheila telling her, 'You have to know someone very well before committing your lives to each other.' Had her mother seen another side of him?

At breakfast the next morning she told Maurice of her decision. She didn't go into any details.

'It's not working out, Dad, and that's what living together is all about – finding out if you're compatible or not and we're not.'

'That's a pity. I thought you were very well suited.'

'So did I!'

'I'm sorry.'

So was she, but she held her comments, thankful that he hadn't pried any further.

The aborted trial had made the headlines for all the dailies and Anne couldn't avoid being drawn into conversation about it. She was glad that she had to be in court at eleven. She'd escape and have her coffee there. That was a mistake. Everyone she met mentioned it and she was relieved when her clients arrived. They hadn't a clue about her personal life or the fact that she had been intimately involved with a senior barrister. All they cared about were their immediate worries and she grudgingly admitted to herself that they were real problems, much worse than hers. She put her own out of her head and concentrated on the agitated woman before her.

Anne was trying to negotiate new maintenance terms for this ex-wife, the mother of the defendant's two children, one of them disabled. The woman had learned that her former husband had applied for a working visa to Australia, and with his record she was sure once he left the jurisdiction his erratic maintenance would probably cease altogether. They had already been back in court for non-payment of the original terms. That episode saw arrangements being put in place for deductions to be taken at source from his salary. Then he lost his job and they ceased altogether. Their younger child needed special care and therapies that prevented Anne's client from taking up full-time work. These were not cheap either and the waiting list for public services was horrendous. The original agreement had seen him still retain ownership of half the family home. The ex-wife was given permission to live there until the children were no longer dependent, or she had a new partner co-habiting with her. There was no such clause on his conditions and he had promptly got involved with another woman. Now he intended making a fresh start with her and leaving his problems behind in Ireland.

Anne was arguing that Zoe's child would always be dependent and that the home should not be sold but be signed over in its entirety to her client. That way, if he should disappear into the outback, she at least would have some security. Proceedings were to continue the next morning.

She put everything into her arguments and was exhausted by the end of the day. She took a taxi back directly to her father's house.

'I feel like a displaced person,' she told him, as he produced dinner for her. 'I've always called this place home, even when I lived in my own apartment, but it's not really, is it?'

'It'll always be that,' he told her. 'You could move back in.'

'I'll never do that. Haven't you always told Gabby and me that there's no going back. In time you may meet someone that you'll want to share your life with and you won't want your daughter playing gooseberry,' she said.

'That'll never happen. No one could replace your mother.'

'You can never say never.'

He laughed. 'God, everything I ever told you is coming back to bite me.'

'See how well I listened to you!' she replied.

It was a week later, after days of medical reports, works records and statements from medics and physical therapists regarding future treatment for their child, that Zoe's errant spouse was ordered to sign the house over unconditionally to her. Anne was thrilled with this outcome. Just seeing the relief on her client's face was reward enough and reaffirmed why she had decided to do law as her second choice. It was only then that she allowed herself to think about her own future.

Daniel had vanished from her radar. There had been no further communication from him. How could he just switch off like that? How could she have been so wrong about him? Maurice insisted that there was no problem with her storing her possessions at his place, but she was reluctant to do that. Although he was an independently minded man it would be too easy to fall into the role of his companion and that wasn't a long-term solution for either of them.

She rang Dee. 'If the offer is still there can I come and stay with you for a bit? My own place will be vacant in seven weeks, and realistically I'll need another one to freshen it up before moving back. Is that too much of an imposition?'

'It's perfect and you'd be doing me a favour. With Charlie's trial coming up I'd welcome the moral support. I'm actually coming around to feeling sorry for him. He's not a bad person underneath it all. I'm lonely here even though I'm surrounded by nice things and have every comfort I could ever need. I can't begin to imagine what it must be like for him in an impersonal, rented flat, knowing that it will probably get worse.'

Anne agreed, remembering the fun her parents had had with the two of them, and the holidays they'd all shared together.

'You can't dwell on that. You weren't involved.'

'I know that,' Dee said, 'I'm sorry you didn't work things out with Daniel. I liked him, but as I've proven to the world, my judgment in men is definitely suspect. What made you change your mind about coming here?'

'Dad did. I want him to move on but he won't do that if I'm back there. Already he's slipped into the habit of talking constantly to me about the good times Mum and he had, and whilst I know it's part of the grieving process, it's not healthy to focus only on the past. When he's in that frame of mind he becomes melancholy, yet when he's in the office or when Darcy brings Samantha around, he's like he always was.'

'I've noticed that too.'

'I'm not sure if having me around so much is a good idea for either of us. Does that make sense? I don't mean to be selfish, but I fought a long battle to be accepted, not only as his daughter, but as a colleague and an equal, and I don't want to forfeit that.'

'That doesn't sound the least bit selfish to me. It's very astute, and for what it's worth, I think you're making the right decision. Maurice will probably find someone else in time – widowers generally do in my experience – and so will you, Anne. You are sure about Daniel?'

'Absolutely. I don't want to go into it, but trust me, he's not who I thought he was. Right now I have to figure out how to pack up that part of my life and extricate it from his apartment!'

'It wouldn't be unreasonable to ask him to let you leave your things there until you have your own place back again.'

She nodded. Dee was probably right but she wanted to sever her personal ties completely. She'd put her things into storage in the interim if necessary. She'd send him an email asking when she could collect her clothes.

She still hadn't come to terms with how he could declare undying love one minute, and seem to mean it, and then turn it off the next. His words had been spoken with such venom. He'd made no further effort to contact her since asking her to leave. Every time her phone beeped she thought she might see his name pop up. Should she answer it? What would she say? But she needn't have wasted her energy worrying, as he didn't. She felt lost, aimless and lonely. Without having Daniel to comfort her, she also missed her mother more than ever.

Darcy was incredulous when she told her. 'I wondered why you didn't want me to ask him to stand for Samantha with you.'

'Things were good then, but I was hesitant and I didn't know why. I never felt it was forever with him, but I wanted it to be.'

'Perhaps he's just too focused on his work. I'm sure he didn't mean to belittle you.'

'I think he did, Darcy. I'm beginning to think he did it to break off the relationship …'

'Well, if he did he's gutless and you're better off without him.'

'I've been coming around to that mind-set myself too. I know he's a bit driven at times. He sees himself going all the way to the top, but I would never get in his way. I would have been so proud to stand by him.'

'I know you would, but perhaps he's one of those men who doesn't like being eclipsed by the women in his life. He probably resented you getting noticed – and you have been in the news a few times lately – more than he has, especially with the prenuptial agreement case. Your clients made history with that one, having their agreement recognised.'

'I can't believe he'd be so petty.'

Darcy didn't reply and her silence told Anne that was exactly what her friend was thinking.

'Hey, look on the bright side,' she said. 'For once Gabby had no reason to be jealous of you. You've no boyfriend to whisk you away for weekends and no penthouse in which to entertain us all. For once she can feel better than you – she has a husband, even if he is as dull as they come.'

They laughed. 'You're right, you bad bitch.' They giggled like they used to. 'I hadn't though about that. At least someone will be happy about it!'

'That's the spirit.'

That week when Peadar came in to see Maurice it was to tell him that another offer had been put on the table.

'Whoever it is means business – it's not for a percentage this time, but for a total buyout of the company. Whoever it is wants full control and the discretion to hire and fire as they wish when the deal is complete.'

'I don't like the sound of that. It feels somehow like a threat.'

'I thought the same, but that's the way business seems to have gone – not letting loyalty stand in the way of a good deal.'

'And is it a good deal, Peadar?'

'Financially yes. A very tempting one, but I need you to be behind me if I decide to take it. I'm old school and am not about to renege on what I told you. If you want it all it's yours.'

'You sound as though you're tempted.'

Peadar paused. 'It's a heck of a lot of money, but I don't need any more at this stage of my life. When I die I suspect some distant relatives will come out of the scrub and fight over my legacy. I won't be here to see it but I need to make decisions soon. I'll not be around forever and I would hate the state to get its hands on any more of my life's worth than is necessary.'

'You know if Anne weren't involved I might be tempted to get out of the business altogether too. Eoin is retiring shortly and we're thinking about taking the bikes abroad and doing a trip. Maybe it's time we did it, but if I agreed to sell I'm selling her future too.'

'She's an adult. She's also a very competent solicitor. They may want to hold on to her. If not, she'd have no problem getting work anywhere in this town.'

'I agree, but the timing is wrong – she's got a lot going on, what with losing her mother …' He trailed off; there was no need to mention Daniel.

'She'll probably go off and get married on you any day soon and have her own family,'

'Possibly but that wouldn't stop her career.'

'In my day it would have,' Peadar said and Maurice smiled to himself. Although his older colleague professed to be a reformed sceptic as to women's abilities in a male world, he still had a way to go when it came to the equality of the sexes.

'Let me think about this. I never thought I'd hear myself say that, but I am curious and I have to say I'd feel a lot more kindly disposed to it if I knew who the bidder was. Could we make it a condition of the sale? That we'd know before we agreed to anything.'

'I doubt it, but we could try,' Peadar replied. 'I'll go back to them and ask.'

'Meanwhile I'll pick my moment to talk it through with Anne.'

'I'm off to the place in Provence for a few weeks. You can let me know then what you think when I get back.'

'Won't it be very hot at this time?'

'Probably, but a bit of heat on the old bones won't do them any harm. I need to sort out my affairs over there too – you know what succession laws are like in France. If everything's not tied up in fancy bows and sealed in wax they'll tax and contest it.'

Father and daughter didn't have that conversation for several days. Daniel had replied to her email and she went around with Darcy on Saturday morning to clear her things from the penthouse and pack anything she could. They arrived at Dee's with numerous suitcases and a sleeping Samantha in her car seat.

'If I ever want to run away, can I come here too? You have a beautiful home,' Darcy said as they sat down to freshly baked scones and shortbread, while Dee cooed over a smiling baby.

'Of course,' Dee agreed, 'but that's not likely to happen, I hope.'

'So do I,' said Darcy.

They emptied the suitcase and put all Dee's clothes away before she headed to her father's house to collect the rest of the things she'd left there.

Maurice collared her in the hallway.

'I need to run something by you. You needn't say anything – I just want you to have a think about it.'

She was surprised that he would even consider giving up his company, but she could understand what was driving him to such a radical change of heart. The unexpected happenings of the past few months had made her more introspective than ever. She promised him that she'd consider the options.

And she did. She thought of little else for the next few weeks. Was she getting a second chance? Was it time to step away from the law and the seedy individuals she sometimes came across, and from a certain seedy professional too?

Did she want to start working for someone else? She argued that she wouldn't have to. With what Maurice promised her she could well afford to set up on her own, maybe in a female practise specialising in women's issues. If she had learned anything it was that there were many, many women out there who would support such a practise. Definitely the concept had possibilities and she was sure that Paula could be persuaded to jump ship with her if it ever happened.

'I'm not going to mention anything to Gabby,' Maurice had said, 'until I've made my decision, although I can't see her objecting. She'd probably be delighted to get cash in hand without having to wait for me to pop my clogs.'

Anne had to agree.

She was as curious as her father about the bidders and on impulse she rang Alan Seavers. They arranged to meet in a wine bar in town for a drink the following night.

'Have you heard anything further at your end?' she asked him when they met.

He seemed to hesitate before answering. 'Not a dickey bird! What about you?'

'Apart from getting this anonymous offer to buy us out completely, no.'

'What does Daniel think about that?' Again the hesitation.

'I don't know and I don't really care about that. We're not together any more.'

'Oh, since when? Is it appropriate for me to commiserate?' he asked.

'A few weeks and commiserations aren't necessary.'

'Was it before or since the offer was made?'

'What has that to do with anything?' she asked.

'Just curious, that's all. How are you, about the break-up, I mean? You seemed so solid together.'

'And you should know that you should never trust appearances. It was just a bit unexpected, though. Enough about me. How are they treating you in the *Chronicle* since your scoop? Did they give you a big bonus after all the publicity they got?'

'Never. I'm still a lowly reporter, a very frustrated lowly reporter, who one day will wake up and wish he had got out of it years ago. Meanwhile I'm starving – have you time to grab a bite to eat, or are you busy?'

'No, I'd love that.'

'Let's go to the Italian next door.'

She relaxed and enjoyed herself, happy at how easily they got on, and reminiscing about college days and fun they had shared together.

'What about your writing?' she asked. 'Are you doing any?'

'Not at the moment. Filling in as crime correspondent doesn't allow much time for creativity, but I will get back to it some day. It's all I want to do and right now it won't pay the bills. I submitted a play for consideration for the Dublin Theatre Festival so I'm keeping my fingers crossed. Nothing might come of it.'

'Don't give it up – you're too good to do that.'

'I won't. Meanwhile I'll keep buying the lottery tickets.'

'You'd probably have a better chance with the play.'

Chapter Twenty

A few weeks later Maurice took an international call. It was from a hospital in France. When he came through to Anne's office she knew something was wrong.

'Peadar's in hospital. He was admitted this morning. It sounds serious.'

'Isn't he still away?'

'He's in Aix-en-Provence. I've got to go over. The old boy has no one – we're the nearest thing to family that he has.'

'Of course you must go. Paula will sort out flights for you. What happened?'

'They didn't tell me, just that he was asking for me.'

'Go home and pack a bag. I'll let you know the arrangements when we make them.'

He went directly to the airport from the house and that evening he rang to fill her in.

'It's not good news, I'm afraid. Apparently he has a brain tumour; he's known about it for a few months now but never told anyone. That's why he was anxious to tidy his affairs up.'

'What are they doing for him? Can he be treated?'

'I get the impression there's nothing they can really do for him, but make sure he isn't in pain. They won't give a time frame but reading between the lines I think we're talking about a matter of weeks. I'm going to try and make arrangements to have him brought back to Dublin. If that's not practical then I'll stay with him till it happens.'

'Oh, Dad, that's so unfair, and so soon after Mum. Will you be alright on your own?'

'I'm a strong old turkey. Don't worry about me, I'll be alright.'

'Where are you staying?'

'At the farmhouse. The housekeeper and her husband have everything under control and are fussing over me. I think they're almost as old as Peadar, and loyal to the last. It's about thirty minutes from the hospital and Pierre, the old boy, drives me in and insists on collecting me too.'

'I'm glad to hear that. Be sure to give Peadar my love and you, look after yourself.'

'I will, and you too. Tell Gabby, won't you? She's not answering her phone.'

'I will.'

It turned out that Peadar knew exactly what was going on and that he'd been sorting his affairs for quite a while. Despite their close business relationship, Maurice was surprised at the extent of the property. They talked openly, and when he suggested that Peadar might like to be brought back home, he agreed.

'I'd like that, but you'll not get that organised in a hurry,' he said. 'If I've learned anything about this country and its people, it's that they love nothing better than a bit of bureaucracy and form filling. What we can do with one page takes them twelve.'

'Don't worry, old friend, I'll get on it straight away.'

'It's not that urgent. I'll be around for a few weeks yet.'

'I sincerely hope so.'

'He wasn't joking about the red tape,' Maurice told Anne a few days later. 'I doubt we'll have all the permits and medical reports in order for a few more days.'

'I don't like the idea of Dad taking all that responsibility. I think he's hardly left the hospital since Tuesday,' she told Paula

'The courts are closed for the next few weeks and there's nothing in your schedule that can't be handled by someone else. Why don't you go over to him?'

She thought about it for a few minutes and decided to do exactly that. She phoned Gabby and told her of her intentions.

'Gabby, I'm going to head off in the morning to be with Dad. Would you like to come too?'

'I'm not likely to leave my husband already when I've only just married him. Besides, with all the expense of the wedding and the honeymoon, I can't really afford to.'

'Don't worry about the money. I'll pay.'

'Always doing the Lady Bountiful act, aren't you. We're not skint. Paul can well afford a poxy airfare to France. That's not the issue.'

Anne sighed. She was never going to win with her sister.

She went ahead with her plans alone. The thought struck her as she waited to check in at the airport that she had hoped her next trip would be jetting off somewhere nice with Daniel. She pushed it away.

As Anne's flight made its way to Marseilles, Peadar and Maurice were discussing business.

'I'm drawing a line under all my dealings today, and after this I want no more discussions about business of any sort. There'll be time enough for you to do that when I'm gone.'

'Are you absolutely sure about all this?'

'Absolutely. Didn't the shrinks verify my sanity for you?'

The previous day he had sold his share of Cullen–Ffinch to Maurice for a nominal amount. Maurice had protested at the ridiculously low sum.

'They did, and I still think if this ever gets out that I'd be accused of taking advantage of you in your present condition.'

'That's why I've had everything drawn up over here and verified by my current physicians, so that there can be no disputing the legality of these contracts once you signed them and they were witnessed. My lawyers in Aix-en-Provence did the same with my French affairs, and there's a proviso that Marie and Pierre should always have their home on the estate for the duration of their lives.'

'You're being extraordinarily generous, Peadar, and you've thought of everything.'

'Don't canonise me yet. I've enjoyed the benefits of it all and it pleases me to know others might enjoy some of it too. You know what they say – there are no pockets in a shroud and I've no intentions of letting it all be flushed away in death duties.'

'I wish more people thought like that.'

'Let's just say I've been lucky to have had this time to be a philosopher, and to reflect on what and who were important in my life, and to act on it.'

Just then Anne appeared, having come straight from the airport, and she looked surprised to find Peadar awake and perfectly lucid, propped up on a pile of pillows. She kissed him and he held on to her hand and joked about her arrival.

'I must be bad if you've come this far.'

'I wanted to make sure they are looking after you properly. Are you in pain?'

'They are, and, no, thankfully I'm not. I'm really very comfortable. But they're talking in whispers around me – that's always a bad sign too.' He laughed. 'Don't look so worried. I've had a good innings and there are much worse ways to go than with what I have.'

'We don't want you to go anywhere.'

'I'm glad to hear you say that, and I'm glad you're here. Your father and I have been doing a lot of talking. I can still do that too, but if I try to stand my balance is gone and I keel over. And I'm likely to fall asleep any minute, so accept my apologies in advance. Anyway as I said we've done a lot of talking and made some decisions.'

'Try not to wear yourself out any more today,' she said, rubbing his arm.

'The egg timer is running out, Anne, and as you know I'm a realist. It would be nice to have had a bit longer, but overall I can't complain. I have few regrets and I'm ready to move on.' She squeezed his hand and he returned the pressure before closing his eyes. 'Not everyone is fortunate enough to be able to say that.'

'I hope I'll be able to do the same when my time comes,' said Maurice.

'So do I.'

He closed his eyes and she looked anxiously at her father. Then Peadar said, 'I'm OK, just tired. It happens more often now. Anne, promise me something.'

'I will.'

'Promise me that when your time comes to shuffle on, that you can say the same, that you've fulfilled your dreams and have no regrets. We can't alter fate but we can soften it with pockets of fulfilment, and contentment, however small.' He opened his eyes and smiled at her. 'They are the cushions we all need in life. Remember that, the philosophy of an old man.'

'I will, but I'm afraid we've exhausted you, Peadar. We'll go and let you get some rest.' She kissed his forehead and Maurice took his hand and said, 'I'll be back later.'

'There's no need, I'll not die tonight,' he said with a glint in his eye. 'Trust me!'

Alan Seavers leafed through the bits of paper he kept in the warped drawer in the noisy newsroom. He wasn't very happy. He hadn't been honest with Anne Cullen when she'd asked him if he had any further insights into the buyout offer. He hadn't told her that he knew the name of the principal: it was Clive Kilucan – Daniel's uncle. Something had made him hold back on sharing this information. Now he questioned if he had done the right thing.

He was torn. She was more than a friend to him and he wasn't at all sure if he was protecting her by his non-disclosure. His investigative instinct told him there was more to this offer than there seemed on the surface. Kilucan was a Senior Counsel, self-employed, very well respected by his peers and clients, and if his lifestyle was a reflection of his success, then he had definitely made it to the top echelons. Why would he want to acquire Cullen–Ffinch at this stage in his career? Unless he were acting for Daniel and it was Daniel who wanted to take them over.

When she had told Alan the whole story about what happened between the two of them he was baffled. He was sure there was a connection between why Daniel had dumped Anne so nastily and the new buyout bid. It seemed to be more than just a coincidence.

He rummaged in the drawer, found another out-dated press release and began scribbling his thoughts on the back of it.

Maurice and Anne returned to the farm late in the afternoon.

'I had no idea this place was so big,' she exclaimed as they drove into a gravelled yard, the yellow pebbles warm and reflecting the sunlight. A long villa was shaded by a group of large sprawling trees, its blue shutters half closed against the glare. Potted geraniums popped with colour all over the place, in groups, on an old millstone, in a disused water trough and on either side of the entrance door. 'It's absolutely charming.'

'In parts. The outside looks good, but it's quite out-dated inside. I don't think Peadar ever did much to it after his parents died.'

'But it looks well cared for.'

'It is that, and the vineyards are rented to his neighbours so it more than pays for itself.'

Marie and Pierre, the resident housekeeper and caretaker who had been there for years, came out to greet them and to hear the latest from the hospital.

'If luck is on our side we should be able to travel on Monday or Tuesday.'

'*Pauvre* Monsieur Peadar, what will we do when he is no longer here with us?' Marie said. Anne could sense their fear. It was the only life they had known for over forty years, possibly longer, and they were terrified that they would be evicted when the place was sold, and that was surely inevitable in the circumstances. She wondered if they had children, but didn't like to ask.

'You mustn't worry about that now. It's important that we make these few weeks as easy as possible for him.'

'*D'accord.*' A tear slid down the old woman's cheek and she wiped it away with the corner of the apron she had removed as she walked towards them. It was obvious she cared for Peadar.

'Why don't you go and visit him, I'm sure he'd love to see you?'

'But you must be hungry. I have prepared a meal for you.'

'Thank you, I can smell something delicious, but we can look after ourselves, can't we, Dad? You go. We'll be fine.'

Marie hesitated for a minute and her face broke into a grin.

'Just a quick visit then and thank you, mademoiselle,' she said, adding, 'Monsieur Maurice knows where everything is.'

And he did. They ate and chatted before going for a walk around the property. A ginger cat slid elegantly past them and in through the door.

'Is he, she or it allowed inside?'

'That's Abricot. I believe he's a timeshare cat.'

'A what!?'

'A timeshare cat! He shares his time between Marie's house and here and he doesn't like sharing his seat with anyone. He'll come round to you in his own time.'

She laughed.

The vines were fresh and the irrigation system gurgled quietly beneath their twisted trunks. The air was warm and smelt of damp earth.

'It's beautiful here,' Anne said. 'I love that the house hasn't been modernised. I don't think it's old-fashioned at all. It oozes character and charm. I think I'd call it quaint.'

'It's much bigger than it looks from the front. Come and I'll show you the rest of it.'

The bedrooms were furnished with beautiful, large, old pieces and woven cane chairs. Tapestries and embroideries added richness to the china knick-knacks and ornaments.

'That room is off limits,' Maurice told her as they reached the end of a corridor.

'Why?'

'I never asked,' he replied. 'I just know it's always kept locked.'

'How typical of you, Dad. My curiosity would have got the better of me.'

'Sometimes it's best not to be too nosey.'

'Perhaps it had something to do with the little boy he lost.'

'Like I said, sometimes it's best not to be too nosey.'

'That's put me back in my box. Come on, give me the grand tour.'

The house had appeared to be a bungalow from the front, but it was built like a U-shape, with two long, double-storey extensions on both ends at the back. These enclosed a cobbled courtyard with rambling roses, honeysuckle and a gnarled old olive tree. From here the landscape sloped gently upwards and the vines covered this in tidy lines. A little to the left there was another house – a pretty cottage set against a backdrop of tall poplars.

'That's where Marie and Pierre live.'

'They'll miss him terribly.'

'They will. Despite what he says, he never did realise one of his dreams, or his father's either for that matter, of having his own wine, bottled under the Ffinch–Ffinch label, but he loved this place. He called it his refuge.'

'I can understand why. It's perfect.'

'I learned more about him in the last week than I knew in all the years working with him. He talked about his childhood. Later he and his student friends used to earn a few bob helping with the harvest. Then everyone used itinerant workers and they used to sleep in those long sheds over there, before moving on to the next farm. The same ones came every year and the end of *vendange* parties seem to have been pretty riotous affairs. That was back in the days when they did everything by hand and crushed the grapes by treading on them. It's all mechanised now.'

'Ffinch–Ffinch wine … that has a certain ring to it.'

'Oh, he wouldn't have called it that – he wanted it to be *Le Bouvreuil* – the Bullfinch, a play on words!'

'Did he ever try to make it happen?'

'I don't think so.'

'What'll happen it all now? I mean when he's gone?'

'You know how organised Peadar is. He has all that in hand.'

'I was surprised to find him so well.'

'He put on a brave face for you. He tires very easily.'

'And what about you, Dad? This can't be easy.'

'It's not, but there's nowhere else I'd rather be. It's Peadar's time.'

The next few days went by between hospital visits in a frenzy of paperwork, phone calls and red tape and even Anne could see a change in him over that short period.

She helped Marie pack his personal things and could see how upset she was at having to say goodbye to the employer, who was obviously so much more to her and her husband than that. He was, and had been, their life for longer than any of them remembered.

'You will let us know when … when it happens?' she asked, always direct.

'Of course we will. I promise,' Anne said, hugging her tightly and shaking Pierre's hands. He held them and then hugged her.

Marie watched. 'He always talked about you like a daughter. Your sister, no, but you, yes.'

As planned, they flew home in the air ambulance the following Monday and Anne was allowed to accompany them. Peadar was awake for most of the journey, and, always the gentleman, he made sure to praise the seamless efficiency of the crew and medics involved.

'We're not new to this,' the young doctor told him 'In 1870 wounded soldiers were airlifted in hot-air balloons from the Siege of Paris.'

'In 1870?' Anne thought she'd misheard.

He nodded. '*Vraiment*.'

'So I can relax now!' Peadar replied.

An ambulance was waiting on the tarmac and, once the final checklist and handover had been completed, he was driven straight to hospital. The journey took a lot out of him, and despite being exhausted he kept telling them how glad he was to be home. He was moved to a hospice a week later and drifted in and out of sleeps that got longer and longer as he shut gently down.

Chapter Twenty-One

During this time Maurice refused to discuss the future of the company individually with any of the heads of department. He was determined to keep the status quo while Peadar was still alive. He and Anne had several long meetings, which led to lots of speculation.

Paula brought coffee in to one of these. 'Everyone is wondering what's going to happen when old man Ffinch dies,' she remarked. 'It's bound to bring changes, isn't it?'

'There's no need to worry,' Anne said. 'When it happens I'll address the staff. I'd be happy if you didn't make any other comment for the moment.'

Two days later Peadar slipped away in his sleep, with Maurice by his bedside.

His funeral was a large affair, stopping traffic in Donnybrook as the cortege left the packed church and made its way to the cemetery, the same one where, only a few short months earlier, many of the same assembly had gathered for Sheila's burial.

Maurice, flanked by his two daughters and Darcy, spoke a few words at the graveside, totally forgetting his train of thought halfway through and beginning again, only to stumble in the same place. People understood and some clapped when he finished.

Obituaries for Peadar Ffinch Junior appeared in several of the newspapers. These reminded readers of his and his father's achievements and his reputation for fairness. These tributes were peppered with phrases like 'one of a kind', 'old school professional' and 'a gentleman's gentleman'.

He died as he had lived, in an orderly, organised fashion, and he had passed the baton to Maurice.

The following Monday Maurice called a meeting of the staff and told them about the offer that Peadar had received to sell out before he died and how he had rejected it, leaving him as sole shareholder.

'I want to assure you all that, despite anything you might read in the papers, I have no intentions of accepting that or any other offer. We had never put the firm on the market and those offers were unsolicited. We never found out if they had come from one and the same bidder, or from different ones, and that was a motivating factor in not entering into negotiations of any sort. I'd be lying to you if I said the idea of selling hadn't been discussed.'

A murmur of surprise went around the meeting room. It had been a closely guarded secret, one that, it seemed to Anne, had been well kept.

He continued. 'I want to make it crystal clear that I'm staying on, but that I'm letting Anne take over my role and my shares. It's a gentle handover, as I'm not ready to walk away just yet. All your jobs are safe and secure and will continue to be and, whether or not we diversify somewhat or expand our cyber crime division, those decisions will be up to her. From now on she's in charge and I'm there as her back up. If you have any questions I'll be happy to answer them.

When they had dispersed he said, 'Anne, I'd like to take you out to dinner tonight – to celebrate your new role. There's something else I need to talk about too and I think Gabby should be there as well.'

'Do you really feel like celebrating and must we have her along?'

'Yes to both of those. Are you free?'

'Of course I am, Dad,' she replied, wondering what else he had up his sleeve.

'Don't look so worried. You're well up for the new role.'

'I'm not worrying, honestly,' she said with a grin. 'I'm just wondering now that I have the power should I evict you out of your salubrious office and let you have mine.'

'Not a chance, young lady, that's not negotiable. I'll ring your sister and book Les Frères for seven thirty.

She rang Alan at lunchtime and told him that they had broken the news of the offer.

'It might smoke the bidders out, right enough.'

'Keep your ear to the ground,' she said.

They'd talked a few times since the evening they'd had a meal together and she was quite surprised when he immediately asked her to meet him that afternoon. They arranged to go for a quick coffee in the local shopping centre at three.

'I wasn't entirely honest with you the last time we met, Anne. I did have some information but when you told me about you and Daniel splitting up I didn't mention it. I know and knew then who your bidder is. It's Clive Kilucan.' He paused. 'I believe they're related in some way.'

'What? Why didn't you tell me that, Alan?'

'I've just told you. I didn't know if it had anything to do with your break-up and I didn't want to make things any worse.'

'Why would it?'

'I don't know – the timing just seemed too coincidental to a suspicious mind like mine.'

'What do you mean, coincidental?'

'It's kind of delicate, Anne, and I don't want to offend you, but could his interest in you have been motivated by a desire to acquire the firm?'

'Good God, don't hold back, Alan. What sort of a twisted question is that? Are you suggesting he couldn't have liked me for who I am, but that he just wanted to get his hands on the firm?'

'I told you it was delicate.'

'You must have a very low opinion of me.'

'You know that's not true.'

'I thought you were a friend.'

'I am, believe me.'

'I don't. I can't.' She opened her bag, took out a ten-euro note and put it on the table. 'That's for the coffee,' she said and left.

She had an empty feeling in the pit of her stomach. She was angry that Alan had been able to put into words something that had been hovering in the depths of her mind. Something she hadn't let surface. Had Daniel been using her, hoping to get information on the breakdown of the shares? She remembered the day of Samantha's naming ceremony how tetchy he'd been about Maurice not discussing business with him. In hindsight he had always brought the discussion to how Maurice had proceeded through his career – obviously trying to find out how much of the company he actually owned. He was cunning, she had to hand him that. He never asked her those questions outright. He'd been annoyed too when he discovered that she hadn't told him about something that her father had asked her not to discuss with anyone. She remembered his 'I don't have to tell you everything' remark, and it suddenly had a new significance. He was hitting back at her because unwittingly she wasn't playing along.

It was when she informed him that Maurice and Peadar intended to hold out for a better offer that he dropped her like a hot coal. And now she discovered that his uncle was behind the whole thing. The man who had sat beside her at that awful dinner party where Daniel's ex-girlfriend had done her best to humiliate her in front of everyone. The offer had already been made by then. They both must have known that, yet nothing had been said. Was it really Daniel who wanted to own them, and not Clive Kilucan? Was Clive the front man? What sort of fool was she not to have twigged?

She felt more dejected and rejected than ever. How could either of them, much less her partner and lover, have sanctioned the offer when her mum had just died? The offer that Peadar had described the timing of as lacking respect and decency. What a callous, calculating bastard he'd turned out to be.

She didn't feel like going out anywhere that night. She tried to reach her dad but his phone was switched off. She longed for normality to return, whatever normality was any more, and although she was enjoying living with Dee she was also looking forward to getting back into her own apartment. She wanted her own space again.

At times she missed Daniel, the chats and the closeness, and all that their intimacy had entailed, but as the days wore on she realised the manner of his scheming and his dismissal of her was so hurtful that it now eclipsed the good times in her mind.

She went home to change and met Dee in the kitchen.

'How do you think Maurice is coping with everything? Does he seem a little ... remote or distracted to you?' Dee asked her.

'I hadn't noticed, but there has been lot of upheaval in his life. I suppose it's only natural. Why did you ask?

'Oh, I don't know. It's something and nothing. It's just that he doesn't seem to be taking care of himself like he used to. He called here the other evening with sauce all over his tie and shirtfront and when I mentioned it he just dismissed it as though it were nothing. The Maurice I know would never have been seen anywhere like that. Charlie used to envy him, said he was always so dapper and well turned out, he made him feel like a peasant. The other day he looked, well, a bit unkempt.'

'That doesn't sound like him at all. He's always so fastidious.'

'Forget I said anything. Maybe he was just embarrassed.'

'I'll give him a good once over later and see what I think,' she said, as the taxi pulled up outside Dee's house. 'Don't expect me back. I'll stay over there with him tonight.'

Chapter Twenty-Two

She seethed every time she thought about Alan's comments, and now, as if the day couldn't get any worse, she had to face Gabby. How would she react to the news about her promotion, she wondered, as the car made its way along the Stillorgan dual carriageway towards town.

Her father's announcement, although she knew it was coming, had put a stamp of finality on her future in law. She felt it trapped her more than ever because now she would have the responsibility for so many others' futures as well. She wished she could just walk away, but she wouldn't do that to her father. Mostly she enjoyed her job, but the prospects of doing it until she reached Maurice's or Peadar's ages unnerved her. Had this restlessness anything to do with the disillusionment Daniel had caused her? Was that what she really wanted?

What if she ever met someone who wanted to marry her, and not for her business assets either, but someone who loved her and wanted a family with her? What then? Would she be able to juggle those two lives? Would she want to? She dismissed these thoughts. She had inherited genes from both her parents, genes of stoicism and commitment, which prevented her from putting herself first.

Maurice was already at the table when she got there, her sister arriving a few minutes later.

'You've changed your hair, I like it,' Anne said as they sat down.

'Yes, one of the girls at the club recommended her hairdresser and I decided to try him. I'm very pleased with it. Now, Dad, what's this all about?'

'Let's order some drinks and food first and I'll tell you.'

He outlined the changes he had explained in the office that morning to her.

Anne could see the rage building up on Gabby's face. 'You're retiring? This is very sudden, is it not?'

'No, I'm not really, just gently easing off so that I can take a bit of time to do a few things I've always wanted.'

'So she's going to get everything when you're gone?' she uttered. 'Isn't that just typical? The Golden Girl wins again.'

'It's not like that,' Anne said.

'That's what it seems like to me.'

'Simmer down and hear me out,' their father said, more sternly than usual. 'I have to think of the staff, the way Peadar thought of me. I don't want the company falling apart when I'm gone, so I've decided to give Anne the fifty-one per cent share and you'll get the remainder.'

'That's not fair.'

'Maybe not, but it's my decision. It is her livelihood and career and she deserves recognition for that.'

'She gets paid handsomely, doesn't she?'

'She does, and so would you if you had done the same. She

knows the company inside out and can make informed decisions about it. If you want to take equity you can sell your portion to her or an outsider, and the company will still survive, albeit with a new partner. This way nobody loses.'

'That's not how it seems to me.'

'It worked perfectly for Peadar and me over the years, and thanks to his unbelievable generosity, you'll both benefit considerably more than I ever thought any of us would.'

She didn't reply. Over their main course he began to explain Anne's new role as managing director.

'I suppose I should congratulate you,' Gabby said, half raising her glass.

'Thank you. It's all a little unexpected, but really it's not going to be too different on a day-to-day basis.'

'That's what she thinks!' Her father chuckled. 'But you're not going to get rid of me that soon.'

'That's good,' said Anne, glad that the awkward moment had passed and Gabby seemed to have been mollified. 'Now what about you? How are you adjusting to married life? You certainly looked relaxed and glowing.'

'I'm enjoying it, as for glowing that's from the tan I got on honeymoon, and being out on the golf course today. I took a day off to play in an away and the weather was glorious.'

'How is the house coming on?' Anne asked.

'We're getting there – we'll have you over when the curtains arrive. In fact, we're planning on having a house-warming party but not until after mid-September. There are too many things happening at the club over the summer and with Paul's dad being captain he likes us to attend as many of them as we can.'

'Well, I'll look forward to that,' Maurice said. 'I can't quite get used to having a son-in-law.'

'Or me a brother-in-law.'

They ate in silence for a few minutes and Anne wondered was there some other reason Maurice had brought them together. He had told her his plans earlier that day and it didn't make sense to insist on a meeting outside the office, unless he just wanted moral support. She decided not to tell him about Daniel's possible involvement in the takeover bids, not in Gabby's presence anyway and not tonight. She couldn't take her gloating, not after Alan's reaction.

When dessert arrived, as though reading her mind, Maurice cleared his throat and said, 'There is something else I need to tell you, and I know you're not going to like this, Gabby, but you have to believe me—'

'You're not ill, Dad, are you?' Gabby asked. 'I couldn't bear it if you were.'

'No, not at all. You don't have to worry on that score. But I have to tell you that this had nothing whatever to do with me. Peadar has left the villa and farm in Aix to Anne, with a provision than Marie and Pierre can live on there for the rest of their days. He gifted their cottage to them until they're both gone, then it reverts back to what is now your estate, Anne.'

'What?' Anne was speechless.

Gabby wasn't. As it sunk in, she exploded with rage.

'I don't believe this. I can't believe this. As if my sister getting the lion's share of the firm was not enough, she now gets a place in France and you expect me to believe you didn't cook this up between you when you were over there?' She looked at them with murderous malevolence and raised her voice. 'What sort of idiot do you think I am?'

'You're attracting attention, Gabby,' Anne said, nodding towards the other diners who had stopped talking to hear what was going on. 'I can assure you I knew absolutely nothing about this until now. I'm totally shocked.'

'And you expect me to believe that?'

'Whether you do or not, it's the truth. It was never discussed with me. I'm flabbergasted. Dad, are you sure it isn't a mistake?'

'Positive,' he said. 'Peadar had all the paperwork done when I got over there.'

'But he had a brain tumour, for Christ's sake! He wasn't of sound mind to make decisions like that. The will could be contested.'

'It could, Gabby, but it would be futile. I made the same argument to him myself, but he had taken the precaution of having it witnessed and medically endorsed several months ago, when he was first diagnosed. He wanted to be sure there would be no such confusion.'

'It's just not fair. How am I going to tell Paul and the O'Reillys? They don't understand how we are treated so differently.'

'Is that what you and they think?' Maurice said quietly. 'That's news to me.'

'I wonder if they'll change their minds when you tell them you'll inherit forty-nine per cent of Dad's business?' Anne asked.

'I have to agree with your sister, Gabby. You know, when I tackled Peadar about leaving the villa to Anne, I was concerned that some people may have felt that I could have taken advantage of him when he was poorly, but I never expected that judgment to come from my own flesh and blood. I have to say I'm very disappointed.'

'Not half as disappointed as I am in both of you, thinking you can soften me up with a measly dinner and a compliment about my hair.' She spat the words out, pushed her chair back, called for her jacket and stormed out without so much as a thank you to the waiter who had fetched it for her, or a backward glance at the suddenly-quiet dining room.

Maurice sat back in his chair and she could see how distressed he was. 'I knew it wouldn't be easy telling her that, that's why I wanted you both together when I did it, but I'm genuinely delighted for you, especially as I saw your reaction to the place when you saw it. I just wonder how you could be so different from each other.'

'So do I, but she's not going to change now, unless marriage mellows her. I just can't believe this has happened. A few weeks ago I'd never even been to that part of France.'

'And now you own a piece of it!'

'I can't believe it. It hasn't sunk in yet. Why me?'

'Peadar had the height of respect and regard for you, because you stood up to him. He liked someone who could challenge him.'

'Can I ask you something, Dad? I don't understand why you didn't tell me about the villa before the promotion. It might have coloured my acceptance.'

'It might and I think Peadar knew that too. He wanted to ensure the future of the company and let you have time to reflect on what you wanted to do. He left everything in order over there so you don't have to make any snap decisions.'

'I don't understand ...'

'The vines and land are to stay leased out to his neighbours for another year and the house and farm will still be managed by Pierre. There's funding there to pay for all eventualities for the next twelve months and by then the rental accrued in the interim will cover the following one, so you don't have to worry about it.'

'He really was methodical, wasn't he?'

'The best, but he was wise too. I think he made the right choice.' He raised his glass and said, 'A toast to my old friend, may he never be forgotten.' She lifted hers and clinked it.

'He's certainly made sure of that in this family.' They smiled at each other.

'Now what are we going to do about that sister of yours?'

'Mum would say, "Leave her to simmer down a bit and see if we can talk to her rationally then." I'm sure she'll change her mind when she realises she can go there for holidays. She can even bring the O'Reillys with her!'

He sighed. 'If it doesn't madden her even more.'

'It's been some day, and now it's time for a revelation of my own.' She repeated what Alan had told her and he was shocked.

'I hate to admit it, but at times Daniel almost seemed too good to be true. He did ask an awful lot of questions about the business any time we talked and I did find that irritating. I figured if he was your choice then I had no right to say anything. You've no idea how I miss your mother to talk to about things like that. I never really realised that there was an ulterior motive. In hindsight though …' He stopped. 'In hindsight perhaps you had a lucky escape. You deserve better.'

Better than being dated by someone who was only interested in his own goals and not in her, for herself? She remembered Alan's words and felt deflated again. She felt she had lost him as a friend that day. The dynamic of their relationship had changed and she wasn't at all happy about it.

As though reading her mind Maurice said, 'Don't let it come between you and your friend. Remember it's not always the messenger's fault.'

'I know that,' she answered but she was too hurt to give in to that just yet. 'Dad, I'm wrecked. That was some whirlwind of events. Can we call it a day and take a taxi home?' They got their jackets and her dad went to the men's room. Anne was waiting for him when she felt a hand on her shoulder and the maître d' asked discreetly if he could have a word.

'I'm afraid your bill has not been paid.'

'But I saw my father putting the notes in the folder.'

'Yes, so did I, but he took them back out again and put them in his wallet when you went to the rest room. The waiter was watching him. It happens sometimes after a diner has made a scene.'

A scene? God, Gabby flouncing out. What was he implying – that they were deliberately trying a scam?

'There has to be some mistake? Are you sure?'

'Absolutely, but we can check the CCTV footage together in the office if you like.'

'That won't be necessary,' she said fumbling in her bag, embarrassed, and producing her credit card. 'Please put it on this, and accept my apologies. He must have got confused. He's been under a lot of strain lately. His business partner just died.' She heard herself justifying whatever had happened and realised how lame it sounded. Maurice joined her at the desk just as she was getting her receipt.

'Oh, thank you, Anne, but this was going to be my treat,' he said and she saw the two staff members exchange a knowing look. He never mentioned it in the taxi. She'd have to have a word with Gabby about not upsetting him so much.

'The place is a bit of a mess,' he apologised when he opened the door and turned the lights on. He always said that, even though his idea of a mess was the weekend newspaper or supplements being strewn on the sofa, or a few fliers on the hall table.

This time, though, it really was a mess.

There were cups in the sink with tea and coffee remains growing bearded mould inside them. Plates with half-eaten sandwiches, congealed food and biscuit wrappers decorated other surfaces, and the tip-up bin was filled to capacity, the lid not properly closed. The rancid odour of stale food permeated from the kitchen through the other rooms. Dead flowers drooped in yellowed water, their shrivelled petals forming circles on the surfaces beneath them.

He didn't seem to notice any of this as he asked if she'd like a cup of tea before going to bed.

'Why don't you go on up and I'll bring you one?' she said.

She was shocked. She didn't know what to say. Her father's ideas of fastidiousness were higher than most. When had he started to let things slide? Could this be a symptom of grieving? She remembered Dee's conversation about his soiled shirt and tie and wondered how she hadn't noticed. She'd have to keep a closer eye on him.

She opened the conservatory doors and the kitchen windows and set about cleaning up and disinfecting the surfaces. She took towels off the floor in the bathroom and when she went to put a wash on she found he had never emptied the previous lot and everything in it was covered with black mildew spots. They must have been in there for weeks and were beyond rescue. She checked the refuse collection days on the calendar that her mother always stuck on the little cork noticeboard by the back door. She opened the fridge and threw fruit and half-used cartons of out-of-date food and milk into some bags and took them outside. She managed to squeeze them into the bins, which had obviously not been emptied for several weeks. She wheeled them out by the side of the garage and onto the road for the following day's collection.

It was a beautiful, balmy, starry night and, as she looked up at the sky, for the first time since arriving back at the house she allowed herself think about the villa in France – her villa. What she wouldn't give to be there right now. How pleased Sheila would have been at this quirk of fate. They could have holidayed together there. She missed her so much. She would probably have gone over with Dee too. She felt her eyes well up. She wiped a tear and went back inside, feeling very much alone. She closed the windows and locked the doors.

It was almost two when she went to bed, her mind whirring. She'd have to talk to her father about getting someone in to clean for him once or twice a week, something he had previously resisted, insisting he was quite capable of looking after himself. And he had been too, but whatever had got into him, if he let the place get into that state again he was likely to give himself food poisoning, or worse.

'Well, don't some people have all the luck,' Paula said when she told her about Peadar's legacy.

'It hasn't sunk in. I haven't even told Darcy yet.'

When she got around to doing that Samantha was demanding her mother's attention and she couldn't talk to her.

'Ring me when you can – I've got news!' Anne told her. 'Big news!'

'Sorry. No matter how big it is, it's not as urgent as this child. I'll get back to you!'

When she did she apologised. 'Time and nappy changes wait for no man. Now, what's this big news?'

'You're talking to the new owner of a villa in France.'

'You never said you were thinking of buying abroad.'

'I didn't, because I wasn't. It's a gift.' She told her about the latest developments in her life.

'My God, that's *fantastique*, Anne! Company director and a property owner. You'll be too grand to talk to me soon.'

'Never.'

'I can see you there, picnicking on the terrace, gingham cloths and bowls of cherries.'

'Good old Darce, you've got great imagination, but I like the sound of that.'

'Dare I ask – how did Gabby take the news?'

'Just as you'd expect, with the reaction of a martyr and a victim. She was furious and flounced out of the restaurant in a rage. I have to confess I've been afraid to contact her this morning. Dad was so upset he walked out without paying and they collared me when I was leaving. All very embarrassing.'

'That's awful. Let her cool down.'

'That's what I'm doing; I just don't know how long it will take. She's convinced that we influenced Peadar because he didn't know what he was doing.'

'Twisted twit – that's typical of her. Is Maurice there? I haven't been over to see him for a few weeks what with him being away and the funeral and all that and it's time little Samantha had a few more cuddles before she forgets him.'

'He'd enjoy that. He's not in yet, but should be shortly. I'll get him to give you a ring.'

She phoned Gabby a couple of times over the next few days. She wanted to try to sort things out. Every time she thought of her sister she thought of Sheila and what she would make of them not talking to each other. Family had always been so important to her. Dee tried to mediate and was told, albeit politely, to back off. The weekend came and went with no further communication. Then Anne got a call that took her focus off it completely.

She was in her office with a client. They were composing a victim's impact statement that they would deliver in court. Her phone buzzed and she looked through the glass window between her office and Paula's. It wasn't like her PA to interrupt her when she had anyone with her. Paula raised her hands in an 'I had no choice' kind of gesture, and Anne excused herself and picked it up.

'Is that Anne Cullen, Maurice Cullen's daughter?' an officious voice asked. Fear gripped her as she waited to be told her father had collapsed or had been knocked down, or crashed the car or worse.

'It's the Gardaí, here in College Green. We have a Mr Maurice Cullen here with his. He claims he is your father.'

'He is. Is he all right? What happened? Is he hurt?'

'No, he seems perfectly fine to us.'

'Then why are you ringing me?'

'He's been arrested.'

'Is this a joke?' she exploded and was tempted to hang up, but something made her hold on, her clients looking quizzically on.

'What? What for?'

'Shoplifting.'

'What? When? OK. Yes. Yes, of course I'll come down right away. Thank you.'

She apologised and explained there was an emergency and that one of her associates would finalise the statement with them. They said they understood and she excused herself and ran out into the street to hail a taxi – she'd never find parking near that Garda station.

Maurice was looking a little shamefaced when she was taken in to a small room to him.

'Dad, what happened? Tell me.'

'I don't know really. I was in the bookshop, looking for a book that was reviewed in the paper on Sunday. I found it and the next thing I knew I was being asked to go back inside the shop. I offered to pay, but they wouldn't hear of it. The manager pointed to a sign that said "Shoplifters will be prosecuted". I told him he had no right to accuse me in front of other customers and he replied that the Gardaí had already been called and that it was out of their hands. They shouldn't be allowed behave like that to law-abiding citizens.'

'And had you walked out without paying, Dad? Perhaps they made a mistake. Anyone can get distracted. It seems a bit heavy handed to me, to waste your time for a book,' she said to the officer who had been standing behind her, listening. She knew his face from the courts too.

'He also had a packet of thank-you cards and a diary, which he'd put in his inside pocket. They have him on their security cameras and had been watching him doing it.'

'I don't understand,' she said, completely confused. 'My father is an honest man. He's never been in any kind of trouble. He just buried his business partner last week.'

'We know who he is, and we are aware of the circumstances,' the officer said, 'but wearing a suit doesn't make a crime any less of one. The shop has agreed to let it go and, as we have no record on file of any misdemeanours in the past, we have also agreed. Just make sure that he knows he can't expect leniency of any kind if there's a reoccurrence. In fact the shop has said they'd prefer to do without any further custom from him. He has to understand that and stay away from there in future.'

'I haven't disappeared. I'm sitting here listening to you, so stop talking about me as if I were a child or invisible, or both,' Maurice chimed in. 'It's a load of nonsense. I can't understand the fuss. I forgot to pay. It's that simple. Have you never done that? I'm sure I'd have realised it when I got back to the office. I'd have paid the next time I was in there.'

'That's what they all say.'

'Well, I'm not a "they", whoever they are, I can assure you,' he said indignantly and stood up. 'Is this over now?'

'I certainly hope so,' the Garda said and he went around to hold the door open for them to leave. 'Thank you for coming down,' he said to Anne and whispered, 'Often one embarrassing incident like this is all it takes to stop this kind of thing happening again.'

She thanked him. She was annoyed at his suggestion that it might happen again, but relieved that he had been so understanding. What had possessed her father? She didn't know what to make of it. They walked back to the office together and he told her he was sorry for dragging her away. Then he changed the subject as though nothing had happened. His easy dismissal of his behaviour made her wonder if he had done this kind of thing before and got away with it. Was the incident in the restaurant the previous week purely coincidental? She hadn't mentioned that to him since. She'd come across professionals who stole for the kicks, not from necessity. But Maurice? Surely not.

Gabby still wasn't returning her calls so in frustration she texted.

'Ring me. Urgent. Dad in trouble.' She didn't hear from her until that evening and without waiting for her to say what the trouble was she began a tirade.

'If this is some sort of ruse to try and placate me it's very underhand of you.'

'Gabby, not everything in this life is planned or organised to suit or to discommode you. I needed to tell you about Dad. I don't think he's coping with life very well at the moment.'

'Perhaps he has an uneasy conscience about the way he's treated me.'

'What sort of diatribe is that? Will you listen to yourself? Dad has always been perfectly fair to us, and to Darcy too.'

'Are you going to tell me he's given her the house now.'

Exasperated, Anne blurted out, 'Dad was arrested today.'

'Jesus Christ. He's not in custody, is he?'

'No, he was let go.' She explained what had happened. 'I felt like a parent who is called in to the headmaster to defend their child, who just happens to be the class bully. I literally didn't know what to say to them, or to him.'

'Could you imagine that getting out in the golf club or into to the papers? The tabloids would have a field day.'

'I never thought about that.' She had to bite her tongue from reacting. Did Gabby never think about anything else apart from her bloody golf club? As if any of her shallow so-called friends would give a damn about her anyway, apart from making her the butt of that week's hot gossip.

'There's something else …' She filled her in on what had happened after she'd left the restaurant. 'Be nicer to him, Gabby. He's very vulnerable right now and I think he might welcome a phone call from you. He said he hasn't heard from you for a while.'

'I'll think about it.'

'And maybe not mention that you know about this little episode.'

'You sounded just like Mum there – this little episode – she never called anything as it was. Now I have to go, I have a bridge lesson.'

Darcy's reaction was one of genuine concern. 'How embarrassing for him. The poor devil has been through a lot lately. His mind was probably miles away, or on some case or other.'

'You're right. I just hope he's not going to make a habit of it.'

'Relax, he's not very likely to turn into a kleptomaniac overnight,' her friend assured her. 'I'm sure lots of people do that at some stage in their lives. What did Gabby say?'

'You can probably guess.'

'I suppose all she's concerned with is the shame if that got out? Am I right? The O'Reillys would be *mortified*!' Darcy said imitating Gabby's mother-in-law. '"She'll never get on the social committee if this gets out!" I swear, Anne, that one needs to get a life – her world is about the same size as that golf course.'

'You're bad.' Anne laughed, relieved that she had been able to tell someone and to get a different perspective on the whole incident. 'She's off to play bridge.'

'An opportunity to show off, no doubt.'

'At bridge? I don't think she's that good yet. She never showed any interest in it when Mum and Dad tried to teach us.'

'But it's not really about bridge is it? I heard some women discussing this at the doctors when I brought Samantha for her vaccination. One remarked how she'd hate the weekly fashion parade with everyone discussing who was wearing what. Another chimed in with it's not the clothes they notice – it's the hands. She said she hated her hands and her stubby nails. Do you know what the other one told her? She said she needn't worry about that – they wouldn't be looking at those – they'd only be looking at the jewellery she'd be wearing. Can you believe it?'

'I suppose it depends where you play, but that's enough to put anybody off.'

'Except the likes of Gabby.'

Maurice had given them the choice of Sheila's jewellery and

Gabby had opted for two of her rings, an emerald and a two-diamond stone twist that had belonged to their grandmother.

'You're right there,' said Anne. 'Now I'd better get back to work. Thank you for cheering me up.'

'Don't worry too much about Maurice. He'll be fine.'

The Garda station incident blew over without consequence and was never mentioned by any of them for a long time.

With the courts being on summer recess, Anne didn't bump into Daniel and was relieved about that, although she was determined to confront him when she did.

Alan hadn't been in touch either and she found that upset her more, although she still wasn't ready to forgive him. The truth hurt and she was still sore at the implication of what he'd said. Her social life had been curtailed seriously once Daniel and she had severed connections and, since Darcy was so busy with Samantha, she missed the girly nights out they used to share.

The highlights of her social calendar were drinks on a Friday night with Paula and a few of the women from the office. Dee, who was always flitting from one event to another, insisted she accompanied her occasionally, to a gallery opening and another time to a piano recital in the National Art Gallery. For her birthday she and Darcy met some college friends and they had a meal in one of their old haunts. During the evening Alan came in to the restaurant with a female companion. He came over and said hello to them, but his dinner date went straight to their table so he didn't introduce her. He enquired how her father was keeping and returned to his table. The women were still sitting at theirs when he was leaving and he waved across the room as he left.

Chapter Twenty-Three

'I still have my eye on this office,' she teased her father, as he opened and closed the drawers in his leather-topped desk. 'And on that wing-backed chair. Maybe I'll pull rank on you after all and move in here. We can still share Paula.'

'Not a chance,' he said looking up at her. 'These go with seniority not with rank.'

'What are you rummaging for? You're like something demented there, opening and closing the drawers.'

'My passport. I'll have to go back over to France in the next few weeks to sort a few things out. I promised Peadar I'd look after the disposal of his papers, his personal effects, etc. It's time I took care of them, but I can't seem to find it. Did you see it anywhere at home? You didn't put it anywhere, did you? I've searched everywhere to no avail.'

'No, I didn't notice, but then I wasn't looking for it. I'm sure you've put it somewhere for safety. Did you check in your jacket pockets and your wheelie bag? I often leave mine in there after a trip and forget about it till I'm going somewhere.'

'I don't know if I checked them.'

'When do you intend travelling?'

'I was going to get Paula to check flights to Paris and decide then. Your mother and I loved Paris.'

'Why Paris? Surely Marseilles is nearer?'

He looked at her steadily. 'That's what I said, Marseilles. Would you like to come over with me?'

'I'd love to but I can't take time off just yet. My apartment is ready for me to move back into this weekend and I want to start taking my things out of Dee's. I'll take a few weeks in August and go over and familiarise myself with my estate,' she joked. 'I was thinking that I might ask Darcy and Richard if they'd like to join me. They didn't plan any holidays this year with all the additional expenses of a baby.'

'That would be lovely for them, if a bit on the hot side. Tell them I'll cover their airfares. That'll take the pressure off them.'

'That's very generous of you. Dad.'

'Just don't tell Gabby, I can't take much more of her victim complex.'

'I won't.' She handed him a sheaf of papers. 'I've looked over these papers like you asked me to, they just need your signature.'

'Great, the estate agent needs them this afternoon. They're closing the sale later. First I have to find my passport.'

'If it's not here it's obviously still in the house. I'm leaving early this afternoon to get the hair done and glam up for tonight, but if you like I'll pop in at home on the way to Dee's and have a look. I'm sure it's probably sitting there somewhere staring at you.'

A while later Paula came in to her office. She closed the door behind her. That always heralded something important, or a bit of juicy gossip not intended for general release throughout the office.

'So what's the news?' Anne asked, looking up from her laptop.

'It's Maurice. He's spent the last few hours in a real state looking for his passport.'

'Yeah, he told me he'd lost it.'

'But he has it. I gave it to him this morning when he asked me about finding flights to Paris. He'd left it on my desk a few weeks ago and I'd put it in the safe for security. I told him at the time, but he obviously forgot.'

'Paris? He's not going to Paris. He's going back to Aix so he needs to fly into Marseilles. Has he booked tickets?'

'No, he asked me to, which I thought was strange, as he always does those himself. But honestly, Anne, I don't know how to say this, he seems to be a little, well, a little unlike his usual decisive self. Have you noticed anything different about his behaviour?'

'Thinking about it there have been a few things recently that are a bit out of character, but I put them down to stresses. There have been some huge changes in his life. I'm not really surprised that he was a little bit distracted. I'll keep a closer eye on him.'

'The break will do him good,' Paula said. 'It's probably exactly what he needs.'

'I wouldn't mind one myself, but I need to get my move done and get back to some degree of normality. Dee is terrific but she's always trying to get me out. She says it's tragic that her social life is so manic, while mine is – well, it's pedestrian, I think that's the word she used. Tonight we're off with some of her arty friends to hear a premiere by that composer Michael Gallen.'

'Michael Gallen? Should I know him?''According to Dee he's not the up-and-coming composer that some reviewers claimed, he's arrived – in more ways than one. He seems to be extraordinarily talented. She's been talking about him since hearing him perform in the Dublin Theatre Fringe Festival.

To be honest I'd rather get on with my packing, but she's been so good to me that I can't let her down.'

The National Concert Hall was a sell out and as the choral music and hauntingly beautiful orchestrations wrapped around her she forgot her anxiety at Maurice's behaviour and let herself float along with the composer's sentiments.

'Well, what did you think? Isn't he marvellous? Was I exaggerating?' Dee asked at the interval.

'Definitely not. I'm loving it.' After it was over the foyer was buzzing with praise and positive comments. She was adding hers to some of Dee's friends when she spotted Alan. He was with the same female companion he had had that night at the restaurant. She was sure he had seen her, but he didn't make any effort to come over. She pretended to check her phone, which was still turned to silent, and she saw a message from her father.

'Still can't find my passport.'

The spell was broken. As she sat in the auditorium she had been transported to a different sphere, a magical plane that lifted her above the mundane. Now try as she could, she was unable to put that message to the back of her head. What was going on with her dad?

Later, in bed, she strung the incidences together: the restaurant bill, the shoplifting, the state of the house, the fuss over the passport, the airport mix-up. Of course they were all down to grief. Everyone knew that grief did funny things to people and that everyone reacted differently to it. She knew he'd be fine when he adjusted and, as Paula had pointed out, the break at the villa would certainly help and would put closure on Peadar's affairs.

With that resolved, and phrases of Michael Gallen's ethereal music on a loop in her head, she eventually slept.

She was telling Paula all about it the next day when her dad came in announcing, 'I found it.' He held up the passport. 'Now I must organise the flights to Marseilles.'

'I can do to those for you,' Paula offered, glancing at Anne.

'Thank you, but I'm perfectly well able to book a few flights,' he replied pleasantly.

She and Paula exchanged glances.

'Before you confirm them, let me know when you're going to be away and I'll check the diaries and make sure we don't need you for anything at that time.'

'Sure thing,' he said to Paula.

Relieved, Anne went back to her desk. Normality seemed to have been restored. It was, until the first phone call of the morning. Maurice had failed to sign the deeds she had left on his desk – the ones that were needed to close the house sale the previous evening. They were still in his in-tray.

'You should have told me they were needed yesterday,' was all he had to say.

'I thought I did, Dad.'

'You mustn't have.'

She knew she had. 'Perhaps you could do them now and I'll try and see if I can salvage the situation,' she suggested. The buyers were threatening to pull out of the deal. She and Paula were left with this mess to sort. After several apologetic phone calls and a good bit of grovelling, Paula had them couriered to their destination. They both hoped it wasn't too late.

Meanwhile Maurice went ahead and booked his tickets without consulting anyone and announced that he was heading off that weekend for two weeks. Paula verified that he had indeed made the bookings for Marseilles. He never made any reference to the unsigned deeds or the panic that had caused in the office.

Gabby answered Anne's calls but never initiated any herself. She did ring Maurice from time to time and fitted him in for hurried visits between golf, work, the club and more golf fixtures. They were still waiting for an invitation to the house. Darcy said it would probably only come on a day that the course was flooded and the clubhouse had been struck by lightning and she had nowhere to go.

Chapter Twenty-Four

She drove Maurice to the airport early on Saturday for his flight to France. Then she headed back to start her move. Laden down with boxes, she arrived at the door of her apartment. She felt she was coming home again. Since Sheila died she no longer felt that way about the house she had grown up in. Its heart was gone.

The complex comprised just three low-rise blocks, three storeys in each, and in the twenty-five years it had been there, the Virginia creeper had snaked its way across the front of the buildings, softening their edges and covering the gable ends.

An award-winning landscape company looked after the grounds; consequently the lawns were always like bowling greens and the shrubbery tamed and styled like well-cut hair. These screened the parking spaces discreetly. The colour schemes of the flowerbeds marked the passing of the seasons. Many of the neighbours had lived there since the apartments were built and most of them were friendly, while keeping to themselves, but there was the security of knowing that if they were needed they'd be there for one another.

Anne smiled as she saw the movement behind Mrs Dunne's curtain. Malcolm Coleman, the chairman of the residents' committee for several terms, had joked that Mrs Dunne, in apartment one, could have saved them all a fortune on the surveillance portion of their annual service charges as she kept such a good eye on the comings and goings of everyone. Her net curtains twitched visibly when any car pulled up or when visitors arrived.

Anne was a carrying a large box of shoes when Mrs Dunne emerged from her door.

'You're back. Is it for good this time?'

'I hope so, Mrs Dunne. How are you?' She was always called Mrs Dunne. If they knew it, no one ever used her first name.

'I'm fine really, but Nicolas Leonard has gone into a home.' Nicolas had the apartment next to Anne's on the third floor.

'Oh, I am sorry to hear that.' He was the most senior resident, a courtly old gentleman who was pleasant to everyone.

'Yes, his hip gave out and he was finding it difficult to walk. He'd had a few falls since you've been gone,' she said, almost accusing her of abandoning him in his time of need. Anne was finding it harder and harder to balance the box.

'I'd love to stay and chat but I have to make a move, I've a lot more to bring in. I'll pop in for a cuppa some evening when I'm settled and hear all your news.'

'That would be grand, or I could come up to you,' Mrs Dunne suggested. 'I hope those foreigners you had in your place didn't do too much damage. I saw the decorators were in when they left.'

Foreigners? That was the first time she'd heard Americans called that. 'No, Mrs Dunne, they were exemplary tenants. I was just giving the place a fresh look. Now I must go – this is very heavy and it's only one of many I have to bring in. See you later.'

She managed to escape and hoped she'd get by the door next time without a repeat performance, otherwise it was going to be a very long day.

The apartment smelled of fresh paint and air freshener. She flung the windows open wide, went on to her balcony and stood there, looking out at her once-familiar view. So much had happened since she had moved in with Daniel. She smiled a wistful smile – so much had happened since she had left Daniel, or more accurately, been dumped by him. So much had happened in a year, good and bad. She needed to remind herself of that.

Dee arrived close behind her. 'No time for daydreaming if we've to get this lot unpacked and put away.'

'I'm just getting a feel for the place. I'm sure you'll be glad to see the back of me.'

'No – I won't. It's been very good for me to have you coming and going. You got me over the worst part of living alone. I hate to admit it, but I miss Charlie and I will miss you. Now don't let me get maudlin.' She produced a bag with milk and croissants. 'I stopped off to get some essentials. There's coffee too. I couldn't remember what kind of coffee you used, so I grabbed some cappuccinos just in case I got it wrong.'

'Perfect. You know I thought I was going to find this place claustrophobic, after Daniel's penthouse, but I don't.'

'You probably would have had you come straight back, but then anywhere would seem confined after that. This is a big apartment.'

'It is,' she said with a sigh, 'that's why Dad persuaded me to go for it at the time, so I could have a spare room as well as a room for my art things. I was taken once I saw the view. I love being able to see and smell the sea. Anyway, it feels great to be back. There's a certain comfort in the familiar.'

'You start putting those thing away and I'll go down and get another box from my car.'

In her bedroom she hung her clothes on the new hangers she had bought and as she was doing this task she realised that she would actually miss Daniel's walk-in dressing room more than him.

'What sort of shallow person does that make me?' she said when she shared this revelation with Dee.

'With *your* shoe collection? A totally normal one I would say,' and they laughed about it.

They made another trip before lunch and filled both their vehicles with more of her possessions. She was struggling with her easel. One of its legs had extended during the short drive and was caught under the passenger seat. She went around to the front to move it forwards. She stretched in to fiddle with the lever, her behind stuck up in inelegantly in the air, when she became aware of someone behind her. Through her legs she just see two well-shod feet and dark-blue denim trousers. She straightened suddenly and banged her head on the frame of the door. She let out a string of expletives.

'I didn't mean to startle you. Are you all right?' the man enquired, fair hair flopping down on his forehead.

She rubbed her head, sore and annoyed.

'What did you think you were doing, coming up behind me like that?'

'I'm sorry. I saw you struggling and was about to offer to help, but obviously I've just made things worse.'

'No, you didn't. I didn't mean to be rude. It's just all this packing and unpacking is doing my head in.'

'In more ways than one it seems.' He grinned and she laughed.

He had the bluest eyes she had ever seen. 'It's always a bit of a mare moving. You're not in Three One by any chance?'

'How did you figure that out?'

'I'm in Three Two. Just renting for a year. I heard on the grapevine I was getting a new neighbour. Here, let me help you with that,' he said reaching in to the back and releasing the easel. 'Are you an artist?'

'No. I'm in law.'

'I better watch myself so. I'm Dean Moore, doctor.'

'You'll be handy to have next door,' she said, pulling another box towards her.

'That looks heavy, let me take it and you take the easel.'

Dee looked surprised when Anne arrived back with Dean in tow. He helped them unload the two cars and when they said they were going over to her house to get the remainder of her things he suggested soup and a sandwich first in the local before that. Anne realised she was starving. It was after two and all she'd eaten was one of the croissants that Dee had brought.

They all took their cars and headed off.

While they were eating Maurice texted to say he had arrived and that Pierre had collected him from the airport as planned.

'I'm glad he did that,' said Dee.

'Got Pierre to collect him?'

'No, that he texted you. I always like to know that someone has reached their destination.'

'I have to confess that I'm a bit concerned about him driving on the other side of the road.'

'You need your wits about you right enough. Has he done it before?' Dean asked.

'Countless times, but he seems to have been a bit distracted lately.'

'I'm sure you're worrying about nothing,' Dee told her.

They ordered and Dean turned out to be witty and entertaining. Before they realised, it was almost four.

'I didn't mean to hold you up so long,' he said. 'I'll leave you to it. You know where I am if you need anything. Please feel free to call any time, if you run out of sugar, cornflakes …'

'I will, and if I can return the compliment the same applies to you. Have you met any of the other neighbours yet?'

'No, apart from the old dear on the ground floor. She seems to be looking out her window whenever I come and go. I'm only there a few weeks and it's amazing how often she has checked her mailbox at exactly the same moment as I opened the front door. She must get an awful lot of post.'

'Mrs Dunne is our resident watcher. She never misses a thing. She's probably seen us going in and out today, and it will be interesting to see what sort of spin she puts on that!'

They laughed and he said, 'Whatever it is, I'm sure worse will have been said about me. It was lovely meeting you both, but I won't hold you up any longer.'

'I had hoped to be finished by now,' Anne told Dee when they got back to her house.

'We had to take a break at some stage,' Dee rationalised. 'Without his help we'd probably only be setting off for the last run at this stage anyway.'

'I really appreciate what you did, taking me in, and the way you've been there for Dad too.'

'Sheila was my dearest friend, I'd have done anything for her.'

'I know, but I'm still grateful,' she said, hugging the older women. They loaded the last bits and pieces and when everything was back in its place in the apartment Dee said she was ravenous.

'Dinner will be my treat.'

'Only if we can we have it here. I'm too tired to think about going out anywhere. Let's order in, sit on your balcony and enjoy the view.'

Anne opened the fridge. 'There's Pinot Grigio and Sancerre chilled. I put them in when I got here this morning.'

'Glad to see you have your priorities right. Go and ring that takeaway and I'll pour this.' Dee opened several cupboards before she found the one with glasses. They sat outside until the lights came on across Dublin Bay.

After Dee left, Anne bagged the cartons, took a shower and got into her own bed, in her own home, surrounded by her belongings and, reflecting over the day, she was very pleased with the way it had gone.

She'd finish off sorting things the next morning and get rid of all the boxes stacked in her hall. She'd also pop over to her dad's and check that he hadn't left any food lying around or wet washing in the machine when he left for France. She had broached the subject of getting someone in to keep the place tidy and he promised that he would think about it while he was away. If he didn't she was going to organise that herself.

She had to prepare mentally for the new working week. It would be the first time she would be in total control of the company, and without her father being physically present. She was determined to show him and the staff that she was quite capable of filling that role competently.

She had to set about getting a life for herself and put the past where it belonged – in the past. Since her mum's death and the whole Daniel saga, she had isolated herself a bit socially, half afraid at how she would react meeting him or his friends. Those situations were not going to change. He was going nowhere and it would be impossible to avoid him indefinitely. It was up to her to get on with her life.

Their paths were sure to cross as soon as the courts were back in session. If anything, he was the one who should feel awkward, not her. She hadn't done anything underhand, but with his sense of entitlement, guilt, she knew, was not something that ever caused him sleepless nights.

She had never followed up on the promise she had made of doing the watercolour of Frank and Alphabet's house. Perhaps when she had her art room sorted she'd contact them. They must know by now that we've split up, she thought, but that's no reason why I shouldn't do it.

She wondered how Maurice was feeling being back in Peadar's villa ... her villa, she reminded herself. That still hadn't sunk in and it probably wouldn't until she went back there herself. The idea excited her. She needed to plan her visit. There was so much she wanted to ask and see about it. When she had been there she hadn't taken it in, never in a million years imagining she would own it some day. She had been occupied with being there for her dad while he organised Peadar's ambulance flight. She didn't think she had even been in all the downstairs rooms, never mind all the bedrooms, and Marie had made it clear that the kitchen was out of bounds. That was her domain.

As she lay trying to remember other details she went off on a tangent. Her future definitely needed some organising. Meeting Dean had added an unexpected twist to the day, even though she might have preferred their first encounter to have been in a more decorous way – and not sprawled across the front seat of her car with her posterior stuck up in the air. She was happy knowing that he was only down the corridor if she should need him. He'd make a pleasant neighbour. The previous one had kept very much to himself, exchanging pleasantries when they met, but little else. He was a nice old man and she must find out from Mrs Dunne where the nursing home he had moved into was and pay him a visit. Every Christmas she'd been there he left a gift at her front door. It was always the same, a candle scented with lavender, his late wife's favourite flower. She always had a bottle of Paddy whiskey for him.

Perhaps she should invite Dean for a drink or a meal for his help. She might even have a few friends over to celebrate moving back in and ask him along. A drink might be more casual than a meal. She didn't want to give him the wrong impression.

She sighed. That was something she had planned to do when she moved in with Daniel, but life had got in the way and she'd never had the parties she'd imagined having. The more she reflected the more she could see that she had lived those eleven months to his beat and mostly in the company of his friends. Apart from integrating with her parents, for reasons that were now so obvious, he hadn't made too much of an effort with Gabby, Paul, Darcy or Richard, or any of her other friends that he had met. She had learned a valuable lesson and she wasn't going to be duped again. She sighed. She was going to be in control next time.

She woke late and looked around her familiar surroundings. It felt so good to be back. She took her tea out on to the veranda. It always seemed odd to her how you could sense it was a Sunday morning. Sunday mornings sounded different. They were quieter, the hums and echoes more accentuated, periods of stillness punctuated by the sporadic sounding of bells from neighbouring churches. It was warm but was going to be one those several-seasons-in-one-day type of days. Above the horizon white-edged grey clouds shuffled about, letting patches of blue show promisingly through. A scavenging of gulls screeched and dive-bombed the choppy waves. She had an urge to take out her sketchpad, but resisted. There was something she needed to do first.

She phoned Darcy. 'I hope I'm not ringing you too early.'

'Early? With a baby? My little bundle of joy doesn't know the concept of time. She and I saw the dawn break as she let the whole world know that cutting teeth is no fun.'

'I'll come around.'

Darcy opened the door holding a howling, red-faced Samantha. 'Poor little thing,' Anne said, taking her. Samantha nuzzled into her neck, quiet for all of six seconds before she started off again.

'What about her poor sleep-deprived mother?'

'You do look wrecked.'

'Thanks. I am. Richard is great, but he's up to his eyes with the Leaving Cert papers and he needs to keep alert for that. He's asleep now. He did the early part of the night with her and the pair of them stayed down here on the sofa, and there wasn't a peep out of her, little madam that she is, but of course he was awake since five too. When he's up I'm heading for a long soak and a few hours' kip. I never thought they'd become the most desired things in my world.'

'Would you like me to take her for a few hours?'

'That's sweet but I don't think she'd be any happier. When she gets distressed like this she wants no one but her poor frazzled mother.'

'That's understandable. And I've been so preoccupied that I'd completely forgotten he was correcting papers. They must be nearly at the end. Aren't the results out soon?'

'Thankfully, yes. They'll be released in a few week, then I'll sleep for Ireland.' Samantha wriggled and squirmed and Darcy took her back and rocked her gently.

'I'll make some tea.'

'That's exactly what I need. She's exhausted and so am I. She's bound to nod off soon. I don't know how people go back to work immediately after having a baby. Even though I'd give her away right now, I don't think I would cope with putting her in a crèche every morning if she were upset like this.'

'You're lucky you both have teachers' holidays.'

'I know. It may have lousy pay, hence Richard marking the exams, but there are compensations.'

'How would you fancy a break in France, at *my* villa before you go back to work? I'm going over for the last two weeks in August and I'm dying to show it to you.'

'God, Anne, are you serious? I could think of nothing I'd like more. I've been sitting here wondering if there would ever be anything more in my life than nappies and feeds. I'll have to ask Richard about it though. Funds aren't exactly flush at the moment.'

'You needn't worry about that. Dad said he'd look after your flights.'

'I can't let him do that. He's too generous.'

'No one asked him to – he offered – he enjoys doing things like that for us.'

'But I'm not even his daughter and your folks have been so good already helping us with the deposit for the mortgage, and—'

'You're part of our family, Darcy, and always will be.'

'I often wonder what would have happened me if they hadn't rescued me. I'd probably have ended up in a foster home. I never used to wonder about that, but it's surprising what comes into your head when you're sitting up in the stillness of night nursing your baby. What would happen to her if we were to be killed in a car crash like Mum and Dad?'

'God, Darcy, don't even think like that.'

'I can't help it.'

'It's only natural that you would. I suppose that's what they mean when they talk about maternal instinct – a primal need to protect your young from anything hurtful.'

'I wish they had been here to see her and for her to get to know them, and your mum too. Maurice is the nearest thing to a grandfather she'll ever have.'

'And he loves that. She's been so good for him. Life often throws us off course, but you and Richard have her and each other; enjoy that. There'll probably be other little Samantha's running around in time. Don't waste any of it worrying about the what-ifs.'

Darcy raised her eyes to heaven. 'Other little Samantha's! Not if this one continues like this. A squealing baby is the best contraceptive ever.'

'It won't last forever. Think about the trip. It would be great for us all. A bit of sunshine, those cherries in a bowl on a gingham cloth on the terrace that you dream about …'

'Yes, please. God, I can't believe I'm thinking about it, but even if I have to take in laundry we'll manage it. We will,' she said, savouring her tea as though it were vintage wine.

'You won't have to do that. It won't cost you anything once you're there. You'll be my guests and, as Gabby keeps reminding me, I'm Lady Bountiful now, whoever she was, and, according to her description of me to Dad, I'm now able "to engage in ostentatious acts of charity to impress others".'

'She's such a jealous weapon. She should be thrilled for you. Seriously, though, for the sake of familial relationships do you think you should let her have a stay there before me? Will this not cause even more animosity between you two?'

'She doesn't need an excuse, and if she ever did before the villa business, that situation is not going to go away, so she'll have to get used to it.'

'I'm not going away either, but I still think maybe you should offer.'

'In summer time? What about her fixtures and her fourballs and aways, to say nothing of her blazer days? I think not.' They laughed and realised that Samantha had finally gone asleep. As though her unexpected silence had acted as an alarm clock, Richard appeared on the stairs a few minutes later, hair tossed and looking only half awake. Darcy told him about Anne's offer and his immediate reply was, 'I knew you were right making her Samantha's fairy godmother. I could think of nothing I'd rather do before facing back into the classroom. Will we go? *Oui! Oui! Oui! Merci!*

'That's settled then. I'll get back to you with flights.'

'We'll have to get missy a passport. I hope we have enough time,' he said,

'I hadn't thought of that,' said Darcy. 'I'll sort that out tomorrow.'

'I'll go online and see what we need.'

'I'm going to head off to let you get on with your day.'

As Anne was leaving, Darcy said, 'I never even asked you if you moved back in yesterday.'

'I did and it was great waking up there this morning. I have a new neighbour too, who seems very nice. He helped me and Dee yesterday and we all went to the pub at lunch time.'

'Oh, tell me more?'

'Do you never give up?' Anne laughed. 'Go. Put that child down in her cot, and luxuriate in that bath you've been craving.' She kissed them goodbye and left.

Later in the afternoon, when she had stocked up with groceries and disposed of all the cardboard boxes, she opened her laptop and looked at availability of flights. She bookmarked a few and sent a text with the options to Darcy. She didn't want to phone in case she had finally got to sleep.

On impulse she typed in Dean Moore's name and found his records. He had qualified in Dublin and done the usual internships, before specialising. He had spent a few years working with Médecins Sans Frontières and had returned recently from humanitarian work with Syrian refugees in camps. That would explain the sun-bleached hair, she thought. She smiled to herself. Why am I doing this? She closed the laptop and went to organise her clothes for the morning.

Nothing untoward happened during her first week in charge and, before she left for the weekend, Paula said, 'I told you you'd be well able to fill your father's shoes. The rest is probably all he needs too – a complete break from the office.'

'Don't let him hear you say that. He's not ready to retire yet. I think he'd go loopy with no structure to his days, and I agree with you. He's had so much on his plate lately.'

'He'd probably get used to doing less in no time at all, meeting other old boys in the same situation,' Paula said.

'This is a good trial – if he enjoys himself away from this place I'm hoping it will be easier to persuade him to take more time off. I heard him planning a road trip with Eoin. Eoin's sixty-five in a few months and he has to retire as a consultant at the hospital.'

'What a crazy system when they're crying out for more staff.'

'It is, but from a purely selfish point of view if he's not working either then Dad's more likely to take time out. You know how they love their bikes.'

She had just over two weeks to go before heading to France. Maurice would be back at the weekend before that and, although they spoke regularly on the phone, she was dying to hear all about it. There was so much she wanted to ask.

'How are you getting on with all Peadar's personal things? Is it difficult going through them?'

'There's not too much involved. I'm going to bring home the property deeds and other legal documents so we can keep them safely filed. He had everything as it should be. Regarding his personal effects, Marie has been stoic, really stoic, and she's been at my side sorting his clothes. I think she may even be more upset by it all than I am, if truth be told. She keeps telling me how good I am for being here. She doesn't seem to realise that I consider it a privilege to do this last service for him.'

'Don't let her change anything until I get there and see it again.'

'She said the same. I thinks she's afraid you'll come over and turn it into a minimalist, modern pad.'

'Tell her she need have no fear of that. I loved what I saw.'

'She'll be glad to hear it.'

'How are you finding the driving?'

'No bother at all, except that I keep getting lost at one roundabout and find myself going off on a detour through the surrounding countryside. It's happened me a few times so I've got to explore further afield. I'll mark it on a map to show you where it is when you get here. That way you can avoid it. Otherwise I've been having a fine time. The French know how to live. They appreciate life in a way that I think we've lost in Ireland. It's beautiful over here. You'll absolutely love it.'

'I know I will, and you must feel free to go over any time you like.'

He laughed. 'I will.'

'I can't wait. None of us can. Darcy is having a hard time getting Samantha's passport processed in time – they don't consider it an emergency.'

'Yes, she told me. She rang me to thank me for covering their flights.'

'I did a company letter for the passport, saying their trip had to do with a legal matter. Not entirely the truth but sufficiently close to stand up, I hope.'

'Well done, I'm sure between you you'll get it sorted. Now my nostrils are twitching. Marie has something delicious ready for me to eat so I'll say goodbye. See you on Saturday.'

'Tell her I'm looking forward to getting to know her and Pierre properly.'

'They're excited about having you as their boss, and about having a baby here. I don't think there's been anyone young here for years.'

'They're excited too. As regards being a boss – I'll have to think about that. Now I'll let you go, Dad, take care on that roundabout.'

'I will. Say hi to Gabby if you're talking to her. I keep missing her. Bye, love.'

She hadn't heard him so carefree since her mum died – carefree and optimistic. Passing over the baton to her must have lifted a lot of responsibility from his shoulders.

On an impulse, when she went home that evening she knocked on Dean's door.

'I've no cornflakes or sugar,' he said when he opened the door.

'Good, because I don't need either.'

'But I'm making a stir-fry and just opened a palatable Sauvignon Blanc, if you'd care to join me?'

'Oh, I was coming to ask you if you'd like to have a drink some evening, to say thank you for helping me.'

'You thanked me the other day, and I'd love to take you up on that offer, but only if you'll come and help me eat – I always cook too much.'

'It smells good. Can you give me five minutes to drop these things in next door?'

'Five minutes,' he replied. She smiled, and went back to her apartment to freshen up.

She had only been in her neighbour's one a dozen or so times when Nicholas Leonard had been there and it always seemed dark and cluttered, furnished with quality pieces that were too large for it. It was obvious that when he had downsized from his Mount Merrion home he hadn't wanted to part with them. Whoever the landlord was now had replaced these with contemporary pieces in light woods and the whole apartment had a completely different feel to it. Dean had set a second place at the table and had the bottle already chilling in an ice bucket.

'I thought you were vegetarian,' she said as he served her chicken stir-fry. 'Didn't you just have a salad sandwich the other day?'

'I suppose you could call me a flexitarian. Sometimes I do, sometimes I don't. I've worked in some pretty dodgy places and experienced Montezuma's revenge, Delhi belly and all sorts of other euphemistic ways of describing it, so now I have a more cautious attitude to what I eat.'

'That's u nderstandable. Y ou've o bviously t ravelled a l ot,' s he said, afraid she'd let slip that she'd googled him. He told her about his work and how he had become involved in the whole Syrian war fallout, about the conditions in Zaatari camp in Jordan. 'It's hard to comprehend the extent of it.'

'No one thought it would drag on so long. When did you get back?'

'About six weeks ago. I was totally burned out. Food is in short supply. We never had enough drugs, bandages, syringes or dressings, and supplies were often looted or damaged en route.'

'It must be heart-breaking looking into a father's or mother's eyes, watching them watching their children suffer and not being able to do anything for them.'

'It is, but what's even worse is looking at kids, and adults too, who are traumatised by the reality of what war does. Little kids who witnessed things they should never see. And all that to end up with no security or a place to call home. Sorry, I know I'm off on a rant, but even at this remove, it's hard to get those little faces with their blank stares out of my head.'

'I can't begin to imagine what it must be like. It makes my job sound like a doddle. What are you doing since you came back?'

'My field is orthopaedics. I've secured a place as a consultant, but the vacancy is not free for a while; meanwhile I'm filling my time sorting my life out, doing the odd locum and stand-by at that hospital, recharging the batteries and catching up with friends and colleagues.'

'We all need to do that every now and then.'

'You're right there. Now I've been monopolising the conversation. What about you? You said law was your area of expertise – do you specialise in criminal, corporate or what?'

'No, the company handles those and more. Family law is my bag.'

'I'm sure that can be taxing at times too.'

'He was so easy to talk to,' she told Darcy the next day when she rang to see what was happening about Samantha's passport, 'and he seemed genuinely interested in what I was saying.'

'Does this mean you're getting over Daniel?'

'They don't even deserve to be mentioned in the same sentence. I've come to realise that Daniel was totally conceited, ruthless, arrogant, pompous and self-absorbed.'

Her friend laughed. 'Don't hold back.'

'I haven't finished yet,' Anne continued. 'The impressions I had of him when I was a student were actually the right ones. I'll trust my instincts in future and not be blinded by flattery.'

'And what are those same instincts telling you about Dr Dean?'

'That he's a very genuine, interesting and kind person.'

'That's a good starting point,' Darcy said. 'Did you arrange to meet again?'

'Yes, he's coming to me for cornflakes next.'

'Jaysus, you didn't – did you? Did you stay for breakfast?'

'Of course I didn't. It's just a joke. And do you know what I like about him? He doesn't want to go to fancy restaurants. He's quite happy to stay in and enjoy the company.'

'And are you?'

'Last night was one of the most enjoyable I've had in a long time.'

'And I thought Richard and I were the only ones turning into couch potatoes – and we have a good excuse.'

'We'll change that when we get to France. I'm delighted the passport is on its way.'

'So am I. I could never have gone away without her. Did you see Alan on the telly last night? Of course you didn't. I forgot you were otherwise engaged.'

'What was he on for?' Anne asked.

'It was on some arts show. Apparently one of his plays has been accepted for the Dublin Theatre Festival. I thought I'd book for us, as a tiny thank you.'

'There's no need for thank-yous, but that sounds great.'

She felt a bit guilty about Alan. He had only been looking out for her and protecting her from finding out what a conniving sod her partner was; yet she had taken it out on him. She hated falling out with anyone. That was Gabby's form, not hers. She really owed him an apology. Perhaps she should give him a call and congratulate him, and clear the air at the same time.

That evening she talked to Gabby and told her about the plans she had made with Darcy.

'I knew you'd be tied up with fixtures well into the autumn, but I'd love you and Paul to come over then. I might even try and schedule another week off at the same time, if you didn't mind my company.'

'It's your house, you can do what you like, but it would have been nice to have been asked first,' was her reply.

'Darcy did suggest it but I honestly didn't think you'd mind.'

'I don't mind. I wouldn't have expected anything else.'

Trying not to show how her barbs hurt she continued. 'Have a chat with Paul and come back to me on it.'

'I'll wait for the right opportunity. He's not exactly happy with my family right now, not after the way I've been treated.'

As Anne sat there wondering what Gabby's problem was, she couldn't hold back any longer. 'I can understand how this legacy could rankle, but you must know that you can use it any time you like. What I can't understand, Gabby, is why you have such a spleen against me. What makes you feel you've been short-changed all your life? We were always treated the same. We had the same education and opportunities. I just don't get what the problem is.'

'That's not how Paul and the O'Reillys see it.'

'Then maybe you'll tell me how they do. Pray, enlighten me, please.'

'Don't try to be clever with your legalese, looking down your nose at me.'

'What do—' Anne heard the phone go dead. Gabby may be her sister but she had really crossed a line this time. Needing to vent on someone she rang Darcy and retold the conversation.

'I wouldn't mention it or your invitation to her again. That girl has problems.'

'I think you were right when you told me she was born angry.'

'And jealous, Anne. She was born jealous too. I'd love to be a fly on the wall when she's giving her version to Paul. Forget about it. She'll probably ring you tomorrow and apologise.'

'No, that's something you would do, Darcy, but not our Gabby.'

She had intended to contact Alan, but was in no frame of mind now. She had arranged to cook for Dean on Saturday and tried to focus on what she would serve.

When it came around she was well into her preparations when he knocked on her door.

'I'm sorry, Anne. I have to cry off tonight. I've just been called in to the hospital. Sod's Law, isn't it? It's the first emergency I've had since I came back.'

'No problem, we can do it again, or if you're not too late pop in when you're finished. It's fish so I can cook that up in a few minutes.'

She went to bed at eleven. He hadn't been in touch.

On Sunday she heard Alan Seavers' name being mentioned on

'What It Says in the Papers' and it reminded her that she still needed to clear the air between them. She'd do it this week before she went away.

The opportunity arose on Monday morning as she drove to work. She heard him being mentioned again for some report or other that he had written for his paper. It was too early to call him so she dictated a reminder to herself to do it at eleven.

Maurice was back at work that day and they had a good chat. He seemed to have enjoyed himself, despite the purpose of his trip, and was full of talk about taking his motorbike over on the ferry and doing a bit of touring.

'You'll need to watch out for your roundabout,' she reminded him.

He looked at her blankly.

'You know, the one you told me about, where you kept missing your turn,' she prompted.

'I haven't a clue what you're talking about,' he said. 'The signage is very good in France, and so is the wine. Get Pierre to recommend some local ones for you. There's nothing like insider knowledge.'

Her phone beeped a reminder to contact Alan and he excused himself and went back to his own office, telling Paula he had brought her back some chocolates, the pralines Peadar used to buy.

'Anne,' was all Alan said when he answered his phone.

'Alan, I want to apologise for the way I reacted when we last talked.'

'Thank you,' he replied, not making it any easier for her.

'I overreacted and I realise you were only trying to protect me from the truth, but I wasn't ready to hear that then.'

'That was very obvious.'

'I'm sorry, Alan, truly I am. I'm heading off to France at the weekend for a few weeks – maybe we could have a drink before or after that.'

He seemed to consider this before replying. 'What about Thursday?'

'Thursday's fine with me, and thank you.'

She felt awkward when he walked in. Normally she'd kiss him, as she did with anyone she knew, but somehow it didn't feel right this time. Instead she asked him what he'd like to drink.

'Just a soda and lime,' he replied.

'Are you on the dry?'

'No, antibiotics. Now, tell me, do you want to talk about the Daniel and Clive Kilucan business or is that topic to be the proverbial elephant in the room?'

'No, we can talk about it. I really am sorry for taking it out on you. I'd be lying if I said I wasn't hurt by your suggestion that he'd been with me for ulterior reasons. I was shocked. I see now how right you were and I feel such a gullible fool.'

'You're neither gullible nor a fool, Anne, and you're certainly not the first woman to be taken in by a smooth-talker like him. I've seen him in the courtroom and he's mighty impressive.'

'Don't remind me. Did you ever find out anything else?'

'Apart from confirming that Kilucan was definitely acting for Daniel, I know that an offer has been made to Benton & Benton in the same covert manner as the one Cullen–Ffinch received.'

'Have you reported on this?'

'No. I didn't want you to think I was poking around in your affairs, just keeping old wounds exposed, but if you've no objection I'll run it. It's a good story.'

'Do. I'd love to be there to see Daniel's face when he sees it.'

'It might cause a bit of public speculation as to the nature of his relationship with you. Are you prepared for that?'

'Let it. In fact, if you want a quote I'll give you one, saying how I didn't know he was the person behind the offers, even though we were living together at the time. That should show him up to his fine friends, and in his true colours, too.'

'Are you absolutely sure about this?'

'Never surer.'

'Why don't I run it on Saturday? You'll be off on holidays and by the time you get back the story will be dead.'

'Perfect. Now that we've got that out of the way, I'm starving.'

'Will we go next door and have a plate of pasta?'

'And you can tell me what's been happening in your life. I hear your play was accepted and I'm curious too, that lovely lady I've seen you with, is she someone of significance?'

'Teresa? Good God, no. She's a colleague and I was her decoy. She's been shadowing one of those dodgy property dealers, a guy who got into NAMA, and who should be living on a three-hundred-euro-a-week allowance, something that would be impossible with the lavish lifestyle he continues to enjoy. What's happening with you?'

They chatted about his play and she filled him in about her majority shareholder news and her unexpected legacy.

'If you ever need anywhere to hide out for a while you're welcome to it,' she informed him.

'You might be sorry you told me that. This job is doing my head in. I feel more and more discontent every day. I've contemplated the idea of taking a year off, getting away from all the low-lifes and scumbags I encounter every day and being free to try writing – not journalism.'

'Maybe you should just go for it.'

'There's always some reason not to – and ironically this play is the current impediment. But if it's a success I'm hoping they'll give me a commission for another.'

'You're just looking for excuses.' She laughed.

'Probably.'

'I'm glad we're friends again.'

'So am I,' he said, reaching across the table and covering her hand with his. 'I missed you and our chats.'

'Me too.'

She did manage to take Dean out for a meal before she set off, to thank him for his help. She found his company very enjoyable. He told her more about the stints he had spent working with Médecins Sans Frontières and with the other humanitarian organisations.

'It doesn't leave you much time for a personal life, does it?' she asked.

'You're right there. It takes a special partner to put up with all the absences. It also takes a while to readjust to normal life again when I come back here. The last relationship I had broke up because of all of the above. I offered to move out, it was less disruptive that way, hence I've ended up as your neighbour.'

'I could have got worse, I suppose.' She laughed.

'You could,' he agreed. 'And what's your excuse for being single?'

'It's boring, but similar in some respects. When you helped me with my things I was moving back here after a break-up too.'

'I thought you'd been living with your friend, Dee.'

'I had. Dee was my mum's closest friend. She's actually my godmother too, but I was only with her temporarily after getting my marching orders, and while I waited for the lease on this place to expire. I'd rented it out. I've owned it for several years and lived here since then, with the exception of most of the past one. Now it's time to move on.' She heard herself saying this and hoped she hadn't given the impression of being a desperate female in need of a male, any male. 'I'm not looking for a relationship. I'm perfectly happy with my own company. It's platonic all the way from here on for me.' That sounded even more desperate to her ears.

He smiled. 'Ditto.'

As they walked back to their block, she thought it had been a good week: she'd sorted things out with Alan; her dad seemed to be back to his old self again; and her new neighbour had turned out to be a very unexpected and pleasant addition to her life.

Chapter Twenty-Five

The heat hit them as they stepped off the plane at Marseilles. Pierre was waiting for them when they exited the arrivals hall. Anne went to greet him, telling him she was sorry that he had lost his friend and employer and that she knew how much Peadar had valued him. He thanked her, took her hands and shook them for so long that she thought he'd wring them off. She introduced her friends and he greeted them formally. He got a beatific smile from Samantha, who had slept throughout the flight and was ready to charm everyone again. '*Elle est mignonne,*' he said, smiling back at her and taking the car seat from Richard.

He packed their baggage efficiently in the people carrier and drove them through the outskirts of the city into verdant countryside where rows of vines made criss-cross patterns on the landscape and the sky was cloudless blue. He seemed to relish his role as tour guide.

'Did you grow up around here?' Richard asked him.

'Provence is my country. I was born on a farm not far from Le

Refuge. Marie, my wife, and me, we went to the same school when we were small. We fell in love. Then we married. We never had other boy or girlfriends. We never travelled much; there was no need to. We have everything we need here.' He smiled.

'That's sounds like a very romantic story, Pierre,' Anne said.

'It's beautiful and so French. Are all Frenchmen as romantic?' Darcy asked.

'Most of them, if you believe what you read,' he said, a twinkle in his eye. 'We are also supposed to be the best lovers in the world. Now our reputation is in doubt.' They were all listening to him as he negotiated a *route nationale*, flanked by fields of tall sunflowers. The ones on their right had their backs to them, and the ones on their left were facing them, glowing like thousands of golden suns.

'Why is that?' asked Richard. 'Have we been trying to compete with a fable?'

'I hope not, but there is a school of thought which says we are now the worst lovers in the world because we have such a reputation to uphold that the young men worry that they may not be able to live up to the expectation of the ladies and they can no longer perform. I am glad I am older.' They laughed. 'It's true,' he insisted.

'That takes the pressure off,' Richard replied.

'There is much to see and do around here. If you want, I will show you. If you prefer to go without me, *d'accord*, but if you want me to accompany you then I am at your disposal.'

'It sounds wonderful. I had no idea it was so picturesque,' Anne said.

'Last time you were here, Madam Anne, you didn't see anything.' That was true. 'You have to visit Marseilles, especially the Vieux Port. I believe the shopping is world class but not for Marie. She has no time for boutiques with a little selection and large price tags.'

'I can understand that,' Darcy said. 'But maybe we can go

window shopping there some day and show Samantha what she can aspire to.'

'We flew in over the bay and saw the islands in the distance. It was quite spectacular,' Anne remarked

'All the vines – we're right in the heart of it. I'd love to do a wine tasting in a local vineyard, if that's possible, and if the schedule allows,' said Richard.

'There is no schedule. This is holiday time – to come and go as you like, or to sit around all day doing nothing,' Anne told him. 'Of course you must do a wine tasting. It's almost compulsory.'

'She is right. This is the place of sunflowers, lavender, olive trees and wine, very good wine,' Pierre said, taking his hand off the steering wheel to gesture the emphasis on 'good'.

'I can't really believe I'm here,' said Darcy for the second time.

'This is a new adventure for me,' said Anne, 'and I'm really glad you are here, all of you, to share it.'

Pierre indicated and turned into a driveway. The villa came into view.

'Is this it? My God, I thought it was going to be like a little cottage – this place is huge!' Darcy exclaimed. 'You never said.'

'I never said it was small, but I couldn't really remember too much as we were on the go all the time when I was here, between the hospital and dealing with bureaucracy.'

'I can't wait to see inside,' Darcy said, jumping out just as Marie appeared, wiping her hands in a snowy white apron that seemed to envelope her.

'Madam Anne, welcome to your home. We are so happy to have you and with your friends and the *bébé*. Where is she?' she asked peering into the back seat to see her.

'That's the first time I have thought about it as my home,' Anne said, and it was at that moment she began looking on it as such.

It was charming, the warm cut-stone draped with creepers, the blue-grey wooden shutters providing further contrast. She saw it though different eyes. This was hers. It belonged to her. And she had done nothing to merit it. The tubs and window boxes were filled with petunias and geraniums; mature trees that she couldn't identify offered shelter from the overhead sun. She felt an urge to go in and explore; a curiosity to open doors and cupboards and familiarise herself with the geography of the place, the furniture, the contents.

As though reading her mind, Darcy said, 'I want to see everything.'

'I'll show you to your rooms, if you like,' said Marie. 'Leave your luggage. Pierre will take them in for you. When you're ready you can go on through to the terrace and I'll bring the tray out. I've made some pastries and the coffee is ready.'

Inside felt much cooler and it took a few minutes for their eyes to adjust. It was like stepping back in time: lace cloths covered little tables and there were ornaments and old photographs everywhere. Large gilt-framed paintings filled the wall space and there were several vases of flowers placed around the hallway that led to the terrace.

'It's wonderful, absolutely wonderful,' Darcy said. 'I wouldn't change a thing if it were mine.'

Marie nodded in agreement. 'I am glad to hear you say that.' She told Darcy to go and freshen up. 'I'm sure you're dying for some coffee.'

'Are those your vines?' Richard asked, finding Anne looking around when he emerged into the sunlight a few minutes later.

'Technically I believe they are, although they are leased out to a neighbour.'

'How much land have you actually got?'

'I couldn't tell you. I'll be meeting the guy they've leased the vines to at some stage and have to meet the solicitors too. That's just one of the questions on my list. Maybe you'd like to sit in on that meeting with me, if you wouldn't mind. Two heads would be better than one and you might be able to ask things I wouldn't even think about. And help with translations if I get stuck.'

'My pleasure. And if there's anything else you want just shout. This really is some place, and quite deceptive from the outside. It's cleverly designed the way it steps down at the back, yet still looks like a tall single storey from the front.'

'I read somewhere,' Anne told him, 'that the houses around these parts were built a certain way to protect them from the mistral wind, and I think that blows from the north, which would make this terrace south-facing.'

Darcy emerged with Samantha and put her in her buggy. 'Jaysus, girl, you landed on your feet with this place. It's magical and huge.' She spotted the table when she turned around. 'Oh my God, a bowl of cherries on a gingham cloth! Have I died and gone to heaven? Nice touch. Did you organise those?'

They all laughed at her.

'I couldn't *not* do it, you painted such a vivid picture. You had my mouth watering at the thought,' Anne said.

'And *tarte aux fraises*.'

'You're like the proverbial child in the sweetshop hopping from one thing to another,' her husband teased.

'I can't help it. I love this place already. I love the terrace, that old olive tree, the flowers, the vines, the view. Everything. And I've only taken in a fraction of it.'

'You've taken in more than I have,' Anne said.

'I've only just started. I love the olde-worlde feel to it and all the little knick-knacks everywhere. I'm glad Samantha isn't crawling yet – she'd demolish everything. I could just see this in one of those glossy interiors magazines – authentic vintage French chic. Our bedroom is magical. There must be ten pillows and cushions on the bed, which is enormous.'

'It is marvellous, isn't it? Peadar's parents spent a lot of time here, before eventually moving over, and his mother obviously had a very good eye. He said he hardly changed anything.'

'There are some lovely pieces of furniture in the hallway,' said Richard.

'Wait until you see the rest of it,' Darcy told him. 'You should have sent us snaps of it.'

'Would you believe I don't have a single one. I never took any when I was here. It didn't seem appropriate. I never thought then that I'd be back here again at any stage. And you know what Dad thinks of social media. He never uses his phone camera. I'm not sure he'd know how.'

'Well, I'll be taking plenty,' Darcy said, producing her iPad mini and clicking away.

Pierre came to join them with a bottle and some glasses. 'I'll take you for a walk around later if you like,' he offered, 'but first you must try this wine. Your grapes went into this.'

After a while Marie and Darcy took Samantha inside for her nap. 'This room has always been called the nursery. It was little Rory's room when he was a baby,' Marie told them. 'Rory was Monsieur Peadar's son, his only child. He didn't survive into adulthood. He got polio in the epidemic in the fifties, in Ireland.'

'How sad,' Darcy said.

'They took him here to recover, but he didn't make it.' The older woman sighed.

'It's a gorgeous room.'

A mosquito net, tied back with a pink satin ribbon, which Marie must have bought specially for their visit, hung like a canopy over the cot. It was dressed with beautiful linen, and a very finely crocheted blanket. 'That's fabulous.'

'Monsieur Peadar's mother was very *doueé*, very gifted, with her hands. Most of the handcrafts were done by her,' she explained, as she closed the shutters against the sun.

'You've obviously looked after them very well over the years,' Darcy said.

'I have. They are very precious, heirlooms really. It's nice to see that you appreciate them. Most young people want everything to be easy care. They don't want what their mothers used and they don't appreciate the skills that went into pieces like these. Is it the same in Ireland?'

'I think so.' She told Marie what had happened to her parents. 'I wish I had more of my mother's things. I think people thought they were being kind by disposing of them in case they reminded me and made me sad. I wish they hadn't now.'

'That's a shame. But you now have this precious little one and you have to make memories for her to cherish. We were devastated when little Rory was taken from us, but Madame Ffinch, Monsieur Peadar's mother, was strong, stronger than the baby's mother. She left Monsieur Peadar for another man and we never heard from her again. Madame's handcrafts kept her going. I can still visualise her sitting under the old olive out the back working her needle furiously and singing to herself.'

'What a charming picture you paint. I can almost see her from your description.'

Marie smiled. 'I'm talking too much, but I have to say it's lovely having guests and especially having a baby here again. Is she always so placid?'

'Don't let her fool you!' Darcy laughed as they watched her fall asleep, exhausted by the journey. 'She has her moments.'

'Go out and relax, Madame Darcy. I will keep an eye on her. I will call you when she wakes.'

'I know I keep saying it but I really do think I've died and gone to heaven. Thank you, Marie. I feel I've been liberated.' They laughed.

'Go, make the most of it.'

She went back out to the terrace where Richard and Anne were chatting over a different wine. 'Rosé, Richard?' she said. 'I never saw you drink rosé before. Is there a sup for me?'

'Sure. It's a locally produced rosé and comes with Pierre's seal of approval,' Anne said. 'Try some, then we're going to walk the land with him. He's just gone to do something first.'

'Spoken like a real lady of the manor,' Richard said to her, with a laugh. 'Peadar may not have made many changes inside, but the farm certainly appears to have been modernised and well maintained.'

'It does. I'd love to think that I could do the same if I keep it.'

'What do you mean, if you keep it? You can't possibly think about selling it.'

'It may not be practical, Darcy. I have to go over the books with Pierre before I make any decisions.'

'Is that why you're not as excited as I am about it?' her friend asked.

'I hadn't realised I wasn't.' Anne paused for a few seconds as though considering what her friend had said. 'Yes. Possibly. Probably. You're right. I have to think with my head, not with my heart, so I need to keep detached. I have to look on this as a business venture and see if it's going to be a viable one. If it is I'll get attached then. I promise.' She laughed.

As they walked between the precisely planted rows of vines up to the top of the hill she checked her phone. Alan had mailed her about his piece on Daniel and his uncle Clive's offer to Cullen–Ffinch. He used her comment about being kept in the dark despite cohabiting with him. There was a lot of reaction and much speculation. Ossie Benton of Benton & Benton was also quoted as saying, 'we value transparency above all else, so in the light of these revelations, we would not consider any association with the current bidders, either now or in the future.'

'I'm delighted Daniel got his comeuppance. Now forget about him,' Richard said. 'That's all in the past. Concentrate on the future and on all this.'

'This is the best vantage point. From here, Anne,' Pierre explained, 'you can see the boundaries of your property to the right, just where those lavender fields begin.' Darcy caught her eye and winked her approval. Irregular patches of vivid purple stood out against others of yellowing grain. 'That's the house where Marie and I live over there, and can you see the other cottage beyond that, at the road? That's also yours. So are those two large sheds and the other buildings behind them in the yard. That's where wine used to be produced right here on the estate. They did that until just after the last war. Nowadays it's all handled by a cooperative.'

Anne was astonished. She had had no idea it was such a large concern. She had thought the vines sloping from the end of the garden were hers, but hadn't realised that they marched down the other side of the hill too.

'Who lives in the other cottage?'

'No one right now, but it would make a perfect *gîte*, if you wanted to rent it out. I've arranged for you to meet those involved in a few days; after that we'll go though the accounts. I hope you'll find them all to you satisfaction.'

'I'm looking forward to it, and I'm sure I shall.'

He walked them towards the long low sheds where the itinerant grape pickers used to sleep when they arrived every season to work there and on neighbouring farms. When they eventually reached them, Pierre explained, 'There are old presses in one. Peadar didn't want to get rid of them. He felt they were part of agricultural history. He hated to see things like this being lost for posterity.'

'I can see why,' Richard said. 'They certainly add character to the place.'

'He liked the old ways, oak barrels and manual harvesting. He had no time for stainless steel and plastic corks.'

Just listening to him Anne was coming around to the notion that she had a lot to learn about being a landowner, or *une propriétaire terrien*.

Marie was cradling Samantha when they got back. 'If you want to feed the little one first, dinner will be ready in half an hour.'

'I haven't even unpacked,' Darcy protested.

'I've done that for you all.'

'Marie, I want to take you home with me,' she said hugging the petite woman.

'I think I may have first call on her,' said Anne.

Later Marie announced dinner by sounding a brass gong that stood on a long console table in the hallway. The table was covered with photographs, mostly black and white, and Anne wanted to pick each one up and discover the story behind the elegant people who were captured there, in a parade of fashions, hairstyles and groupings. She inhaled deeply. Was this really hers now? All of it? Her only regrets were that she couldn't thank Peadar in person for his wonderful generosity, or share it with her mum.

They sat down on tall, woven cane-backed chairs in the dining room to enjoy the meal. There was a charming elegance about it all and Marie served several tasty courses with imaginative garnishes.

'You don't have to put out the best china for us while we're here,' Darcy said to her friend, 'I'm not used to eating off a highly polished table, with highly polished cutlery, gleaming stemware and matching dishes, condiments and platters.'

'I think this is Marie's way, so I'm not going to knock it, besides I don't think there are any odd mugs in her kitchen. I think they might only have best china here!' She laughed. 'They! Listen to me. I'm still finding it hard to get my head around it all – that this, all of this, is not theirs, but mine!'

During dinner Richard said, 'It's a pity Maurice put you in charge before you got this place.'

'Why do you say that?'

'Because I think if I had been given it I wouldn't have gone back at all.'

Darcy agreed. 'Maybe that's why he did – to protect his business first.'

After dinner they sat on the terrace and sipped wine, listening to the sounds of the frogs and crickets and smelling the smells of the sun-warmed earth as the irrigation system bubbled into action between the rows of vines.

After a few days Anne was beginning to feel less like she was visiting someone else's home and less like a child who could look but mustn't touch. She had been reluctant to go wandering in and out of rooms or opening drawers, especially when Marie was around. She felt that was somehow violating her space, so when Marie left for the local market on the third day Anne seized her chance to have a good browse.

While she was doing this, Darcy joined her, having put Samantha down for her morning nap. Richard was off somewhere with Pierre. They had become bosom buddies, chatting away in French. At both gable ends of the wings that formed the courtyard boundaries there were matching archways with two steps leading up to the largest bedrooms at the end. The sun flooded in through the windows, which were shaped mimicking the internal arches. Through the lace curtains, it made patterns on the tables and the armchairs that furnished these spaces.

Anne found herself being drawn back again to a display table that held lots of personal knick-knacks: an intricately carved fan; an old prayer book with an ivory cover; a lady's pistol with a mother-of-pearl handle in its original mother-of-pearl box; a theatre programme from L'Opéra de Paris; and a chunky gold chain with a heavy seal attached. There was also a framed picture of a little boy with a lock of white-blond hair curled at the bottom.

'That must be Rory's,' said Darcy.

'Rory?' Anne enquired.

'Peadar's son, the little boy who died of polio.'

'God, Darcy, I never knew his name or what happened him. How did you find that out?'

'Marie told me. She loves talking about times past and I think having Samantha here has brought back a lot of old memories for her.'

'It must be hard for her seeing me, a complete outsider, swan in and take over her domain.'

'You're not a stranger to her and she doesn't feel you're taking over. She said she feels you've always been part of the family. Peadar talked a lot about Maurice and you. She's even heard about me too.'

In all there were six bedrooms upstairs, two with en-suite bathrooms that were as big as most modern bedrooms. 'They must take an hour to fill,' remarked Anne, looking at the enormous freestanding bath, with its claw feet and brass fittings.

'And I imagine they must have been the height of sophistication when they were put in, with those big showers and all that brassware. Can you imagine all the polishing they'd need?'

Four of the bedrooms were large, large enough for a desk and chair, a small sofa or chaise longue, a fireplace, a dressing table, a chest of drawers as well as an enormous bed. The smaller ones were good-sized doubles. There was a walk-in linen room, filled with pristine ironed piles, all labelled: *les draps de lit*; *les taies d'oreiller*; *les couvre-pieds*; *les draps de tables*; *les serviettes*; *les serviettes de table* etc. An eclectic collection of art work decorated the walls and there were more old photographs everywhere.

'I must get Marie to tell me who these people were, before they're forgotten forever. From what I hear, Peadar's mother was quite a socialite, even after she was widowed, always having houseguests and entertaining. It seems to have been a real party house back in the day.'

'You'll have to keep the tradition up,' Darcy said

'I will, if I keep this place.'

'Don't talk like that.'

'Right now it seems a very daunting prospect. It must cost a fortune to upkeep and run, never mind paying staff.' Her friend agreed. 'It might be madness to hold on to it.'

On the ground floor the large kitchen was a throwback to a different era with rows of gleaming copper pots and pans hanging over a solid wooden central island. A stockpot simmered gently on the stove top, filling the room with a herby aroma. Off this room there was a large scullery and a walk-in pantry.

'Just look in here,' Darcy called, 'there are enough jams and chutneys to feed an army.' And there were: rows of conserves, all labelled meticulously and dated.

Apart from a formal sitting room and dining room, there was a music room with a lacquered baby grand taking centre stage while stacks of old sheet music were arranged in bundles. Beyond this, in the last room on the corridor, Anne was astonished to discover a room full of art materials: dozens of completed and half-finished sketches were pinned to walls and lay in frames around the base of the walls. They were discussing these and speculating on who had done them when the men came back.

'I see you've discovered Peadar's guilty pleasure,' Pierre said. 'He never let anyone see these.' Anne remembered the locked door when she had been there with Maurice, but she had put it completely out of her mind.

'Who did these?'

'Peadar, and his son, Rory. When he was ill he took him back here from Ireland to convalesce and over a few months they used to spend hours in this room together. That was when they thought he'd recover. Those were sketches of *les bouvreuils*, bullfinches, that they were doing together for the Ffinch wine they promised they'd produce together some day when he recovered.'

'I never knew he painted,' Anne said, studying some detailed pen and washes of birds.

'He didn't – not for years – but in the last three or four he took it back up again. He used to tell me it was one of his few regrets – that he should have got out of law altogether and done art professionally.'

'I know that feeling. Did he ever try making his wine?'

'No, his heart wasn't in it after he lost the boy.'

Walking closer for a better look she wished again that she had taken more time to get to know the real Peadar. 'He could have made a living out of these. These are seriously good,' said Anne.

'He told us you painted.' That surprised her. 'You must do something for the house while you are here,' Pierre said.

'I doubt there'll be any time,' she replied, suddenly feeling like an intruder in this private space. She wasn't sure she was ready to move in and paint amid Peadar's memories and personal effects, yet she had an overwhelming urge to bring the room to life again.

Over the next week Pierre impressed her with his knowledge and the methodical way he worked. He knew the running of the villa and land inside out and was able to back this up with statistics and figures. He also seemed to know everyone for miles around, making her transition from visitor to landowner a smooth one. When her father told her that everything had been taken care of for twelve months so that she wouldn't have to worry about it, she hadn't really given it much thought. Now the more she learned, the more she realised what a blessing that was. She would never manage otherwise.

She phoned the office to update him on how things were going. 'I knew you'd love it! How are Darcy and Richard enjoying themselves?'

'Fantastically – they're off in Aix-en-Provence today, exploring. She's taken countless photos of the house. She even sent some to Gabby, telling her she has to see it for herself. I'm not sure if that was a good move. Gabby will probably feel her nose is being rubbed in it.'

She heard him let out a sigh. 'She'll have to get over that.'

'I just wish Mum was here to see it. She'd have been in her element.'

'She would and she'd have been so happy for you.'

'I'm meeting the guys who have the land leased later on today and we've been invited to one of the neighbour's for dinner this evening. Marie insists on babysitting.'

'Tell them to expect me next month, if that's OK with you. Eoin and I will definitely head over with the bikes for a week or two and use it as our base. We're trying to persuade Paddy to come along too.'

'I'm delighted to hear that, the Hell's Angels on tour again. And, Dad, you don't need to ask my permission to come here, ever. I want everyone to come and enjoy it.'

He laughed. 'I'll be only too happy to do my bit!'

'I was a little concerned about Marie and Pierre having to do more work when there are visitors. I suggested getting in extra help when they need it but they assured me that it's their job and they prefer being busy.'

'I think they mean that too.'

Her neighbours had invited another couple over and by the end of the evening new friendships had been formed despite Pierre warning 'We French don't embrace foreigners too quickly, but, because of your connections with the Ffinch family it may be easier.' And that had proven to be the case.

Over the next few days she spent hours going over every detail of the property with Pierre, and often with Richard too.

'I'm still not sure if I could afford to keep it. Perhaps I could sell off some of it and keep the house,' She told him.

'You'd still have to maintain it and from what I can see there's no need to make any snap decisions. It's in a very healthy state, but think about it. You may look at it all differently when you're back home,' Richard advised.

'I know I will.' She laughed. 'I also know that as soon as I get back I'll wish I was still here.'

'Me too,' he agreed.

Chapter Twenty-Six

Anne was at her car when she remembered the truffles and hazelnut pralines she'd got for Paula. She went back to her apartment to get them. It was grey and windy and many of the schools were back that morning after the summer holidays. The traffic on her journey to work reflected this. There were delays everywhere and umbrellas blew inside out, caught by the sudden gusts. As she sat in her car she fantasised about being back at the villa, eating a crusty, buttery croissant with Marie's homemade apricot jam. She let out a deep sigh, reversed into her parking spot, and dodged others rushing to get to work. She shook her umbrella and put it in the stand inside the door.

'What's been happening in my absence?' she asked, depositing the chocolates on Paula's desk.

'Nothing that we couldn't handle,' she answered, but Anne sensed an undercurrent. 'There's a follow-up on your family-violence case – Perdita, the mother with the child who took her husband back to give him yet another chance. Well, he's beaten her again and her son; he broke his guitar across her back. He's out on bail and there's a temporary barring order in place. I've left the notes on your desk.'

'The cowardly bastard. I knew he'd do it again. His type always does. Who has been handling it?'

'Maurice, but I don't think his heart is in it. He seems preoccupied. He keeps going on about a charge on his credit card statement for a purchase he insists he never made.'

'Did you check it out?'

'I tried to, but as he reminds me every time that he's quite capable of doing that himself. Then the next day he tells me about it all over again. Maybe you could have a word with him.'

'Thanks, Paula, I will. I'm sure there's a reasonable explanation.' Paula didn't answer.

She didn't have to wait long before he came in to her office. She was reading through the details of the assault on Perdita's file and she felt her heart sink. It hadn't taken much to bounce her back to reality.

'You're looking very well after your break,' he said.

'I was spoiled. Pierre and Marie are real treasures. They run that place like clockwork.'

Without any further preamble he put a bank statement down on the desk and said, 'I don't know to tell you this, but I think Darcy has been using my credit card.'

'What? You must be mistaken, Dad. She'd never do that.'

'That what I thought, but she has. I know because I checked. It's there in black and white,' he said shoving the statement across for her to see it. 'She bought airline tickets for France and paid for them with my money.'

Anne studied the figure and the date before saying, 'Dad, they are the tickets you paid for, for her trip with me. Look, mine is on my statement and the dates match.'

'Why did she not pay for you? Was she afraid you'd rumble her?'

'Oh, Dad, Darcy would never do anything like that. Those purchases were made after you told me you'd take the tab for their fares.'

'I never said such a thing. You must be mistaken. I never gave her permission to use my card.'

'She didn't. I made those bookings and I put theirs on your card and mine on my own one.'

'She never asked my permission. I don't ever remember having that conversation with her.'

'You didn't, Dad. You told me to do it. Don't you remember how delighted she was at your generosity? She called around with Samantha and brought you a casserole and a lemon cake to say thank you. I was there when she came.'

'I do remember the lemon cake.' He paused for an instant as though trying to recall. 'But she often brings me lemon cake, which is more than can be said of that sister of yours. She arrives, one arm longer than the other, and never thinks of bringing me anything. Have you talked to her since you got back?'

'No, I left a message for her.'

'I wouldn't expect to hear back, if I were you. She's still spitting fire at your good fortune. She's been very odd with me lately,' he added.

'I'm not going to get into that with her. The sooner she learns that life is not a competition then the better for her. She has so much when you compare her to this poor Perdita woman. She doesn't realise how lucky she is.'

Paula arrived with coffee. 'You're right there.' She had opened her pralines and put some on a plate.

'Keep those for yourself. I brought some for the rest of us.'

'I couldn't wait any longer.' She laughed.

'I'll have one,' said Maurice, reaching over. He put sugar in his coffee and said, 'Now let's talk about this credit card business. Why do you think Darcy used it without telling me? After all I've done for that girl?'

She looked at her dad, as though seeing him for the first time, and then at Paula who had a look that said: 'do you see what I mean?'

'Leave it here, Dad and I'll deal with it. I'm sure it's a simple mistake,' Anne said, trying to buy time, but he wasn't going to be fobbed off.

'How could she have got my PIN number?'

'She didn't, Dad. Don't worry. It's probably a mistake on my part. I made the bookings and probably got them mixed up. Just let me deal with Perdita's case first then I'll look after it,' she said.

'If you're sure,' he said reluctantly.

'I'm sure,' she answered much more confidently than she felt.

As he went back to his own office she heard him say, 'I don't know why she'd do that to me.'

When he'd crossed the hall to his office Paula closed the door to hers, came back in and sat down. Before Anne could say anything she began her speech, one, Anne realised afterwards, that had taken some courage and some rehearsal to deliver.

'We've been colleagues and I hope more than that for a long time and I feel I have no choice but to speak out. Maurice's behaviour has become erratic and he is definitely having problems with his memory. I'm not comfortable any more handling any of his financial affairs in case he turns on me and accuses me of stealing. He's very influential and if that happened no one would take my word over his.'

'I'm sure that would never happen. He trusts you implicitly.'

'You would have said the same about Darcy, wouldn't you?'

'Probably. Definitely, but why didn't you say something before?' asked Anne.

'I wanted to, but it's not easy.'

'When did you begin to notice it?'

'Very soon after your mum died, but I put it down to the grieving process. He kept asking me for the code for his phone. I wrote it down so many times. He still doesn't remember it or that it's on his tablet. He doesn't need the code for that because it's thumbprint activated, but that doesn't seem to have registered either. He frequently asks me to send mails for him or to open attachments. It's like the simple things he's done every day have been wiped away.'

'How could I never connected have these incidents …?'

'That's probably because you're grieving too, and so much else has been going on in your life and around you. There have been other things too – the shoplifting episode, the to-do about his passport and—'

'The c onveyancing p apers h e s wore I n ever g ave h im, t he washing left in the machine. What does that say about me? How could I not have noticed, Paula? I've been so preoccupied with Daniel, Mum, my move. And I criticise Gabby. Maybe I'm just as bad.'

'That's n onsense. You've n o r eason t o f eel g uilty. M aybe y ou didn't want to admit there could be a problem. They s ay t hose closest are often the last to realise these things, but Anne, whatever is causing it, he needs to see someone. Prevention is better than cure. I know that's a cliché and how you hate those, but he could be a danger to himself and to others driving around if his mind is on other things. He told us he drove the wrong way around a roundabout last week. He was thinking of you in France and indicated to turn right instead of left. Fortunately the car behind blew at him and he realised his mistake. But it could have had disastrous consequences. It's very serious, Anne, can't you see why I had to tell you?'

'I'm beginning to realise that, and I'm glad you did.'

'I hate saying these things to you, just when you're back from holidays, but I can't pretend they aren't happening, and this business with the credit card is another step. He won't listen to reason.'

'He did tell me he'd pay their airfares.'

'I know. I was beside you when he said it, but it's as though he has blocked it out of his mind, or forgotten completely.'

'I'll talk to Eoin. He'll be able to point me in the right direction, and Paula, thank you. I know this can't have been an easy thing to do.'

'You have Perdita coming in at eleven, so you'd better read through her file before that,' she said, 'and don't look so worried, I'm sure it can be sorted. It's been a hell of a year so far and I'm only on the periphery. I can't begin to imagine how all that stress has taken its toll on Maurice.' She smiled. 'But he'll be fine.'

Anne checked the clock. She took her phone out of her bag, scrolled down and punched in Eoin's private number. It went to voicemail. She didn't leave a message. She tried his rooms and was answered by a secretary with attitude. 'No. It's not possible to speak with Mr Maleady. He's in theatre all day. Would you care to make an appointment?'

'Please let him know I called and ask him to ring me on this number at his convenience.'

'Mr Maleady doesn't return patients' calls,' came the imperious reply. Really? She wondered if Eoin knew this. 'Can you phone him back in the morning, between ten and twelve? He'll be in attendance in his rooms then.'

'No, I can't. I'm not a patient and he will return this one.' She was furious. They would have no clients if they treated theirs like this. 'Please make sure you give him the message.'

'I can't guarantee—'

'I'm not looking for a guarantee, I just want to know that you'll do your job and pass my message on, thank you.'

'That is part of my job – to vet Mr Maleady's calls.'

'Well, please prioritise this one.'

'What is the nature of the urgency?'

'It's a personal matter and one that I have no intention of discussing with you.'

'There's no need to be rude,' came the curt reply.

'Ditto, and good day,' said Anne, and hung up. She felt a degree of satisfaction. Who did that woman think she was? Eoin not returning calls? This was the man who often stayed around the hospital all night to watch over a patient who was giving post-op concern and who frequently cancelled his Saturday 'bike' mornings with her dad and Paddy so that he could do a visit or meet with someone's family. And he had come running when Maurice needed him. No wonder so many consultants had a bad rep and were considered out of touch with their patients, if their secretaries were anything like his one.

Anne returned to the file in front of her. She was no more in the frame of mind to address it but she had to put Perdita's problems to the fore. She needed her and Anne was determined to try to make her see reason this time. The morning was turning into a horror story, one that seemed more than a world away from the one she had left on Friday. Was it only last Friday? She turned her phone to silent as Paula showed her client in.

She was shocked at how much the woman had aged since the beginning of the summer. She looked physically stooped and cowed. She smiled at Anne, but the smile didn't reach her eyes. They had a haunted look about them, and they kept darting towards the door as though searching for a way out if she had to flee suddenly.

'How have you been managing?' Anne asked her gently.

'Not too badly. I've given up the contract cleaning job.'

Anne knew she was the area supervisor for a large company and before she could ask her why, Perdita continued. 'I had to. I was afraid leaving Johnny alone with that man. I've got a job helping out at the local crèche. It's only for several hours a week, it doesn't pay well but at least I'm sure of that money if nothing else comes in and I know Johnny is safe.'

That had to be a big decision to make. Anne made some notes.

'And Johnny? How is he? Is his asthma as bad as ever.'

'It's worse. The doctor tells me it's stress-related and even I can see that. He's so anxious whenever his dad is around that he can hardly breathe. He resents having a sickly kid and he makes snide remarks all the time about him being tied to his mother's apron strings and the like. That just makes it worse. We have to get away from him. It was bad enough before, but now that he's getting violent with him it can't go on.'

'No, I agree entirely. From what I see the physical abuse seems to be getting more frequent and more violent,' she said glancing at the file.

'That's because Johnny is starting to stand up for me and he can't take that. It shows him up for the coward that he is.'

'But Perdita, we've been here before. If we do press charges, and I strongly advise that we do, are you going to change your mind again and give him another chance? It's unlikely that he's going to change and someone will get seriously hurt if this continues. Let's hope for a custodial sentence – that will give you all some respite. The other priority is to secure the house for you both and to ensure he cannot come anywhere near it ever again.'

'That sounds almost too good to be true. And if Johnny's asthma improves I could take more mornings at the crèche, even do some full days. He'll be in secondary school next year. The other company told me I can come back any time I like, but the hours aren't ideal for a single parent.'

'Have you discussed the consequences of a barring order with Johnny? He needs to know that he may not have free access to his father when he gets out.'

'He knows that and right now he hates his guts. He says he never wants to have anything to do with him again.'

'I can't say I blame him, but he may change his mind when he's older.'

'If he does that's OK by me. He's entitled to have a relationship with his father, but only if his father is capable of respecting him and treating him properly.'

'Leave it with me,' Anne said. 'I'll put things in motion and get back to you as soon as I have more information.'

A little later Anne called her sister to tell her what had been happening with Maurice.

'I can't talk now,' Gabby said. 'I'm rushing out the door. I'm meeting some girls from the club for lunch. I'll catch you later.'

'Don't you ever go to work?' Anne asked.

'I'm on flexi-time now. Got to go.' And she did.

Anne rang Dee to ask her opinion.

'I didn't like to say anything, but he has been doing a few odd things lately,' she told her. 'He told me he was going to see Charlie at his flat but turned up at my door an hour later. He said he couldn't remember where it was.'

'But he's been there several times,' Anne said.

'I know. That's what worried me. He rang one night and asked me what the code was for his house alarm.'

'Had it been changed?'

'No,' said Dee. 'He just couldn't seem to remember that either.'

Anne had thought the day couldn't get any worse and now she had learned this. How had she missed so much? Had she let the whole Daniel business overshadow everything else in her world? She thought she had dealt with it. She needed to get out of the office for a while to think.

'Take the afternoon off. I can keep things going here. You don't have to be in court until tomorrow afternoon and you know that case inside out,' Paula said, and, seeing the doubt on Anne's face, added, 'you can always phone me if you need me or vice versa. Go on.'

It was still raining when she left and was as dark as a November day. When she parked she saw Dean getting out of his car, juggling with an oversized golf umbrella. He waved. 'The tan suits you,' he called, 'but why the great big frown?'

'Don't ask,' she replied. 'I thought you were starting your new job this week.'

'I am, but not until Wednesday. Have you had lunch? I've just stocked up on a few healthy options, and a carrot cake.' He grinned and she felt her face relax. He held the umbrella over her. They both saw Mrs Dunne's curtains twitch as they headed for the front door. 'We're safe. She's already checked the post box this morning,' he said and he winked at her. 'Let's give her something to brighten her day.' He put his arm around her and planted a kiss on her forehead, before opening the door and letting them in. 'You're a troublemaker.' She laughed. And he replied, 'I know.'

She kept the conversation light, much lighter than she was feeling. She told him about France, the house and the old vineyards. They were eating couscous with cold lamb, baby tomatoes and tzatziki when she heard her phone buzzing. She went to the counter to get it out of her bag. It was Eoin.

'I have to take this. I'm sorry,' she said.

She outlined her concerns about her dad, then listened to Eoin speak. 'What are you telling me?' she asked. 'He could have had a stroke and not be aware of it?' She sat down again. This could not really be happening. She lost her concentration for a moment, mouthed 'sorry' again to Dean and tuned back in to hear Eoin say, 'It seems as though these things are not isolated instances. On their own they don't amount to much, people get confused, fixated about things like their finances or medications even, but there seems to be a pattern emerging here.'

'Too many for them to be coincidental,' she said.

'I think perhaps yes. And I think it's time we found out what is going on, Anne. I'll have a chat with one of the geriatricians here and we'll organise some scans and assessments.'

Dean busied himself, as though not listening, but it was impossible to pretend he hadn't heard. When she had finished her conversation he waited for a few seconds and asked, 'Do you want to talk about it?'

'No, that's not fair on you. I bet everywhere you go when people hear you're a doctor they ask for a bit of advice. I don't want to lose our friendship by becoming one of those characters.'

He put his hand across the table and covered hers, saying, 'Don't worry, that'll not happen.' There was such sincerity in his eyes that she felt something letting go inside her and she knew that moment that she could trust him.

'You'll have gathered that was about my dad. He's behaving weirdly. That was one of his best friends. Eoin Maleady. You probably know him.' He nodded. 'He seems to think it could be a TIA, or series of them, whatever they are.'

'It's a mini stroke, a transient ischemic attack, or TIA for short. Don't look so worried. They tend not to kill brain tissue or cause any permanent disabilities. Often people have one or more of these at a time of stress and then they never get any more. He'll need a bit of monitoring and investigation, but that's purely precautionary.'

'But how do they happen?'

'They're caused by a temporary lack of blood flow to the brain. Sometimes they only last a few seconds. Often the person who has them doesn't even notice. He's in good hands with Eoin Maleady,' he said, but his words offered little reassurance.

It was just registering that Eoin hadn't seem surprised at all by her call or by her line of questioning. He must have noticed something too. She felt a sense of foreboding she had never felt before and wished above all else that her mother was there to talk to. As though sensing her distress, Dean said, 'Why don't you go and lie down for a while and try not to worry.'

She wished people didn't say that. It didn't lessen the anxiety. It just reminded her that she probably did have cause to feel that way. He walked her to the door and said, 'I'm here if you feel the need. I do make house calls in exceptional circumstances and if they are in my immediate neighbourhood.' He grinned and leaned over and kissed her on the cheek.

When she went back into her own flat she phoned Darcy and told her what had been happening, leaving out the bit about the fuss Maurice was making over her airline tickets for France. She rang Gabby again and left a message telling her to ring her as soon as she was free.

'Do you want to come around?' Darcy asked. 'The house is a

mess. I'm still unpacking and I'm trying to get a bag, or bags, ready for Samantha for crèche in the morning. She needs so much you'd think she was going away for a week.'

'Oh, Darcy, I'm sorry. I completely forgot you went back to work today. How was it?'

'Hectic, mad, disorganised and wonderful to be back, but I missed her like mad. I couldn't wait to get out to pick her up. I don't think she even knew I was gone, the ungrateful little minx! Come around for a cuppa.'

'No, you sound tired and I've had a few glasses of wine with Dean. I'll catch you later in the week.'

'Oh, a few glasses of wine with Dean, indeed, and in the middle of the afternoon!' They laughed, and Anne replied, 'I'll let you know if there are any developments.'

She stood looking out into the dark and focused on the raindrops running in little rivulets down the outside of the glass. It still hadn't let up and everywhere was sodden. Sometimes the drops had a free run from top to bottom, at other times they collided with each other, causing a diversion and finding a new path. They moved at different speeds too. Is that how the circulation works? Could the blood find new pathways if areas were blocked, she wondered. These thoughts were interrupted by her doorbell. She pressed the speaker and was surprised to hear Gabby's voice. She seldom called on her, announced or unannounced.

'It's open,' Anne said and she went to let her in. She hadn't expected to see Paul standing beside her.

Without preamble her sister asked, 'What's the emergency?'

'What emergency?'

'I got your message and a call from drama queen Darcy saying you needed to see me urgently, about Dad, but not to phone him. What's going on?'

'She must have misunderstood,' Anne replied, knowing full well she hadn't. 'I am concerned about him though. He's been acting oddly and that's worrying. Something's not right. Eoin is going to organise for him to see a geriatrician to have him assessed.'

'Assessed for what exactly?' Paul asked.

'I'm really not too sure. He thinks maybe he's had one or more mini strokes in the last while,' she explained,

'While you were off sunning yourself in your estate in France, you mean?'

She clenched her fists – she was not a violent person, but sometimes the urge to give her sister a good slap was overwhelming. She unclenched them and said quietly, 'No, I think it goes back further than that, to the day he was taken in to Pearse Street for shoplifting.'

Gabby reddened and looked flustered. She shot a look at Paul, who appeared baffled by this revelation. It was apparent that this was the first he'd heard about that incident. Before he could say anything, her sister continued. 'He hasn't done it again? Please tell me he hasn't.'

'No, there have been a few other things though. Have you noticed anything different?'

'No, but then I don't live in his pocket like you do.'

She let that pass.

'Can anything be done?'

'Dean said it will depend on the results of the tests.'

'Who's Dean?'

'My neighbour, next door. He's a medic.'

'How is he involved? Is he treating Dad?'

'No, he's not. He's just a friend. He says it could all be caused by high blood pressure or it—'

'Blood pressure – for God's sake, doesn't every old person have that?'

'Dad's not old. He's not seventy yet.'

'Stop trying to split hairs. What difference does a few weeks make? Seventy is old. What will we do if he has a major stroke and he can't do things for himself? I can't mind him.'

'We'd better make sure he doesn't have one then. Hadn't we? So don't upset him.'

'I knew you'd make it out to be my fault.'

'It's nobody's fault, but please don't mention anything to him about being concerned. He'd hate that. Let's leave it to Eoin to handle it his way.'

'She's right, Gabby. He must be used to situations like this,' said Paul. She nodded in agreement.

'We were going to organise dinner at the golf club for his birthday,' she said. 'Should I hold off doing that?'

'I would, not because of anything that's happened, but because I think he's deliberately trying to avoid the occasion altogether and the easiest way of doing that is by going away. He and Eoin are taking the bikes to France.'

'I can understand that,' Paul said, before Gabby could offer an argument.

'They can't be too concerned if that's the plan. I knew Darcy was overreacting. Could we not have discussed this on the phone?'

Before Anne could remind her that she'd left her two messages and if she'd returned either they probably could have done so, Gabby looked at her watch and said, 'God, is that the time? We have to go – I need to get my beauty sleep. Flexi-time has its advantages, but it means I'm on the early shift tomorrow. I'm in at six.'

'Don't wake me when you're leaving.' Paul stood up and said to Anne, 'Let us know if we can do anything.'

'I will and thank you,' she said letting them out.

Words whirled around in her head. Don't worry, permanent damage, restraining orders, assessments, domestic abuse, blocked arteries, custodial sentences, scans and tests, memory lapses. They jumbled and made no sense as she lay there in the dark, tossing and turning, the rain beating against her windows. If she didn't get to sleep soon she'd be no good to Perdita in court the following afternoon.

Chapter Twenty-Seven

The judge on the bench that day was not known for leniency in domestic violence cases and, as expected, he handed down a custodial sentence. He then pronounced, 'You have left me with no alternative but to have the family home used to secure a future for your wife and for the son whom you have deprived of a happy and carefree childhood so far. He can never get those years back, nor can his mother. Therefore the judgment of this court is that the property will be put in her name solely with immediate effect. This will in no way compensate either party for the wrong they have had done to them, but it may make their future somewhat better.'

Anne left court delighted with the outcome. Perdita hugged her and thanked her for her support.

'It's your time now. Make sure you make the most of it.'

'Oh, I will, I can assure you of that.'

'I don't know how she'll manage the repayments,' Anne told Paula. 'I suppose she could rent out a room or—'

'Stop, will you? That's not your problem. You've just given that woman and her child their lives back. You're not expected to do any more.'

'That's easier said than done. I can't just switch off like that. She's the same age as me and she's lived a lifetime more. I have such a cushy number by comparison.'

'I know. You're too soft. You can't feel guilty because you got the good hand.'

'It is unfair.'

'Life is unfair, but what you've just done has made a difference, a real difference to her and Johnny's future. It's up to them now.

Minutes after she left she got a text from Alan: 'Congratulations, that was a good day's work. Where have you disappeared to?'

He must have been in the courtroom. She hadn't noticed which members of the press corps were there. She realised how much more preoccupied she was with her father than she had thought. She opened her car and climbed in, but before she could reply Alan sent her a follow-up.

'Are you at a loose end?' She was exhausted but she knew Alan would lift her spirits.

'Yes,' she texted back, 'but I don't feel like going out. Come over to me. I can rustle up something simple.'

'What time?'

'Now, if that suits.'

'It does.'

She smiled to herself. It was a glorious autumn evening, the sort that made it impossible to remember what the previous day had been like. The traffic was reasonably light too.

Eoin had phoned her while she was on her way back to the car. He'd told her he had lined up some tests and a consultation for Maurice.

'I don't know how I'll tell him. I know he'll be upset that we're doing this behind his back.'

'You don't have to worry. I've already done that. I told him we'd have to have a once-over before we take the bikes to France.'

'And he fell for that?'

'No, I embroidered it a little. I said he should take advantage of getting it done for nowt while I'm still on the staff here and he fell for that.'

'You're wily,' she'd said. 'I really appreciate you doing this for us.'

'Don't embarrass me,' he'd said with a laugh.

'I have to file a few paragraphs on the case,' Alan said when he arrived, 'then I'm all yours.'

'Work away. I've things to do in the kitchen.' She left him to it.

When they were eating, he said, 'I'm dying to hear all about France. Did it live up to expectations? Have you got any photographs?'

'It did, and I have, but I want to hear about this play of yours first. Have the rehearsals started yet? Darcy has got tickets for the two of us.'

'They have.' As he went on to outline the plot, she thought about how Alan had been a constant in her life since college days. They had always had a special bond, and they had mixed in the same set, witnessing each other's relationships, break-ups and unrequited loves. They knew everything about each other and their families. She was so glad they had made up. She had missed him when they had had the fracas over Daniel. It had hurt, but in her heart she knew that whatever happened in her life he would always be there for her. And she for him.

He looked at his watch and exclaimed, 'I didn't realise it was so late. I didn't mean to stay so long.'

'That's as much my fault. I enjoyed the evening very much,' she said as she opened the door for him. He leaned over and kissed her cheek as the lift doors opened, and Dean emerged. 'Thanks again, that was just like old times,' he said, nodding at Dean before the doors closed behind him.

'Someone special?' Dean enquired. She smiled. 'Yes, I suppose you could say that. How was your first day?' she asked, as she stifled a yawn.

'Very good, but you look dead on your feet. We'll talk again.'

'Thanks. Night night.'

Chapter Twenty-Eight

Maurice hadn't mentioned the chat he'd had with Eoin or the tests that had been arranged to either of his daughters. But he had noticed some unsettling occurrences and had discussed some of his concerns with Peadar when sitting all those hours at his bedside. He told him how he kept forgetting his PIN numbers and the code for his newfangled phone. In voicing these anxieties he had admitted to himself that there was something amiss. Always pragmatic, Peadar had told him to get himself checked out. He promised he would, but he hadn't. He was terrified that they would put a name on what was happening to him, and he wasn't ready for that, not yet.

The realisation that he wasn't fooling anyone anymore was dawning. He was aware that Anne, and Paula too, were watching him carefully. There had been another few episodes that he'd managed to conceal from them. He couldn't remember what they were right now, but he knew they involved Dee and that nice man from the alarm company. Charlie was still listed as one of their back-up numbers. He told her he'd change that. Had he? He couldn't remember if he had or not.

Apart from noticing a declining interest in work matters, he felt just like his old self. He had told himself that was natural. After years at the helm he was just entitled to ease out of the role, passing on responsibilities, as Peadar had done to him. However, he knew he couldn't run away forever from whatever was happening, and although he dreaded being told something he didn't want to hear, he was going to have to face up to it sometime. He let Eoin think he believed his line about getting an MOT before he retired from the hospital, but in fact he'd already decided to get help once he'd got back.

He was getting excited at the prospect of going to France again, and his first road trip since Sheila died. He'd turn seventy while over there and he made his daughters promise there were to be no surprises on his return. He didn't want a party or a fuss of any kind. He assured them that one of Marie's delicious dinners would be celebration enough. The girls agreed that was a good idea, even though Gabby had shown no interest whatever in Anne's villa. She never discussed it with him and he knew her well enough to know this jealousy towards her sister must be killing her.

'I won't be in tomorrow,' he told Anne. 'I've gone through the diary with Paula and it seems I'll not be missed. I've a few things to organise for going away.'

'That's fine, Dad. That's why you put me in charge.'

'You're right,' he said, not divulging the real reason for his absence. He was scheduled to get his results and wanted time to reflect on them quietly, whatever they might be.

His appointment with the neurologist was at the private clinic where he had had an MRI and other motor tests done the previous week.

'I see you've come alone today, Maurice,' was the consultant's greeting, as he extended a hand.

That activated an alarm somewhere deep inside him. Why shouldn't he be alone? He was about to make a reply, but found he couldn't think of a single thing to say.

'Do take a seat.'

The mahogany desk lay between them, impersonal and benign, and Maurice wondered how many worlds had been changed by whatever news had floated across it in one-way traffic? Was his about to become one of them?

'You know why we've been investigating. We wanted to confirm or rule out evidence of TIAs and I'm happy to tell you that you have not been experiencing any of these, or indeed a stroke of any kind.' He paused for this to sink in.

Maurice spoke first. 'I sense a "but" coming next.'

'There is a but, and I'm afraid there's no easy way to give you this news, but the brain imaging has shown up Alzheimer's disease.'

'That is my worst nightmare.'

'I can understand that and I'm sorry to be the bearer of such news.'

Another pause. This time Maurice held back.

'I'm sure you're aware, there is no cure as yet for Alzheimer's, although great advances are being made all the time in this, as in all neurological disorders.'

'So what's my prognosis? How long do I have before I go do-lally altogether?'

'They would not have been my words, Maurice, and I know it's a shock. I can't give you a definitive answer. No one could. Would you like to go away and have a think about it? Talk it over with your family and come back to me with any questions you may have once it has sunk in.'

'I've thought of little else in the past few months, since I first started noticing changes.'

'What were the first signs that made you suspicious?'

'When I could no longer distinguish between banknotes, even though the number is printed on them. I couldn't count the change in my pocket either. Individually I can distinguish them, but when I try to add them up or pay for something I just go blank.'

'That fits the pattern alright.'

'I was arrested for shoplifting because I couldn't remember how to pay or whether I had paid, so I panicked and walked out and got caught.'

'That's not as uncommon as you may imagine. Has it affected your work so far?'

'I'm sure it has. I no longer think I have the clarity of vision to make that judgment. I have noticed though that I put off filling in forms and doing my accounts. I'm terrified of them. Is that serious?'

'In themselves these things are not, but what is more concerning is the shrinkage in the brain tissue that your scan has revealed. Normally people with this disease have had it for a length of time before it manifests any signs of memory loss or cognitive difficulties. In some cases it's more progressive. Indications would suggest that your condition could be termed as rapid onset. I'll give you some literature to read and pass on to your family, then we can talk more about the way forward and how to manage the progression.'

'Can it be arrested?'

'I wish I could say yes, but I can't. Effectively plaques and tangles spread throughout the brain and cause damage, because they interrupt or destroy the circuitry. In your case the shrinkage is a further worry.'

'Can I do anything?'

'Medically there is no magic potion for the treatment of Alzheimer's. Every case is different but we can deal with the symptoms as they arise. If I were in your shoes I would put my affairs in order and make my wishes very clear to all concerned. In my experience, that saves an awful lot of family problems when it comes to issues such as care. Do these things while you have clarity of thought. And Maurice, I'd also consider appointing someone you can trust as your legal guardian, someone who also knows these wishes and can act in your best interests. But who am I telling?' He smiled. 'You know more about these things than I do.'

'It's a bit different when it's your own affairs you have to consider. I never wanted to be a burden on my children, or for my life to end up like this.'

'None of us do. Try not to focus on the worst aspects. It won't all be bad, but you will have to curtail some of your activities. I understand from Eoin that you're one of his biker friends and that you have a trip planned. Frankly if he were not going with you I honestly would be advising you to cancel this, and put the car and bike up on blocks, but in the circumstances I think you should look on this as your last hurrah on the bike. As regards driving your car, I'm afraid I'm going to have to veto that.'

'So my insurance would be null and void if I were to ignore your advice.'

'Yes, and as you indicated to me, you are only too aware of how your cognitive impairment is already beginning to affect your ability to recognise landmarks and follow directions.' He stopped talking to let this sink in.

Maurice looked down at his hands, pushing the cuticle of

one thumb back with the nail from the other. 'It's worse than I thought,' he said.

'I'm afraid so. I wish I could tell you progress will be slow, but the indicators are that it won't. Are you going to be all right? Is there anyone I can call for you? Or I could give Eoin a shout, he should be out of his clinic round about now.'

Maurice nodded.

'I'll just pop down to his secretary and find out the state of play. I'll be back in a few minutes.'

The consultant put his hand comfortingly on his shoulder as he passed by. It had seemed to be a good idea not having anyone with him when he got the news, but now that he knew the extent of it, it didn't seem like such a smart one. He should have asked Dee to come with him. She knew what discretion meant. He'd have to tell the girls and he hadn't a clue how he was going to do that.

Chapter Twenty-Nine

Maurice asked them all to come to his house the following Saturday. Anne was pleased to see fresh flowers in the hallway and the house looking tidy and lived in again. Reluctantly agreeing to allow a cleaner in one morning a week had made a difference, and the woman Dee had recommended seemed to be doing a good job. She wasn't surprised to see that Dee was already there, scones and tea at the ready.

Darcy came in, a bag of baby accoutrements hanging from her arm, followed by Richard carrying a smiling Samantha in her seat. 'It's like planning an Arctic expedition to go anywhere,' he said, gently putting his daughter down on the floor and turning the seat so that she could see everyone. 'I never knew babies took up so much space or needed so much stuff!'

After all the usual comments on how big she was getting, who she looked like and on her curly hair, Gabby arrived on her own. She left no one in any doubt as to her frame of mind as she made her dissatisfaction known about having her weekend plans disrupted. She looked around the room, then said, 'Dee and Darcy here too – this is a real family council. Has someone else left my sister another legacy, a house or a parcel of land? If not, why the command from on high?'

No one answered that, then Darcy said, 'I see Paul's not with you.'

'Not everyone can drop everything at a moment's notice. He and his dad are playing in the Father and Son competition. They're defending their title, although no captain has ever won it while he held the office, so they're hoping to be the first to do it.'

'Let's hope they do,' Dee said cheerfully. 'Now your father has something to tell you, but let's sort out the tea and coffee first.' She smiled encouragingly at him. He'd talked to her the previous day and asked her if she'd give him her moral support. She had been honest with him and admitted that she had been worried too.

'In one way,' he'd told her, 'it's a relief to have it out in the open, but I don't mind admitting that now that it has a name I'm terrified.'

'You wouldn't be normal if you weren't, but you have to tell the girls and Darcy too. You'll need all of us and we'll be there for you.'

'Thank you, Dee. You're wonderful. I can understand why you and Sheila were such good friends.'

'No one knows what's ahead, so just live for today and make sure you enjoy it by making it count.' Together they'd planned this meeting and now that those who meant everything to him were gathered around he couldn't back out of it. He had to tell them, knowing his news was about to crash into their worlds, affecting all of them in some way or another.

Maurice refused a scone, took a sip of his tea and launched his grenade.

He could see the shock registering on their faces as he finished his little speech.

'... I'm sure – no, I know – that you've all noticed some of the silly things I've been doing.' He looked from one to another.

'Dad, at first we thought that you were just a bit distracted after losing Mum and then Peadar,' said Anne, who was now sitting with Samantha on her knee. Samantha kept trying to pull a chain from around her neck. 'But now – when did you start noticing anything was wrong?' she asked.

'At Gabby's wedding actually, when I forgot my speech.'

'Did you? I never noticed,' Gabby replied. Anne nodded and he knew she was remembering.

'Maurice, that was probably the most stressful thing you ever had to do in the circumstances. I was surprised you managed to get through the day at all,' Dee said.

'I don't want platitudes. I'm an intelligent human being. I know what is going on and what I have to do. I dried up at Peadar's graveside too and there have been lots of other little things. I had my suspicions and now that they are confirmed I don't want to be wrapped in cotton wool. In one way I wish Sheila was here to be by my side, but on another level I'm glad she's not. She'd have hated watching me deteriorate. We often talked about things like that. We had made a pact never to put the other in a home unless there was absolutely no other solution. We always promised to be there for each other.' He seemed to go off somewhere in his mind, and when he spoke again, he said, 'She had an easy and gentle death.'

'Dad—' Gabby began.

'I told you the last thing I need is for you all to be pussy-footing around me,' he snapped. 'Now, I have things to do, so off you all go and get on with your day and let me get on with mine. I'm not gaga yet.'

Confused and shocked, no one moved. He stood up and took

his car keys out of his pocket and handed these ceremoniously over to Richard.

'That old Ford of yours will hardly get through another NCT. I'll not be needing the Audi anymore so take it. It's yours.'

'I can't do that.'

'I can. I'm not allowed drive any more so you'll be doing me a favour, taking temptation out of my way.'

'Should we tell people?' Darcy asked.

'Not yet. For the moment let's keep it as family business. It'll get out soon enough.'

'What about France and your bike trip?' Gabby asked.

'That'll be my last hoorah on the highway, and I'm only allowed do it because I'll have the boys to shepherd me,' he said.

'Are you sure about the diagnosis, Maurice? It all seems to be happening very fast. Doctors sometimes get things wrong,' Richard said.

'They do, but they haven't this time. I've seen the scans and Eoin has explained everything. The professor is happy to meet any of you and talk you through it. Now take the car and enjoy it.'

He could see the disbelief on all their faces. 'Don't look at me like that. I'm not deluded. I've had a bit of time to mull over such things and I told Eoin I was going to do this. I discussed my plans with Dee also, so that you know it's not a whim.'

'Wouldn't you rather give it to Paul?' Darcy asked.

'No, Gabby got her mother's car. Anne has her fancy convertible. Now it's your turn. I can't have my honorary granddaughter driving around in that old rust bucket.'

'It's not that bad.' Darcy laughed. 'How can we thank you?'

'By making sure I'm never out of lemon drizzle cake. Now, as I said, I have things to do.'

Chapter Thirty

Anne felt the bottom had fallen out of her world, again. First her mother, then Daniel, then Peadar and now her dad. In a flash she understood why he had made the changes to the company, putting her in charge before telling her about the villa and her inheritance. He knew what was happening to him before they did – and they thought they were fooling him by pretending there was nothing strange about his behaviour of late. She should have guessed. That was also why he never mentioned the shoplifting episode or the passport fuss again. He was always methodical and today was typical. He had planned how to drop his bombshell, and then dismiss them to come to terms with it and deal with the fallout as they saw fit. He didn't want to be drawn into further discussion or into going over and over his behaviour of late.

She stopped at the supermarket and walked around the aisles like an automaton. When she got back home to the apartment she had no recollection of having bought any of the items she took out of the bags. She opened a bottle of wine and poured herself a large glass. She downed it as she stood on her balcony looking out at the sea, the wind whipping white tops on the waves. Her mind had stopped working. She wanted to hide somewhere, to feel protected. She wished she could hide in a roll of bubble-wrap or feathers, somewhere warm and safe, somewhere that would prevent anything else sharp or painful getting anywhere near her.

She poured another glass of wine and sat down at the kitchen table, amid her shopping, and cried. What was going to happen next? What would happen when Maurice could no longer cope on his own, never mind be left alone?

She couldn't think straight. She heard the lift doors open and knew Dean was back home. He'd started back full-time at the hospital during the week and she wondered how it had gone. Then she remembered she was supposed to be cooking for him that night. Maybe she should cancel. She stood up and began clearing away. She must have been functioning on some level as she shopped because she had the makings of a proper meal. She decided against cancelling. It would probably do her good to have company and stop her from wallowing in self-pity.

By the time Dean appeared, behind a huge bunch of pink gerberas and white gypsophila, she had collected her thoughts, and had another glass of wine. She was resolved that she wasn't going to spend the night talking about her or her father's problems, so she asked him about his new role at the hospital.

'It's strange to be back. It's a totally different environment than working in conflict zones, knowing that trained personnel, scans and theatres are all at my disposal, not to mention simple things like antibiotics and other medicines. It's a different buzz altogether. Out there the challenges were much greater and it was so frustrating when the humanitarian aid convoys were ambushed and simple things like bandages and dressings were stolen. The idea of having my own secretary, or PA, as I believe I should call him or her, is quite foreign, almost indulgent to me.'

'I hope you don't get a harridan like Eoin's. It would be easier to get into the White House than to try to have an unscheduled chat with him.'

'Some of them do go overboard, especially the older ones – they like to think they are in charge of us too.'

'Well, make sure that you don't get one like that.'

'Maybe you should vet the applicants for me.' He laughed. She filled the glasses again and answered, 'I might like that.'

After they had finished eating they moved over to the sofa.

'You never mentioned your dad or his results? Am I reading too much into that or should I mind my own business?' he said.

'It's your night off – let's not talk about it.'

'Because …?' Dean urged.

'Because it's your night off.'

'Friendship doesn't keep office hours,' he said, taking her hand and she felt her eyes fill up. It was as though he had released the switch that opened her emotions. She let it all out, her frustrations, her anger, her hurt, her fears. She stood up to get another bottle of wine, but he held on to her hand and wouldn't let go.

'I think maybe we've had enough of that.'

She wobbled slightly and fell back down beside him. She looked at him and leaned over. 'You're so nice, Dean Moore, so damned nice. And I haven't even experienced your bedside manner yet.' She began kissing him and it took a few seconds before she realised he was not reciprocating. He held her from him gently.

'I think it's time you got some rest. We'll talk tomorrow.' He stood up and helped her to her feet. She swayed and he led her to her bedroom and sat her on the bed. She lay back and he lifted her legs in, straightening them before pulling the duvet over her.

He kissed her on the forehead and said goodnight. She heard him moving around the kitchen as she drifted into oblivion.

She woke around noon, her head splitting and her mouth as dry as an old rag. She needed to get some water and it was then that she noticed she was fully dressed. She noticed that the place had been tidied and everything put away, and that there were four empty wine bottles on the sink. No wonder I feel awful, she thought. Then fragments of the day before began filtering back. The family conference, her dad's news, dinner with Dean. Oh Jesus, tell me I didn't come on to him. Tell me I dreamt that bit. The more she tried to convince herself it hadn't happened, the more she knew it had. Her phone beeped, a text message.

'Thought you mightn't answer your phone, so here's the story. Lunch in the pub at two. I need to tell you something. I have to do something first. See you there. Dean x.'

She couldn't pretend she hadn't got it, he'd see it had been delivered and read. The curse of smartphones; sometimes they were just too smart. It was better to get it over with. She showered, drank the best part of a litre of water and decided to walk to the pub. The fresh air might help her hangover and she wanted to be there first.

She saw him come in, looking fresh and alert, no sign of a hard night about him at all. He smiled and greeted her with a kiss on the cheek. 'Lovely dinner last night. Thank you. My turn next.' He was being perfectly normal. She had just about convinced herself that maybe she had imagined it all when he said, 'About last night …'

'Dean, I am so embarrassed. I never meant that to happen. I don't know what I was thinking. I'm so sorry. I had far too much wine. I don't normally drink like that, but I think I must have had a bottle or more before you came in.'

'It's all right, Anne, there's no need to apologise. You had a difficult day and if anything I should be the one saying sorry. I just hope you didn't think I was leading you on. That was never my intention.'

'Of course I didn't. It'll all so embarrassing.'

'Please don't let it be. I love your company and want to be friends with you long term, but Anne, I have to tell you, I'm gay.'

'You're gay?' she repeated.

'Yes, I am. It's not something I shout about – despite gay marriage and Ireland's so-called liberal attitudes to such matters, there are not too many surgeons who advertise the fact.'

'No, there aren't,' she agreed. 'I never had an inkling. Have you got a partner?'

'Not at the moment. When I came back it was after a nasty break-up. I told you about that.'

'Yes, I remember now, but I never twigged that it wasn't a female.'

'I hope I didn't give off the wrong messages.'

'You didn't, Dean. I promise you. I value your friendship, very much, and I was afraid I'd ruined that. I hope I haven't. I was just so upset yesterday.'

'I know that, Anne. Just forget it ever happened,' he said.

'I'll do my best,' she replied, but she had the feeling it was not something she was going to forget easily.

'So we're good?' he said.

'We're very good, and thank you.' She smiled.

Anne and Maurice had a chat with Paula and they decided that they should call in the senior members of the firm and tell them what was happening. Maurice was happy to let her conduct the proceedings.

'I'd like to formally appoint you, Vincent, as my second in command, if you're willing,' she told him, in front of his peers.

'I'd consider it an honour,' he answered. Vincent had joined the company straight after getting his degree and was still in his early forties. He was well versed in its practises and was totally dependable, as well as being an easy and obliging colleague.

Anne added, 'For obvious reasons we don't think it necessary to make Dad's condition public knowledge just yet.'

'I'd appreciate discretion until we can't avoid it any longer,' Maurice said. 'Anne will co-handle any on-going cases for the moment, and we'll gradually disperse my clients amongst the rest of you.'

After some questions he told them, 'I'll be away for a few weeks and when I come back I'd like to carry on for as long as I can and trust you'll let me know when I'm failing to keep the standards up.' His smile indicated there would be no more discussion, but throughout the day Anne was aware of conversations stopping and of inane remarks being made when she came upon any of the staff talking.

Life went on pretty much the same over the next few weeks and Maurice left for France with Eoin and Paddy. Alan had become a more regular part of her social life again and she looked forward to the time they spent together. He represented normality where that had become something of a rarity. She told him about her faux pas with Dean.

'I think you're making too much out of it. If you had asked me I would have thought he probably had designs on you, so my gaydar let me down there too.'

'I'm embarrassed every time I think about it.'

'How come you never came on to me like that?' he teased.

She didn't have an answer. Alan was her friend, her mate, her confidante. She just didn't see him in that light.

His play was a great hit at the Theatre Festival and she and Darcy took him out for a few drinks afterwards.

'You've no excuse to stay in the world of crime any longer,' Anne told him, 'you know you can do it. Go and follow your dream to write full time.'

'One of my teachers always told us "*festina lente*". I never listened to him in school but I remember him telling us that, over and over again. I think he was trying to encourage us, but it had the opposite effect. So in his memory I'm going to do just that and wait until the end of the run, then I'll take six months' unpaid leave and see how it goes. That way if I've nothing to show at the end of it I'll still have my poxy job to go back to!'

'I can't wait for your next one. The nosey neighbour character in that was priceless,' said Darcy. 'You could turn it into a sitcom, even a series, based around her.'

'I wish you were writing the reviews,' he said, as he hailed a taxi.

'I'm so looking forward to the weekend. It's my turn for a sleep-in – no ungodly early alarm wakening me to get Samantha ready for crèche.'

'I'm not on until Sunday night's shift,' said Alan, 'so it'll be a leisurely one for me too.'

'And I don't have to worry about Dad being away. It's such a relief knowing he has Eoin and Paddy with him.' Anne wouldn't let herself think any further than a few days ahead. Eoin was keeping her posted. She talked to Maurice most nights and noticed how he had difficulty remembering the names of places they'd been, or where they'd had lunch. She knew she needed to savour the peace of mind while she still could.

On Sunday she organised her clothes for the week ahead, had a good long soak in a scented bath and went to bed early. She was drifting off when her phone rang. It was just after ten.

'Have you been watching the news?' Darcy sounded agitated. 'There's been another gangland shooting. There are several injuries and one of them is a journalist. I think it's Alan.'

'What? Are you sure?' She was already out of bed. She stood there for a minute. She didn't know what to do, or who to call. Who would give her information? She grabbed her dressing gown and ran next door to Dean. He'd know what to do. He brought her in and made a few calls.

'It seems he got caught in the crossfire and took a bullet in his thigh and another in the lower leg. The tibia is broken but that's not the cause for concern. The one that went in higher up severed the femoral artery and he lost a lot of blood. He's in surgery now. That's all I can tell you. I'll ring again in a little while.' He tried to comfort her, but she was distraught.

'I can't lose him. You know that, don't you? I can't. I just can't.' She stood up. 'I want to go to the hospital, Dean, to be there when he wakes up.'

'I don't think that's a good idea, Anne,' he advised. 'He'll be out of it for a good while and even then he'll be pretty groggy. Why not try and get some sleep and go in first thing in the morning?' But she was having none of it. She insisted on going in. 'You're not driving - you're in shock,' he told her.

'Then I'll take a taxi.'

'I'll drive you. Go and get something warm to wear – it'll be a long night.'

At the hospital their footsteps echoed noisily as they hurried along the quiet corridors. They stopped when they reached a door with

Strictly No Admittance emblazoned across it. Dean keyed in a number and a click announced the latch had opened. Despite the late hour when the rest of the world was dark and sleeping, this space was brightly lit and buzzing with activity. A few uniformed and armed police turned to watch them approach.

'How did you get in to the unit? There are absolutely no visitors permitted here,' the nurse at the duty desk informed them, looking up from her writing and over at the Gardaí.

'We're here to see Alan Seavers, this is—'

'When Mr Seavers is back with us, he'll be in the high dependency unit and only next of kin are admitted, when they allow it. You may go back out the way you came in,' she said in dismissal and turned to her work.

Anne looked at Dean who was opening his wallet. For one insane second she thought, he's not going to try to bribe the woman, and in front of the police too? Surely not. He produced his hospital ID card and spoke with an air of authority. 'I'm Dean Moore, recently joined your staff, and this is Anne Cullen, Alan Seavers' fiancée.'

The nurse looked up again and he continued, 'I've done some locum work here over the past few months. I'm sure some of your colleagues can verify that.'

'It's OK, Mr Cullen, I do recognise you now. I'm sorry. It's just been a manic night so far.' She looked at Anne and said, 'Please follow me, you can wait in here. He should be down in an hour or so.' She indicated a small side room with some utilitarian high-back chairs and a low table with a few dog-eared magazines scattered on top. When they were alone he said, 'I'll get us some tea and see if I can find out anything more for you.' He returned a while later carrying two polystyrene cups of tea. He put them down and she closed the door over.

'Well?'

'The surgery went as well as can be expected. They're bringing him back to us now.'

She stood up.

'Not so fast. They'll have to do the handover and get him settled in the unit before you can go in. It won't be too long.'

'Fiancée – where did that come from?' she asked him.

'It was the best I could do to get you in.' He smiled. 'When I saw the armed guards I knew you hadn't a chance of seeing him otherwise.'

'I'd better text his sister and tell her not to land me in it, although her flight's not due in until after seven.'

"You'll be safe enough. By the time she gets in from the airport the staff will have changed over. I just hope the shock of finding himself engaged won't finish him off altogether.'

She smiled back. 'I'm so glad you're here,' she said. 'I suppose the Gardaí are here to interview him.'

'There could be others involved or injured too. I didn't ask.'

The door opened. 'You can go in for just two minutes. Only one of you. I'm afraid I can't do anything about the Gardaí being present there – they have their job to do, too. Don't expect him to be responsive or to make much sense. He's lost a lot of blood and the anaesthetic is still wearing off.'

She followed and heard the nurse say to the one writing notes by his bed, 'Dean Moore brought this patient's fiancée in to see him, although I'd have thought he'd have more sense.' Anne froze, fear gripping her as she saw Alan lying in this hostile environment, connected to tubes and machines that beeped and flashed to a rhythm of their own. He looked waxen under the oxygen mask and she had to hold back her tears. She stood looking at him without saying anything. She reached down, took his hand and squeezed it. 'I'm so sorry you're hurt. You have to get better. I couldn't bear it if anything happened to you. I couldn't.' She wiped her eyes with the back of her other hand and was sure she felt a slight pressure from Alan's. She squeezed it again as the nurse hovered and fiddled with the flow mechanism on a drip, leaving her in no doubt that she was in the way. 'Alan, It's Anne. I love you. Please get better. I couldn't live without you. I'll be waiting outside when you wake up,' she said, before leaning down and kissing him slowly on his forehead. She let his hand go reluctantly.

Dean was outside the door, talking to the other guard. He put his arm around her. 'Now that you've seen him I think you should go home and get some sleep. Alan will be out of it for a few more hours and he'll need his rest when he comes to.'

'I told him I'd be here. I don't know if he could hear me, and even if he didn't, I want to be here when he wakes.'

'I can't stay with you, Anne. I have to get some shut-eye. I'm in theatre at half-past seven in the morning, and I'll be no use to anyone if I don't, but I'll look in on you here before that.'

'I wouldn't expect you to stay, Dean. I've already made too many demands on your friendship and your time. I'll be fine.'

'I'll get you a fresh brew and I'll see if I can inveigle a blanket and a pillow out of the night sister for you.' He gave her a comforting hug. 'It'll be all right. I promise you.'

After he left to spend what was left of the night on a bed somewhere in the hospital, she tried to get comfortable on the slippery chair. She wondered what had made her realise her real feelings for Alan. She had told him she loved him and she knew with positive conviction that she did. Had he heard her? If he had would he remember, or had she just committed another gaffe like the one she had with Dean? Could she have destroyed their friendship by her unexpected declaration?

She had never been in any doubt that he fancied her. God knows he had made many declarations over the years, but she hadn't ever looked on him as being more than a good mate. Reflecting, she couldn't figure out when her feelings had changed to much more than deep friendship. She could pinpoint a definite shift after they had fallen out over the Daniel business. That had shaken her and she had missed him more than she had ever imagined and she wanted him more in her life, but still kept him at a distance.

I'm going to have to stop blaming everything on grieving, she thought. Life is going on all around me and I keep ignoring the signs. I've known him for over ten years and from the very beginning we always enjoyed each other's company, and at parties and gatherings, no matter who we were with, we always gravitated towards each other. That has to count for something special.

What if he never wakes up?

I can't think like that.

I've been such a fool, using our jobs as an excuse to keep him at arm's length, pushing him away, feeling jealous when I saw him with another woman. I've been walking around with my head in the clouds, she decided, before eventually falling into a fitful sleep. She was woken by a hand on her arm, shaking her gently. It was the nurse. 'He's awake and asking for you. You can talk to him for a few minutes, but that's all.'

She was surprised to find him completely lucid even if his voice sounded a bit slurred. She felt embarrassed by it now.

'Good timing this, wasn't it?' he said. She was puzzled. 'After what Darcy said on Friday I had decided I was going to tell them in the paper tonight that I wanted to take six months off to work on a new play. And I was quite happy to forego my salary and give it a go. Maybe now I'll get it with full pay.' He grinned at her. 'Maybe even with a bit of compensation thrown in.'

'You always look on the bright side, although I'd hardly call anything bright about being shot at in the line of duty.'

'The bonus is that I suppose I can call myself a proper crime journo now,' he said, 'being wounded in action.'

'I don't know how you can laugh at that. Think of what could have been.'

'And think of what can be now. This is just the push I needed. A bit extreme, I'll admit.'

The nurse came back in and gave her her marching orders.

She met Dean on the corridor. 'I believe he'll live,' he said with a smile, 'although I guess you have that figured out by now. You look wretched though. Go home and get some rest. I'll check on him when I'm through in theatre and report back to you.'

Darcy phoned her after dropping Samantha off at the crèche.

'It's all over the news. Not life threatening, they're saying. How is he?'

'I think he'll be out of work for a while. Dean says he may have nerve damage, but they won't know that just yet. I'm just so grateful that he's alive … Darcy … I did something stupid and rash.'

'What did you do?'

'I told Alan I loved him.'

'And about time too,' she replied. 'I'm glad you've come to your senses. It was so obvious! That'll make him recover quicker than any surgery. There's the bell, I have to get to class. Talk later.'

'But he didn't hear me …' she said to herself

Chapter Thirty-One

Her father came back from his biking trip, full of the adventures the three of them had had, and with bits of news from Marie and Pierre.

'They think we should go over and spend Christmas there in the villa. They said they love having people there and don't relish the place being empty for the holiday.'

Christmas. It was months away and Anne couldn't bear the thoughts of it. It wouldn't ever be the same again for any of them. How could they put up a tree and decorations and do all the celebration bits – that had always been Sheila's department. She loved Christmas and everything about it. She'd have started shopping by now ...

'That sounds like a plan. Maybe you could get around Gabby and Paul to join us. We could invite Dee along too. What do you think, Dad? It would be a change from Bad Gastein for her.'

'Leave it with me,' he said. 'I'll organise it. Don't look so worried. I'll let you check the plans before I book anything.'

That's what he said, but they both knew there was no guarantee that he would remember to do that. Whether he did or not it was good for him to have some projects to keep him occupied, since he had cut down his working week to three days. No one asked outright what he was going to do with the others, but he made it known that he had plans, plans to catch up with other retirees, the odd game of golf, long leisurely lunches, keeping the garden as Sheila would have done, and reading, lots and lots of reading.

Instead of easing Anne's mind, she now had the additional worry of what he would get up to, or where he might wander to, with no one to supervise him, although he was back three weeks and settling in to the new self-imposed regime with apparent ease. She was happy when he told her he was meeting an old friend for lunch and said he was going to enjoy a glass or two of good wine. He assured her that he wouldn't use the car. Had he forgotten that he had given it to Richard? Eoin had suggested that they should confiscate the keys of his motorbikes in case he took a vagary and went off on one of them alone.

Anne was filling Paula in on Alan's progress over soup and sandwiches in the kitchen that they all referred to rather grandly as the canteen. No one could argue that it was a step up from the cramped one they had had in the old Georgian building, and it did have a great view down over the canal, but canteen was stretching it a bit. Her phone buzzed. She had it on silent for her lunchtime, but checked it anyway.

'It's Daniel.'

'Your Daniel, as in *Daniel* Daniel?' Paula asked with eyebrows raised. 'What does he want?'

'I don't know.'

'Are you going to answer it, or will I?' She reached out but it stopped vibrating at that moment.

'What is he ringing me for?'

'To apologise for being such a prick? To ask you to come back? To offer to buy us out again? To get your legal opinion on something? How the hell do I know, Anne? Ring him back and find out!'

'I certainly will not!'

The phone began buzzing again and his name popped up. She answered it as she would any call. 'Anne Cullen, Cullen–Ffinch.' She hadn't spoken to him since the day she had left his apartment and had often wondered how she'd handle this first contact. Even thinking of him brought up an explosion of emotions – a mixture of hurt, anger, hatred and disappointment at the forefront.

'I'm with your father, Anne,' he said without any preamble. So that's who he was lunching with, was her first thought, then why was he lunching with him, and why had he kept that a secret?

'Oh, I hadn't realised …'

'He doesn't, eh, he doesn't seem to be quite himself.'

'I'll come and get him, what restaurant are you in?'

'Restaurant? I'm in the foyer of the Criminal Courts. I found him wandering around looking lost and disoriented. He keeps saying we have to catch up and that I must come to dinner with your mother and him sometime.'

She didn't know what to say to that. This was something new.

'I think he may have had a turn, Anne.'

'Thank you for contacting me, Daniel. He hasn't been himself lately. Can you stay with him until I get there? I'll leave straight away.'

'No, let me take him to you. It'll be quicker. I don't have my car but I'll call a taxi.'

She thanked him again and looked at Paula. No words were needed between the two women. Yet again Anne realised life was taking control of her, not the other way around, and she knew she'd have no say in the course it had plotted out for her or her dad.

It seemed an age before they arrived at the office, Maurice walking in breezily ahead of Daniel saying, 'Look who I bumped into. He gave me a lift back here and I was just saying he must come over with you to see Sheila and myself again soon. It's been too long since we did that.'

Paula's face registered disbelief, but before she could correct him Anne stepped in.

'That's true, Dad. It has been a while. Now let's not detain Daniel any longer. I'm sure he's as busy as ever,' she said ushering him back out into the hallway. 'Thank you for getting him back safely.'

'I think he needs to be checked out, Anne. I think he may have had a stroke or a turn of some sort. He's very confused. He didn't seem to know who he was or what he was doing there in the courts when I spotted him. I suggested he ring you and he said he didn't know where to find a phone, yet he had his one in his hand.'

'He has Alzheimer's.'

'Oh, Anne, I'm really sorry to hear that. How long have you known?'

'Officially only seven or eight weeks, but there were definite signs before that. We just hadn't joined them up.'

'Look, I know it all ended nastily between us, but you don't deserve this, any of you. If I can do anything at any stage give me a shout. I'm genuinely fond of the old boy and of you too, Anne, despite how it finished.'

In other circumstances she would have reacted to this – the nastiness was not of her making, and she didn't need his expressions of devotion, but she didn't have the energy to take him on. For a split second she wanted him to be there again, a steady shoulder to lean on. But only for a split second. She told him she appreciated what he had done and thanked him again.

'I mean it, Anne, if there is anything …'

And if there is ever anything … you'd be the last person on earth I'd call, she thought, as she went back to her office before his taxi had pulled away.

'Dad, I thought you were having lunch with an old colleague today.'

'I knew there was something I was meant to do.'

'Did you put it in your diary?' He looked at her blankly, as though he hadn't a clue what she was talking about. 'Your lunch appointment – maybe you wrote it in the diary.' Still nothing. 'What about your phone?' He had put it on his desk beside his keys and newspaper. She reached over and saw several missed calls and messages from his friend Craig.

'Dad, why didn't you answer this?'

'I don't know. Maybe I didn't hear it. I don't know what all the fuss is about. I'm not hungry anyway. Now I need to go to the gents.' He excused himself.

This was all happening far too quickly but she didn't know when or what the next episode would be. She stood there feeling lost and fearful of what lay ahead.

When he returned he said, 'Your mother would have reminded me if she were still here. She was great about things like that. I suppose I'd better give Craig a ring and rearrange things.'

Just like that he was back in the present, lucid, fully functioning and with no recollection of having met Daniel.

As her dad's cognitive abilities were deteriorating at an alarming rate, Alan was making slow but steady and very promising progress.

His days were filled with exercises, physiotherapy and assurances that his injured leg would work properly again. She visited him every day and took him out for a change of scenery frequently. He flirted with her and with the nurses, and she found herself feeling jealous of his new relationships.

He never referred to Anne's comments in the hospital and part of her was relieved, as she began to accept that he hadn't heard her. Telling him as she did could have jeopardised the closeness they always had. She was prepared to have him in her life as her best friend rather than not at all, but in reality she now wanted more. Much more.

Why had it had taken the realisation that he might have died from the shooting to bring about her epiphany? How could she have been so blinkered? Her happiness had been under her nose all along and she hadn't recognised it.

She told Dean how she had managed to complicate her life in a way her ditzy sister never did hers.

'Gabby always knew what she wanted and went after it. Simple as that. While I, on the other hand, wouldn't know where to start to change the easy relationship I have with Alan. Where would I begin letting him know that I'd like to move it on to another level. How do I know he'd want to?'

'Has he ever given you any indication he does?'

'Lots and lots of times he told me he was in love with me, and lots and lots of times I laughed it off. His timing was awful – he usually did it when I had a boyfriend or he'd just finished with some girl or other.'

'Maybe he got tired of being rejected,' Dean suggested.

'Or maybe he isn't interested any more.'

'I've only known him a short while, and for what it's worth, I think you're great together. You should let him know how you feel. You owe that much to both of you.'

She wasn't sure about that at all.

'I thought this was going to be easy,' Alan said, as they walked along the seafront at Sandymount; he still using crutches, his lower leg encased in an oversized cast. 'I thought that once I was free of the manic newsroom deadlines I'd spend my time sitting at my laptop, being inspired by my muse. I hadn't factored in the distraction of pain or the sense of claustrophobia that confinement brings with it. They've almost destroyed any bit of creativity I had.'

'That'll pass. Why don't you go to the villa and recuperate there? You might even get your inspiration back and if you don't, the change of scenery won't do you any harm. It's beautiful and peaceful. Marie and Pierre will take care of everything you need.'

He thought for a bit and his face broke into a wide grin.

'You're fabulous, Anne. Do you know that? Just the thoughts of that have lifted my spirits. Would you, or could you, come over and spend a bit of time with me?'

'There's nothing on this earth I'd rather do,' she said truthfully, 'but with the way things are with Dad I'm afraid to make plans. I couldn't leave him on his own for any length of time. Besides we're going over for Christmas.'

'No Austria this year?'

'No. I think maybe it's time to make new traditions now that Gabby's got a husband. Darcy and Richard will be doing their Santa Claus bit, Dee and Charlie are apart, which leaves Dad and me as the odd ones out.'

'You might find that I'll have taken up squatters rights by then.'

'You'd be more than welcome. When do you think you'll be able to travel?'

'I'm not sure about that, but it will be the first question I'll ask the physio tomorrow.'

She laughed and wished she could just down tools and go with him. Why hadn't she realised how carefree her life was before? Now it was filled with complexity and uncertainty.

Work was becoming an inconvenience too. She found it hard to concentrate, to try and block out what was going on in her personal life. Instead of seeing the faintest glimmer of hope at the end of the proverbial tunnel, the tunnel seemed to be getting narrower and longer and there was no sign of any chink in its blackness. It was in this frame of mind that she bumped into Perdita, her former client, on the street. She almost walked by her.

'Anne. You're miles away. It's Perdita.'

'Hello. You look well. How have you been?'

'Happier and poorer than ever, but I'm so grateful to you.'

'There's no need for that. And Johnny?'

'His asthma has almost gone since the sentencing. He's not missing any school as a result. He got an A in maths recently. You'd think he'd won the Fields Medal, he's so proud, and he's joined the chess club.'

'Congratulate him for me. Has the crèche worked out for you? Did you get more hours?' As she posed this question she realised that Perdita could be the answer to some of her problems.

'Not really, a few but they're irregular, so I can't rely on them.'

'I may have a proposition for you. Have you time for a coffee?'

An hour later they had struck a deal: Perdita would drive her father when he needed to be taken to his club, social events or lunches on the days he didn't come in to the office; she would also look after the house and prepare a hot meal for him.

'This arrangement isn't mine alone to make. I have to run it by him first and by my sister, but I'll get back to you as soon as I can.'

'Anne to the rescue again!' Perdita laughed.

She smiled and felt the muscles in her face relax. She hadn't realised how pent up she had become, constantly fearing what calamity the next phone call would herald, and trying to dismiss the feeling she was being left to shoulder most of it on her own.

Prior to this encounter she had asked her sister to meet to discuss a care plan for Maurice. Gabby had bridge that evening so the meeting was scheduled for the following one.

'He doesn't need to know we've discussed this. Just act as though you were passing and decided to pop in to see him. Darcy will be there too.'

'Darcy's not strictly family.'

Not this again, she thought in exasperation. If Gabby had any sense at all she should be delighted to have an extra body on our team, any extra body. 'I don't think you realise how serious the situation is becoming, or how rapidly things are changing for Dad.'

'You always exaggerate. I'm sure it's not that bad.'

Anne chose not to answer that. She'd fill her in when they met. 'See you around half six.'

As it happened Gabby got a first-hand idea of how things were evolving when she arrived early. She found the door open and no sign of her dad anywhere. She went into the garage, the shed, the garden and all the rooms, but there was no sign of him. She rang his number and heard the phone ringing out in the kitchen. She ran, only to find it sitting in the sink. When Darcy arrived she found Gabby in a panic. 'We've got to take our cars and drive around the locality and look for him.'

'He could simply have forgotten to close the door when he

went out,' said Darcy calmly. 'He could just be out talking to a neighbour, or gone to borrow something. I'll knock on a few doors.'

'Shouldn't we phone the Gardaí?'

'Not yet, let's explore our options first.'

'Something could have happened him. We can't take that chance. We should let Anne know too.'

'I'll call her,' said Darcy. 'You start with the cul-de-sacs.'

Before Gabby had a chance to go looking, Maurice came back with some roses, one of his fingers bleeding. 'I picked these for Sheila. Is she with you?'

Gabby burst out crying.

'What's wrong, Gabby? Where's your mum?'

'Mum's dead, Dad,' she cried. 'Mum's dead!'

'Oh, no one told me that. You can have the flowers instead.' He handed them to her.

'They're very pretty, Maurice,' Darcy said. 'Where did you get them?'

'In a garden around the corner. Where Marty Beagan lives. I don't think she saw me pick them. She's never there. That woman is a powerhouse and she's in everything except the crib. Mary Clerkin, who lives opposite her, might have seen me though. I'm not sure. Any chance she gets she's outside taking every blink of sun, or photographing her flowers. She always has her camera with her.'

Darcy and Gabby stood looking at Maurice as though he had landed from another planet. Anne had come in behind them and heard the end of this.

'Well, Dad, for a man who never gossips or takes any interest in the neighbours that was some news flash.'

He smiled when he saw her. 'Hello, Anne. Did you know your

mum is dead? No one told me.' Gabby burst out crying again. He ignored her this time.

'Did she call out for me? Where was I?'
'I'm not sure, Dad. I'm going to make some tea and fix up that cut on your hand. You must have caught it on a thorn.'

He stared at the blood as she washed and dressed it, then he looked up and seemed surprised to see them all there.

'What a lovely surprise, all my girls together. Only Sheila missing, and little Samantha too.' No one knew what to say. Then he announced, 'Do you know what I'd love to do?' They waited. 'I'd love to have some pizza, the one with ham, peppers and pineapple, and a glass of white wine. We haven't done that for a long time. Let's order some. Your mum might be here by the time it's delivered.'

It was a long night and by the end of it Gabby was only too pleased to learn that Perdita was coming on board. Maurice agreed quite readily to the extra support, saying he missed his car so a driver sounded great.

'I want to make it quite clear that I don't want or need to be chaperoned or spied on every minute of every day. I'm not a child and I don't want to be treated as one. But I'm happy you'll all want to help if the time comes that I'll need it.'

He was back with them again. 'I must put those flowers in water. They're not from my garden, are they? Thank you, whoever brought them. They're lovely.'

'We don't want to crowd you either, Dad, or curtail your freedom, but we need to know you'll be safe.'

'I'm hardly likely to get lost, am I?' he said and no one reminded him of the Daniel incident.

'So that's all arranged, I'll come over on Saturday and spend a few hours with you and Perdita, let you get to know each other.

She might have her son with her. He's learning chess. Maybe you could show him a few moves.'

'Maybe,' he replied.

'And I know I'm always welcome so long as I bring my lemon drizzle cake,' Darcy said.

'And your daughter,' he said and they laughed.

Anne nipped out at one point and went around to Marty Beagan's house to explain about the roses and about Maurice's condition. She couldn't have been more understanding and promised to spread the word among the other neighbours and ask them to keep an eye on him and out for him.

Gabby didn't make such a song and dance about her social calendar as she normally would, while all this was going on. It was clear that the evening had been a reality check for her. 'Can we get some more backup?' she asked when her dad went upstairs for something.

'Let's not push things any more. We've given him a lot to digest tonight. We'll see how Perdita works out and keep our fingers crossed that he doesn't get any worse too quickly,' said Anne. 'He's lucky he has so many interests and several good friends, even Charlie.'

'Do they keep in touch?' asked Gabby incredulously.

'They do. Dad stood by him, now he's doing the same. They have lunch together every week.'

'Does Dee know that?'

'Of course she does. And she's been there for Dad all along. In fact, she noticed things weren't right before I did,' Anne replied.

Chapter Thirty-Two

'It seems that I'll have my fit-to-travel pass in three weeks' time, and if I'm still welcome at the Cullen estate in Provence I'll start packing my bags,' Alan told her when he called at lunchtime the next day.

'Of course you are and that's terrific news. You'll love it there.'

'Let me take you out for a meal tonight, to thank you in advance, if you're free.'

'No thank-yous necessary, but a meal sounds great,' she replied.

'I'll reserve a table and get back to you.' When he did it was to tell her, 'I've booked Les Frères. I thought we should go French to mark the occasion and to get me in the mood for this unexpected treat.'

Her heart sank. She hadn't told him about the humiliating situation in which she'd found herself there with her father. Her life these days seemed to be peppered with embarrassing situations that she hadn't talked about. Perhaps they wouldn't recognise her, or there might be a different front-of-house manager on duty that night. Trying to put these thoughts aside, she went home early to have a bath and relax before her date.

They had a drink before dinner in a little bar just around the corner from the restaurant and Anne told Alan what had happened on the previous occasion.

'Things seem to be progressing pretty quickly there, don't they? That can't be easy for you, Anne.' His concern was genuine and she felt tears welling and her voice breaking.

'I'm sorry, I didn't mean to upset you.' He wiped a tear from her cheek. He hugged her and held her until she regained her composure and could talk again.

'You didn't, Alan. You know, you don't really notice it when it's an isolated incident, but when you sit down and start adding these up it's kind of a shock. I worry all the time about the next stage and the one after that. It's all moving too fast, and coming so soon after losing Mum …'

'What will you do long-term?'

'I'm just being an ostrich. I know Dad has the rapid-onset variety so it may not be so long-distance at all and long-term is almost inevitable, as he's physically strong and fit. It will become impossible to run the company and look after him twenty-four hours a day.'

'You and Gabby could always go part-time and share the responsibility.'

'Unfortunately she's of the mind-set that that's what money is for. Now, what am I doing monopolising our time talking about me? Please shut me up. Tell me what you are going to be working on when you get to France … a new play, another poetry collection, a novel?'

'Let's go in to the restaurant first.'

It was the same maître d'. He welcomed them, before recognition dawned. She was about to offer an explanation when Alan stepped in. 'Jacques, I believe you have met my friend, Anne Cullen.'

'Any friend of yours, Monsieur Alan, is always welcome.' She looked in surprise. Alan hadn't said he knew this man, yet it appeared they knew each other pretty well. 'She was here with her father recently. Such a terrible shame the way Alzheimer's has affected him and so quickly too.' He left it at that and followed Jacques to their table in the corner, handing his crutches to him.

'That was clever, the way you got that in,' she said. 'I was afraid he was going to ask me to leave.'

'I'd like to see him try.'

They talked and laughed and discussed the villa.

'Would you not come over with me for the first weekend even, to see me settled and show me the ropes? Surely between all Maurice's friends someone could be around to keep an eye on things.'

'You've no idea how good that sounds. Leave it with me and I'll see what I can organise.'

'I might get preferential treatment from your staff when they know they're not just dealing with anybody.'

'My staff? God, Alan, that's so not me. And why would you warrant special treatment anyway?'

'As your fiancé, of course!' He grinned at her as she blushed to an unflattering shade. 'Before I came to properly I heard the nurses saying something about my fiancée coming to see me. Please tell me I wasn't delirious!' She didn't know what to say, so she said nothing. He reached his hands out to her and she took them and held them tightly.

His gaze never faltered as he said, 'Tell me you meant it, Anne. You know I love you and have done since I first met you. I'd given up telling you because I felt I never had a chance, and when Daniel arrived on the scene I became resigned to never being with you. I thought I was hallucinating in the hospital. Dean has since assured me that I wasn't. I knew then I hadn't imagined the rest. But I need to know, Anne, did you mean it?'

'I did, I do.' She grinned back at him. 'Oh yes, Alan, I do. I never meant anything more in my life'

'That sounds like marriage vows, and I haven't even proposed yet.' He laughed. 'But I would if I could go down on my gammy knee. Oh, what the heck, you were never a girl for convention anyhow. Anne, we've wasted so much time. I just want to be with you, spend the rest of our lives together. You might even consider marrying me one day.'

'I just said yes to dinner and now I find myself being proposed to.'

'Is it too soon to declare all this? It's just that I've been doing a lot of thinking and looking at you losing your mum, the situation with your dad and my accident. I wanted to be sure you were feeling the same, but I can't wait any longer.'

'I don't want to wait either.'

'If that's a yes to my proposal then, I have to tell you, my prospects are decidedly shaky. I may not want to go back into journalism; in fact, I know I won't. I want to write full-time so I'll never be rich.'

'Then you have to know that my prospects are equally shaky. I'm getting to dislike my job more each day and want to run away from every legal book and law reform report. I hate what's happening to Dad. No, worse than that, I resent not knowing what's ahead and not being able to be in control of my life. That doesn't show me in a very good light, does it?'

'I'd say we're evenly matched.'

'But Dad is going to need my attention more and more …'

'And I want to be there to help you with him.'

'It's easy to say that.'

'I'm ignoring that! I know what he means to you and I'm in.'

'If I say yes, am I going home engaged?!'

'Yes, but without a ring to prove it. Do you want a long engagement?'

'Cut to the chase, why don't you?' She laughed.

'Do you want a long engagement?' he asked again.

'No, it's been too long already. I just want to elope.'

'Perfect. But we haven't even slept together,' he said quietly, aware that they had already attracted the attention of the diners at the next table.

'Then we'd better rectify that as soon as possible,' she said. 'We can skip dessert and go back to mine.'

'I'd better make sure to pay the bill first.' He winked and called for his crutches.

Their first time making love was a fumbled mixture of laughter and tenderness, of passion and lust. The cast on his leg brought some restrictions they hadn't expected and he promised, 'Next time it will be better.'

'It won't, because I'm not waiting until you get rid of that,' she said, reaching for him again with a longing that needed to be satisfied. In the afterglow she realised that there was a light at the end of the tunnel and that it didn't seem too far away at all.

'Dad, would you mind if I didn't have a conventional wedding, but just did it very quietly?' she asked after she broke the news to him in the office the next day.

'Would I mind? Nothing would make me happier. Never again do I want to go through the circus production your sister put on. If it wasn't for her I'm convinced your mother would still be here.'

'Dad, don't ever let Gabby hear you say that. It would destroy her. Besides, you don't really believe that.'

'In my heart I do, and that's not the do-lally bit of me talking, either.'

Anne believed him. To change the focus she told him she was going to go to Provence with Alan for a weekend. Between Darcy and Dee, and hopefully by then Perdita also, they'd be there to keep an eye on him while she was gone.

Her news caused ripples in the office, with everyone clamouring to wish her well.

'I told you you should marry him a long time ago,' Paula said. 'It was obvious to everyone you had a special connection.'

'You also told me I wouldn't do any better than Daniel!'

'OK, I admit that was a bad call, and everyone is entitled to one of those. But I like Alan. That's the difference.'

Anne had a meeting with the heads of the departments and told them that she'd be needing more time off in the near future; therefore she was putting Vincent in place as acting MD until further notice.

Both Darcy and Gabby were incredulous when she phoned them.

'I'm so happy for you, Anne, I thought you'd never come to your senses. It's been so apparent to everyone but you. Congratulations. I can't wait to tell Richard.'

Her sister sounded genuinely pleased for her. 'If I can do anything for you, let me know. There's a lot of work in planning a wedding.'

'Thanks, Gabby. I appreciate that. It'll be something small and soon. I want Dad to give me away while he's still aware of what he's doing.'

'That's a good idea. Oh, by the way, we've decided to come over to your villa for Christmas.' Anne had not been expecting that.

She texted Dean, knowing he was in theatre that morning. 'I'm engaged!! To Alan. Thank you, Cupid. A xx.'

He replied with a string of smiley and thumbs-up emojis.

Dee's reaction was typical of her godmother: 'This calls for champagne and more champagne to welcome Alan into your clan.'

Chapter Thirty-Three

It was late afternoon when they touched down at Marseilles. Pierre was waiting at the airport to meet Alan and Anne. If his congratulations were warm and genuine, Marie's surpassed them. She had made a special engagement cake and fussed over Alan, ushering him in and making sure he had a comfortable seat, enough cushions and a table close by.

'I could get used to being spoiled like this,' he told her, and added, when she left the room to fetch coffee for them, 'I think I'll keep the cast on a little longer if it has that effect, but I'm afraid to move now in case she thinks I'm a fraud!'

The ginger cat appeared and eyed Alan disdainfully before walking away towards Anne. She was allowed stroke him until he purred.

'Who's that?' asked Alan. 'He looked at me as though I'm sitting in his seat.'

'You are. It's Abricot; he's their timeshare cat. Don't ask! Anyway, Marie and Pierre go back to their house when they've served dinner. I'll give you the grand tour then.'

'If we have the place to ourselves I may have other ideas. After all I only have you for the weekend.'

'You're incorrigible,' she said.

'No, just insatiable. I can't get enough of you. I can't honestly believe that we got here.'

'And I can't fathom how it took us so long.'

'The responsibility for that, *ma cherie*, was all your doing.'

'Then I have some making up to do.'

'You'll get your chance soon enough. I promise. I can see the house properly tomorrow!'

They did go to bed shortly after dinner and after only a cursory look around the villa.

'It's very impressive and I'm so glad I proposed before seeing this or you might have thought I had designs on your estate.'

She laughed as she led the way upstairs. 'Thank you for making me smile again. I feel as though a dark cloud has just evaporated.'

The journey had taken more out of him than he had thought it would, but he wasn't too tired to show Anne how he felt about her. He was up the next morning before she was awake and he went outside to look around. He explored the long low sheds where the itinerant grape pickers used to sleep when they arrived every season to work there and on neighbouring farms. He discovered the old winepresses in another, and by the time he came back, Anne could see he was all fired up about something, and that he didn't want Marie to hear what it was.

'From your demeanour,' Anne said, 'I'm expecting you to tell me you've just had a blinding flash of inspiration and that you'd like me to leave today so you can begin working on it straight away.'

'No, Anne, I'll wait until Monday for that. But it's here. The solution to all your problems. It's here, right under your nose.'

She didn't know where this was leading.

'A studio, Anne, accommodation, scenery, a garden for your dad. You always said your dream would be to run an art school or an artist's retreat. Well, here you have it. It's all out there, in your own back yard. Of course you'd probably have to get planning permissions for structural changes and the like, but the basic fabric is there. You could do what you really want to do, paint again, and you could have your dad live with you.'

The more he talked the more she realised he had spotted something that she had missed. Something that Peadar had obviously seen when he gifted the property to her. She tried to recall what he had told her when she visited him in hospital. Something about not having regrets when she came to shuffle on.

She knew, and had known for a good while now, that, even though she was good at it, her heart wasn't in law. It had never been. She had conformed and given in to subtle and not-so-subtle pressures when she aborted her degree course in the National College of Art and Design. That decision had given her parents, and in particular her mother, great pleasure, yet it was her father who had originally encouraged her to prepare a portfolio for consideration for that course in the first p lace. W ould h e understand if she changed horses at this stage? She had a feeling he probably would.

While she had been lost in thought Alan sat, his coffee cup in his hand, watching her. He was already sketching ideas in his mind.

After breakfast they went outside again, walking and talking, stopping and talking, weighing up possibilities.

'It's a huge decision, Alan. I'm not sure I could do it, or ask you to, either. Have you thought it through? Do you really want to start your married life living with your father-in-law? That situation won't get any easier.'

'I'm marrying you because I love you and that encompasses the for-better-and-for-worse bit. It won't be one-way traffic – you don't really know my family and their foibles yet. There's my neurotic mother, who is working her way through the medical dictionary, and my xenophobic father who won't fly anyway; consequently you'll become very familiar with Cornwall. My sister, well, you've met her and she's reasonably normal! Your dad comes as part of the package, I know that, and I'm more than happy to accept that and be there for both of you. As regards moving – I can write anywhere – I just want to spend the rest of my life with you, wherever that happens to be.'

'And then there's the firm. Is Dad capable of discussing all this logically?'

'From my perspective he knew what he was doing when he put you in charge and handed the reins to you officially. He and Peadar had talked it all out and I think that was his way of relinquishing his control and letting you take over – of giving you the authority to do things your way.'

'Perhaps. But that still leaves me wondering do I have the right to dispose of it?'

'Only you can answer those questions.'

'And Marie and Pierre. How do you think they'll feel about turning this place into an artists' retreat? I'd have to consult them too.'

'They might be delighted to see it coming to life again.'

'They might, but I need time, Alan. I'll have to choose my moment to talk to Dad.'

'There's no need to rush anywhere. You take all the time you need, Anne. It's just an idea.'

'Just an idea.' She laughed. 'Just an idea, Alan! And you expect me to forget you ever mentioned it. It's an idea that's already causing seismic waves in my head and potentially in my life too.'

It was his turn to laugh.

'And you've been standing on that leg for too long now. Rest for a bit and we'll get Pierre to drive us around and show you the sights and find somewhere nice for lunch. Who knows, we might even get the opportunity to bring up the studio idea with him and test the waters!'

'Don't look at me like that. I'm not getting involved any further.'

'That's great. You'll stay here and relax while you send me back home tomorrow night, my head in a tailspin.'

'You won't hear another word about it from me. I've said my bit.'

'I'm going to ask Marie to come in to you. She wants to fix up your physio appointments for you.'

'I don't think she'll let me away with much.'

'She's just looking out for you. Anyway, it'll give you two a chance to bond and I can relax knowing you're in good hands.'

'You needn't worry about me – I can't wait to ditch these sticks and get back to normal again. I'm determined to get rid of the limp before I make you Mrs Seavers, which I'd like to do as soon as we can.'

'It would have been good if we had been able to do it before Christmas. We could have had the ceremony at home and then all come here to celebrate together.'

'There's nothing to stop us doing things in reverse order. Let's have the celebrations and make it legal as soon as we can after that,' he said. 'Is there any chance we'd get some wriggle room on the three-month waiting time, what with your dad's worsening condition?'

'It's a possibility … neither of us have been married before or lived abroad. I'll look into special dispensations when I get home.'

The weekend seemed to pass by in a flash and a much more carefree Anne reluctantly flew back in Dublin.

'I'll expect news on your masterpiece very soon,' she told Alan before she left, 'but take it easy – remember you're here to recuperate.'

'I'll see you in a few weeks.'

'I thought you were supposed to be taking a long break over here.'

'I was, but that was when you offered t o l et m e s tay. Th en we were friends. Now, especially after the last few days, I can't bear the thoughts of being away from my betrothed! Two weeks, three max, before I go mad without you, but I will start writing. I promise.'

She found herself smiling a lot on the plane as she remembered their love-making. She was missing him already, his touch, his smell, his warmth and his passion. Looking back at the last month it hadn't been at all strange making the transition from friends to lovers. She collected her bag and went straight to her dad's from the airport.

'Did you bring Sheila back with you?' was his greeting. That brought her down to earth with a bump.

'Not this time, Dad. Not this time,' she replied. He accepted that and said, 'Tell me about France. Did Alan like the house? And Marie and Pierre, how are they?'

She filled him in on all the news and enquired if Perdita had been in.

'I like that woman. She's very intelligent and she doesn't treat me like a child the way Gabby sometimes does. Her young lad Johnny and I played chess. I let him win twice, but then I beat him.'

'You used to do that with us.'

'I did – I think it's important to realise that you can't always win or be good at everything. It seems to have worked with you; I'm not so sure about your sister. She hates losing at anything.'

He wouldn't hear of her staying overnight.

'Leave me have my independence while I have it. I know it'll slip away soon enough.'

She squeezed his arm. 'You're doing great, Dad.'

'I am, aren't I?'

She was pleased to see Dean open his door when she got out of the lift. 'Just wondering how the patient survived the travelling?'

'Good really. It's tiring using the crutches, but there were no ill effects.'

'He won't need them for much longer and the rest and change of scenery will do him good.'

'I'm not so sure he'll be doing much resting. He's a man on a mission. Do you have a minute to chat or have you an early start?'

'I'm not in until after lunch tomorrow.'

They talked until one in the morning. When Anne went in to work on the Monday she had her mind set on a definite course of action.

Chapter Thirty-Four

Over the next few weeks Alan and Anne were in constant contact with each other, spending hours every evening on Skype. He was as good as his word and never referred to the idea of an art school or studio again, although she could sense it in the air between them. She didn't mention it either and had to stop herself from doing so on a few occasions.

She did, however, chat to her dad several times to make sure he understood what she was suggesting. She met Eoin and told him of her possible plans. She got his professional take on his friend's mental state. Eoin also provided the necessary documentation to back up her request for a special marriage licence.

'It's inevitable that Maurice will need twenty-four-hour care, and supervision. I can't put a time span on that, but realistically that's happening quicker than any of us would have liked. Ideally he will continue to thrive in a familiar environment, and more importantly surrounded by people who mean something to him, so the sooner he makes the transition the better it will suit him.'

'I was quite prepared to give up work and become his carer if that's what it took. I wouldn't ever put him in a home, Eoin. That'll never be an option.'

'I think he knows that, Anne.'

'So you really don't think moving him to France will be too much for him to cope with?'

'Not if he has you there with him along the way. He knows the set-up in France and has happy associations with it. From a practical point of view the layout of the villa would suit all your needs, as he could have his own self-contained quarters, ones that would be easy to secure if necessary.'

'It's such a relief to hear you say that. It's so sad to think about what's ahead for him.'

'Alzheimer's is a cruel disease, and it's often harder on the carers. Keep him involved as much as you can. You have to embrace the days and enjoy the good ones together while you can. There will be rough ones ahead.'

'You won't lose touch, will you?'

'Of course not. I'll even come and visit too, as often as you'll have me. Now go and try to get that wedding organised.'

'He's so excited about it we've decided we're going to go ahead with the day, even if we can't get a special licence. Then it can all be rubberstamped when it eventually comes through. It was always Dad's wish to walk both his daughters down the aisle and Gabby's wedding was too soon after Mum's death for him to enjoy any of it. We're going to give him his day.'

'Gabby. I need to see you,' was the message Anne left for her sister.

Uncharacteristically Gabby phoned back within the hour.

'Is there a problem?'

'I hope not, but it depends on how you look at things. Can we meet? I don't want to do this on the phone.'

'OK. Will Darcy be coming along too?'

'Would you mind if she did? It would save me having to go over the same thing twice.'

'No, that's fine. It'll be nice to see her.'

Was this really her sister talking? Had marriage done this to her? Or was it her father's illness that had impacted on her normally aggressive attitude? Perhaps she shouldn't be so hard on her. After all, it had taken Alan's accident for her to realise what he meant to her. Maybe the same had happened to Gabby

'I hope you haven't booked your flights yet,' she told them.

'You haven't changed your mind about having us, have you?' asked Gabby.

'No, but Alan and I are getting married on the twenty-third.'

'The twenty-third of what?'

'Of December – this December – and flying out immediately afterwards. We're going to have our celebrations at the villa. Dad probably won't remember any of it in a few months' time, but it's important to me to have him there by my side.'

'So you got the special licence?' said Darcy.

'Not yet.'

'What about Dad?' asked Gabby.

'What about him? He'll be coming too and that is why I wanted to see you. Alan and I are planning to move to France permanently and want Dad to come and live with us. I've run it past him a few times and he's excited about it, but I don't want to step on your toes, Gabby. If you're not happy about it then we'll leave things as they are and I'll give up work and go back home to keep an eye on things.'

'I wasn't expecting that,' she said. 'What about the firm? Who'll run it?'

'As Dad signed it over to me, I'm legally entitled to sell it, unless you want to buy me out and put someone in charge of it. If not, I will sell it and give you your share.'

'But you can't practise law in France,' said Darcy. 'Wouldn't you have to do exams?'

'I don't intend to.'

'Is Dad happy about this?'

'He says he is. He loves France and he loves the villa, but you'd have to come over often and see him.'

'Of course I would.'

'I know I just sprung this on you and I understand that you'll need time to think about it all,' Anne said.

'I won't. He's never been happy at home since Mum died and I have to admit I hate going into the house ever since too, but if you're sure it's what he wants then let's do it.'

'But Anne,' Darcy insisted, 'what are you going to do? What about Alan's job?'

'I'm going to do what I always wanted to do – paint and open a studio and art school, with painting holidays in the summer months. Alan can write anywhere and we can look after Dad at the same time.'

'My god, that sounds absolutely perfect! When did you decide on this?'

'It was Alan's brainchild. He just reminded me of what I'd always wanted from life. He's asked Dean to be his best man too and I think if he hadn't I would have. He played a big part in us getting together, finally.'

'Finally!' They laughed.

'Is he going to join us in France?' Darcy asked. 'I'm looking forward to getting to know him better.'

'No, he can't. He's last man in so he's on duty at the hospital for the holidays.'

Chapter Thirty-Five

The fires were crackling, the villa beautifully decorated. The curtains and shutters were drawn against the night. Anne had suggested that they have the celebratory wedding meal on Christmas Eve and not on the night of their arrival and Marie had gone to town on the preparations. She had obviously spent much of the run up to the day polishing silver and preparing the formal dining room for the traditional *le reveillon* meal. She wouldn't let anyone in there until the gong had sounded, then she opened the door ceremoniously.

What met their eyes was a tastefully set table, in red and white, candles flickering everywhere and a sideboard groaning under the weight of no less than thirteen desserts.

'Did Sheila make these, Marie?'

'No, Monsieur Maurice. They are a Provençal tradition and represent Christ and the twelve apostles,' she explained. 'The *Bûche de Noël*, or Yule log, is extra.' There was nougat, both white and black, candied fruits, quinces, dates, nuts and tangerines among them. Before they got to the desserts there were several courses, all accompanied by carefully chosen wines. During the meal Maurice asked a few times, 'Is your mother coming along later? I want to tell her about the wedding. You looked beautiful.'

'Yes, Dad, later,' Anne replied. They had all learned that he was happy once he had an answer. Explanations didn't have the same effect.

Gabby was quiet, but Anne noticed she and Paul exchanging smiles now and again. She was glad that her sister was happy. Darcy noticed she hadn't touched her wine all evening and whispered it to Dee. When she got Gabby on her own she asked if she had a secret she might like to share. She grinned. 'Yes, but not tonight. This is Anne and Alan's celebration, so don't say a word, please. I'll tell them in a few days.'

'That's wonderful—' she began to say, but Gabby shushed her as Alan appeared with his sister, Megan, in tow. He announced that in keeping with French tradition they were going to open their presents at midnight, and not wait until Christmas morning.

Megan was almost completely hidden behind a stack of gifts. Paul grabbed one before it hit the floor.

'If you think this is bad just remember I had to lug them to Dublin from Cornwall first and then get them here and wrap them. So you'd better like them.' They laughed.

'I hope you don't expect me to wake Samantha up for this,' Darcy said.

'I don't think she'll be able to tell the difference if we leave her asleep,' said Richard.

They all gathered around the Christmas tree and began exchanging packages of interesting shapes and sizes. Alan handed Anne a large envelope. She looked at it quizzically.

'Go on, open it,' he urged.

She did and took out a sheaf of drawings – with a cover page showing one of Peadar Ffinch's paintings. It was one of those they had found in the room he had kept locked. One of the ones that he and his young son had hoped would be the Ffinch–Ffinch wine label in the future. Emblazoned above the beautifully coloured plumage of the bullfinch were the words Le Bouvreuil Art Studio & Gallery.

'Le Bouvreuil … I'm not familiar with that word,' Megan said.

'It's finch,' Anne said, 'and we've kept it to honour Peadar Ffinch who left me this wonderful legacy. And who knows, maybe one day we'll try producing the wine he had hoped to make; if not, then his name will live on here in the gallery.'

'He'd really appreciate that,' Maurice said.

Alan made space on the table. 'I did these sketches when I was here convalescing and I got a mate to scale them up properly. I wanted to keep them as a surprise until you had definitely decided it was what you wanted to do. Of course they're only preliminary ideas – the decisions are yours to make.'

'Alan, they're wonderful. What a unique and thoughtful present. I couldn't visualise what it would all look like. Now you've done that for me, you've made it all come alive.' They all crowded around to see the drawings.

'That's the artists' studio, with lots of long windows for natural light and with views of the vines and the hills,' he explained.

'When Dad and I came here first,' Anne told them, 'you could see fields of lavender and sunflowers from the terrace. Do you remember, Dad?'

'I do,' he replied.

'They're our first memories too,' said Richard.

'And what's this?' asked Gabby, picking up another page.

'It's where the wine presses are. I thought it would make a

wonderful gallery, to show off Anne's and other artists' work, or for holding exhibitions. This space can be easily achieved while retaining the original stone walls and the old wine presses in the middle.'

'That sounds wonderful,' said Dee. 'Quite unique. Do you intend running residential courses?'

'That's the long-term plan,' said Anne. 'But we'll have to build up to that.'

Alan showed them how the former accommodation in the long low sheds, where the workers used to sleep, could be converted into self-contained units.

'They're mightily impressive,' Richard said and Paul agreed. Maurice lost interest and went back to see what else he could find under the Christmas tree.

'What about Maurice? How does he fit into all this?' asked Paul.

'If all goes according to plan, Perdita will come out with Johnny at Easter and see what they think about coming over permanently to help us with Dad and with the running of the place. It would be too much to expect Marie to take on the extra chores and there's a vacant cottage on the land that would be ideal for them.'

'When will you start work on it?' Richard asked.

'If these plans match the expectations and meet with the approval of Mrs Seavers –' Alan laughed '– I like the sound of that ... then we can begin looking for planning permissions and necessary permits.'

'If my husband ... Funny, I like the sound of that too.' She smiled at Alan. 'If my husband gets his way we'll be starting in the morning.'

'On Christmas Day?' said Gabby.

'Well, maybe on the twenty-sixth!' she said as she studied the painting again.

'It all sounds very exciting,' said Gabby. 'You'd never have guessed old Peadar had so much to him.'

'No, you wouldn't,' her sister agreed. 'He made me promise him before he died when my time came to shuffle on – his words, not mine – that when my time came to shuffle on that I'd have fulfilled my dreams and have no regrets. I didn't realise then that he had plans to make it all happen for me.'

Maurice came back into the room in his pyjamas, or rather his pyjama top over his shirt and trousers. 'I'd like to propose we refresh our glasses and raise them in a toast to my dear friend Peadar and my wife Sheila, who are no longer with us.'

Standing side by side Anne and Alan knew it was going to be hard. This was a bittersweet moment. Their wedding celebration, their first Christmas together, the first without her mother, and with a father who, though very much present, was becoming more and more absent … There could be no denying that there were difficult times ahead.

She raised her glass and did as Peadar had bid her do. She remembered the philosophy of an old man who'd told her, 'We can't alter fate, but we can soften it with pockets of fulfilment and contentment, however small. They are the cushions we all need in life.'

As she looked around the room, his former home warm and festive, and saw the faces of those she loved most in the world, Alan's arm around her waist, she knew that this was one of those pockets of fulfilment and contentment to be treasured always, and she sent him heartfelt, silent thanks, wherever he was.

Acknowledgements

It's such a privilege to be a small part of Team Hachette Ireland. They are all professional and dedicated cogs in the well-oiled wheels that are necessary to bring any book from an inkling of an idea to its publication, and to getting it there on the bookshelves for you to buy.

There are too many to single out, so please forgive me when I mention my editorial director, Ciara Doorley, who has enough faith in me to allow me write what I like to write without interference!

Huge thanks to Joanna Smyth, editorial and communications manager, for her affable attitude to my queries.

And Red Rattle Design – thank you for another evocative cover.